THE GOLDEN AGE OF

CRIME FICTION

PETER HAINING

The Plot Thickens: a classic illustration by Norman Rockwell
from the front cover of the *Saturday Evening Post*, 8
September 1923. (©The Curtis Publishing Co.)

THE GOLDEN AGE OF
CRIME
FICTION

PETER HAINING

PRION

This is a Prion Book

First published in 2002

This edition published in 2012 by Prion
An imprint of the Carlton Publishing Group
20 Mortimer Street
London W1T 3JW

10 9 8 7 6 5 4 3 2 1

Visit our website: www.prionbooks.com

Text © copyright Peter Haining 2002
Design © copyright Prion Books Ltd

A CIP catalogue record for this book is available from
the British Library.

ISBN 978 1 85375 869 0

Design by Grade Design Consultants, London
Scanning by Chris Scott, Text Box Graphics
Printed in Dubai

CONTENTS

Foreword vii

CHAPTER **1** Cold-Blooded Killers & Hot Penny Bloods 2

CHAPTER **2** The Yellow-Back Crime Fighters 26

CHAPTER **3** Dime-a-Dozen Sleuths 46

CHAPTER **4** The Rivals of Sherlock Holmes 66

CHAPTER **5** Enter the Private Investigators 96

CHAPTER **6** The Poets of Tabloid Murder 128

CHAPTER **7** The Mean Streets of Crime Noir 158

CHAPTER **8** The Spies Who Came In from the Cold 184

Index 211

FOREWORD

There are stories of the 'detection' of criminal activities which date back two thousand years and more. Accounts of astute people capable of interpreting clues and cross-examining suspected wrongdoers can be found in the Bible and among Chinese tales from as early as the seventh century. In the *Apocrypha*, for instance, the story of Susanna and the Elders tells of Daniel, who questions and convicts two elders of false testimony and rescues an innocent young girl from death; and recounted in *The Exploits of Ti Jen-chieh* (630–700) are the cases of a Chinese magistrate whose successful enquiries enable him to become an influential statesman in the T'ang dynasty. Both Daniel and Ti Jen-chieh are prototypes of the modern detective, yet neither are described as such. That tag would have to wait many years – until the middle of the nineteenth century, in fact – when the art of detection, or 'ratiocination', was first labelled and utilized in fiction by Edgar Allan Poe, now rightly acknowledged as the 'father of the detective story'. Poe, in five unique short stories, started what has become with the passage of time one of the most absorbing, challenging and exciting of all literary genres.

The entire evolution of detective fiction can be summarized in three words: *whodunit*, *howdunit* and *whydunit*. The first refers to the pure puzzle story in which a detective – amateur or professional – solves a crime and brings the criminal to justice. In the *howdunit*, the focus shifts to the method by which the crime was committed; and in the *whydunit* the psychological motives of the criminal are paramount in the story.

Crime, of course, can be committed in any number of ways and can take place in any sort of environment, from the everyday suburban home to the murky world of espionage. This sense of artistic freedom has challenged the writers of detective stories, often resulting in the creation of heroes who are now household names. Indeed, between Poe and the era of James Bond, *all* the elements that make up the modern stories of crime and detection evolved. It is my pleasure to depict those authors who have been responsible for this classic era in the pages that follow.

PETER HAINING, London

Cold-Blooded Killers & Hot Penny Bloods

COLD-BLOODED KILLERS
& HOT PENNY BLOODS

The man who invented the detective story was a deeply disturbed American writer and poet named Edgar Allan Poe. Believed by some of his biographers to have been an alcoholic and drug user, his life dogged by poverty and hopeless love affairs, Poe created the first major detective in fiction and in just five stories laid down the ground rules for the detective story. His own nature was a mixture of intelligence and arrogance; he was obsessive and at times his behaviour bordered on the insane. Yet, in his tragic life cut short before he reached the age of 40, Poe's work ensured him recognition as probably the greatest American writer of the nineteenth century and the acknowledged 'father' of the tale of detection. He was a genius, and his *oeuvre* gripped the imagination of generations of readers and of all writers of detective fiction.

The influences which led to the remarkable achievements of Edgar Allan Poe (1809–1849) have been much debated; two events in his life, however, seem to be especially significant. Born in Boston, the son of two professional actors, David Poe and his English-born wife, Elizabeth, he was orphaned while still a child following their sudden death from tuberculosis. The boy was raised instead by wealthy foster parents, educated for a while in England and then at the University of Virginia. Here he displayed a talent for prose and verse – publishing his first book of poetry, *Tamerlane & Other Poems*, in 1827 – and, the evidence suggests, started to develop his interest in crime that would have such a profound effect on literature.

In 1825 a jealous husband, Jeroboam

Above: The 'father of detectives', C. Auguste Dupin, sets about solving *The Murders in the Rue Morgue* (1841) in an illustration by Byam Shaw.
Below: Later French edition of the *Mémoires de Vidocq* (1828–1829) which probably influenced Edgar Allan Poe.

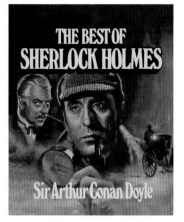

Left: The first detective partnership in crime fiction: Auguste Dupin (right) and his American friend – who bears a strong resemblance to Poe – pictured by the American artist, Charles Raymond Macauley.
Above: Sherlock Holmes and Doctor Watson followed in the footsteps of Dupin and his companion.

Beauchamp, killed the Attorney General of Kentucky, Solomon Sharp, for seducing Beauchamp's wife, Anne. While Beauchamp was awaiting execution, Anne committed suicide. So distraught was the husband at hearing this news that he tried the same thing, instantly providing the press of the day with a sensational story which would soon be called the 'Kentucky Tragedy'. The young Poe was among those who became absorbed by the events and he used them as the basis for a blank verse drama, *Politan*, relocating the setting to Rome and making the wronged couple English. Although five episodes were published in *The Southern Literary Messenger* between December 1835 and January 1836, the story was never completed. At much the same time, Poe is also believed to have read a series of sensational articles, 'Unpublished Passages in the Life of Vidocq, the French Minister of Police' in *Burton's Gentleman's Magazine*, to which he was also a contributor. These were extracts from the ghost-written, highly romanticized *Memoires* of François Eugéne Vidocq (1775–1857), a criminal turned thief-taker who coined the phrase 'set a thief to catch a thief' and founded the Police de Sûreté in Paris (published in four volumes during 1828–1829). Elements of both these American and French sources are found in Poe's ground-breaking short stories.

The first of Poe's five tales, 'The Murders in the Rue Morgue', appeared in *Graham's Magazine* in April 1841. Set in Paris, it introduces the Chevalier C. Auguste Dupin, a somewhat eccentric but highly intelligent and scholarly young man of excellent family who has fallen on hard times. Dupin is fascinated by crime and meets an American who also shares his interests, and the two take up residence in a curious old mansion at 33 Rue Dunot in the Faubourg St-Germain district. It is here that the Chevalier begins his career as a solver of crimes. The first is the baffling case of two women who have been brutally slain while in a locked room in the Rue Morgue. To aid his deductions, Dupin and his friend walk the gas-lit streets of Paris deep in conversation. Poe describes the method by which the amateur investigator finally solves the killing as 'ratiocination' – rationalizing the facts one by one – the term 'detective' not yet being in use. The result is the first analytical detective story: the detection in it more interesting than the crime. Poe's introduction of the companion-as-narrator device was to prove the precursor of many such alliances – most famously Sherlock Holmes and Doctor Watson – while the dumbfounded police officer (Holmes' Inspector Lestrade) and the concept of the 'Locked Room Mystery' would also echo down the ages of detective fiction.

The forthright and occasionally arrogant Dupin – regarded by many critics as an idealization of the author himself – returned the following year in 'The Mystery of Marie Roget', a story about the discovery of the body of a young shop girl floating in the River Seine. Published as a three-part serial in *Snowden's Ladies Companion*, November 1842– February 1843, it too is a landmark story – the first example of the armchair detective exercising his cerebral powers (Agatha

Christie's Hercule Poirot with his 'little grey cells' being an archetypal example of the tradition). Throughout the story, Dupin sits behind the closed shutters of his library studying the newspaper accounts of the girl's death which are brought to him. He wears dark green glasses to avoid any distractions, and to aid concentration he smokes a meerschaum pipe. This second case was based on a real-life murder, that of Mary Rogers, a pretty American clerk, found in the Hudson River in August 1841 – a mystery still unsolved at the time Poe proposed his solution: that it had been a crime of passion.

A year passed before Poe wrote a third case, 'The Purloined Letter' for an annual publication, *The Gift*, issued in October 1844. Dupin again breaks new ground: here the Prefect of Police in Paris appeals to him for help in finding some documents stolen from the royal apartments – and Dupin succeeds in doing so after only the most cursory inspection of the premises. With this story,

Right: A horrifying picture of the killer in the Rue Morgue by American artist Francis Simpson Coburn.
Below: The discovery of the body in *The Mystery of Marie Roget* (1842–1843).

Dupin playing the armchair detective in *The Mystery of Marie Roget* and proving to be the precursor of Agatha Christie's Hercule Poirot.

Poe introduced the 'concealment in the most obvious place' ploy, which has since been popular with many other writers. It has also been argued that this story, with its reference to the activities of secret agents, is a prototype of the modern spy story such as the adventures of James Bond.

Two other tales of detection by Poe deserve mention, though Dupin appears in neither. 'The Gold Bug' (*The Dollar Newspaper*, June 1843) describes the efforts of William Legrand to decipher a cryptogram in order to locate some buried treasure. 'Thou Art the Man' (*Graham's Magazine*, July 1844) offers no less than four precedent-setting elements: an anonymous narrator (foreshadowing Dashiell Hammett's 'The Continental Op' and his ilk); the earliest use of ballistics; false clues laid by the guilty man; and the murderer ultimately exposed as the least likely suspect. Together with the three Dupin cases, these stories –

Another Byam Shaw illustration for Poe's *The Gold Bug* (1843).

Poe's mystery of *The Purloined Letter* (1844) is regarded as a prototype of spy stories like those of James Bond.

The anonymous narrator of Poe's *Thou Art the Man* (1844) foreshadowed Dashiell Hammett's famous Continental Op.

The first American detective novel, Charles Burdett's *The Gambler*, or, *The Policeman's Story*, (1848) was a pointer to the 'yellow-back' memoirs of policemen like Walter's *Recollections of a Detective Police-Officer* (1856).

all written in a period of just over three years – anticipated virtually every type of detective-crime story, and their impact will be evident in almost every page of this book. Auguste Dupin, 'the father of detectives', has been portrayed on the screen in a number of adaptations of varying degrees of faithfulness, notably by the American actors Leon Ames, Patric Knowles and Steve Forrest, and the English classical actor Edward Woodward.

The first writer to be inspired by Poe's tales of ratiocination was another American, Charles Burdett (1815–1878), who also took the facts of Mary Rogers' life and death – in particular the seductive elements of her character – in creating *The Gambler*, or, *The Policeman's Story*, published in 1848 and generally accepted as the first American detective *novel*. Despite the importance of this book, copies are of the utmost rarity, and very

little is known about its creator beyond the facts that he was born in New York and, like Poe, was a journalist who turned to writing articles, short stories and historical novels based on American history. Burdett is believed to have reported on the discovery of Mary Rogers' body for his newspaper and then to have decided to use the theme for a novel in which he also moralizes at some length about the 'dire perils' of gambling. In a preface to the book, the author states that all the events described in it are true and the facts were given to him by one of the police officers who investigated the crime. This practice was to become commonplace among the authors of detective 'memoirs', such as *Recollections of a Detective Police-Officer* by 'Walters' (see *passim*) which became very popular during the 'yellow-back era'.

Poe was also an important influence on a

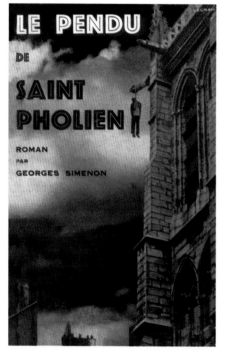

The French author Émile Gaboriau introduced the *roman policier* with novels like *Le Crime d'Orcival* (1867) which Georges Simenon turned into a hugely successful genre of its own.

French writer, Émile Gaboriau (1832–1873), who is credited with inventing a particularly Gallic form of detective fiction, the *roman policier*, later brilliantly extemporized by Georges Simenon. Gaboriau's keynote contribution was a detective, Monsieur Lecoq, who appears in five novels, beginning in 1866 with *L'Affaire Lerouge*. Like Poe, Gaboriau had read the fictionalized life story of Eugène Vidocq, and the similarities between the reformed thief and Lecoq are too striking to be mere coincidence. As a young man, Lecoq loses his father while studying to become a lawyer and, thrown on his own resources, is on the verge of a life of crime when he manages to get a job with the Sûreté, quickly displaying a formidable ability as a detective. He only plays a small part in *L'Affaire Lerouge*, in which an amateur detective, Père Tabaret,

deserves most of the credit for tracking down the brutal killer of an old woman. But in *Le Dossier 113* (1867), Lecoq takes centre stage in unravelling the mystery of a banker's wife who has succumbed to blackmail in order to keep secret details of her daughter's birth. For the first time in fiction, Lecoq uses a number of specialized techniques during the enquiry, in particular the study of footprints and a means of detecting whether or not a bed has been slept in! A third adventure, *Le Crime d'Orcival* (1867), reveals Lecoq as a master of disguise and – in his own words – 'the best and most famous detective in the world'. Two more novels further enhanced his stature – *Les Esclaves de Paris* (1868) and *Le Petit Vieux des Batignolles*, published after Gaboriau's death in 1876 – as did a silent movie version of *Le Dossier 113* made in

France and a Hollywood production in 1932 with Lew Cody as the man from the Sûreté.

These five novels by Émile Gaboriau undoubtedly deserve to have earned him better recognition in the history of crime fiction than he is generally given. Born in Saujo, he was initially intent on a career in the army but, growing disillusioned with his lack of promotion, quit the service and got a job as secretary and assistant to the writer Paul Ferval, who produced hundreds of serial stories for the *feuilletons*, or serial leaflets, in the leading French newspapers. Many of Ferval's stories contained elements of crime, and Gaboriau was regularly dispatched by his employer to collect first-hand information from the prisons, courts and morgues of Paris. In 1859, though, the pupil became the master and began to write his own serials. After several moderately successful romances, Gaboriau hit on a winning formula with *L'Affaire Lerouge* and thereafter all his titles became very popular, as Chris Steinbrunner and Otto Penzler have noted in the *Encyclopedia of Mystery and Detection* (1976):

'Gaboriau moved ahead of his contemporaries by focusing attention on the gathering and interpreting of evidence in the detection of crime, rather than the previously emphasized sensational commission of it. The *roman policier* which he invented was instantly copied by scores of prolific French hacks, most of whom followed a standard pattern: a brutally murdered victim is found; a police officer demonstrates ingenuity in solving the crime, which inevitably is connected with old family scandals; the villain is usually a handsome nobleman, often of illegitimate birth.'

Across the Channel in England, millions of readers had been devouring their own version of the *feuilleton* since the 1840s. These weekly

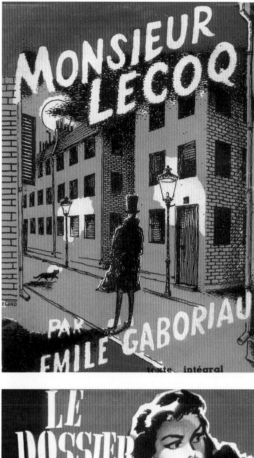

Gaboriau's most popular novels, *Monsieur Lecoq* (1869) and *Le Dossier 113* (1868), have frequently been reprinted.

serial stories also featured tales of murder, scandal and detection (with the added spice of some blue blood) and had become infamously known as 'penny bloods' because of their price and front page illustration depicting a moment of high drama and bloodshed. The eight-page periodicals, sniffily denounced in some quarters as 'penny packets of poison', were issued by a group of publishing entrepreneurs based in and around Fleet Street in London who took advantage of the recent invention of the rotary printing press and ever-increasing literacy levels to pour out a stream of fiction catering to every taste. The 'bloods' were all written by versatile hacks able to meet the weekly deadlines – although the success or failure of their serials depended entirely on sales. If these fell, the publication would stop with its next issue and the author

would be obliged to bring even the most complex plot to an immediate conclusion. The 'fierce' engravings on the front page of each issue were an undisguised sales ploy and quite often pictured a scene that did not actually materialize in the story!

One of the most popular authors of these serials was Thomas Peckett Prest (1810–1879), described by one contemporary as 'a morbid genius with a wonderful imagination'. Born into comparative affluence in Durham, he initially worked creating lyrics for the stage before being recruited into the stable of writers employed by the king of the 'penny bloods', Edward Lloyd, based in Salisbury Square, just off Fleet Street. Prest had a particular interest in tales of mystery and horror, and among his early successes were *The Maniac Father* (1842) and *The String of Pearls* (1846), inspired by the murders of Sweeney Todd, the Demon Barber of Fleet Street, and the first novel about this recurring subject in crime literature.

Prest's most popular 'blood', though, was *The Old House of West Street* (1846), a sprawling tale of mayhem and murder which ran for over 800 pages. The story was based on a real house of ill repute, the Red Lion in West Street, Clerkenwell, which for years had been the headquarters for all manner of highwaymen, thieves and lawbreakers including Jonathan Wild, Jack Sheppard and Jerry Abershaw. Several murders were committed on the premises – the bodies of the victims were tipped unceremoniously into the Fleet Ditch behind – and there were numerous secret passages, sliding panels and trap doors to help the guilty escape from the law. When the premises were finally pulled down in the mid-1840s, Prest seized on the Red Lion as the basis for his long and bloody saga, which

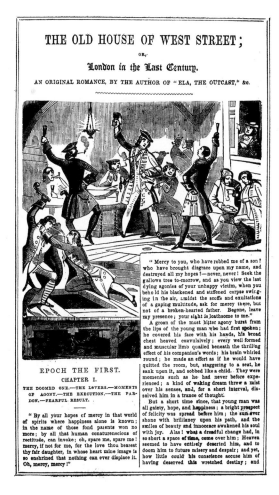

The Old House of West Street (1846), one of the most popular 'penny bloods' by Thomas Peckett Prest, who also wrote the first account of the serial killer Sweeney Todd.

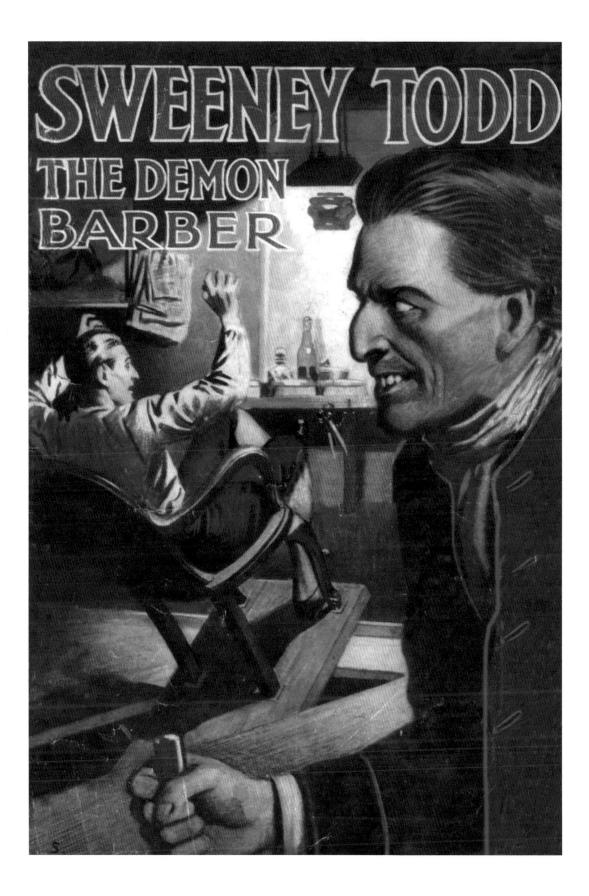

Malcolm James Rymer was another best-selling author of 'penny bloods'. His weekly adventures of *Edith Heron* (1861) were accompanied by a free colour plate.

features the resourceful villain Dick Jones, an escapee from Newgate Prison who remains hidden despite repeated searches by the police. Although vast quantities of *The Old House of West Street* were printed to satisfy public demand, few copies exist today. The following year, Lloyd and Prest had another long-running success with *Newgate*, a highly sensationalized account of the famous London prison and some of its most notorious inmates; then in 1851 they fictionalized another gruesome mass-murderer's story, *Sawney Bean, the Man Eater of Midlothian*. When Lloyd died he was almost a millionaire, while Prest ended his days in poverty, a victim of consumption.

Another of the best-selling 'penny blood' authors was Malcolm James Rymer (1804–1882), whose name was for a time thought to be a pseudonym of Prest: Rymer has subsequently been confirmed as the author of the horror classic *Varney the Vampire* (1847), for years wrongly attributed to the other writer. Rymer was born in the Scottish Highlands, trained to be an engineer in London, but was attracted to authorship and provided stories for Lloyd for several years before taking his talents to a rival, John Dicks, who paid him substantially more money. For some

years he specialized in tales of Gothic horror, including *The Black Monk* (1844) and *Ada, the Betrayed* (1845), before turning to novelizing true crimes with the story of the husband and wife murder team, Maria and Frederick Manning, who were hanged before a crowd of 50,000 people in November 1847. Rymer's greatest success came in 1860 with *Edith the Captive*, and its sequel, *Edith Heron* (1861), in which his beautiful young heroine escaped one fate worse than death after another at the grasping hands of highwaymen, footpads, evil noblemen and the arch-villain Jonathan Wild. A unique feature of the second serial was the issue each week of a free colour plate of a dramatic scene intended as a sales attraction: a crude precursor of the modern pin-up. Needless to say, these plates are now extremely rare.

Among other 'penny bloods' that proved very popular with Victorian readers were *Melina the Murderess* (1848) by an erstwhile reporter, Septimus Hunt, which recounted the adventures of a young woman who ultimately shoots and kills the soldier who has seduced and betrayed her; *The Mysteries of London* (1849), a pot-pourri of crime and criminals in the city's underworld by George W. M. Reynolds, a man described by Cyril Pearl in *A Victorian Patchwork* as 'a spiritual ancestor to Mickey Spillane and Ian Fleming'; and *The Merry Wives of London* (1850), a mixture of villainy and illicit passion written by James Lindridge who earned a reputation as a 'pseudo-pornographer' because of this penny serial with its suggestive illustrations, again the forerunner of British hard-boiled writers like Hank Janson.

Fascinating though the 'penny bloods' were, their authors added very little that was new to the crime genre. The next important development came through the work of two close friends who are also recognized as among the finest British novelists, Charles

A desperate woman at the mercy of a criminal in
The Mysteries of London (1849) by George W. M. Reynolds,
described as 'a spiritual ancestor to Mickey Spillane'.

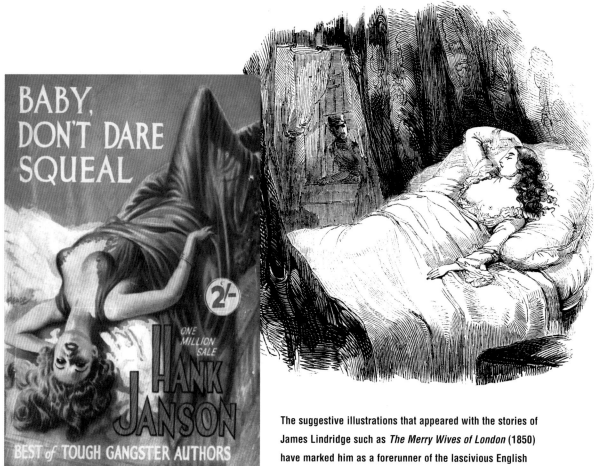

The suggestive illustrations that appeared with the stories of James Lindridge such as *The Merry Wives of London* (1850) have marked him as a forerunner of the lascivious English gangster writers like Hank Janson.

Dickens and Wilkie Collins. Dickens is credited with creating the first significant detective in English literature in the shape of Inspector Bucket in *Bleak House* (1853), while Collins' novel *The Moonstone* (1868) has been described by T. S. Eliot as 'the first, the longest and the best of modern English detective novels'. While both statements are open to dispute, the importance of the two authors' work in the genre should not be underestimated, as the durability of their books has proved. It is also interesting that several of the authors' most important detective stories were first published in America.

Crime, mystery and detection are to be found in a number of the novels of Charles Dickens (1812–1870) who had his first brush with the law as a child in Portsea when his father, a navy clerk, was imprisoned for debt. The young Dickens was forced to earn his own living for several years, before an unexpected legacy freed his father and enabled him to continue his education. After jobs as a lawyer's clerk and reporter, he began contributing sketches signed 'Boz' to the *Morning Magazine* and then achieved lasting fame with the comic masterpiece *The Posthumous Papers of the Pickwick Club* (1836). Dickens' interest in the detection of crime surfaced in a series of articles he wrote about the Bow Street Runners and the London police force, the result of spending several days and nights on the beat with local officers for the magazine he edited,

Charles Dickens' Inspector Bucket in *Bleak House* (1853) has been called 'the first significant detective in English literature'.

All The Year Round. His experiences of low life were invaluable when he came to write *Oliver Twist* (1838) and then the story of *Barnaby Rudge,* which focuses on two murders and the flight from justice of one of the main suspects. This mystery was published as a serial in 1840, and after the first episode had appeared, Edgar Allan Poe wrote an essay accurately predicting the outcome of the plot, complete with its twists and turns. When shown this article, Dickens is said to have exclaimed, 'The man must be the very devil!'

Inspector Bucket took his place in the halls of crime literature when the serialization of *Bleak House* began in 1852. Here again, Dickens had created an unforgettable character: a stout, middle-aged man who is patient and hardworking in the detection of crime. He wears a monocle, is prone to waving his finger when explaining his methods, yet invariably remains calm and collected, no matter how frantic the activity going on around him may become. At a stroke, Bucket became the prototype of the honest, competent and unexciting copper that has since been seen in countless detective stories up to and including Chief Inspector Morse. Like Dupin, Bucket has a habit of wandering around the vicinity of any crime and has a keen eye for human foibles. He displays a special pride in solving the case of the Jarndyce fortune – even if the discovery of a will comes too late to help the heirs so desperately awaiting their inheritance.

Dickens' next foray into crime, *Hunted Down,* appeared in 1859 and was based on the sensational case of a poisoner, Thomas Griffiths Wainewright, who had murdered his sister-in-law for her insurance and was then discovered to have killed others as well. In the novel, Mr Sampson, the manager of a life insurance company, plays detective after he begins to suspect that a client has killed one of his nieces and is now poisoning another. Curiously, after its serialization in England,

the story was first published as a book in America in 1861 by the T. B. Peterson Company of Philadelphia. It was not, though, until 1870 that Dickens started another crime novel, *The Mystery of Edwin Drood,* a tale of opium addiction, frustrated passion and suspected murder. Tragically, he died after completing just six chapters. The real mystery of Edwin Drood remains what Dickens intended the resolution of his tale to be – a puzzle that has since attracted the ingenuity of a number of British and American crime writers.

It is interesting to speculate what Dickens' friend Wilkie Collins (1824–1889), who outlived him by almost 20 years, might have made of the plot if he had attempted to finish *Edwin Drood.* Indeed, with his interest in crime

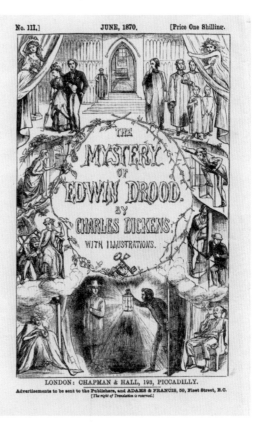

An early issue of Charles Dickens' serial crime story, *The Mystery of Edwin Drood* (1870), which he did not live to complete.

fiction, the thought must surely have crossed Collins' mind – but perhaps like so many others he believed the only satisfactory resolution had been lost with Dickens' death. His own achievements, though, ensured him a place of distinction: two masterpieces of detection, *The Woman in White* (1860) and *The Moonstone* (1868), plus several more novels and short stories in which crime is prominent.

Wilkie Collins' life was not unlike that of Poe: he had an unsettled childhood and education, suffered from bad health, took to opium, and died a disgruntled figure, having never been able to repeat the success of his two great detective novels. Born in London, the son of a landscape painter, he nursed ambitions to follow in his father's footsteps, but instead studied law. During this period he met Charles Dickens and was soon collaborating with him on articles and stories for *All The Year Round*. Collins broke into the world of crime literature with a trio of ingenious short stories and a 'first'

Right: Several of Wilkie Collins' ground-breaking crime short stories were collected in *After Dark* (1856).
Below: *Who Is the Thief?* by Wilkie Collins was first published in America in *The Atlantic Monthly* in 1858.

– the first humorous detective story. 'A Terribly Strange Bed' was the first of these, about a gambler who finds himself trapped in a bed which smothers its victims. It was followed by 'A Stolen Letter' which was clearly influenced by Poe's story 'The Purloined Letter', and a murder-mystery, 'Who Killed Zebedee?' These stories were later collected in *After Dark* (1856). Collins' ground-breaking comic tale 'Who Is the Thief? – Extracted from the Correspondence of the London Police' was written in 1858 and first appeared in the April issue of the leading American magazine, *The Atlantic Monthly*. It consists of a series of letters passed between Chief Inspector Theakstone, Sergeant Bulmer and an amateur detective, Matthew Sharpin, who very nearly

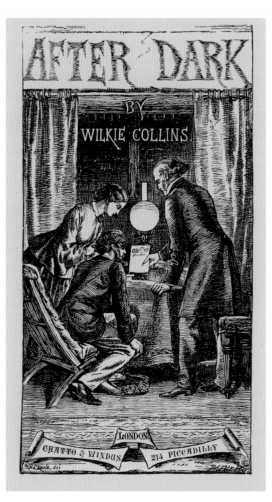

sabotages a police operation to catch a robber. The story made its first appearance in book form as part of a collection, *The Queen of Hearts*, published by Hurst & Blackett of London in 1859.

The following year Wilkie Collins stunned the reading public and critics alike with *The Woman in White*. There was an intriguing element to this story of an heiress, Laura Fairlie, who is the object of a plot by her husband and his villainous friend, Count Fosco, to defraud her, because it was partly based on a notorious eighteenth-century French case and partly on Collins' own live-in lover. The author was already the subject of gossip in prudish Victorian society because he was not married to Caroline Graves, with whom he lived. He then immortalized their first meeting in his novel. This had occurred one evening when Collins encountered Caroline running, screaming, from a house where she had been held prisoner for several months. This dramatic moment with a 'woman in white' became the opening of the story, which detailed the detective work of Laura's lover, Walter Hartright, to defeat the two schemers. The story was first published as a serial in *All The Year Round*, followed by *Harper's Weekly* in November 1859, and was an even bigger success when published as a book by Sampson Low the following year. *The Woman in White* has been dramatized several times for the stage and was filmed in 1929 with Blanche Sweet, followed by Hilary Eaves (1940), Eleanor Parker (1948) and most recently Helena Bonham-Carter (1988).

It was to be a further eight years before Wilkie Collins published *The Moonstone* in *All The Year Round*. The story centres around the search for a huge yellow diamond, the Moonstone, stolen in India and now missing after being bequeathed to Rachel Verinder. Hot on the trail are a murderous trio of Indians determined to return the Moonstone home,

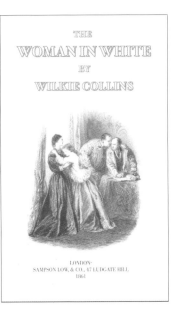

First edition of *The Woman in White* (1860), Wilkie Collins' landmark novel about a plot to defraud a young heiress.

The Moonstone, Wilkie Collins' second great story of detection, written in 1868, has been repeatedly reprinted in paperback. This cover illustration shows Sergeant Cuff discovering a vital clue.

and the custodian of the law, Sergeant Cuff. The policeman is not a very prepossessing figure: thin, elderly, bearded and dressed in unobtrusive black clothes. He has steely grey eyes, though, which never miss a trick, and he brings great energy and perseverance to crime solving. Once again Collins had drawn on real events for his story: the Constance Kent murder case in 1860, investigated by Inspector Jonathan Wicher. Although Kent was acquitted of the killing – ruining the Inspector's reputation – five years later she admitted she *had* committed the crime. Surprisingly, this outstanding story has only been filmed twice – as a silent in 1915 (without Sergeant Cuff at all!) and in 1934 starring Charles Irwin. But along with *The Woman in White*, it continued to sell throughout the 'yellow-back era' and was also one of the first titles to appear in the subsequent 'Sixpenny Paperback' series – the forerunners of today's mass-market softcovers. Three of Wilkie Collins' other novels involving crime and mystery were also popular in these formats: *Hide and Seek* (1854), the mystery of an orphan and her mother; *A Rogue's Life* (1859), about an unscrupulous fortune hunter; and *The Law and the Lady* (1875), based on the baffling Scottish murder case of Madeleine Smith to which the jury recorded a verdict of 'Not Proven'.

Next on the scene was a man described as 'the apotheosis of the police detective in mid-Victorian literature' by Ian Ousby in *Bloodhounds of Heaven* (1876). He is Hawkshaw, a handsome, virile investigator from Scotland Yard with a reputation for no-nonsense crime fighting and equally adept at using his sharp brain or quick fists when necessary. He made his debut in 1863 in a melodrama, *The Ticket-of-Leave Man* by Tom Taylor (1817–1880), the first play in which a detective plays a central role. Taylor was born in Sunderland, studied at Glasgow University and Trinity College, Cambridge, before qualifying as a lawyer and practising in London and on the Northern Circuit. He also began writing for the *Morning Chronicle* and contributing comic sketches to *Punch* – but his real love lay in the theatre and he achieved his first success with a farce, *To Parents and Guardians*, in 1845. Taylor's two best-remembered plays are *The Ticket-of-Leave Man* and *Our American Cousin* (1855), the latter owing its fame principally to the fact that Abraham Lincoln was assassinated while watching a performance at Ford's Theatre in Washington in 1865. *The Ticket-of-Leave Man* tells the story of a Lancashire lad, Bob Brierly, who becomes involved with two criminals, Dalton and Moss, and is unjustly convicted and sent to prison for one of their crimes. On his release on parole as a 'ticket-of-leave man', Brierly is again tempted into villainy by Dalton and Moss but fortunately is saved by the intervention of Hawkshaw, 'the most famous of all the Scotland Yard detectives', who has been on the trail of the two villains for some time, and proves the boy's innocence. A contemporary description of Tom Taylor suggests that he was the model for his hero: 'a man of lithe, sinewy figure, rugged features, a pugilistic jaw and eyes which glittered like steel and fixed those he was looking at with the bull's eye of a policeman's lantern.' During the course of the drama, Hawkshaw reveals a little of his illustrious past as 'the hero of the great gold dust robberies and the famous Trunk-line forgeries.'

Despite this hint of Hawkshaw's career, Tom Taylor never wrote another word about the detective, although on the back of the success of the play it was novelized by a mystery writer, Cecil Henry Bullivent (1882–1961).

Opposite: The career of *Hawkshaw the Detective*, created for the stage by Tom Taylor, was continued in print by crime writer Cecil Bullivent, who was also a contributor to the pioneer British periodical *The Detective Magazine*.

The DETECTIVE MAGAZINE 7ᵈ

April 27th, 1923.   Vol. 1. No. 12.   Fortnightly.

An Incident From "The Shadow on the Blind." (See inside.)

...M AND ROMANCE OF CRIME DETECTION.

Hawkshaw the Detective

THE MAN FROM SCOTLAND YARD

THIS WEEK'S STORY: THE LASS OF MORLAND'S MILL.

The fictionalized cases of the famous American detective Allan Pinkerton such as *The Expressman and the Detective* (1874) directly inspired the 'private eyes' who later filled the pages of pulp magazines.

This book sold so well that Bullivent continued to write cases about the detective until the outbreak of the First World War. As well as developing the Hawkshaw series, he also contributed to the earliest British periodical devoted solely to crime, *The Detective Magazine*, which published short stories and articles by retired police officers, notably two ex-Chief Detective Inspectors, Haigh and Gough. Bullivent's contributions to the ground-breaking magazine included a series of stories about a private investigator, later collected as *Garnett Bell: Detective* (1920), plus *Millie Lynn – Shop Investigator* (1920), one of the first stories of a store detective, and a gangster thriller, *A King of Crooks* (1932).

Well known as Hawkshaw and the other fictional detectives might be, all were almost eclipsed by a real-life character, Allan Pinkerton (1819–1884) who, in the space of a few years, became the most famous detective in the world and founder of the crime-busting agency which still bears his name. Inventor of the slogan 'We Never Sleep' and the logo of a wide-open eye, he and his 'operatives' hunted down law-breakers by the thousand and gave rise to the catchphrase description 'private eye'. Pinkerton waged war on such notorious outlaws as Butch Cassidy and the Sundance Kid and the James Brothers, as well as investigating corrupt public officials and tracking down criminals like Adam Worth, the international counterfeiter, con-man and art thief, who became the model for Sherlock Holmes' arch-enemy, Professor Moriarty. He also published no fewer than 18 books about the agency's achievements which added a new dimension to the history of crime literature and earned their author the epithet of 'the grandaddy of gumshoes'. As for the agency itself, its professionalism, mobility and ubiquity anticipated in many ways the Federal Bureau of Investigations, which was not created until 1908.

Legend has it that Pinkerton read Vidocq's *Memoirs* when he was a young man and this sparked his later career. What is certain is that he was born not in America but in Glasgow, in the notorious Gorbals district, and was apprenticed as a cooper. From his youth he displayed a fiery temper and a hatred of oppression, becoming a militant extremist for the rights of the working man. Not surprisingly, these activities brought Pinkerton to the attention of the law, and in order to escape imprisonment he was forced to flee Scotland in 1842, emigrating to America. In Chicago he found a city growing faster than authority and had no trouble in getting a job in the city's rudimentary police force. Such was the success of the brave, hardworking and dogged lawman in rounding up small time criminals, powerful gangs and even a notorious band of counterfeiters, that in 1850 he decided to set up his own agency. The Pinkerton's National Detective Agency rapidly became the most successful organization of its kind, and today, specializing in security, employs over 50,000 people in over 250 offices in 20 countries.

It is said that Allan Pinkerton was something of a tyrant and a bully to his 'operatives', and although he could be a source of inspiration to them was also capable of firing off hysterical and self-righteous letters to subordinates – especially if he caught them drinking. He also had a somewhat ambivalent attitude towards the law, declaring on one occasion, 'The end justifies the means if the end is justice.' He is known to have authorized illegal burglaries on behalf of clients and advocated the killing of bank robbers on the grounds that juries would not convict them. During the years 1860–1862, he was responsible for the safety of the new President Abraham Lincoln – providing the

kind of protection which the Secret Service offers a president today – and for a time was a spymaster as the Head of Intelligence to General McClellan, operating behind Confederate lines with a small group of trusted operatives gathering military intelligence. When the General was removed from his post for lack of activity, Pinkerton returned to sleuthing, and it seems highly probable that if he had stayed in the job, Lincoln would not have been assassinated. Pinkerton believed implicitly in the *rightness* of his mission to subdue crime: 'I feel no power on earth is able to check me, no power in Heaven or Hell can influence me when I know I am in the right.' Gifted with an inordinate sense of inquisitiveness, he was also quick to accept new ideas to aid him in his work. He established the first 'Rogues' Gallery' of mug-shots and made good use of a new invention, the telephone. The agency also pioneered international crime-fighting by exchanging information with detective agencies in other countries, notably Scotland Yard.

Pinkerton's reputation for incorruptibility shines through alongside his faith in his own moral rectitude in the pages of his books, all issued under the generic title, 'Allan Pinkerton's Detective Stories' by the Chicago publishers W. B. Keen, Cooke & Co. Notable among these works, which were all illustrated with graphic line engravings, are the railway saga, *The Expressman and*

The master criminal Adam Worth, whom Allan Pinkerton pursued, was the inspiration for Sherlock Holmes' great adversary, Professor Moriarty.

the Detective (1874); *The Mollie Maguires and the Detectives* (1877), about the subduing of the IRA-type killers who had terrorized the Pennsylvania coalfields; and his memoirs, *Thirty Years a Detective* (1884). In all of these cases, though, the bravery of Pinkerton's 'private eyes' is very evident – many took great risks and some even lost their lives serving their irascible Scottish taskmaster – and from their ranks emerged one of the greatest of all crime writers, Dashiell Hammett. Curiously, though, Pinkerton made little reference to the fact that he also employed some brave *women*. Unlike his rivals, he was always keen to hire women operatives and believed them to be essential to success in a wide range of cases. The evidence suggests he thought them at least as clever and daring as men in detective work, and it is to Pinkerton's eternal credit that he resisted opposition to such appointments from within his own

organization. The facts show that he employed female detectives almost half a century before the New York City Police Force took on its first women officers.

Despite their undoubted position of pre-eminence in crime fiction today, women writers came late into the genre, and arguments still simmer as to who was actually the first female detective novel writer. The honour lies between two American ladies: Victoria Fuller Victor (1831–1886) who wrote as 'Seeley Regester', and Anna Katherine Green (1846–1935), described variously as the mother, grandmother or even godmother of the detective story. To be strictly accurate, Seeley Regester's *The Dead Letter*, published in 1867, was the first detective *novel* by a female writer, while Green was the first woman to make a career as a crime novelist, starting with *The Leavenworth Case* in 1878. She also created one of the earliest female detectives, Amelia Butterworth, a genteel lady of refined manners and remarkable insight – a forerunner in every respect of Agatha Christie's Miss Marple.

The reason for the arguments about this question are probably due to the fact that very little was known until recently about Seeley Regester, whose name had previously only been seen on historical and humorous novels. Indeed, there were those who believed the author was a man, as much of her fiction was issued by one of the leading 'Dime Novel' publishers, Beadle and Adams, whose contributors were almost solely male. Born in the little town of Erie in Pennsylvania, Metta Victoria Fuller Victor, to give the writer her full name, wrote her first novel, *The Last Days of Tul: A Romance of the Lost Cities of the*

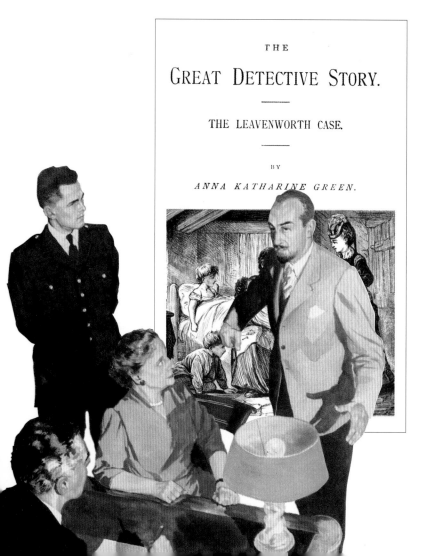

THE

GREAT DETECTIVE STORY.

———

THE LEAVENWORTH CASE.

———

BY

ANNA KATHARINE GREEN.

Amelia Butterworth, one of the first female detectives, making her debut in 1878 in *The Leavenworth Case* by the American author Anna Katherine Green. She was the forerunner of Agatha Christie's Miss Marple.

Yucatan, when she was only 15, and this provided her with an entree into the stable of Beadle and Adams for whom she wrote a constant stream of serials for the next quarter of a century. *The Dead Letter* – in which a murderer is revealed through hints in a mysterious piece of correspondence – owes an obvious debt to Poe's famous story, yet went largely unnoticed after its publication in *Beadle's Dime Library* in the autumn of 1867.

No such journey into obscurity followed the publication of *The Leavenworth Case*. It is the account of policeman Ebenezer Gryce's investigations into the murder of Mr Leavenworth just as he is about to sign a new will – and it caught the imagination of readers for several reasons. Gryce himself is a middle-aged, quietly spoken and competent officer who for all his diffidence has a vast knowledge of esoteric subjects and a keen mind for the 'science of probability'. Critics have remarked that his specialist knowledge of things like types of cigar ash and different grades of writing paper anticipate the more famous methods of Sherlock Holmes, then still a decade away from his first appearance. If Gryce has a problem it is his sense of inferiority. He believes his profession precludes him from ever being considered a gentleman, and is therefore happy to call on the help of his friend, Amelia Butterworth, a lady of considerable social standing who mixes easily in all sections of American society. Miss Butterworth again comes to his assistance in subsequent cases including *A Strange*

Disappearance (1880), *Behind Closed Doors* (1888) and *That Affair Next Door* (1897).

It is perhaps not altogether surprising that Anna Green should have been attracted to crime fiction, as she was the daughter of a well-known New York criminal lawyer, James Wilson Green. However, her early inclinations were towards poetry; she published a collection of verse, *The Defense of the Bride & Other Poems*, in 1882. Four years earlier, however, she wrote *The Leavenworth Case* which, it is believed, was based on an incident from her father's career, as the subtitle, *A Lawyer's Tale*, seems to substantiate. The huge success of this book prompted Anna Green to write further mystery and detective stories, a feature of which is the engrossing deductive and investigative detective work of the major characters, notably Gryce and Miss Butterworth. The authoress later adapted *The Leavenworth Case* for the stage – her husband taking a leading role – and the story was filmed as a silent movie in 1923 and then in Hollywood in 1936 with Donald Cook and Erin O'Brien-Moore as the detective partnership.

The advent of the lady detective was certainly long overdue in America. In Britain, however, the female crime fighter had already been introduced to readers thanks to a new form of publishing, the 'yellow-back' novel, which was not only inexpensive and put popular fiction within the reach of a mass audience, but also provided an ideal vehicle for further developments in the history of crime fiction.

THE YELLOW-BACK CRIME FIGHTERS

Mary Paschal is 'one of the much-dreaded, but little-known people called Female Detectives'. A dark-haired beauty with arching eyebrows and ever-alert eyes, she made her debut as the first lady crime fighter in Britain in the pages of *Experiences of a Lady Detective* published in 1861. The book, with its predominantly yellow illustration on strawboard covered by glazed paper, shows Mary tracking a suspected murderer through a crowded London park. It was to prove a typical example of the publishing phenomenon

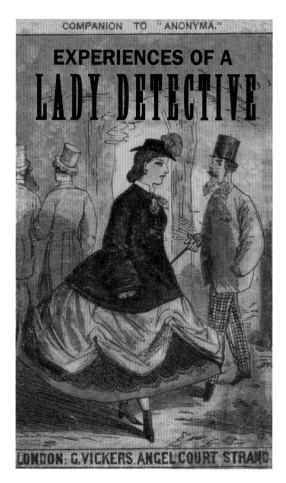

The first of the 'yellow-back' female crime fighters, Mary Paschal, who made her debut in print in 1861.

of cheap fiction that took the British reading public by storm in the 1860s and prospered for almost half a century, a period that has since become known as the 'yellow-back era' after the unmistakable characteristic of the books. Novels of crime and mystery – such as the one about Mary Paschal – were to prove major elements of this incredible success story.

The author of *Experiences of a Lady Detective* was given as 'Anonyma' and the publisher, George Vickers of London, implied in the book and advertizing that the 'experiences' had been written by the heroine herself. Just as the yellow covers were used to identify these inexpensive works, so the idea that the texts were written by real detectives was used to enhance their appeal. Whether Mary Paschal had any basis in fact or not, she is undoubtedly a worthy pioneer of crime fiction. Aged about 40, she is described as having taken up her occupation as a result of her husband's sudden death, which left her penniless. Receiving a mysterious offer to put her 'good birth, education and subtle brain to work in the fight against crime', she has plunged into a life that is strange, exciting and mysterious. 'Soon,' she writes in the book's opening chapter, 'like an accomplished actress, I was playing my part in the dramas which required nerve and strength, cunning and confidence.'

Mary Paschal's cases, in which she describes hunting down two murderers, bringing about the arrest of various crooks and a blackmailer, and also audaciously using her own femininity to bring to justice a wealthy aristocrat who is debauching young girls, sold so well that in 1864 Vickers issued a second volume, *Revelations of a Lady Detective*, in which the intrepid heroine described tackling a further cross-section of rogues and villains, not to

Wilkie Collins' novel *The Woman in White* was one of the early best sellers in the 'yellow-back' format along with his story of a confidence trickster, *A Rogue's Life* (1870).

mention bringing about the downfall of a prominent Member of Parliament who had been using his position to pervert the course of justice and amass a fortune. By all accounts this 'yellow-back', too, was a success, but 'Anonyma' wrote no more tales about the first female detective. Instead, she produced a series of books about London high- and low-life, including a highly embellished 'biography' of a notorious Victorian lady of pleasure, 'Skittles' (a.k.a. Catherine Walters), who bestowed her favours on numerous rich patrons – notably the Duke of Devonshire whom she nicknamed 'Harty-Tarty' – and who is today commemorated by a blue plaque in South Street, Mayfair, which refers to her as 'the last Victorian courtesan'.

The picture of the criminal fraternity that 'Anonyma's' titles offered readers was very different from the subject of the two books credited with starting the 'yellow-back era'.

These were a culinary guide, *Letters Left at the Pastry Cook's* by Horace Mayhew, and *Money: How To Get, How To Keep, and How To Use It*, both issued in April 1853 by a London firm, Ingram, Cooke & Co. The two books with their eye-catching, illustrated covers were in stark contrast to the plain cloth or leather-bound volumes of the time. They were aimed unashamedly at providing inexpensive reading for the masses, and it was the pioneer 'self-help' title, *Money*, with its vivid yellow covers, that gave the entire series its name and established the format that other publishers were soon following. The major players in this area of publishing would soon prove to be Vickers, George Routledge & Sons, Chatto & Windus and Ward Lock; the latter would become even more famous for publishing the first Sherlock Holmes case, *A Study in Scarlet*, in 1887.

The growth of the railways in Britain, from

The English mystery novelist Mrs B. M. Croker set some of her most popular crime stories in India, including the collection, *To Let* (1899).

she produced several crime novels with Indian settings, including *Interference* (1891), *The Real Lady Hilda* (1895), *Terence* (1898) – which was dramatized in the USA – and a collection of detective short stories, *To Let* (1899), all published by Chatto & Windus.

Mrs Croker's main British rival was Helen Mathers (1853–1920), the wife of a distinguished London surgeon, Henry Reeves. Mathers made a notable debut in 1878 with *As He Comes Up the Stairs*, in which a woman wrongly convicted of the murder of her husband and his gipsy sweetheart recounts her story in the condemned cell. The two-

shilling 'yellow-back' edition published by Richard Bentley sold over 100,000 copies in the next decade. Mathers chose courtroom settings for three of her other crime novels, *The Land O' Leal* (1878), *Eyre's Acquittal* (1884) and *Murder or Manslaughter* (1885), in which a Scottish barrister, Hugo Hold, solves the crime. Another of her rare novels in the cheap format is *Stephen Hatton* (1886), an anguished account of a man whose alleged victim is found alive after he has been supposedly executed.

Two American authoresses of crime also proved very popular with the English travelling public at this time. 'Yellow-back' reprints of the novels of Emma Murdoch – writing as 'Lawrence L. Lynch' – and Carolyn Wells, creator of detective Fleming Stone, were as well received in Britain as across the Atlantic. They helped to bridge the gap between the old-style crime novel of the nineteenth century and the heyday of the genre which would follow in the twentieth.

The London publishers Ward Lock enthusiastically promoted the thrillers of 'Lawrence L. Lynch' after securing the rights from a publisher in Chicago, where the author lived. Whether Ward Lock knew that Lynch was actually the Chicago socialite Emma Murdoch Van Deventer (1854–1919) proved immaterial: the books with their striking covers and evocative titles all sold many thousands of copies. *Shadowed By Three* (1879) spotlighted an intrepid private detective, Francis Ferrars, who returned in *The Last Stroke* (1896); *The New*

Fleming Stone, the book-loving American detective created by Carolyn Wells, appeared in dozens of cases including *The Crime in the Crypt* (1928).

'Lawrence Lynch' was the pen-name of the US crime novelist Emma Murdoch Van Deventer, many of whose titles such as *The Last Stroke* (1896) were republished as 'yellow-backs'.

Detective Story: The Diamond Coterie (1884) introduced a dashing criminal investigator, Neil J. Bathurst. *A Mountain Mystery: or, The Outlaws of the Rockies* (1886) is one of the earliest novels to feature an officer of the Mounties, Gordon Stanhope. Murdoch was on her home territory in *Against Odds* (1894) and *No Proof, A Detective Story* (1895), with Carl Masters of the Chicago Police Department solving the first, and a young city lawyer, Kenneth Jasper, turning detective to dig up evidence where at first there seems to be none at all, in the second.

Carolyn Wells (1870–1942) very nearly did not live long enough to achieve a literary career, suffering a debilitating attack of measles at her home in Rahway, New Jersey, when she was barely six years old. For the rest of her life, Wells was virtually deaf but she became a prodigious reader. Her discovery of the works of Anna Katherine Green determined her to become a crime writer. Wells' marriage to the publisher Hadwin Houghton enhanced her literary skills and after producing a parody of Sherlock Holmes for *Lippincott's Magazine* in 1902, she introduced her own hero, Fleming Stone, an intellectual, book-loving man not unlike the hero of Baker Street, in 'The Maxwell Mystery' for *All-Story Magazine*, May 1906. Novels soon followed and Wells produced over 80 mystery stories in all, 60 of them featuring Stone. George H. Doran was Wells' publisher in America and Ward Lock in Britain, both of whom sold large quantities of her work. According to historian Eric Quayle, 'she did much to stimulate renewed interest in tales of detective fiction in the USA and created a vogue for the subject at a time when other styles of sensational novels were increasingly in favour with the reading public.'

Wells was an imaginative writer, creating several other detective heroes including Bert Bayliss, a socialite private investigator, and Kenneth Carlisle, a Hollywood leading man who gives up a career as a silent-movie star to become a crime fighter. Although her work is neglected today, Wells was also responsible for writing the first instructional manual on how to become a thriller writer, *The Technique of the Mystery Story* (1913), in which she argued against the use of impossible murder methods and declared unequivocally, 'The detective story must *seem* as real in the same sense that fairy tales *seem* real to children.' It is a dictate that no successful crime writer can afford to ignore.

Far and away the single most popular crime 'yellow-back' was *The Mystery of a Hansom Cab*, a novel originally published in

Melbourne, Australia, by the author, Fergus Hume (1859–1932), at his own expense. There is, in fact, probably no more unlikely success story in the history of crime fiction publishing than this tale of a brutal crime in which the identity of the killer is actually given away in the preface! Hume had been born in England, but emigrated with his family to New Zealand and then moved on to Australia to practise as a lawyer. In an attempt to augment his income, he asked a local bookseller what kind of book sold best. Hume wrote later, 'He replied that the detective sales of Émile Gaboriau had a large sale; and as, at this time, I had never heard of this author, I bought all his works and

determined to write a book of the same class containing a mystery, a murder and a description of the low life of Melbourne.'

Unable to find a publisher for *The Mystery of a Hansom Cab*, Hume decided to publish the book himself and just about covered his costs on the first printing. One purchaser of the book, however, was an Englishman who evidently had an eye for a commercial prospect. He promptly bought the rights from the author, set up the Hansom Cab Publishing Company in London, and launched the book onto the nation's railway bookstalls. With its simple yellow cover and illustration of a hansom cab, it rapidly sold 350,000 copies, a figure which was doubled when the story was reprinted in America. By the end of the century, *The Mystery of a Hansom Cab* had also been translated into 12 foreign languages.

Hume, who was still in Australia while all this was happening, scraped together enough

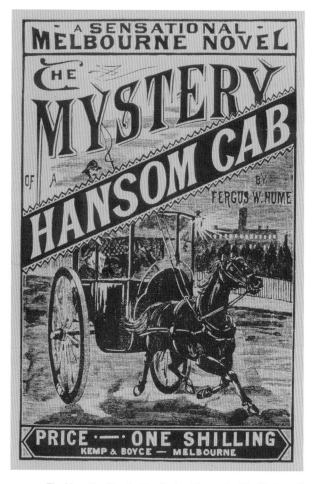

The biggest-selling 'yellow-back' of them all – *The Mystery of a Hansom Cab* by Fergus W. Hume (1886) – and another of the author's popular crime stories, *Madame Midas* (1888).

money for a fare to England and arrived in London to find his book everywhere and his name on everyone's lips. It should have made him wealthy, but having sold the copyright he was not entitled to a penny. Disappointed but not downhearted, Hume settled in Essex and in the years that followed tried desperately to repeat his success, writing over 100 more crime novels – including *Madame Midas* (1888), *For the Defense* (1898) and the optimistically entitled *The Mystery of a Motor Cab* (1908) – but none achieved anything like the popularity of the first book. Today, in most

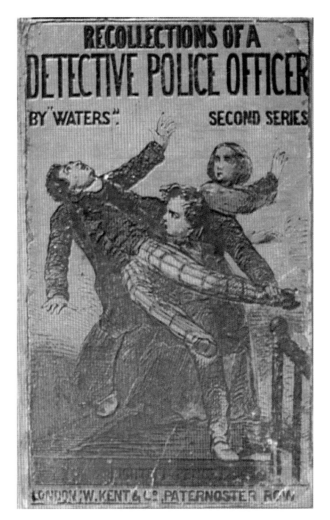

The most popular of the series of 'pseudo-real' police memoirs were those by 'Walters'. This second series of *Recollections of a Detective Police-Officer* appeared in 1859.

histories of crime fiction, Hume is dismissed as a hack whose books are unreadable and whose most famous story was 'tedious from start to finish'. Yet it outsold the works of Poe, Collins and even Conan Doyle for years, and more copies were bought in its 'yellow-back' format than any other title. Furthermore, the original Melbourne edition has the distinction today of being one of the rarest books in the world – only two copies are known to exist.

A very popular sub-genre of the 'yellow-back era' were the pseudo-real police memoirs in which apparently 'retired' members of the force recounted their triumphs in solving every imaginable type of crime from murder to larceny. In fact, most contained little more than a smattering of fact liberally coloured by anonymous authors. This minor phenomenon followed hard on the heels of the establishment in 1845 of the first Detective Police Force by Sir James Graham and was initiated by *The Recollections of a Policeman* by 'Walters' in 1849. Curiously, these stories of a London officer first appeared in *Chambers' Edinburgh Magazine* as a serial beginning in the July of that year; the book form was published in 1852 by Cornish & Lamport of New York. The US text had clearly been pirated from *Chambers'* magazine, and it was to be four years before the first official UK edition, entitled *Recollections of a Detective Police-Officer*, in striking yellow boards, was issued by J. & C. Brown of Ave Maria Lane, London. A second series of *Recollections* appeared from another London publisher, W. Kent & Co., three years later in 1859.

The first US edition in 1852 credited the author as Thomas Walters and carried an explanatory preface for the benefit of readers: 'The Detective Policeman is in some respects peculiar to England. He differs as much from the informer and spy of the Continent of Europe as the modern Protective Policeman does from the old fashioned Watchman. In point of face, he is a preventive as much as a detective. His occupation is as honourable as it is dangerous. Its difficulties and danger give it an odour of the romantic. The record of the "hair-breadth escapes" which follow, is another verification of the old saying, "Truth is stranger than fiction." '

The book claims to be the experiences of a member of the Metropolitan Police who has successfully brought to justice a variety of thieves, confidence tricksters, forgers and murderers. As a result he has been promoted to the rank of Detective and provided with two assistants who are especially useful to him in the second volume of tales. As to the actual author of these books – which have been described by John Carter as 'the most important of the early "yellow-back" books' and by Otto Penzler as 'the earliest short detective stories by an English author' – little is known beyond the fact that his real name was William Russell and he was a minor Victorian author whose books were published almost solely in cheap editions. They ranged in content from domestic tales such as *Valerie Duclos* (1854), to nautical yarns like *Cruise of the Blue Jacket* (1862) – which he signed as 'Lieutenant Warneford, RN' – and various 'memoirs' (*Experiences of a Barrister* [1856], and *Recollections of a Sheriff's Officer* [1860], to name but two), culminating in the ground-breaking work that is his best memorial. The last of Russell's books, *The Valazy Family*, appeared in 1870, and after that all is silence.

Such, however, was the success of *Recollections of a Detective Police-Officer* that it was officially published in a US edition in 1856 by Wentworth of Boston and then reissued in 1864 by the New York firm of Dick & Fitzgerald. There were also German and French translations before it made a third appearance in America, filling the entire issue of *Old Cap Collier Library*, Number 15, June

18, 1883, where it was entitled *The Secret Detective: or, One Night in a Gambling House* and ascribed to 'A London Police Captain'. The publishers of the *Library* – an archetypal 'dime novel' – were Munro's of New York, who will be discussed in the next chapter.

In the immediate aftermath of the success of 'Walters' book, the market was flooded with similar 'recollections'. However, few of these 'yellow-backs' have survived, and it is possible only to note the titles of some of the more significant examples. The energetic publishers Ward Lock appear to have dominated the field in the next decade, first signing up a London writer, Thomas Delf, who was already the unacknowledged pen behind a number of their successful cheap titles, to write a series of similar books. The first of these, *The Diary of an Ex-Detective*, was credited to 'Charles Martel' and featured a former Bow Street Runner named Bolter who recounted a score of lively if largely unbelievable investigations in the capital city. The following year Martel wrote *The Detective's Note-Book* with the same central character, and it is possible he may have written two or three more titles of which no trace now exists. That same year Ward Lock also issued *The Irish Police Officer: The Identification & Other Tales*, by one 'Robert Curtis' who was the hero of his own exploits in and around Dublin. A sequel, *Curiosities of Detection*, appeared in 1862.

Even busier on Ward Lock's behalf was Andrew Forrester, who was responsible for no fewer than three titles in the year 1863 alone. In the first of these, *The Revelations of a Private Detective*, Forrester was himself the detective, but in its successors, *Secret Service: or, Recollections of a City Detective* and *The Female Detective*, both of the investigators were unnamed in the first person narratives.

Clues: or, Leaves From a Chief Constable's Note Book also appeared in the same year, but from an Edinburgh publisher, Oliphant,

Anderson & Ferrier. It, too, was given a stamp of authority, being ascribed to William Henderson, Chief Constable of Edinburgh, although the introduction tempered such notions: 'Most of the so-called "Experiences of Detective Officers" have no foundation in fact, but are only works of imagination, and their interest is mainly due to highly exciting situations and events of a more or less improbable kind woven into a narrative of cleverly written fiction. While the following stories are in certain instances based on facts, the circumstances are not narrated exactly as they took place, but founded on events which have occurred within the writer's experience so that any interest they may possess must be ascribed to the manner of the telling.' Certainly, the book with chapters entitled 'How I Tracked Down the Silk Stealers', 'A Forger's Game of Billiards', 'The Wine Samplers' and 'An Unmitigated Scoundrel', was popular enough to go through two editions.

Another Scotsman, James McGovan, was also a major figure in the era of pseudo-memoirs. Ostensibly a detective who had served the community of Edinburgh with distinction for many years, McGovan now kept busy writing about his exploits. Published by John Menzies, who already had a strong foothold in the railway bookstall boom, the half dozen titles which followed *Brought To Bay; or, The Experiences of a City Detective* in 1878 were actually all the work of a local writer named William Crawford Honeyman. His contribution to the development of the detective story was significant, but once again little is known about him. McGovan presents himself as an energetic and skilled investigator, a feature of his cases being the confessions of the villains – frequently given on their deathbeds or in the shadow of the noose. It seems probable that McGovan/Honeyman used a number of the cases of a formerly well-known Edinburgh detective named James McLevy, who had

Clues, another collection of fictionalized police stories, was published in Edinburgh in 1863.

written his memoirs in 1861 as *Curiosities of Crime in Edinburgh During the Last Twenty Years* and claimed to have taken part in 'no fewer than 2,220 cases'. Despite the outrageousness of many of McLevy's claims and a statement that he was 'the best and most successful detective in Scotland', his book was forgotten until 'James McGovan' used it as the inspiration for *Brought To Bay* and a string of further 'recollections', 'memoirs' and 'records' including *Hunted Down* (1878), which was particularly popular, selling over 25,000 copies in English as well as being translated into French and German, *Strange Clues* (1881), *Traced and Tracked* (1884),

Solved Mysteries (1888), *Criminals Caught* (1890) and *The Invisible Pickpocket*, a posthumous collection drawing on the earlier titles and issued by the London publishing house of Herbert Jenkins in 1922. The popularity of this book prompted Jenkins to inaugurate a reprinting campaign of all the McGovan titles, and with their evocative and colourful dust jackets they found a whole new readership.

What gives the James McGovan titles their special interest, however, is that they were published at the same time as a young medical student named Arthur Conan Doyle was busy with his studies in Edinburgh. The books were advertised on hoardings and copies piled high in the local bookshops to such an extent that the young Doyle could hardly have missed them and, in all probability, read one or more in his spare time. Although it is well documented that Doyle used his teacher, Professor Bell, as a model for his famous detective, several crime historians, myself included, suspect that there is more than a little of McGovan in the man from Baker Street. Both have a highly developed skill at observation and draw their conclusions from the smallest clues. They have huge professional know-how and have developed their capabilities to such a degree that what may seem like luck or coincidence is actually the result of a life-time of observing humanity. The cases of both McGovan and Holmes are mostly told in short story form, too – although the Scotsman does not have a faithful Watson at his side.

Evidence suggests that by the final decade of the nineteenth century, the public appetite for such ambiguous tales was beginning to wane. Ellery Queen, for example, in his bibliography *The Detective Short Story* (1969), has referred to *Stories from Scotland Yard* 'as told by Inspector Moser', published in 1890 by Routledge, as 'one of the last of the Pseudo-Real Life memoirs'. Inspector Moser is said to have been a member of the CID and his experiences are 'retold' by a popular biographer of the time, Charles F. Rideal. Be this as it may, his stories of 'A Diamond Robbery', 'An Aristocratic Wrongdoer' and 'The Career of a French Youth' may well have lacked the necessary excitement – indeed the joint authors confess in the introduction that their stories are 'studiously devoid of sensationalism' – for a substantial part of the first print run was later sold off in paper wrappers at the price of one shilling.

In fact, just a few years prior to this, in 1884, a by-product of the 'yellow-back' had made its first appearance – crime stories issued not in glazed boards but in paper covers selling for a shilling each. These little books, measuring $6^{1}/_{2}$ inches by 4, were the very first paperbacks as we know the term and, because of their content, soon became known as 'shilling shockers'. The books were, though, of good quality paper, sewn and bound into paper covers, sometimes illustrated, and the covers printed in a single colour with decorative lettering. A single title, *Called Back*, by Hugh Conway, which mixed all the elements of crime, mystery and detection, is credited with giving the 'shilling shocker' its greatest initial impetus and launching an era that lasted into the next century.

Called Back is the story of a blind man who is the only witness to a murder. Later his sight is miraculously restored and he marries a girl with telepathic ability who enables him to 'see' the crime again and solve the case. Conway's intriguing story first appeared in *Arrowsmith's Christmas Annual* for 1883, published by a Bristol printer, J. W. Arrowsmith.

Opposite: The exploits of Scottish crime fighter James McGovan were very successful in 'yellow-back' format and several, including *Hunted Down* (1878), were later reprinted in traditional hardback format.

Arrowsmith's
Bristol
Library.

♥

Called Back

By

Hugh
Conway.

Bristol : J. W. Arrowsmith, 11 Quay Street.
London : Griffith & Farran, St. Paul's Churchyard.

PRICE ONE SHILLING.

The first and still best-known of the 'shilling shockers',
Called Back by Hugh Conway, published in Bristol in 1883.

The author's real name was Frederick John Fargus (1847–1885), a local writer of poems and music hall songs who fancied himself a thriller writer and produced a work that, within a year, sold over a quarter of a million copies. Following its initial appearance in the *Annual*, Arrowsmith took the bold decision to republish *Called Back* in a smaller format with a simple paper cover in purple overprinted in blue type as 'Volume One' in Arrowsmith's Bristol Library. The huge sales of the paperback assured the fortunes of both the author and the publisher, who was later to boast on every copy that the Library was 'as necessary to the traveller as a rug in winter and a dust-coat in summer'. Today, the *Arrowsmith's Christmas Annual* containing the first printing of the story has been described by an American dealer in crime fiction as 'perhaps the rarest first edition of Victorian best-sellers'.

Conway wrote several more titles before his death from tuberculosis in 1885. All were published in America, including *Dark Days* (1884), in which the protagonist protects a woman from a charge of murder; *A Dead Man's Face* (1885), about the avenging of a brutal crime; and *A Cardinal Sin* (1886), with its complicated and sensational plot: it was described by a reviewer in *Vanity Fair* as 'all in all, one of the most enthralling pieces of fiction of the last five and twenty years'. Such was the success of Conway's 'shilling shockers' that *Called Back* was adapted for the stage in 1890 and plagiarized and parodied by a number of writers, notably in an anonymous Irish spoof, *U-go Gone-away Hug-away: Hauled Back By His Wife* published in 1885, and by the English humorist Andrew Lang, who enjoyed a *succès d'estime* with *Much Darker Days* written under the *nom de plume* 'A. Huge Longway'. Arrowsmith continued to publish the Bristol Library Series long after the death of Conway – issuing almost 100 titles between 1884 and 1906 – although the firm does have the dubious distinction of having rejected Conan Doyle's *A Study in Scarlet* before it was accepted by *Beeton's Christmas Annual*.

The success of *Called Back* resulted in the railway bookstalls of Britain being deluged with 'shilling shockers' from other publishers anxious to climb on the bandwagon. The books typically ran between 128 and 192 pages in length and tended to contain short novels aimed at catching the eye of commuters with less time to spend reading than the long-distance traveller. Once again the favourite classic authors – unprotected by copyright, of course – were issued in this format, followed by more recent writers Robert Louis Stevenson, Dick Donovan, Rider Haggard, James Payn and Thomas Hardy. In

A highly romanticized version of the Ned Kelly story recounted by 'A US Detective' published in 1885.

1885, Charles Henry Clarke, a resourceful publisher in Warwick Lane, London, launched his sixpenny 'Popular Railway Reading' series and featured crime stories prominently on the list. A popular and now very collectable title was the highly romanticized *Ned Kelly and His Bushmen* written by 'A US Detective'. It describes the exploits of Will Crolius, a young American detective, who is summoned to Australia and there plays a crucial (if completely imaginary) role in bringing Kelly's reign of terror to an end! The outlaw had, in fact, only been executed five years prior to publication, but his legend was already growing at a furious rate thanks to works of fantasy such as this.

Within a decade, some publishers were cutting down the price of their paperbacks to sixpence as well as giving them still more garish covers. Routledge launched a series of *Sixpenny Detective Stories* which claimed to be publishing 'one of the greatest of the writers of detective stories', Fortune du Boisgobey (1821–1891), a Frenchman who imitated Émile Gaboriau in both style and subject, even going so far as to purloin his countryman's famous character, Monsieur Lecoq! Chatto & Windus, though, were probably the leaders in this field with their 'sixpenny wonders' featuring, among others, the works of Émile Zola, Hall Caine, Arnold Bennet, Ouida and Charles Reade, whose masterpiece, *The Cloister and the Heath*, launched the list in 1893 and sold over 350,000 copies. The company's titles were made all the more distinctive by the superb artwork of a team of artists including J. H. Valda, Gerald Leake, Dudley Tennant and H. L. Bacon. The Chatto list included several crime writers such as the evergreen Wilkie Collins, and also made a star of a one-time children's writer, George Manville Fenn (1831–1909) – although he is virtually forgotten today. Family misfortune threw Fenn, born into comparative luxury,

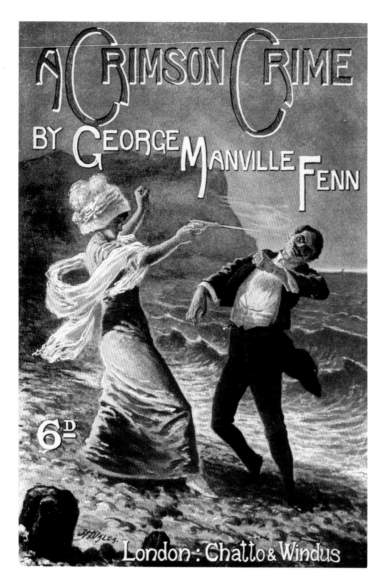

George Manville Fenn was one of the most successful of the 'sixpenny' crime novelists with eye-catching titles like *A Crimson Crime* (1899).

The era of the sixpenny paperbacks also saw the concept of 'faction' novels based on the lives of famous criminals, inaugurated by Charles Henry Clarke and taken a step further. Legendary characters like Sweeney Todd, Jonathan Wild and John Lee, *The Man They Could Not Hang*, proved good railway bookstall titles for the London firm of C. Arthur Pearson. The authors of these highly imaginative and grisly tales received no credit; nor did those who novelized the lives of Charles Peace, *The Master Criminal*, and Maria Marten, the victim of *The Murder in the Red Barn*, for the Mellifont Press. (The liberties taken with this last true crime story were quite staggering: the setting was updated from 1827 to the twentieth century, Maria changed from a country girl to a fashionable young thing, and her lover, William Corder, from an oafish farmer to a squire-about-town.)

One author whose popularity first grew during the 'yellow-back era', and who prospered through the days of the 'shilling shockers' and the sixpenny paperbacks right until his mid-fifties, was Nat Gould (1847–1919). His thrillers set in the world of horse-racing made Gould the Dick Francis of his time. Referred to in the contemporary press as 'The Prince of Sporting Novelists', he is said to have written over 150 novels which sold in excess of 30 million copies. Like Fergus Hume, Nat Gould was born in England and emigrated to Australia where he first tasted literary success. In England, he had been employed briefly in the tea trade and in farming before getting a job on the *Newark Advertiser*. After reaching Australia, he found a place on the *Brisbane Daily Sun*, where he became the racing correspondent. In 1890, Gould wrote his first racing thriller, *The Double Event*, and its success in Australia was repeated in England and settled the direction of his life. Within a year he had returned to England and began

onto his own resources while still in his teens. After a brief attempt to become a teacher, he moved to London and secured work writing stories for children's magazines. His first novel, a mystery, *Hollowdell Grange*, appeared in 1867, and in the years that followed he wrote over 100 more books. His most successful period was in his association with Chatto & Windus, producing titles for the sixpenny list such as *Witness to the Dead* (1893), *A Crimson Crime* (1899) and *Black Shadows* (1902), which are all now much sought-after for their striking covers.

producing the books that were to make his name; the first titles were published by Routledge and then by a variety of other London companies.

All Nat Gould's books display the inside knowledge he had gained as a correspondent in Australia and then augmented by research in England. The style of his 'yellow-backs', such as *The Three Wagers* (1896), *One of a Mob* (1899), and *Warned Off* (1902), may have been regularly criticized by reviewers, and his beautiful heroines, unscrupulous villains

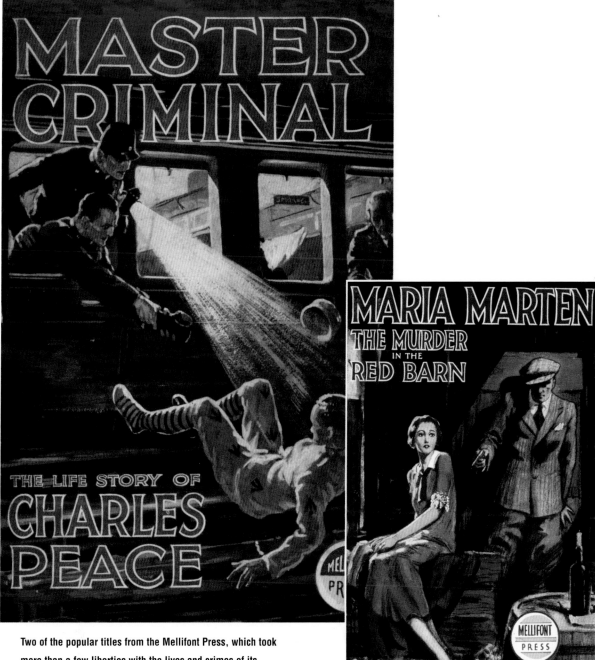

Two of the popular titles from the Mellifont Press, which took more than a few liberties with the lives and crimes of its subjects, including *Charles Peace* and *Maria Marten*.

The combination of horse-racing and crime made Nat Gould the Dick Francis of his age with best-sellers such as *The Three Wagers* (1896) and *One of a Mob* (1899).

Opposite: Paperback editions of Nat Gould's most popular titles continued to be published for years after his death. This edition of *The Pace That Kills* appeared in 1929.

(usually trainers or owners) and square-jawed heroes were often little more than caricatures, but Gould's answer to his critics was to point to his sales figures. He was a master at spinning out the last hundred yards of a race, in which the schemers gloated over a victory only to have it snatched from them in the last few strides. He is also credited with creating the first race course detective in fiction, Valentine Martyn, who made his debut in 1910 with 'The Exploits of a Race-Course Detective'. The title of one of Gould's later sixpenny paperbacks, *The Pace That Kills*, was grimly prophetic. Gould had always been a big spender (like many of the heroes of his books) and wrote to keep pace with his debts. When he died just after the end of the First World War, the 'yellow-back' and 'shilling shocker' had passed into history, but for all his industry and fame, 'The Prince of Sporting Novelists' left an estate of just £7,800.

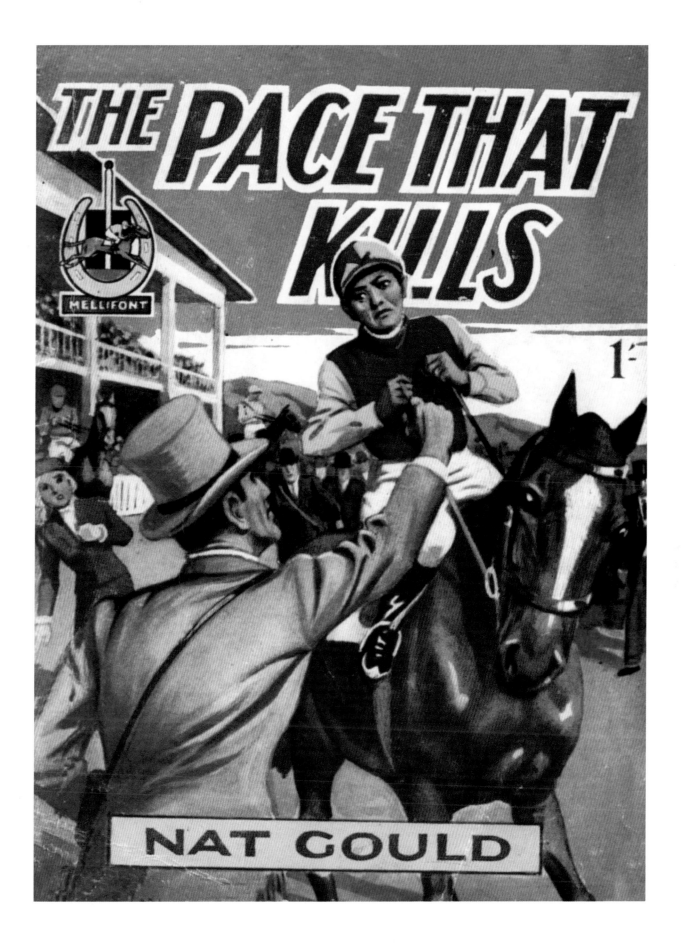

Dime-a-Dozen
Sleuths

DIME-A-DOZEN SLEUTHS

Old Sleuth is a glowering, somewhat intimidating figure with long, curly hair and a bushy beard who peers at the world over wire-rimmed glasses. He dresses in a frock coat, wears a stove-pipe hat and carries a furled umbrella in one hand. A picture of inquisitiveness and determination, he was the first crime investigator to be known as a 'sleuth' and the first detective story hero to appear in a continuing series in the American publications known as 'dime novels' that appeared in the 1860s. They were, in many respects, the US equivalent of the British 'penny dreadfuls'; often as lurid and sensational, though certainly more influential in the development of crime fiction, since they promoted public interest in tales of detection and the way that detectives worked. By their very nature, these publications were as much loved by their readers as reviled by those who campaigned to have them suppressed.

It is probably true to say that the dime novel publishers were the first to sense the American public's interest in crime and tales of detection and appreciate the enormous potential for such stories. Indeed, they turned out literally thousands of titles before the 'legitimate' book trade woke up to the profits to be made in this field. As the young nation grew, millions of readers thrilled to the exploits of Old Sleuth and his rivals Old Cap Collier, Old King Brady and, the biggest star of all, 'young' Nick Carter. The dime novels represented the first mass-produced entertainment industry of importance, and it has been said that they stood in the same relation to the average young American as television does today. Five major companies came to dominate the market, some of whose names are still familiar today, all of them publishing stories of 'sleuths' (the word actually means a bloodhound but was applied in this context to a human detective). The publications themselves are of considerable rarity today.

The man who had the idea of publishing sensational novels at ten cents each was Irwin Pedro Beadle (1826–1882), a New York publisher who operated from 141 Williams Street. Along with his older brother, Erastus (1826–1882), Beadle had set up the company on the strength of a number of song books all costing a dime, which proved a huge success. Sensing that young America might also be in the mood for tales of drama and emotion – as long as they were inexpensive – Beadle devised a format for producing paper-covered novels

OLD SLEUTH.

Left: Old Sleuth, the first crime investigator to be known by the term, who appeared in print in 1872.

on rag-content paper that varied in size from four by six inches to five by seven inches with between 96 and 250 pages. These were followed by weekly 'story papers' or 'broadleaves' that resembled magazines, contained from 32 to 64 pages, and ran serials and novelettes which were later reprinted as dime novels by their astute publisher. Very few of these publications had any illustrations beyond that on the front cover and all were printed in black and white. These story papers sold for either a nickel or a dime. In the first phase of publications, it was stories of life in the Wild West with its legends of Indian skirmishes, heroic frontiersmen and rough and ready characters that dominated the market. But from the 1880s colourful tales of crime and detection became equally popular with readers across the nation.

Beadle launched his first dime novel on 7 June 1860 with an advertisement in the *New York Tribune* which declared:

BOOKS FOR THE MILLION!
A Dollar Book for a Dime!!
128 Pages complete, only Ten Cents!!!
Beadle's Dime Novels No 1:
Malaeska; The Indian Wife
of the White Hunter
By Mrs. Anne S. Stephens

Mrs Stephens (1813–1886) was an assistant editor on a popular New York magazine, *The Ladies' Companion*, as well as a prolific writer of novels. Her inventive and highly moral story of the struggle of the Indian wife of a white hunter in the Catskill Mountains in the early colonial days had originally appeared in the *Companion*. In its new format, *Malaeska* was a popular success, but Irwin Beadle's idea did not really take off until October of that same year when the eighth title in the series was released. It was *Seth Jones; or, The Captives of the Frontier* by Edward S. Ellis

(1840–1916). The author was just 20 years old and a teacher at a school in Red Bank, New Jersey at the time. But the combination of his storytelling skill and Beadle's acumen created a sensation, as Ellis never forgot:

'All of a sudden, all over the country, there broke out a rash of posters, dodgers and painted inscriptions demanding to know, "Who is Seth Jones?" Everywhere you went this query met you. It came fluttering at you in staring letters on the sidewalks. It came fluttering in to you on little dodgers thrust by the handful into the Broadway stages. In the country the trees and rocks and the sides of roofs of barns all clamoured with stentorian demands to know who Seth Jones was. And just when it had begun to be a weariness and one of the burdens of life a new rush of decorations broke out all over the country. This was in the form of big and little posters bearing a lithographic portrait of a stalwart, heroic looking hunter. And above or below this imposing figure in large type were the words, "I am Seth Jones!" '

The result of this unique promotion by Beadle was the sale of over 600,000 copies of *Seth Jones* and the assured success of his company. Initially, Irwin Beadle had only one partner in the business, his brother Erastus, but he was later joined by Robert Adams (1837–1866), whose surname gave the company its more familiar title of Beadle & Adams. In the years until the firm's demise at the end of the century, it published over 7,500 titles and its name became a virtual synonym for the dime novel.

In October 1877 Beadle & Adams launched their most successful series character, the eponymous Deadwood Dick, in the first issue of *Half-Dime Library*, a magazine which initially prospered on a diet of frontier, American Indian and pioneer stories and later, tales of crime and detection. Deadwood Dick's popularity spanned this entire period and

Deadwood Dick was originally a frontier scout who became a city detective and an enduring favourite with dime novel readers. Created in 1877 by Edward Wheeler, the self-styled 'Sensational Novelist', Deadwood Dick later had his own magazine.

during it he metamorphosed from a trapper and outlaw in the Black Hills of South Dakota to a dispenser of rough border justice and finally a detective dedicated to preserving law and order in Philadelphia, Boston, New York and elsewhere. He was created by Edward Lytton Wheeler (1854–1885) a New Yorker who, like Edward Ellis, wrote his first contributions for Beadle when barely out of his teens, and so revelled in his subsequent popularity that he had his stationery printed with the words, 'Edward Wheeler, Sensational Novelist'. A glance at some of his other titles – especially highly-coloured tales of female heroines like *Denver Doll, the Detective Queen* – show that this sobriquet was well deserved. Wheeler later revealed that Deadwood Dick was partly based on a real Western frontiersman, Richard W. Clarke, famous for his slang-filled language and prowess with his fists and six-shooters. The author, whose life was cut short by illness, is believed to have

written 33 of the dime novels about the resourceful Deadwood Dick, although after his death Beadle & Adams had no scruples about getting another author to continue the series under his by-line for a hundred more stories of the frontiersman turned sleuth. It has been suggested that this 'conversion' was brought about as much by the demands of maintaining reader interest in the character as the action of campaigners against the publishers of dime novels.

On the back of the success of Deadwood Dick, another Beadle & Adams writer, J. C. Cowdrick, created a second detective for the list, William West, 'Broadway Billy', who made his debut in the *Half-Dime Library* in 1885. A tall, handsome young man in his early twenties, Billy had two assistants, Seth and Happy Harry, who helped him solve a variety of cases. Together they brought to justice all manner of criminals, blackmailers, bank robbers and even fraudulent mediums in cases

Edward Wheeler also created a popular female heroine, *Denver Doll, the Detective Queen* (1882).

Broadway Billy was another versatile crime buster created in 1885 by J.C. Cowdrick to cash in on the success of Deadwood Dick.

such as *Broadway Billy's Shadow Chase, Broadway Billy's Bank Racket* and *Broadway Billy Among Jersey Thugs.* The series was still more successful when reprinted in Britain by the Aldine Publishing Company as part of their *Tip-Top Tales.*

The Beadle brothers were followed into the market place by two more siblings, George and Norman Munro from Nova Scotia, a pair of men as flamboyant, enthusiastic and litigious as ever worked in publishing. They deserve the credit for three 'firsts' in detective fiction – though they achieved these separately and amid furious quarrels. George (1825–1896) is acknowledged as having published the first dime novel detective story, *The Bowery Detective* by Kenward Philp, which initially appeared in the *New York Fireside Companion* in weekly episodes in 1870, and is credited

with introducing the pioneer serial hero Old Sleuth. (Philp's story was later reprinted in issue 64 of *Old Sleuth Library* in 1894.) For his part, Norman Munro (1844–1894) published the first periodical devoted solely to detective fiction, *Old Cap Collier Library.* The brothers, though united by blood, allowed a great deal of it to be spilt in their publications and came perilously close to spilling each other's.

George Munro had left Nova Scotia as a teenager and headed for New York. There he gained his knowledge of publishing and distribution working with the American News Company and later as a clerk in Irwin Beadle's office when the dime novel boom was just beginning. In 1863 he left to set up his own company just a short way down William Street (subsequently moving to Vandewater Street) and there launched the first of 39 different series of novels and periodicals, beginning with *Munro's Ten Cent Novels*, featuring mainly western novels. Six years later, George published the first issue of the *New York Fireside Companion* which, a year later, introduced *The Bowery Detective*. The unforgettable Old Sleuth was created for the *Companion* in 1872 by Harlan Page Halsey (1841–1907), a local newspaper correspondent who claimed to have actually served in the police. The stories of the eccentric, ageing detective which began with *Old Sleuth, the Detective; or, The Bay Ridge Mystery* were supposedly written 'By Old Sleuth' and became so popular that Munro was forced to reprint them time and time again. The series was first collected in individual volumes in 1885 as the *Old Sleuth Library* and then again in a series of paperback novels, the *Calumet Series*, which began in 1891. By the turn of the century, the redoubtable old detective was still hale and hearty in another series of stories written by Halsey for *Old Sleuth's Own* which Munro issued under the imprint of the Parlor Car Publishing Co. (Shades of the Hansom Cab Company of London here!)

Despite the huge commercial success of Old Sleuth – and another series which Munro had begun to issue called *The Seaside Library*, which reprinted some classic crime titles by Wilkie Collins, Mary Elizabeth Braddon and Émile Gaboriau – George Munro became enraged when anyone else dared to use what he considered his proprietary word, 'sleuth'. Although copyright was non-existent at that time and he plagiarized the works of writers from both sides of the Atlantic as freely as anyone else in the business, Munro immediately instituted proceedings against any

The eccentric, ageing detective *Old Sleuth* had his own *Library* in which he recounted his cases as well as those of equally odd lady detectives such as the dashing Lady Kate.

competitor who dared to use the epithet he claimed to have invented. He went to court 11 times in all to uphold his claim to the synonym – even against his own brother, Norman.

Norman L. Munro had followed in the footsteps of his older brother from Nova Scotia to New York, arriving there when he was 25. Not surprisingly, he got a job with George and proceeded to learn all the tricks of the trade – not to mention sizing up all the profits to be made – until he, too, was ready to set up on his own. In 1873 he opened up premises on William Street just a few doors away from the Munro and Beadle empires. The choice of address was deliberate; the opportunistic young man hoped his periodicals would be confused by the public with those of his brother, and enjoy the same success. The first of Norman's publications was *Ten Cent Irish Novels*, followed by *Ten Cent Popular Novels* and *Ornum & Co's Fifteen Cent Romances* – Ornum being merely Munro spelt

Old Cap Collier was deliberately created in 1883 to rival the success of *Old Sleuth*, but the magazine earned its place in dime novel history as the first weekly devoted exclusively to crime and mystery stories.

backwards. Soon the close proximity of the two Munro establishments was creating friction between the brothers; all the more so when the younger man's range developed quickly to a list of 25 competing titles.

In April 1883 Norman Munro made his major contribution to the detective story genre with the publication of *Old Cap Collier Library*. This was the first dime-novel weekly devoted exclusively to crime and mystery stories, and although the spry old crime fighter of the title only featured in a few of the stories, his signature appeared on a great many more. The real star of the *Library*, though, was Émile Gaboriau with his cases of Monsieur Lecoq who appeared in dozens of issues. An unidentified group of American writers also provided cases for a motley crew of detectives rejoicing in names like Old Broadbrim, the Quaker Detective, Old Thunderbolt, Sergeant Sparrow, Gideon Gaunt and Dick Danger,

whose patch was the same New York streets seemingly kept free of crime by Broadway Billy, but nonetheless heaving with crooks of every shade of villainy. However, when one of Norman Munro's writers introduced the word 'sleuth' into a story, the anger of Norman's brother, George, could be heard the length of William Street. A case was instantly filed by the older brother against the younger and resulted in a lengthy and costly battle in court, as dime-novel historian J. Randolph Cox reported:

'The claim of the sole right to use the word "sleuth" to mean a detective as well as the right to use the family name on the publications was the wedge which divided the brothers once and for all. They ceased to speak to one another, the silence broken only on Norman's deathbed when he requested George settle his affairs.'

Surviving examples of the dime novels and magazines published by Norman Munro indicate that he produced publications as lurid and sensational as those by another major figure, Frank Tousey, whose empire would ultimately be second in size only to that of later arrivals Street & Smith. This same evidence also reveals that Munro, who was briefly in partnership with Tousey between 1873 and 1876, only just beat his associate to the honour of publishing the first all-detective periodical by a matter of a few weeks.

Frank Tousey was born in Brooklyn, New York and had publishing in his blood. His uncle, Sinclair Tousey, was president of the American News Company, and it was here that Frank learned about the importance of distribution and sales promotion. After the brief association with Norman Munro, Tousey left to found his own company, taking with him a periodical they had launched together, *The Boys of New York*, plus its chief writer,

Old King Brady was another unashamed copy of *Old Sleuth*, written by Francis Doughty, and introduced to American readers in 1885.

The New York Detective Library which hit the news-stands in 1883 became well-known for its curious sleuths and for making use of already well-known figures such as the Frenchman Vidocq.

George Small. Under the auspices of his new imprint, Tousey immediately gave full reign to his flair for the dramatic and turned the publication into a purveyor of blood-and-thunder fiction, the covers specifically designed to encourage buyers by their graphic engravings of hooded figures, damsels in distress and any number of heroes in life-threatening situations. It was a formula that could not fail – and one into which stories of crime and detection fitted only too well.

On 7 June 1883, just two months after the appearance of *Old Cap Collier Library*, Tousey issued the first issue of *The New York*

Detective Library, which featured scores of detectives, many of them boasting the most curious names. The following few must suffice but there are dozens more: *New York Nat, the Knife Detective; The Hudson River Tunnel Detective; Harlem Jack, the Office-Boy Detective; The Messenger-Boy Detective Among the Bowery Sharps; Zeb Taylor, the Puritan Detective; Old Humphrey, the Dwarf Detective; Old Sledge, Blacksmith-Detective* and, perhaps most extraordinary of all, *Old Opium, the Mongolian Detective*. By far the most popular of these sleuths, though, was *Old King Brady*, written by 'A New York Detective' who began his dramatic adventures in the *Library* in November 1885 and continued his serial adventures in *The Boys of New York* and complete dime novels. Tousey had instructed his editors to develop a rival to Old Sleuth and Old Cap Collier and the result was a quite different character: plausible, realistic and also the first detective in fiction to have a continuing arch-enemy, the Western outlaw Jesse James. The creator of Old King Brady was Francis Worcester Doughty (1850-1917), born in Brooklyn and a writer for the dime market from the age of 19. Although all the Brady stories were signed with the same pseudonym, it is generally agreed that Doughty contributed the best tales, and his style was so evident that whenever he was put onto other assignments by the Tousey editors, sales of the series dropped until he was recalled.

In fact, Doughty went to a great deal of trouble to give James Brady (the character's real name) a personality which few of his rivals attempted. Brady was not shown as an infallible detective or a master of disguise but as an intelligent man who made mistakes and solved his cases by painstaking enquiry and an intuition based on a lifetime's experience. On his very first case, *The House Without a Door*, Doughty took some pains to describe his hero:

'He was a tall, spare man of about forty, evidently an Irishman. His clothes were plain and ill-fitting and his features large and unattractive, yet for all that there was something about the keen, penetrating eyes, the small mouth and firmly set lips which served to inspire those who met him that they were dealing with no ordinary individual.'

The author also visited the areas where he set his character's cases, and his descriptions of New York, Boston, Chicago and other cities offer a vivid and authentic picture of those places as they actually were at the time. In later stories he was accompanied by Young King Brady who, despite the obvious similarity of his name, was actually no relation at all. In all, Doughty produced 85 of the Old King Brady novels as well as two important books on his hobbies of coin collecting and archaeology. He also wrote the scripts of several silent movies, including the popular Thanhouser Film Corporation serial, *The Twenty Million Dollar Mystery*. Francis Doughty's work been described by the historian E. M. Sanchez-Saavedra as 'among the very best dime novel detective stories'.

The popularity of the *Old King Brady* stories led to the detective being given a partner, *Young King Brady* (who was actually no relation), and the two eventually shared a new magazine, *Secret Service*, first published in 1899 with the innovation of two-colour covers.

Young Sleuth Library, featuring 'New York's favourite young detective' was yet another attempt to cash in on the Old Sleuth market.

Frank Tousey's empire encompassed many genres, as the titles bear witness: *Fame & Fortune Weekly*, *The Five Cent Comic Weekly*, *Wide Awake Library* and the famous *Frank Reade Library* about a boy inventor whose ingenious machines travelled to all corners of the earth. Detective enthusiasts were also catered for by *Secret Service*, which contained stories about both Old and Young King Brady, and *Young Sleuth Library*, an unabashed attempt to capitalize on George Munro's success which featured 'New York's favourite and youngest detective' and his French valet and assistant, Jean Guillaume St. Croix Jenkeau. The success of this series undoubtedly further enraged the veteran publisher – especially when the dime novels were reprinted in England by the Aldine Publishing Company. But one title, *The Five Cent Wide Awake Library*, with its series of

stories about the outlaws Frank and Jesse James, *really* got Frank Tousey into trouble.

The outlaw James boys had captured the imagination of young Americans in a way that no other robbers, murderers or gunmen had done, and they were still very much alive when the dime novel was in its prime. What more natural thing than to turn the pair and their exploits into stories? And who else would think of such an idea but Frank Tousey? Thus readers of the *Wide Awake Library* in 1881 found themselves reading *The Trainrobbers*; *or, A Story of the James Boys* by D. W. Stevens, aka John R. Musick (1848–1901), a prolific Tousey author. Stevens was well-qualified to relate the stories, as he had been born in Missouri and had earlier produced *The True Life of Billy the Kid*, promoted with a free copy of the outlaw's 'Dead or Alive' poster. In the months that followed, Stevens became the virtual 'biographer' of the murderous pair with a string of highly imaginative sequels including *The James Boys as Guerrillas*, *The James Boys and the Ku Klux Klan* and *The James Boys in Minnesota*. In all of these they were increasingly sympathetically portrayed as men seeking justice rather than revenge, anxious to return to the farm. They were even said to be capable of chivalry to all those who did not represent blinkered authority.

The stories proved immensely popular with readers – but also drew the attention of Anthony Comstock (1844–1915), the self-appointed scourge of the dime novel. Comstock was the secretary and chief special agent of the New York Society for the Suppression of Vice (NYSSV), which had begun a campaign in the 1870s, dedicated to putting publishers

Opposite: The fictionalized stories of the outlaws *Frank and Jesse James* by D. W. Stevens which appeared in *Detective Library* prompted a crusade against dime novels by Anthony Comstock.

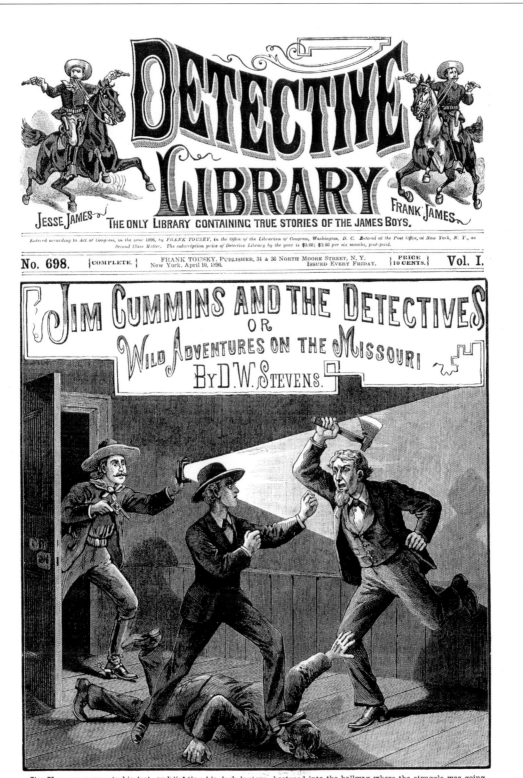

DETECTIVE LIBRARY

JESSE JAMES THE ONLY LIBRARY CONTAINING TRUE STORIES OF THE JAMES BOYS. **FRANK JAMES**

Entered according to Act of Congress, in the year 1896, by FRANK TOUSEY, in the Office of the Librarian of Congress, Washington, D. C. Entered at the Post Office, at New York, N. Y., as Second Class Matter. The subscription price of Detective Library by the year is $5.00; $2.50 per six months, post-paid.

No. 698. {COMPLETE.} FRANK TOUSEY, PUBLISHER, 31 & 36 NORTH MOORE STREET, N. Y. New York, April 10, 1896. ISSUED EVERY FRIDAY. {PRICE 10 CENTS.} Vol. I.

JIM CUMMINS AND THE DETECTIVES
OR
WILD ADVENTURES ON THE MISSOURI
BY D. W. STEVENS.

Jim Younger sprang to his feet, and lighting his dark lantern, hastened into the hallway where the struggle was going on. He flashed his lantern on the scene just as the old man entered with a hatchet in his hand. Bert was a wiry little fellow, and though Tom was much larger than he, he had downed him and placed his heel on his neck.

of dime novels out of business. Comstock, whose name became synonymous with east coast prudery ('Comstockery'), believed that the publications 'corrupted the young by glamorizing criminal behaviour' and were directly responsible for 'the fearful increase of youthful criminals in our cities in recent years'. Coming from a deeply religious Protestant background in rural Connecticut, Comstock was obsessed with what he saw as pornography and wanted to put a stop to all who wrote and published such 'crime breeding stories'. He placed detective dime novels – and especially the James brothers stories published by Frank Tousey – at the top of his hit list of 'obscene literature'.

After Comstock had carried out a number of citizen's arrests on newsdealers selling dime novels and had the courts order their stock destroyed, he turned his attention to Frank Tousey, whose publications were the most sensational. According to social historian Dr John Springhall, Tousey was arrested and interrogated several times by Comstock 'for publishing quasi-pornographic serial novels' and then harassed for publishing the stories featuring Jesse James, Billy the Kid and other outlaw criminals. If Tousey did not cease, thundered Comstock, he would have the Postmaster General refuse to allow them to be sent through the mail. The publisher was now faced with the choice of printing his *Wide Awake Library* catalogue with the outlaws omitted, or substituting other titles which could get past the Post Office Department. He chose the latter course. But Frank Tousey had not got where he was in publishing without being resourceful, and after the 'moral panic' generated by Comstock had died down and Frank James had been tried and acquitted (Jesse, of course, had been killed by Bob Ford in April 1882), he reprinted all of his so-called 'offensive' tales of crime and detection. Dr Springhall adds:

'Outlaw tales dealing with the somewhat chastened James boys returned to the market in 1889 when both Frank Tousey's *Detective Library* and Street & Smith's *Log Cabin Library* began pushing them again. *The Detective Library* eventually ran roughly 200 original adventures of the James gang under the Stevens' by-line, most of them twice, keeping the James boys in circulation for another nine years. A discussion of these outlaw stories has emphasized that they neither wholly glorified nor defamed the bandits, but reflected the societal ambivalence towards the outlaw-hero figure.'

Street & Smith, the last of the major firms to publish nickel and dime detective periodicals, did not take the opportunity to capitalize on the legend of the James boys until after the furore had died down, and their history was altogether different from that of the flamboyant Tousey. They did, though, launch the career of the most famous detective hero in the dime novels and one of the most enduring characters in the genre, Nick Carter.

The two men behind Street & Smith, Francis Scott Street (1831–1885) and Francis Shubael Smith (1819–1887) met while working for *The Sunday Dispatch* in New York. There they discovered each had a dream of running his own publication and consequently purchased the floundering *New York Weekly Dispatch* in 1857. Dropping the word *Dispatch*, the two entrepreneurs, Street the businessman and Smith the editor – transformed the paper by filling its pages with true crime stories and sensational serials, many of which — like *The Vestmaker's Apprentice; or, The Vampyres of Society* and *Maggie, the Child of Charity; or, Waifs on the Sea of Humanity* — were written by Francis Smith himself. Such was the success of the *Weekly*'s new format that Street & Smith were soon issuing a string of other publications: *The Mammoth Monthly*

Reader, The Sea and Shore Series and *Far and Near Series*, all of which drew on the resources of the *Weekly* and its writers.

In the mid-1880s, Smith's son, Ormond, joined the company fresh from Harvard and, soon showing all the astuteness of his father, decided that Street & Smith should get into the dime novel field and challenge the might of Beadle and the others. In 1889 two series appeared: *Log Cabin Library*, which sold for ten cents, and *The Nugget Library*, at half the price. The five-cent novels were aimed primarily at younger readers, with titles such as *His Royal Nibs* by John F. Cowan and *Billy Blight* by Aaron DeWitt. *Log Cabin Library* offered stronger reading matter, cashing in on the legend of Jesse James as well as offering all manner of Western hard-men including 'Gentleman Joe, the Gilt-Edged Sport' who dished out his own rough justice with gun and knife. Ormond Smith also dreamed up a rival for Deadwood Dick in the shape of Diamond Dick Jr (no coincidence in the name!), also aimed at a younger audience, who galloped through hundreds of adventures written by W. B. Lawson, a pen-name for another prolific dime novelist, William Wallace Cook. A third title issued under Ormond Smith's auspices, *The Magnet Library*, launched in 1897, was more closely linked to the detective field in that it regularly reprinted stories by Edgar Allan Poe, Émile Gaboriau, Maurice Leblanc and Fergus Hume.

However, all of Ormond Smith's achievements pale in comparison to the story of how he masterminded the legend of Nick Carter. For some time he had been aware of the appeal of detective stories and encouraged their inclusion in the flourishing *New York Weekly*. One of the authors of these stories was his cousin, John Russell Coryell (1848–1924), a talented writer who had nearly lost his life when the ship he was travelling on to join his family in China was struck by a

typhoon. Safely landed in Shanghai, Coryell's father had got him a job with the consular service. That job entailed Coryell attending the local court, where the endless round of cases of murder, robbery and smuggling made an undeniable impression on him. On his return to America, Coryell worked briefly as a newspaper reporter in Santa Barbara before moving to New York where he found a ready market for his imagination at Street & Smith.

Legend has it that after Coryell had read several of the detective tales in the *New York Weekly*, he told Ormond Smith he could write better stories than any of the existing writers. Amused by his confidence, Smith gave him the go-ahead and shortly afterwards received *The*

Nick Carter, the 'little giant' and master of disguise, created by John Russell Coryell in 1886, began a detective story legend that has never died.

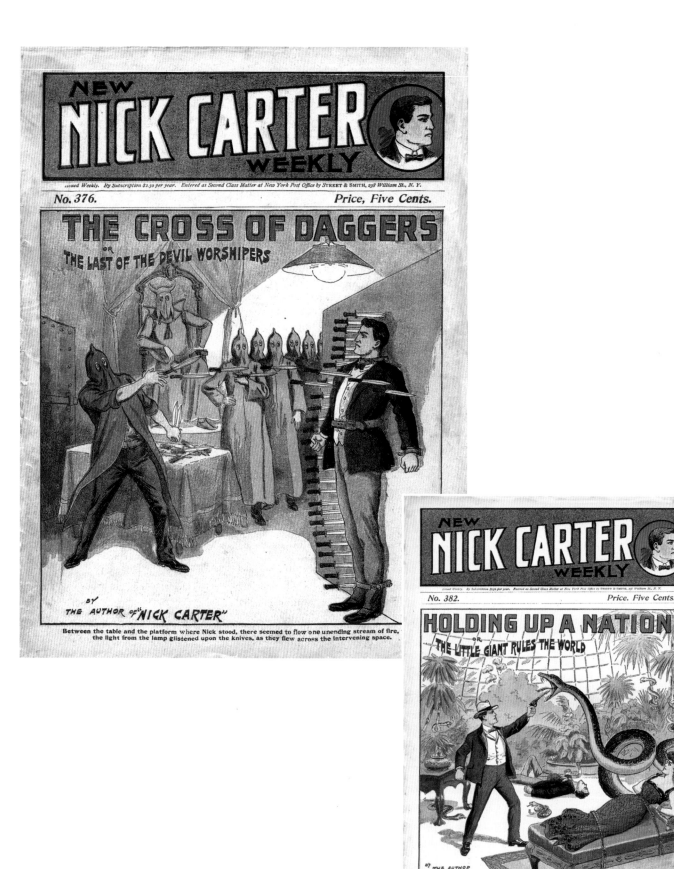

The *Nick Carter* success story was undoubtedly helped
by the decision of publishers Street & Smith in 1898 to
introduce four-colour covers.

Old Detective's Pupil; or, The Mysterious Crime of Madison Square, the tale of a venerable sleuth named Seth Carter and his protégé, Nick Carter. Smith liked the tale enough to commission two more stories from his cousin featuring the same pair, and *Wall Street Haul* and *Fighting Against Millions* were both in his hands before *The Old Detective's Pupil* appeared on the front cover of the *New York Weekly* for 18 September 1886. Perversely, though, Coryell's reward was a long-term contract to write a series of 'High Society' novels under the name of one of the *Weekly*'s most popular writers, Bertha M. Clay. But when letters began arriving at the *Weekly* indicating just how much readers had enjoyed the stories about Nick Carter, Ormond Smith realized he was in danger of missing a great opportunity unless he could find someone else to carry on the detective's adventures. His choice fell on Frederic Marmaduke van Rensselaer Dey (1861–1922), a descendant of a distinguished line of Dutch ancestors, who had graduated from Cornell Law School, practised law but then took to drink and suffered a breakdown. Dey's only method of earning a living proved to be writing dime novels. He happened to be a good friend of Deputy Police Commissioner Faurot of the New York City Police, and with the policeman's inside knowledge was able to give his stories of crime and detection an unmistakable flavour of authenticity. Ormond told Dey that he wanted Nick Carter turned into a serial detective. In his history of Street & Smith, *The Fiction Factory* (1955), Quentin Reynolds has explained what happened next:

'Dey agreed to try it and for the next 17 years he turned out Nick Carter stories as fast as his busy pen could fly. He usually produced a 25,000-word story a week. His first was called *Nick Carter, Detective* by "A Celebrated Author". It seems likely that Ormond Smith had a prophetic vision of Nick's future fame and the fact that eventually there would be a dozen men writing the stories. Nick Carter was an immediate success. No character in fiction, not even Buffalo Bill, could match his amazing versatility.'

The success of this series – and, indeed, the whole raft of Street & Smith dime novels and magazines – was also immeasurably helped by Ormond Smith's decision in the late 1890s that all the covers should be printed in four colours. They were the first company to do so, and the impact on the news-stands, where their publications stood alongside the black-and-white titles of their rivals, was immediately apparent to customers.

In the early years of his unblemished career of crime fighting, Nick Carter was known as 'The Little Giant' because he was small of stature but possessed of enormous strength which earned him comparison with the famous US strong-man, Sandow. He was a man of great intelligence, with a quick mind and a mastery of many languages and skills. His grey eyes took in every detail of a crime scene and his ability to disguise his voice was matched only by his skill at disguising his appearance. Apart from tackling cases of crime in America, he occasionally travelled abroad to solve mysteries that had defeated the finest detective brains, and he confronted an amazingly varied array of villains and criminal masterminds, including the multifarious Daazar, the evil beauty Princess Olga, and the most popular of all his adversaries, Dr. Quartz, who had a penchant for dissecting beautiful girls. Aided by his assistant, Chickering Carter, known as 'Chick', Nick Carter appeared in stories in various formats and as a result was the only important dime novel hero to have survived the collapse of the form in the early twentieth century. Later, he would return in his own pulp magazine to fight organized crime (see

The Classic Era of American Pulp Magazines)
and more recently in paperback where he has
become a suave secret agent with a knack for
seducing beautiful women.

Despite his own problems – or perhaps
because of them – Frederic van Rensselaer
Dey never allowed the original Nick Carter to
drink, smoke, swear or even lie, and whatever
predicament he found himself in, he always
retained his cool and was unfailingly courteous
to women even if they ultimately proved to be
on the side of crime. For his own part Dey,
who looked rather like a Southern colonel
with his aristocratic features and full white
moustache, never quite managed to resist the
drink and became a compulsive gambler too.
The combination resulted in him drinking or
losing much of his considerable income from
Street & Smith for writing over 1,000 cases
and an estimated 20 million words about the
redoubtable sleuth. In the latter years of his
life, Dey apparently suffered from delusions of
grandeur and utilized his imposing manner to
act as a millionaire and try to buy mansion
houses, yachts and even, on one occasion, a
railroad. He was still posing as a wealthy
Californian fruit grower to get credit in a hotel
when he committed suicide, a tragic end for the
man who had played such a vital role in a
detective story legend.

Although dime novels and magazines were
an undeniably American phenomenon, a
considerable number of the stories written for
them were reprinted in a similar cheap format
across the Atlantic and introduced British
readers to the exploits of Deadwood Dick,
Broadway Billy, Young Sleuth and many less
famous characters. These 64-page
publications, which sold at one or two pence
each, were produced by the Aldine Publishing
Company based just off Fleet Street. The
various Aldine libraries with their striking
four-colour covers ran the gamut of subjects
just as the dime novels had done, and although

copies are rare today, they exert a tremendous
fascination for American collectors –
particularly those specializing in crime
fiction.

The founder of Aldine was Charles Perry
Brown (1834–1916), who had been involved in
publications for young people since the age of
19 and began his own line of magazines in
1863 with the *Boys' Journal*. By 1889 he had
become aware of the success of the dime
novel in America and decided to set up his
own company to republish the most
successful titles. The evidence suggests that
Brown loved crime stories – or at least saw
them as the most viable titles to start his list.
He launched the *Aldine Detective Tales* series,
which ran to 348 issues between 1889 and
1906, with the grandiloquent *Brant Adams,
the Emperor of Detectives*. Thereafter followed
a stream of similar *Detective Tales* with titles
like *The Dog Detective; Red Light Will, the
River Detective; The Revenue Detective; or,
Old Rattlesnake; Doc Grip, the Sport Detective*
and *Old Electricity, the Lightning Detective*
as well as more traditional figures in *The
Mysteries of the Night, Running Down a
Double, The Van Peltz Diamonds* and *The
Crimson Cross; or, Foiled at the Finish*,
featuring detective Barton Blake and his
pursuit of criminals branded with the mark of
their evil fraternity. The author, Harlan Page
Halsey, was the stalwart of Old Sleuth tales.

A year later, Brown added a second series,
the *Boys' First-Rate Pocket Library*, which
mainly featured the exploits of Deadwood
Dick as well as historical dramas, maritime
tales and the occasional crime tale with titles
which speak for themselves: *The Vagabond
Detective; or, Bowery Bob's Boom; Bildad
Barnacle, the Detective Hercules* and *Kelley,
Hickey and Company, the Detectives of
Philadelphia*, featuring the partnership of a
man and young boy. Even more occasionally,
Brown tickled the fancies of his adolescent

The most popular dime novels were reprinted in England by the Aldine Publishing Company, beginning in 1889 with the *Detective Tales* series. The Aldine *Boys' First-Rate Pocket Library* republished some of the more unusual of the American dime novel titles such as *Kelley, Hickey and Company, Santa Fe Sal the Slasher* and *New York Nell, the Boy-Girl Detective*.

readers with the cases of some beautiful crime-fighting heroines such as Edward L. Wheeler's *Denver Doll, the Detective Queen; Santa Fe Sal the Slasher* and *New York Nell, the Boy-Girl Detective*. The cover artwork for many of these and other Aldine publications was by H. M. Lewis (who later provided illustrations for Sexton Blake) and F. W. Boyington, a 'specialist' in Wild West stories and the occasional American detective saga though he had never crossed the Atlantic!

Detective fiction was also to be found among the frontier and pirate tales in the *O'er Land*

and Sea Library (408 issues between 1890 and 1905), including several featuring the Beadle & Adams serial detective, Joe Phenix. *Tip-Top Tales* (328 issues between 1890 and 1904) was somewhat smaller in size than the other Aldine titles and, apart from reprinting the cases of Broadway Billy, generally restricted its mysteries to the downfall of crooks in *The Chicago Drummer's Deal* and similar dramas. In all, Brown published nine series drawn from American dime novel sources before deciding in 1901 to expand the range further with titles based on home-grown

The Rivals of Sherlock Holmes

THE RIVALS OF SHERLOCK HOLMES

The appearance of Sherlock Holmes addressing the startled Doctor John Watson with the words, 'You have been in Afghanistan, I perceive,' signified a major landmark in the history of the detective story. Perhaps *the* landmark, because it also helped to turn crime fiction into a serious literary genre. The story, *A Study in Scarlet* by Arthur Conan Doyle, appeared in *Beeton's Christmas Annual* for 1887, and is about a murder in Lauriston Gardens, London, in which the only clue is the word 'Rache' scrawled in blood on the wall above the corpse. It is remarkable because it could almost have been a dime novel plot, featuring two Americans, the businessman Enoch J. Drebber and his arch-rival, Jefferson Hope, a pioneer Western scout turned avenger on the streets of London, with a sub-plot about the Mormon sect. Holmes, the first *consulting* detective, and his companion Watson, are almost secondary characters in a drama that might just have been conceived by Edward S. Ellis or the 'Sensational Novelist' Edward Lytton Wheeler. Nor is this the only occasion on which Conan Doyle found inspiration from America. In *The Valley of Fear*, the last full-length novel which began its run as a serial in the *Strand Magazine* in September 1914, the real hero is not so much Holmes as Birdy Edwards, a Pinkerton operative who infiltrates a group of terrorists, 'The Scowrers', to expose the killer of John Douglas. The parallels between this story and the true-life events when a Pinkerton agent, James McParland, infiltrated the ranks of the notorious Molly Maguires and brought about their downfall, were obvious to all those who had read of the dramatic events in Pennsylvania in 1875.

Sherlock Holmes, like the majority of the detectives who emerged around the turn of the twentieth century attempting to rival his phenomenal popularity, appeared first in a

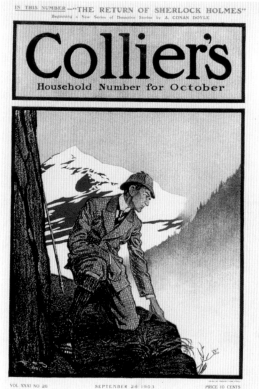

Above: The classic American version of Sherlock Holmes at the Reichenbach Falls drawn by Frederic Dorr Steele in 1903. Left: Sherlock Holmes on the cover of an American dime novel in the *Flashlight Detective Series* published in 1910. Opposite: A montage of images from the Sherlock Holmes stories by the great British artist, Sidney Paget, for the *Strand* magazine.

The Second Stain

The Solitary Cyclist

The Dancing Men

The Hound of the Baskervilles

The Speckled Band

The Reigate Squire

The Boscombe Valley Mystery

The Red-Headed League

The Norwood Builder

The Abbey Grange

The Final Problem

The Bruce-Partington Plans

Classic portrait of the Great Detective by Frank Wiles for the *Strand* magazine's publication of *The Valley of Fear* in 1915.

magazine format far removed from that of the dime novel. These new style magazines were more compact, better printed on quality paper, and profusely illustrated with colour artwork. All the Holmes cases were published exclusively in Britain in the *Strand,* and in the US initially in *Lippincott's Magazine* and later by *Collier's.* Interestingly, some of the stories were also reprinted in dime novel format in the *American Detective Series, Magnet Detective Library, Sherlock Holmes Detective Library* and *The Flashlight Detective Series.* The last title, published by M. A. Donohue of

Chicago, had a curious habit of featuring the Great Detective on the cover of each issue while the mystery stories by prolific dime novelist, Sylvanus Cobb Jr (1823–1887) — such as *Orlando Chester* (1909) and *The Royal Yacht* (1910) — were inside. To be sure, Cobb, the son of a church minister from Maine has been credited with over 300 novels and 1,000 short stories. He was better known than Conan Doyle at the time. His most famous mystery story, *The Gunmaker of Moscow*, was first published as a serial in the *New York Ledger* in 1856, dramatized shortly afterwards by George Aiken, but like much of his work did not appear in book form until after his death.

The creator of Sherlock Holmes, Arthur Conan Doyle (1859–1930), may have become overshadowed by the Great Detective, but there is no doubt that this doctor from Edinburgh who modelled Holmes on his university lecturer, Dr Joseph Bell, is one of the great storytellers of all time. Born into an artistic family of Irish origins, the young Conan Doyle was keen on becoming a writer and wrote some of his first stories while studying at the University of Edinburgh. His first two published stories in 1879 reveal a fascination with America – 'The Mystery of Sasassa Valley' in *Chambers' Journal* and 'The American's Tale' for *London Society* – and it was his admiration for Edgar Allan Poe's Auguste Dupin that made him try a detective story, completing *A Study in Scarlet* in 1887. The story featuring Holmes – whom Conan Doyle had originally thought of calling Sherrinford Holmes – proved difficult to place, and after several rejections was finally accepted by *Beeton's Christmas Annual* for the princely sum of £25! A meeting with the London representative of the Philadelphia publishers, J. B. Lippincott, resulted in a commission for a second story of the Baker Street sleuth, and Conan Doyle duly delivered *The Sign of Four* in the winter of 1889 for

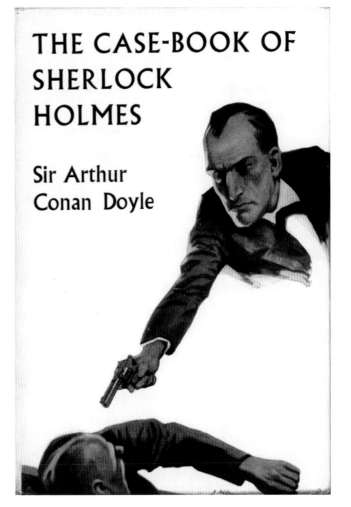

THE CASE-BOOK OF SHERLOCK HOLMES

Sir Arthur Conan Doyle

John Abbey illustrated the dust-jackets for the later collected editions of Sherlock Holmes cases.

simultaneous publication in the English and American editions of *Lippincott's Magazine* in February 1890. The following year, he produced the first of the Holmes short stories, 'A Scandal in Bohemia', for the *Strand* of July 1891. The combination of a detective who employed scientific methods to solve his cases and a 'running' hero to whom readers could become attached was a sensation. The magazine's commissioning of illustrator Sidney Paget for the black and white pictures of the tall, athletic, hawk-nosed figure was another masterstroke and established the archetypal figure still acknowledged as such today. (In America, the persona of Sherlock Holmes was established by an equally talented artist, Frederic Dorr Steele.)

Sexton Blake, who also operated from Baker Street, bore a striking resemblance to Sherlock Holmes in his early days, but later became a much more handsome figure with an eye for the ladies.

After two dozen cases, however, Conan Doyle grew tired of Holmes and, anxious to develop his literary reputation as a writer of historical fiction, attempted to kill off the sleuth in the famous confrontation with his arch-enemy Professor James Moriarty at the Reichenbach Falls in Switzerland. Such, though, was the public outcry at this 'death' – mourners wearing black armbands surrounded the publisher's offices for days on end – that two years later (and tempted by a large fee) Conan Doyle 'revived' Holmes and continued his adventures for a further two decades. The fortune which Sherlock Holmes earned for his creator enabled him to indulge a number of interests, including boxing, skiing, politics, criminology and, as a result of the death of his son during World War One, a fascination with spiritualism and the possibility of life after death. Long before Conan Doyle's

own death, Sherlock Holmes had become the most popular and most imitated character in detective fiction; the books and stories about him were constantly reprinted, translated and adapted in all forms of the media and made stars of numerous actors, notably William Gillette, John Barrymore, Eille Norwood, Arthur Wontner, Basil Rathbone, Peter Cushing and, most recently, Jeremy Brett. So 'real' did Sherlock Holmes become in many people's minds that a cult developed which has continuously studied the 'sacred writings' (as the stories are referred to by Sherlockians) and made the detective's 'home' at 221B Baker Street a mecca for visitors from all over the world.

Opposite: Fetlock Jones, Sherlock Holmes' American nephew, in Mark Twain's parody, *A Double-Barrelled Detective Story* (1902).

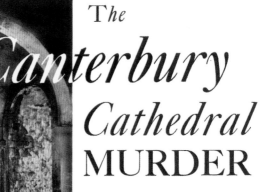

The daughter of Sherlock Holmes and Joan Watson, who made their debut to mystery fiction readers in "The Adventure of the Queen Bee," visit an ancient English cathedral and discover a modern crime in an old setting—the strange case of the silver pencil murder!

By
FREDERIC ARNOLD KUMMER
and BASIL MITCHELL

Baker Street was also the address of one of Holmes' earliest rivals, Sexton Blake, revered by many as the 'schoolboy's Sherlock Holmes'. In a career which spanned over 70 years in comics, magazines and books, over 3,500 of Blake's cases were recorded by nearly 200 authors, including Edgar Wallace, Peter Cheyney and John Creasey. Sexton Blake was created by a Harmsworth Press staff writer, Harry Blythe (1852–1898), in 'The Missing Millionaire' published in *The Halfpenny Marvel* of December 1893. Originally to have been called Frank Blake, he was not unlike Sherlock Holmes in appearance: lean features, a pipe clamped between his teeth, wearing a bowler hat and never without a heavy walking stick. For the story Blythe was paid just £9, which included the full copyright to the character. Sadly, he did not live long enough to see Blake become an enduring favourite with younger readers. One of Sexton Blake's admirers, crime novelist Dorothy L. Sayers, who first read his cases when she was a young schoolgirl, referred to the saga as 'the nearest approach to a national folklore, conceived as the centre for a cycle of loosely-connected romances in the Arthurian manner.' Over the years, Blake moved from the *Marvel* to

Shirley Holmes, daughter of the Great Detective, and her friend, Joan Watson, tackled a series of cases in the US Mystery Magazine *in the early 1930s.*

Detective Weekly, Union Jack and then his own *Sexton Blake Library*, appearing to grow younger as he did so, his clothing varying with current fashions and the pipe giving way to cigarettes. He also gained a young assistant, Edward Carter, known as Tinker, and (in 1956) a pretty secretary, Paula Dane, not to mention developing an eye for beautiful women. Blake was said to be the world's longest serving detective; the last issue of *The Sexton Blake Library* was issued in June 1963.

Hard on the heels of Sexton Blake came a flood of parodies of Sherlock Holmes, enough to fill a library. One of the first authors to utilize such a character in a novel was Mark Twain, aka Samuel Langhorne Clemens (1835–1910), the American author of the classic *Adventures of Tom Sawyer* (1876). In his *A Double-Barrelled Detective Story* (1902), Twain burlesqued the omniscient powers of Sherlock Holmes in a story about the sleuth's American nephew, Fetlock Jones. The US humorist John Kendrick Bangs (1862–1922) also had fun with Holmes in *The Posthumous*

Adventures of Shylock Holmes (1903) which proved as popular as the series of cases about Herlock Sholmes and Jotson written by the English writer, Frank Richards, best-known for his Billy Bunter stories. Perhaps the most bizarre attempt to get on the bandwagon was the series of cases of Sherlock Holmes' *daughter*, Shirley, and her friend, Joan Watson, written by the crime novelist Frederic Arnold Kummer (1873–1943) – author of *The Brute* (1912), *The Painted Woman* (1917) and *Design for Murder* (1936) – which ran in *The Mystery Magazine* in the early thirties. Accompanying the text were photographs of models playing out the dramas of 'The Adventure of the Queen Bee', 'The Canterbury Cathedral Murder' and similar cases.

The United States did, however, provide the first serious challenge to Sherlock Holmes as a scientific detective in the person of Craig Kennedy, who appeared in 26 novels and collections of short stories written by Arthur B. Reeve between 1912 and 1936. At the height of his popularity, Kennedy, a professor at Columbia University who also worked as a consulting detective, was described as 'the American Sherlock Holmes'. Like Holmes, the austere professor is a chemist who uses his knowledge to solve cases and he is one of the first detectives in fiction to use psychoanalytic techniques. In Kennedy's first case, *The Silent Bullet* (1912), recounted by Walter Jameson, a newspaper reporter who subsequently tries to emulate the great man in deciphering clues, he is revealed as a figure of profound intelligence, though not afraid to match his thoughts to action if necessary. He makes use of the latest scientific developments such as lie detectors and portable seismographs and frequently uses disguises.

Kennedy's creator, Arthur Benjamin Reeve (1880–1936), was born in Patchogue, New York, and trained to be a lawyer at Princeton University, but opted

Craig Kennedy, 'The American Sherlock Holmes' demonstrating his skills in *The Azure Ring*, illustrated by James Ruger for *Scientific Detective Monthly* in March 1930.

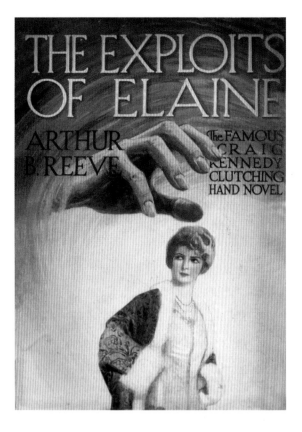

The Exploits of Elaine (1915), the sixth Craig Kennedy
novel by Arthur Reeve, established the detective's fame.

instead for a career in journalism. A series of
articles he was commissioned to write on
scientific crime detection inspired the creation
of Craig Kennedy, and the books quickly
became popular on both sides of the Atlantic.
The sleuth's fame was ensured when the sixth
title, *The Exploits of Elaine* (1915), was
adapted for the screen as a silent serial starring
Arnold Daly as Kennedy and Pearl White as
Elaine. In this story, Kennedy does battle with
a mysterious figure known as 'Clutching Hand',
a scientist with death rays at his command
and the ability to create what is called 'a
poison-kiss epidemic'. He is hell-bent on
depriving Elaine of her inheritance. In one
cliff-hanging sequence, Kennedy brings a dead
girl back to life with a machine, 'Dr Leduc's
Electric Resuscitator'. Similar scientific
miracles also appeared in two sequels starring
White and Daly, *The New Exploits of Elaine*
(1915) and *The Romance of Elaine* (1916).
Although Arthur Reeve accurately predicted

one or two developments in scientific crime
detection, many of his devices quickly became
outdated if not completely implausible.
However, his use of Freudian psychology
some years before psychoanalysis became an
accepted part of crime fighting was a major
achievement, and during World War One,
Reeve helped to set up a special crime and spy
detection laboratory in Washington DC. Like
Holmes before him, Craig Kennedy was played
by a string of actors in the cinema and on
television over the next 30 years, including
Herbert Rawlinson, Jack Mower, Jack Mulhall
and Donald Woods. His last exploits were
published in the famous pulp magazine *Weird
Tales* between 1935 and 1936, illustrated by
the legendary artist Margaret Brundage.

In Britain, the first detective to attain
widespread popularity after Sherlock Holmes
was Martin Hewitt, who made his debut in the
Strand in 1894 illustrated by Sidney Paget.
The great success of the Baker Street sleuth's
adventures had set the magazine's editor,
Greenhough Smith, searching for substitutes
in the inevitable breaks between Conan Doyle's
contributions, and a journalist and dramatist
Arthur Morrison (1863–1945) came up with
'The Lenton Croft Robberies' to fill the gap.
Hewitt could not have been less like Holmes
physically, although he did favour the same
methods. A stout man of medium height with
a comforting smile, he was originally a
solicitor's clerk, but became so successful at
collecting evidence for clients that he decided
to set up a detective agency of his own in an
old building near the Strand. It is Hewitt's
ability to use statistics and resolve technical
problems along with a knack of making the
most of his surroundings – including disguises
– that enables him to solve his cases, all of
which are recorded by a friend called Brett,
'the most remarkable journalist alive'.

Like Conan Doyle, Arthur Morrison
considered the Martin Hewitt stories

secondary to his other writing: realistic novels about the brutality and squalor in the London slums where he had grown up and where he first worked as a reporter. The material about crime and poverty in the East End which he painstakingly gathered for *Tales of Mean Streets* (1894) and *A Child of the Jago* (1896) had a tremendous impact on the sensibilities of Victorian readers and led to a number of important social reforms. The Hewitt stories, Morrison said, were written purely for money, and when, after the success of the first six cases, he was unable to secure a larger fee from the *Strand*, he took the series to *The Windsor Magazine*. Its owners, Ward Lock, later issued the stories in volume form as *The Chronicles of Martin Hewitt* (1895), *The Adventures of Martin Hewitt* (1896) and *The Red Triangle* (1903). In hindsight, it is a pity Morrison did not take his series more seriously, as, with his first-hand knowledge of real crime, he could have set another landmark in detective stories, rather than just following in the steps of Sherlock Holmes. This realistic approach would not, in fact, take place until a generation later with the emergence of the hard-boiled American writers like Dashiell Hammett, Raymond Chandler and others. All of the later magazine and book publications of the Martin Hewitt stories by Ward Lock were illustrated by T. S. Crowther, whose pictures of the affable detective are now considered to be definitive.

Two other writers published by the *Strand* in the hiatus between the Holmes cases were Guy Boothby (1867–1905) and Richard Marsh (1857–1915), who both created arch-villains in the tradition of Professor Moriarty. Boothby's Dr Nikola is a sinister, ruthless man who operates a network of criminals and informers in the London underworld in order to amass great wealth and power. He made his debut in 1895 in the serial *A Bid for Fortune*, brilliantly illustrated by Stanley L. Wood. Wood's portrait of the Doctor with his black cat, Apollyon, perched on his shoulder looks very much like a precursor of James Bond's adversary, Ernst Stavro Blofeld, and his malevolent feline. This picture was used as a poster throughout London to promote later titles in the series: *Dr Nikola* (1896), *The Lust of Hate* (1898) and the dramatic finale, *Farewell, Nikola* (1901). Guy Newell Boothby was an Australian, born in Adelaide, and had tried without much success to write plays down under before moving to England in 1894, where he produced over 50 popular novels of crime and mystery. The success of the Dr Nikola series earned him a fortune. According to historian Maurice Richardson, the villain was based on a charlatan physician, Dr McGregor Reed, who 'practised in

Right: Detective Martin Hewitt also became famous in the pages of the Strand magazine, but his cases were later collected in book form in The Adventures of Martin Hewitt (1896), illustrated by T. S. Crowther.

Above: The arch-villain, Dr. Nikola, who proved himself almost a match for Professor Moriarty in the series of novels by Guy Boothby. Nikola and his black cat, Apollyon, were brilliantly pictured by Stanley L. Wood.

Left: The female anti-hero of Richard Marsh's classic novel, *The Beetle*, published in 1897, the same year as *Dracula*.

Shaftesbury Avenue, stood – unsuccessfully – for both the House of Commons and the United States Senate, and lived to be 91.'

Richard Marsh's anti-hero was female, 'The Oriental', better known as *The Beetle*, the title given to the account of her brutal campaign in London tormenting and mutilating victims until her reign of terror is brought to a violent end in a train crash engineered by 'confidential agent' Augustus Champnell. The story was published in 1897, just a few weeks after the appearance of Bram Stoker's vampire classic, *Dracula*, and earned comparisons with Stoker's novel because of its use of horror and the supernatural – '*Dracula* was creepy, but Mr Marsh goes one, oh! many more than one better,' said the *Daily Chronicle*. Marsh's book also sold just as well for a number of years. Like *Dracula*, it was turned into a stage production and filmed in 1919 with Leal Douglas and Sidney Atherton. However, unlike the sociable and popular Bram Stoker, Richard Marsh was a secretive man whose real name was Richard Bernard Heldmann, and whose career was chequered with rumours of womanizing and even a term in prison. Critic Hugh Greene has said that 'he [Marsh] seems to have been a man haunted by demons'. Born in St John's Wood, London, Heldmann began his writing career contributing adventure fiction for boys to *Young England* and *Union Jack*, after which he wrote over 60 mystery short stories for the *Strand*, signing himself Richard Marsh. His first novel under this name, *The Devil's Diamond*, appeared in 1893, but it was not until *The Beetle* that he became a best-selling author, especially after the book was issued in America by G. P. Putnam in 1917. Many of Marsh's subsequent titles were in a similar gruesome vein – earning him the accolade 'Master of Grand Guignol' –

but he did write several more stories about the courageous Augustus Champnell including *The Datchet Diamonds* (1898), *An Aristocratic Detective* (1899) and *The Chase of the Ruby* (1900). In 1911, the *Strand* published a series of short stories entitled 'The Experiences of a Lip-Reader', about Judith Lee, a teacher of the deaf, who uses her highly developed facilities to solve crimes. The series was warmly received by the magazine's readers, and Marsh wrote a further batch of Miss Lee's cases which were collected as *Judith Lee: Some Pages from Her Life* (1912) and *The Adventures of Judith Lee* (1916).

Stanley L. Wood, who provided the unforgettable illustrations for the Dr Nikola stories, was lured to the *Strand*'s great rival, *Pearson's Magazine*, to provide the pictures for the series of adventures of Don Quebrania Huesos, 'The Bone Smasher', a grim Spanish nobleman whose mission in life is to rob the evil rich and help the poor. The stories of Don Q, as he was known, were written by Hesketh Prichard (1876–1922), an Englishman born in India who spent much of his life travelling and infused all his fiction with his experiences of wild and remote places. The first collection of The Bone Smasher's exploits, *The Chronicles of Don Q*, appeared in 1904 and was followed by several more until the nobleman took his leave in *Don Q's Love Story* in 1909. The popularity of the series inspired a London stage version in 1921, and Douglas Fairbanks later played the character on screen as an adventurous rogue in *Don Q, Son of Zorro* in 1925. Prichard is also credited with having created the only backwoods detective, November Joe, in a series of adventures which drew on his travels in America, first published in the US as *November Joe; The Detective of*

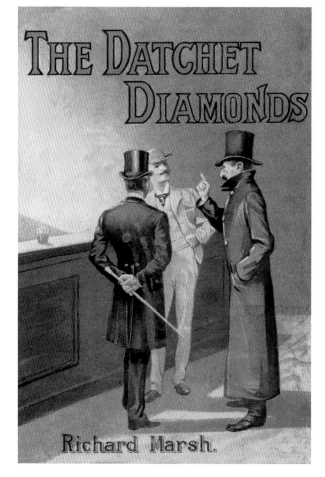

Above: Detective Augustus Champnell, who appeared in *The Beetle*, returned in several of Richard Marsh's other crime thrillers including *The Datchet Diamonds* (1898).

Right: Stanley L. Wood also illustrated the first publication of Hesketh Prichard's stories of the vengeful Spanish nobleman, Don Q, for *Pearson's magazine* in 1904.

the Woods in 1913. The author wrote further stories about Joe for *Pearson's Magazine*.

Undoubtedly, though, the most famous character in the literature of roguery – and an adversary who would have surely tested the metal of Sherlock Holmes – was A. J. Raffles, the gentleman cracksman. He was created by E. W. Hornung, a relative of Arthur Conan Doyle, and his birth might almost have been predestined, according to novelist Brigid Brophy: 'Hornung took his brother-in-law's detective pair, Holmes and Watson, and reincarnated them on the wrong side of the law as Raffles and Bunny, who pursued the business of getting a living by the entirely logical method of stealing it.' What is beyond dispute is that Raffles, the handsome, cricket-playing thief with faultless manners, a stylish residence at the Albany in the heart of London's West End, and a passion for poetry and Sullivan cigarettes, inspired a whole school of adventurers on the borderlines of the law, from Leslie Charteris' 'The Saint' to James Bond. A man who could have succeeded in almost any career, Raffles has settled for crime and, aided by his devoted chronicler, Bunny Manders, uses his wit and charm to gain entry to the homes of the rich and famous and relieve them of their valuables. He is a master of planning, has an ability to stay cool no matter how tight a corner he finds himself in, and is unfailingly generous to his friends. Unlike his brother-in-law, Hornung was able to kill off Raffles fighting bravely for his country in South Africa and resisted all blandishments to revive him: although after his death, his literary executors did give permission for the cracksman to be revived as a somewhat reformed, two-fisted crime-fighter, in a new series of adventures written by crime novelist Barry Perowne.

Raffles' creator, Ernest William Hornung (1866–1921) was born in Middlesborough,

Yorkshire, but spent his childhood in Australia, later turning these experiences into his first stories when he returned to England. Here he began contributing to the *Cornhill Magazine* and *Temple Bar* and made friends with another young writer whose sister, Constance Doyle, he married shortly afterwards. In the late 1890s Hornung had the idea of exploiting the public's preference for glamorous criminals – a factor evident from the days of Robin Hood – and in 1899 he published the first series about *The Amateur Cracksman*. The tales captured the imagination of readers on both sides of the Atlantic and prompted stage adaptations as well as a number of films starring the leading men of their times: John Barrymore, Ronald Colman and David Niven. The hardcover editions of Hornung's other Raffles books, *The Black Mask* (1901), *A Thief in the Night* (1905) and *Mr Justice Raffles* (1909), were illustrated in Britain by Cyrus Cuneo, and in America, by F. C. Youd, who perhaps better than anyone captured the period of the stories and the style of the debonair masked burglar. The US editions of the books were published by Charles Scribner's Sons.

America's major rival to Raffles was Jimmie Dale, an anti-hero with multiple identities, created by Frank L. Packard. The Dale series was initially published in the *People's Magazine* and *Detective Fiction Weekly*. Dale was a wealthy socialite who played the part of a cracksman known as 'The Gray Seal', leaving adhesive-backed seal motifs to indicate his presence, as well as an underworld criminal referred to as 'Larry the Bat', and an artist with a drug problem called Smarlinghue. Conceived in the same tradition as Raffles, Dale often commits crimes to correct injustice and

Opposite: The gentleman cracksman, *Raffles*, was created in 1899 by Sir Arthur Conan Doyle's brother-in-law, E. W. Hornung, as an antidote to Sherlock Holmes.

'The Thinking Machine', Professor Augustus Van Dusen, who uses his vast intelligence to solve the most complex crimes, including 'thinking' his way out of an escape-proof cell.

Professor's career in *The Chase of the Golden Plate* (1906) but Futrelle's fame was assured with *The Thinking Machine* (1907) in which Van Dusen accepts a challenge to 'think' his way out of an escape-proof cell in Chisholm Prison. Several more stories about the eccentric professor followed until the fateful day in April 1912 when Futrelle and his wife sailed off for a holiday on the doomed liner, *Titanic*. The writer died heroically saving his wife as the vessel sank. Several unpublished stories about the Thinking Machine were later discovered among Futrelle's effects and published in *Ellery Queen's Mystery Magazine*.

As the first decade of the twentieth century rolled on, the rivals to Sherlock Holmes grew

in number and variety. After the gentleman cracksman and armchair detective, readers were introduced in 1905 to the first clerical detective, the gentle, genial but very shrewd Father Brown. The chubby Roman Catholic priest from Norfolk with his round, moon-like face, who believes his mission is to save wrongdoers and bring criminals to justice, has been described by Ellery Queen as one of the three greatest detectives in literature (the other two are Dupin and Holmes) and his creator, G. K. Chesterton, as one of the 'most ingenious and skilled writers of crime fiction'. Father Brown's unique way of solving crimes is to think himself *inside* possible suspects: 'and when I'm quite sure that I feel like a murderer, of course I know who he is.' Although the priest's first name is never revealed beyond the initial 'J', a clue may lie in the fact that he was based on a clergyman friend of the author, Father John O'Connor, an Irish priest who lived in Yorkshire, and whose tales of the evils he encountered in the course of his parish duties staggered Chesterton.

Like many important writers, Gilbert Keith Chesterton (1874–1936) was largely unhonoured during his lifetime, but is today regarded as one of the finest minds of his time for the diversity and brilliance of his writing. A study centre devoted to his work has recently been opened. Chesterton was a larger-than-life figure, weighing nearly 20 stone and frequently seen around London dressed in a cloak, a pince-nez and slouch hat, with a sword-stick in his hand. Born to comfortably-off parents, he studied art for a time at the Slade School, but left to get a job in publishing. He started to produce a constant stream of journalism and essays on politics, religion and literature as well as crime and mystery stories – inspired

Opposite: The mild-mannered but very astute detective Father Brown as depicted by Sidney Seymour Lucas in *The Wisdom of Father Brown* (1914).

PIERRE LAFITTE & Cie, Editeurs

Les Aventures Extraordinaires
Joseph Rouletabille, Report

Le Mystère
de la Chambre
Jaune
par
GASTON LEROUX

59e Édition

THE MYSTERY OF
THE YELLOW ROOM
GASTON LEROUX

THE
FRIGHTENED LADY

IT IS
IMPOSSIBLE
NOT TO BE
THRILLED
BY
EDGAR
WALLACE

Above & above right: The French and English editions of Gaston Leroux's classic *The Mystery of the Yellow Room* (1907), the first and most important 'locked room' crime novel.

Right: Leroux's *Mystery of the Yellow Room* was the first story to use the 'least suspected person' theme, later much utilized by Edgar Wallace in novels such as *The Frightened Lady* (1932).

by an admiration he had possessed since childhood for Sherlock Holmes – culminating in the creation of Father Brown. The first story, 'The Blue Cross' was published in *The Storyteller* in September 1910, followed by five more before the series was taken over the following year by *Cassell's Magazine*. The publishers later issued 12 stories as *The Innocence of Father Brown* illustrated by Sidney Seymour Lucas, who also provided the pictures for the second volume, *The Wisdom of Father Brown* (1914). Three more collections appeared in the years leading up to the author's death, the very last Father Brown story, 'The Vampire of the Village', appropriately appearing in the *Strand*. Chesterton, like Conan Doyle, had grown tired of his inoffensive little character but enjoyed collecting the proceeds of the sales to augment his other less profitable work. He also lived long enough to see the first of several film adaptations of Father Brown in 1934 with Walter Connolly, but not the defining version, *Father Brown*, starring the versatile Alec Guinness in top form in 1954.

It would be wrong to imagine that the only rivals to Sherlock Holmes came from Britain and America. In the space of just four years, a group of French writers — Gaston Leroux, Maurice Leblanc, Pierre Souvestre and Marcel Allain — all added keystone works to the crime fiction genre. Chesterton, who was familiar with the works of the first two, described them on one occasion as 'the red and white gentlemen' – the expression referring to Leroux's fiery red hair and beard. All four were journalists – labelled hacks by some of their contemporaries – but created characters whose fame has long outshone many of the so-called literary works of the same period. The first of this quartet, Gaston Leroux (1868–1927), has enjoyed a revival of interest in recent years as a result of Andrew Lloyd Webber's musical version of *The Phantom of the Opera* Leroux's 1911 story of Erik, a crippled musical genius who promotes the career of a young singer at the Paris Opera. The original novel is, though, far from the best of Leroux's work; that accolade belongs to *Le Mystère de la Chambre Jaune* (1907; translated as *The Mystery of the Yellow Room* in 1908), widely acclaimed as one of the first and most important 'locked room' mystery novels and the first use of the 'least suspected person' theme later utilized by Edgar Wallace and Agatha Christie. It features a remarkable young police reporter-cum-amateur-detective, Joseph Rouletabille, whose admiring acolyte, Sainclair, is frequently amazed by his friend's brilliant flashes of insight and follows in his shadow as Rouletabille solves the mystery of how a girl has been assaulted and wounded in a sealed room in the middle of Paris.

Gaston Leroux brought his training and experience as a journalist to the writing of his novel. Born in Paris, he was apparently a rebellious teenager regularly in trouble with the local gendarmerie. His first job was working in a lawyer's office, but his real interest lay in writing. In 1890 he managed to get a job as a legal chronicler on *L'Écho de Paris*. Leroux's skill at describing famous trials caught the eye of the editor of *Le Matin*. He was given a commission to travel around Europe, and the reports he filed from numerous trouble spots earned him an enviable reputation which he used to sell his early works of fiction. All were sensational in tone and usually first published as serials in French periodicals – *La Double Vie de Théophraste Longuet* (1903), for example, was a Gallic version of *Dr Jekyll and Mr Hyde* – but it was the appearance of the 'locked room' mystery first serialized in *L'Illustration* in 1907 that really brought him to public attention. In writing it, he explained later, 'My intention was to go one better than Conan Doyle and

American edition of Gaston Leroux's Cheri-Bibi novel, *Dark Road*, translated in 1924.

make my mystery more complete than even Edgar Allan Poe had done.' A competition run by the newspaper challenging readers to solve the mystery of the yellow room before the final episode produced not a single correct entry! Leroux swiftly created another case for Rouletabille, *Le Parfum de la Dame en Noir* (translated as *The Perfume of the Lady in Black* in 1909), which was followed by six more exploits of the young sleuth who became known as 'the prince of journalists and detectives', taking him across Europe and even into Russia before a final adventure in his native Paris, *Rouletabille Chez les Bohémiens* (1922). The original novel, *The Mystery of the Yellow Room*, has been filmed several times, most notably in America in 1919 starring Lorin Baker. Leroux also deserves to be remembered for his series of adventure

mysteries about the tragic Cheri-Bibi, a man sent to Devil's Island for a crime he did not commit, who returns to avenge himself and others who have been the victims of injustice. These titles, which began with *Les Cages Flottantes* (translated as *The Floating Prison* in 1913) and continued through *Palas et Cheri-Bibi* (translated as *Dark Road* in 1924) to *Le Coup d'État de Cheri-Bibi* (translated as *The New Idol* in 1928) were all published by John Long in the UK and The Macaulay Company in America, with two of the stories reaching the screen starring John Gilbert and Pierre Fresnay.

Maurice Leblanc (1864–1941), the second of the French quartet of crime writers, followed an almost identical career pattern to Leroux. Leblanc acknowledged his debt to the inspiration of Arthur Conan Doyle by actually pitting his popular anti-hero, Arsène Lupin, the 'Prince of Thieves', against a parody of the Baker Street detective in the second title in the series, *Arsène Lupin contre Herlock Sholmes* (1908). Lupin is a gentleman crook, not unlike Raffles, although his style is different and he is blessed with a Gallic sense of humour. Young and handsome, he is a rather brazen villain, mocking the law who charged major crimes to him and his gang whether or not they are responsible. Not surprisingly, Lupin has to use a variety of aliases and disguises, as the author is at some pains to explain in the first of his adventures, *Arsène Lupin, Gentleman Cambrioleur* (1907): 'What is he like? I've seen him perhaps 20 times, and each time he's been different. Only his eyes, his figure, and his bearing have been the same.'

Leblanc, who was born in Rouen but educated in Berlin and Manchester, studied

Right: *Arsène Lupin*, the 'Prince of Thieves' who takes on a thinly-disguised parody of Sherlock Holmes in one of the many novels about his exploits by Maurice Leblanc (1908).

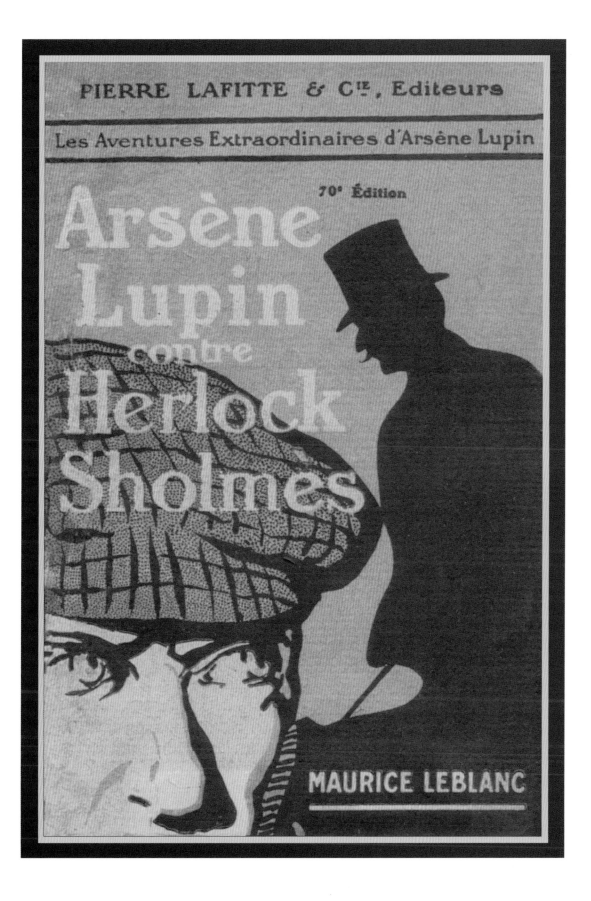

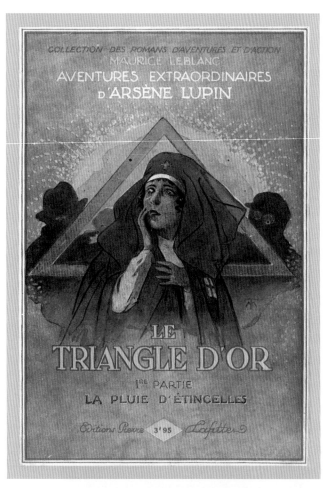

law before working as a police reporter on several Paris newspapers. He turned effortlessly to writing for the popular periodicals and drew on his knowledge of crime in the creation of his roguish anti-hero, whose fast-paced adventures and amusing asides appealed to the taste of French readers. The stories were often published as paperback serials by Editions Pierre Lafitte, the covers stunningly illustrated by either Maurice Toussaint or Robert Broders, whose work undoubtedly helped promote the sales of Lupin's *'aventures extraordinaires'*, like *Le Confession de Arsène Lupin* (1912) and *Le Triangle d'Or* (1917). All were later translated into English for British and American editions. For much of his career, Lupin is a thorn in the flesh of the French police – particularly Lenormand, the chief of the Sûreté, whom he actually impersonates in one story – but later goes to the aid of the harassed officers (unbeknownst to them, of course) and finally sets up his own detective agency. There have been numerous films based on the Lupin stories, starring David Powell, Wedgewood Newell, John Barrymore and Melvyn Douglas.

'Fantômas the Mysterious' was a sinister French rogue dressed in impeccable evening clothes and mask, with a taste for brutality and death, who enjoyed a similar fame to Arsène Lupin in a series of 32 adventures that began in 1911. He, too, was the creation of newspapermen, Pierre Souvestre (1874–1914) and Marcel Allain (1884–1969), who met by chance in the hubbub of Parisian journalism and created a legend that would bring admiring quotes from writers as diverse as Jean Cocteau, Raymond Queneau and James Joyce, who declared the series to be 'Enfantomastic!' Souvestre, who came from a

Left: The paperback serializations of Maurice Leblanc's Arsène Lupin novels were often illustrated by the wonderfully evocative Maurice Toussaint (top) or Robert Broders (below).

'Fantômas the Mysterious' was a sinister French rogue created by Pierre Souvestre and Marcel Allain, whose adventures were continued by Allain after Souvestre's sudden death, concluding with *Fantômas Captured* in 1926.

well-to-do family in Brittany, and his Paris-born collaborator had both studied law before entering the world of journalism. Their paths crossed on *L'Auto*, one of the first magazines to deal with the new craze for motoring. They soon met with publisher Artheme Fayard, who was looking for a series of mystery novels. On receiving the manuscript of the first novel, *Fantômas*, which introduced the 'King of the Night' spreading terror through Paris, with his mistress, Lady Beltham, and his implacable foe, Inspector Juve, Fayard decided to promote the book lavishly. He covered Paris with posters of a masked man in evening clothes looming over the city, a silver dagger in his hand. The effect on the public was electric and the campaign continued with the publication of each subsequent novel – all written at white-hot speed, sometimes in a

matter of days – as sales soared. By the following year a *Société des Amis de Fantômas* had been founded and the first of five movies appeared, produced by the legendary silent serial director, Louis Feuillade. Translations into numerous languages followed, including English. The books were published in Britain by Stanley Paul and in the US by Brentano's, the most popular titles were *The Exploits of Juve* (1912), *A Royal Prisoner* (1913) and *Slippery as Sin* (1914), which featured Tom Bob, an intriguing American detective described as 'the hoodlum policeman'. Pierre Souvestre died of influenza in 1914 and Allain was called up to the armed forces at the outbreak of World War One, halting the series until after the conflict. Allain then produced another 11 Fantômas novels, concluding with *Fantômas Captured* in 1926. He lived long enough to be fêted for his remarkable collaboration and see the republication of a number of the most popular titles.

Three more important rivals to Sherlock Holmes emerged in Britain before crime fiction took off in an entirely new direction. They were a diverse trio: the distinguished Dr John Thorndyke, considered by some to be *the* greatest medico-legal detective; Max Carrados, the first blind investigator; and the everyman sleuth, Philip Trent, described by H. R. F. Keating as 'the first of the ungreat detectives, the human ones'. It has been suggested that the classically handsome Dr Thorndyke with his keen eyesight and physical dexterity might just have preceded Sherlock Holmes if his creator, Richard Austin Freeman (1862–1943) had picked up a pen after conceiving the idea for a medical detective while he was a student at the Middlesex Hospital Medical College. Since his childhood in London's Marylebone district, Freeman had been intrigued by medical jurisprudence, but he allowed the idea of Thorndyke, formerly a lecturer at St Margaret's Hospital with a highly specialized approach to crime solving, to lie germinating until the success of Sherlock Holmes gave him the impetus to begin the series with *The Red Thumb Mark* in 1907. This was followed with a collection of short stories in *Cassell's Magazine* in 1908 which were collected as *John Thorndyke's Cases*. Although Freeman, unlike Conan Doyle, was less ready to admit there had been a real-life original of Thorndyke, he did concede that his character bore a resemblance to Professor Alfred Swaine Taylor, the author of *Principles and Practices of Medical Jurisprudence* (1865), which he had read as a student. Armed with his

The adventures of the renowned medico-legal detective Dr. John Thorndyke were illustrated by Howard K. Elcock with photographic clues in *Pearson's magazine*, and later collected into hugely successful hardback and paperback editions.

A SECOND CLUE THAT HELPED TO BRING THE CRIMINAL TO JUSTICE.

This is a micro-photograph of bulbous hairs such as John Thorndyke found on the hair-brush in the stolen bag. This rare condition of the hair is known as *Trichorrexis nodosa* and is characterised by these swellings on the hairs. These form weak spots and here the hair eventually breaks, the broken ends having a brush-like appearance.

'inevitable green case' and accompanied by his aide, a former student, Dr Christopher Jervis, Thorndyke tackles all his case with painstaking care. A unique feature of the magazine publication of the later stories in *Pearson's* were photographs of clues which the doctor had studied in solving the crimes. These pictures, along with the illustrations by Howard K. Elcock, have become as firmly identified with Thorndyke as those of Sidney Paget with Sherlock Holmes. The doctor's cases continued to appear regularly during the 1920s and 1930s, many of them based on little-known scientific facts that Freeman reasoned his readers would be unaware of. He apparently even tested the workability of some of the substances and contraptions he used, in a laboratory installed on the top floor of his home in Gravesend. It was here that he died in 1943, defying illness and the nightly German bombing raids to complete the final Thorndyke novel, *The Jacob Street Mystery*.

Max Carrados, the first and still the best blind detective, was introduced by author Ernest Bramah to British readers in a series of short stories in the pages of *Pearson's* in 1913, evocatively illustrated by Warwick Reynolds. A year later they were assembled as *Max Carrados*, which Ellery Queen applauded as 'one of the ten best volumes of detective short stories ever written'. What makes Carrados such a fascinating character is the manner in which he uses his other senses — hearing, touch and smell — to discover clues, sense human emotions and solve his cases. Wealthy from an early inheritance, the amateur detective can pick and choose those enquiries he wishes to take up, aided by his manservant, Parkinson, who acts as his eyes, and a friend, Louis Carlyle, a private enquiry agent, who

Stories of Max Carrados, the first blind detective in crime fiction, created by Ernest Bramah, were brilliantly illustrated by Warwick Reynolds in both magazines and books.

possesses invaluable knowledge of the law absorbed from his days as a solicitor. Carrados can read newspaper headlines by the touch of his fingers, recognize people by their voices and often disarm suspects with his humour and generosity. Author Ernest Bramah Smith (1868–1942) was, by contrast, an extremely reticent man, and little is known about him beyond his birth in Manchester. He was the son of a warehouseman, and there is some evidence that he tried, unsuccessfully, to become a farmer before taking up the position of assistant editor on the popular periodical *Today*. During his subsequent literary career – in which he dropped his last name – he wrote several novels about the life of a Chinese minstrel, Kai Lung; a handful of fantasy books, and three collections of Max Carrados stories plus a novel, *The Bravo of London* (1934). The stories of the sightless detective have continued to gain admirers and, apart from occasional paperback reprints, several of his cases have been dramatized by the BBC

starring Simon Callow.

The final rival of Sherlock Holmes, Philip Trent, was everything the man from Baker Street was not. Ordinary, friendly, quietly humorous and tactful, he was created by E. C. Bentley as a deliberate reversal of the trend (started by Conan Doyle) for detectives who were extremely serious, humorless, almost superhuman, their talents matched only by the eccentricity of their behaviour. In a word, he wanted to 'humanize' the detective story, and the result, *Trent's Last Case*, published in 1913, was greeted by the *New York Times* as 'one of the few classics of detective fiction', while Bentley himself later came to be acknowledged by critics like John Carter as 'the father of the contemporary detective story'. Edmund Clerihew Bentley (1875–1956) was born in London and became a life-long friend of G. K. Chesterton when they met as pupils at St Paul's School. After studying law and qualifying for the bar, Bentley opted to follow Chesterton into journalism and, though by no means as prolific, did make his mark as an editorial writer on the *Daily Telegraph*. He also invented a verse-form which became known as the clerihew after the pen-name 'E. Clerihew' which he put on the first volume of verse, *Biography for Beginners*, published in 1905. It was at this time that he began to plan his assault on the traditions of the detective genre which he had been studying for years, and he mapped out a plot while walking each day between his house in Hampstead and office in Fleet Street. *Trent's Last Case* was accepted at much the same time in Britain by Thomas Nelson – where another of his friends, John Buchan, was a director – and by The Century Publishing Company in America.

Bentley's hero, Philip Trent, is fairly young, an artist by profession, and politely curious about crime in a way that gains him respect rather than resentment from the police. He is also fallible in a manner that his predecessors were not, and in *Trent's Last Case* he not only falls in love with Mabel Manderson, the beautiful widow of a neurotic American millionaire who has been murdered, but offers a solution to the crime which is completely wrong! The American publishers were not happy with Bentley's title and suggested *The Woman in Black*. Their editor, Henry Z. Doty, is credited with persuading Bentley to change the original name for his hero from Philip Gasket. The book, though, was a great success on both sides of the Atlantic and translated into numerous languages, at which point Century Publishing reverted to the original for their reprints. More curious still, apart from a small group of short stories all published in the *Strand* between 1914 and 1916, in which Trent successfully solved a number of crimes he was asked to investigate by Sir James Molloy, the managing director of the *Record* newspaper, Bentley produced only two more books about his ground-breaking detective. Whether this was by design or because he had just run out of inspiration is still debated today. *Trent's Own Case* did not appear until 1936 and was co-authored with a friend, H. Warner Allen. The story presented the hero himself as the chief suspect in the murder of an elderly philanthropist. *Trent Intervenes*, which was published two years later, consisted of the earlier short stories plus eight new cases that had been published in the *Strand* with illustrations by Jack M. Faulks. Nevertheless, E. C. Bentley's legacy, small as it may have been in terms of works, was to indicate a new way forward for the detective.

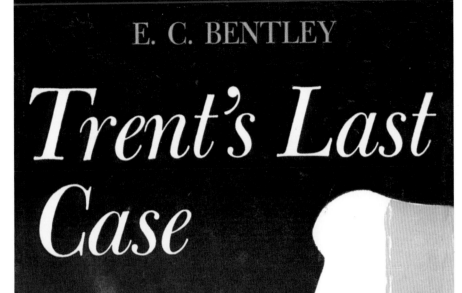

E. C. BENTLEY

Trent's Last Case

One of the masterpieces of detective fiction of all tim

THE WOMAN IN BLACK
By E. C. Bentley

E. C. Bentley's ground-breaking novel, *Trent's Last Case*, which 'humanized' the detective story, was first published in America in 1913 as *The Woman in Black*. It was some years before the US publishers reverted to the book's more familiar and enduring title.

Enter the Private Investigators

ENTER THE PRIVATE INVESTIGATORS

In 1914, as the pall of battle-smoke was beginning to gather over Europe, a young American answered a small ad in a Baltimore newspaper inviting applications for operatives for the famous Pinkerton's National Detective Agency. The young man's name was Samuel Dashiell Hammett (1894–1961) and his decision was profoundly to affect the history of the crime story, as well as produce two of the most famous detectives in all fiction: the Continental Op and Sam Spade. When Hammett began his literary career he brought a first-hand knowledge to his craft, as his biographer, William F. Nolan, has explained: 'He was able to bring the gritty argot of the streets into print, to portray authentically the thugs, hobos, molls, stoolies, gunmen and cops, political bosses and crooked clients, allowing them to talk and behave on paper as they had talked and behaved in Hammett's manhunting years.'

Hammett himself appreciated the importance of immediacy when he was writing about his nameless San Francisco detective, the Op, and the hard-boiled private eye, Spade. 'The novelist must know how things happen,' he said some years later, 'not how they are remembered in later years – and he must write them down that way. And the more direct their passage from street to paper, the more lifelike they should turn out...'

Viewed with the benefit of hindsight, Hammett's life as the originator of a new form of crime story was almost preordained. A moody, critical, complex man with a personal code as unyielding as the fictional code he made his characters live by, his contribution to the genre has been hugely influential – a statement graphically underlined by the fact that most of his work is in print, and also available in dozens of translations.

Hammett was born in St Mary's County, Maryland, of mixed Scottish and French ancestry, the family name being an Americanized version of De Chiel. He was something of a non-conformist from his early teens, leaving the Baltimore Polytechnic Institute when he was just 14 and, easily bored, drifting from one job to another until he spotted the small advertisement. He commented on this defining moment: 'An enigmatic want ad in a Baltimore paper took me into the employ of Pinkerton's – prior to this I was the unsatisfactory and unsatisfied employee of various railroads, stock brokers, machine manufacturers and canners by whom I was usually fired.'

The job of a detective proved exciting and stimulating, demanding patience, adaptability and nerve, and it also took Hammett to a number of new cities in pursuit of criminals. The young agent was not long in winning his first promotion when he captured a man who had stolen a Ferris wheel. He also proved himself adept at taking on a new identity – he posed as the secretary of the Civic Purity League to obtain information on one occasion, and on another spent three months in hospital trying to get information from the suspect in the next bed. Hammett reminisced later:

'Detective work is often ridiculous. There's great humour in it. I was shadowing a man who finally got lost in the country – and I ended up stepping forward to direct him back to the city. On another occasion, the situation was reversed; I was trying to peer into the upper story of a road-house when part of the

Opposite: Cover of Dashiell Hammett's most famous novel, *The Maltese Falcon*, which was first serialized in *Black Mask* in 1929 before appearing in the Alfred A. Knopf hardcover edition.

porch crumbled under me and I fell, spraining an ankle. The proprietor of the road-house gave me water to bathe it in!'

Hammett had to face physical danger on a number of occasions and he carried lifelong scars on his legs and an indentation on his head which had been given to him by a violent criminal. He tracked down a window-smasher in Stockton, California, arrested a forger in Pasco, Washington, and got so close to a gang of drug dealers in San Diego that one pusher even offered him a job in the narcotics trade. His two biggest cases were an assignment in 1919 to track down debonair swindler Nicky Arnstein, who had fleeced scores of victims of over a million dollars (but handed himself in before he could be arrested), and to investigate the notorious case of the film star Roscoe

The stories of the *Continental Op* which had appeared in *Black Mask* were also collected into book form as in this Dell edition from 1945.

'Fatty' Arbuckle, charged with the rape and murder of a young actress, Virginia Rappe. Hammett believed the charges were 'a frame up arranged by some of the corrupt local newspaper boys', and was pleased when Arbuckle was finally cleared after three trials. Already, though, he was growing tired of the arduous life of a private detective and began to write short, true-crime articles for magazines. He sensed, too, that some of his cases might provide the raw material for short stories, and in October 1922 sold his first tale to *Black Mask*, one of the new type of magazines to be found on American news-stands with garish covers and pulpwood text paper that for the next 20 years would provide a new era of cheap reading for a mass audience just as the dime novels before them had done. Although many other pulps carried crime fiction – a substantial number solely devoted to it – *Black Mask* deserves a place of pre-eminence as the magazine that developed what has been called 'the first truly original style of American detective fiction'.

Hammett's story was called 'The Road Home' and features Hagedorn, a detective who is hired to bring back a criminal on the run and during the chase is tempted with a bribe from the fugitive. Hammett chose not to put his real name on the story but signed himself 'Peter Collinson', utilizing a piece of current slang – 'He's a Peter Collins', meaning 'He's a nobody'. A year later, after writing three more crime stories as Collinson, Hammett produced the first-person story of a nameless operative from the Continental Detective Agency in San Francisco. The story 'Crooked Souls' (later reprinted as 'The Gatewood Caper') appeared under his own name. Within months, the Op had become one of the most popular characters in *Black Mask* and Hammett's literary career was under way.

The Op was a mixture of the author himself and James Wright, Assistant Superintendent of Pinkerton's Baltimore office and Hammett's former boss, whom he had grown to admire greatly. Hammett deliberately kept the Op nameless, 'because he's more or less of a type and I'm not sure that he's entitled to a name. I've worked with several of him.' Over the next seven years, until 1930, Hammett sent the sleuth out to track down killers, investigate robberies and find missing persons, all of which confirmed him as the leader of the new 'hard-boiled' school of detective fiction. Apart from the short stories, the Continental Op appeared in three novels, *Blood Money* (actually two linked adventures from *Black Mask*, 'The Big Knockover' and '$106,000 Blood Money', both published in 1927), *Red Harvest* (1929) and *The Dain Curse* (1928).

The creation of this fat little detective alone would have ensured Dashiell Hammett's place among the greats of crime fiction, but in September 1929 *Black Mask* began the serialization of a new hard-boiled story, *The Maltese Falcon*, introducing private eye Sam Spade, a man with a face like Satan, a cynical wit and a method of cool, direct action, the like of which had never been seen before. When the five-part serial was published as a novel the following year it immediately became a best-seller and was hailed by several critics as *the* best American detective novel. Unlike the Op, Sam Spade had no prototype, although Hammett admitted, 'He is idealized in the sense that he is what most of the private detectives I've worked with would *like* to have been.' Casper Gutman, the fat man seeking the elusive gold and jewel-encrusted statuette of the title, was based on a man suspected of being a spy whom Hammett had shadowed around Washington D.C. The story of Spade, the archetypal hard-boiled private dick and arguably the most famous sleuth of the twentieth century, has subsequently been filmed several times, most notably in 1941 starring Humphrey Bogart and directed by

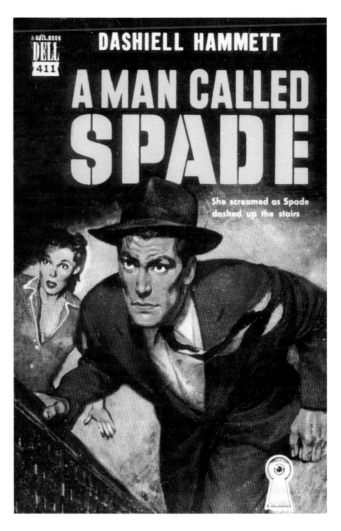

Sam Spade, Hammett's archetypal private eye, appeared in only a handful of short stories which were collected as *A Man Called Spade* in 1946.

John Huston. Despite this rapturous reception, Hammett wrote only three more short stories of his great anti-hero, collected as *The Adventures of Sam Spade* in 1944.

The success of *The Maltese Falcon* landed Dashiell Hammett work in Hollywood, but although he had little regard for the film industry, he moved there and there is little doubt his creative writing suffered as a result, not helped by his heavy drinking. He became embroiled in left-wing politics and was called before Senator Joseph McCarthy's enquiry where he refused to confirm or deny that he was a communist. He did, though, publish a number of short stories – the best collected in *Dead Yellow Women* (1947), *Nightmare Town*

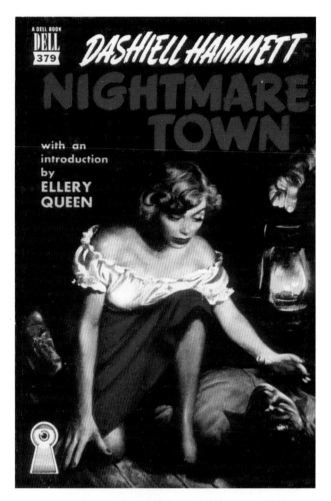

Above: *Nightmare Town*, which was issued in 1948, contained some of the best of Dashiell Hammett's hard-boiled short stories.

Below: Panel from Dashiell Hammett's newspaper cartoon series, *Secret Agent X-9*, which began syndication in 1934 as a rival series to Chester Gould's strip about the incorruptible *Dick Tracy*, who first appeared in 1931.

(1948) and *Woman in the Dark* (1952) – and created the semi-humorous exploits of a retired private detective, Nick Charles, in *The Thin Man* (1934). Hammett ran into trouble with the law because of a particular question-and-answer episode between Nick Charles and his wife, Norah: 'Tell me the truth, when you were wrestling with Mimi, didn't you have an erection?' – 'Oh, a little.'

Hammett was also responsible for producing a newspaper cartoon strip, *Secret Agent X-9*, launched in 1934, which graphically illustrated the violent adventures of a nameless FBI agent. It was drawn by Alex Raymond, later to become famous for his *Flash Gordon* series. The assignment had been offered to him by King Features, which was looking for a rival to *Dick Tracy*, the first successfully syndicated detective strip, which was created and drawn by Chester Gould (1900–1985) and appeared in 1931. A former commercial artist, Gould had devised the incorruptible sleuth as 'Plainclothes Tracy' for the *Chicago Tribune* syndicate with an infallible credo in the era of Prohibition, 'I decided that if the police couldn't catch the gangsters, I'd create a fellow who could.' With 'Plainclothes' dropped by the *Tribune's* editor in favour of the slang term for a detective, the result was a phenomenally popular serial with some of the most colourfully named villains in the history of crime fiction – including Splitface, Flattop, the Blank and Pruneface, to name just four. At its height, *Dick Tracy* appeared in over 800 newspapers around the world, with an enthusiastic readership in excess of 100 million.

For *Secret Agent X-9*, Hammett was guaranteed complete editorial freedom as well as a substantial fee. He proceeded to create the tough-guy agent in his trenchcoat and snap-brim hat who hurtles from one scrap to another confronting all kinds of villains along the way. Although generally overshadowed by Hammett's other work, the series ran for several years and copies of the original strips are now very collectable.

Although Dashiell Hammett is generally credited with creating the first hard-boiled detective, the accolade, strictly speaking, belongs to another *Black Mask* author, Carroll John Daly (1889–1958), who had a story in the same December 1922 issue that carried 'Peter Collinson's' 'The Road Home'. His tale was called 'The False Burton Combs' and it, too, recounted the exploits of a nameless sleuth who 'made his living against law breakers'. Just as Hagedorn predated the Continental Op, so this hard-boiled character proved to be the prototype of Daly's famous crime-buster, Race Williams.

As the creator of a private eye, Daly was about as improbable as Hammett had been inevitable. Born in Yonkers, New York, the son of comfortable, middle-class parents, he was a quiet, scholarly young man who developed a love of the theatre in preparatory school and then enrolled at the American Academy of Dramatic Arts. Although he did appear on the stage in a number of small productions, Daly seemed better suited for management and, realizing that the arrival of the movies provided lots of new opportunities, he became the owner and operator of the first film theatre in Atlantic City. The films that he screened fired Daly's imagination and, with the advent of the pulp magazines offering a market for stories, he decided to try his hand at crime

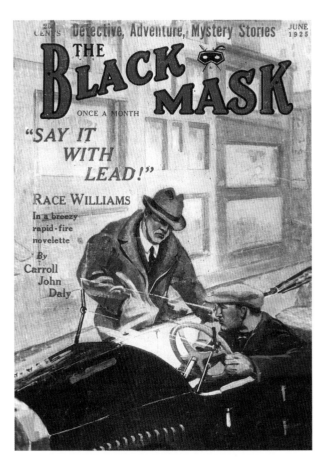

The first hard-boiled detective, Carroll John Daly's Race Williams, who bludgeoned his way to fame in the pages of *Black Mask* from 1922.

fiction. He developed a terse, adjective-filled style of writing clearly influenced by the caption frames in silent pictures, and in October 1922 his first story, 'Dolly', was published by *Black Mask*. It featured Three-Gun Terry Mack, a private eye who spoke and fired his gun in the same staccato style, and it was followed two months later by the anonymous sleuth of 'The False Burton Combs'.

But it was in July 1923 that Daly hit the jackpot with 'Knights of the Open Road', introducing Race Williams, a rugged, fearless and occasionally violent private eye who lives by a strong moral code of right and wrong and is never afraid to take the law into his own hands when the police do not act quickly enough for his liking. The detective has previously been a reporter, photographer, insurance investigator and professional gambler, and at the age of 30, his muscle-packed frame and the glint of danger in his eyes earns him the respect, even fear, of men, and the admiration of women. Williams is also an incredible marksman and can fire his pair of .45s simultaneously, creating a single hole between his adversary's eyes.

According to Carroll John Daly, Williams' justification for gunning down gangsters and criminal masterminds is simple enough: 'I'm what you might call a middleman – just a halfway house between the cops and the crooks. I do a little honest shooting once in a while – just in the way of business, but I never bumped off a guy who didn't need it... You can't make a hamburger without grinding up a little meat.'

Despite the bravado of his characters, Daly himself led the quietest of lives, rarely leaving home, hating physical exercise of any kind, and letting his teeth decay badly because he was terrified of going to the dentist. Only once did this meek persona drop, when he was arrested for carrying a concealed weapon tucked into his belt. It turned out to be a big Race Williams-type .45 – though no one ever knew him to have an enemy!

Although Daly must be acknowledged to have created the first-person narrative hard-boiled private eye in Race Williams, his stories have none of the style and characterization of those by Dashiell Hammett, and even if he was reckoned to be the most popular *Black Mask* writer for some years, he ultimately fell out of favour and spent the last years of his life in California writing for the comics. Some of the Race Williams cases also appeared in the rival pulp, *Dime Detective*, and a few of novel length were published in hardcovers, including *The Third Murderer* (1931), *The Amateur Murderer* (1933) and *Murder from the East* (1935).

A rather more enduring success awaited another writer who made his first contributions to the pulps at this time. Erle Stanley Gardner (1889–1970) sold his first story in 1923 and became famous as the creator of Perry Mason, the best-known attorney in fiction and the hero of more than 80 novels that started with *The Case of the Velvet Claws* (1933). The Perry Mason character went on to generate countless films and TV series, which starred Warren William, Donald Woods and Raymond Burr. Born in Massachusetts, Gardner travelled widely as a child with his engineering father and very nearly ran into trouble with the law as a teenager when he promoted some unlicenced boxing matches. After studying for the law and then gaining a reputation for successfully defending hopeless cases, Gardner began augmenting his meagre income by writing for the pulps. His tales of gangsters in the Prohibition era were immediately popular with readers of *Argosy*, as were his curious adventures of Speed Dash 'The Human Fly', who travelled the world solving cliff-hanging mysteries in the pages of *Top-Notch*; the exploits of Ed Jenkins, the 'Phantom Crook' in *Black Mask*; and con man Paul Pry who regularly appeared in *Dime Detective*. Along with the work he wrote as A. A. Fair, Charles M. Green, Kyle Corning, Les Tillray, Carleton Kendrick and Charles J. Kenny, Gardner was one of the best-selling writers of his generation; the sales of his mystery novels were for a time second only to those of Agatha Christie.

The third benchmark private eye in the development of the hard-boiled tradition was the wise-cracking gumshoe, Philip Marlowe – 'Trouble is my business', his catch-phrase – whose fame deservedly matches that of Sam Spade. Marlowe was the creation of Raymond Thornton Chandler (1888–1959), and he differs from most of his contemporaries in that he is a thinker rather than a man of violent action, and his college education has given him a love of poetry, classical music and solving chess problems. He runs a one-man detective agency

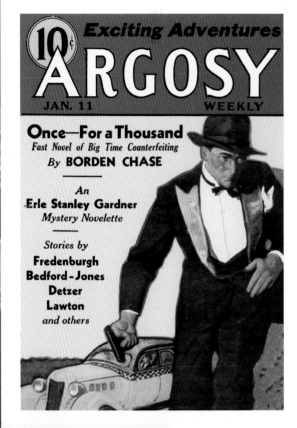

Above: Later stories of Race Williams appeared in *Dime Detective,* which also published some of Raymond Chandler's earliest hard-boiled yarns.

Right: Erle Stanley Gardner, who became famous as the creator of Perry Mason, made his crime debut with hard-boiled stories for pulps such as *Argosy*. He also shared front-cover billing on *Dime Detective* with Raymond Chandler's story *The Lady in the Lake*, about a private eye, Dalmas, who would later metamorphose into Philip Marlowe.

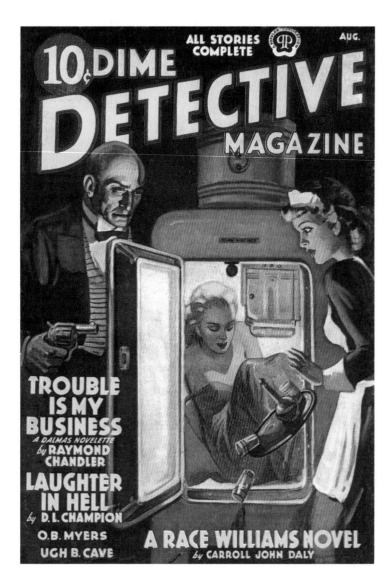

Raymond Chandler's *Trouble Is My Business* appeared first as a Dalmas novelette in *Dime Detective* magazine before being changed to a Marlowe story for book publication.

in Los Angeles, forever on the verge of insolvency, yet he never takes on a case of a dishonest client and puts the requirements of justice before his fees. He has an unshakeable ability to match violence and brutality (even against himself) with a flippant response. Chandler offered this word portrait of Marlowe to an enquiring admirer in 1951:

'The date of his birth is uncertain. I think he said somewhere that he was 38 years old, but that was quite a while ago and he is no older today. He was born in a small California town called Santa Rosa about 50 miles north of San Francisco. Marlowe has never spoken of his parents, and apparently he has no living relatives. I don't know why he came to

southern California, except that eventually most people do, although not all of them remain. He is slightly over six feet tall and weighs about 13st 8lb. He has dark brown hair, brown eyes, and the expression "passably good-looking" would not satisfy him in the least. I don't think he looks tough, but he can be tough. If you ask me why he is a private detective, I can't answer you...'

Chandler himself was born in Chicago, the son of an alcoholic railway engineer ('an utter swine') who abandoned him and his mother when the boy was just seven. His Irish mother then took him to England, where he was educated at Dulwich College and then briefly worked for the Admiralty before becoming a

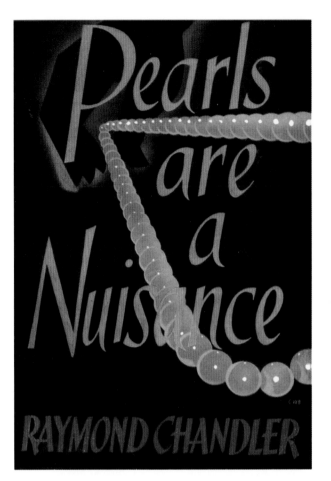

The best of Raymond Chandler's early stories appeared in collections such as *Pearls Are a Nuisance* (1953) and *5 Murderers* (1944).

journalist with the *Daily Express*. He also began contributing the occasional item of prose or poetry to *The Academy* or *The Westminster Gazette*. After service in World War One with the Canadian Gordon Highlanders, Chandler returned to America where he failed to restart his journalistic career and instead became involved in the oil business. The onset of the Depression and his own weakness for drink ruined this career, and in despair he turned to the pulp magazines as an outlet for his dark and cynical imagination. After five months of work he sold his first story, 'Blackmailers Don't Shoot' to *Black Mask* in December 1933. Chandler maintained later that the criterion for the pulps was 'a demand for constant action – if you stopped to

think, you were lost, and when in doubt, have a man come through a door with a gun in his hand.' In fact, what he developed was a prose style that was terse, idiomatic and functional.

During the years that followed, Chandler found a regular outlet for his stories in *Black Mask* and occasionally *Dime Detective*, writing a total of 20 hard-boiled novelettes which featured a mix of private eyes with names like Dalmas, Malvern and Mallory, who would all later transmogrify into the moody, introspective Philip Marlowe. These pulp stories were later collected in paperback anthologies including *5 Murderers* (1944), *Trouble Is My Business* (1951) and *Pearls Are a Nuisance* (1953), a volume first published in England and now a rare Chandler item.

In 1939, Chandler used the hard-won expertise he had developed in writing these stories – as well as some of the actual texts – in turning his hand to novels. The first of these books, *The Big Sleep* (1939), a 'cannibalization' (his word) of 'Killer in the Rain' and 'Finger Man', had Marlowe tackling the case of a dying millionaire, General Sternwood, who is being blackmailed; and the second, *Farewell, My Lovely* (1940), also a composite of several pulp stories, featured the problems of a wealthy Beverly Hills family and their collection of imported jade which tested his mettle to the full. The newspaper reviewers who had previously ignored his work in the pulps now heaped praise on these novels and helped to make Chandler a household name. The distinguished critic Howard Haycraft complimented him on his articulate prose and described *Farewell, My Lovely* as 'the best hard-boiled mystery since the works of Dashiell Hammett'. When the novels were published in England they were praised by a number of leading literary figures who realized their importance including J. B. Priestley and W. H. Auden, and Chandler was delighted to find himself considered a novelist rather than just a mystery writer.

Further Philip Marlowe novels followed, *The High Window* (1942), *The Lady in the Lake* (1943), *The Little Sister* (1949) and *The Long Goodbye* (1953), confirming Chandler's stature when the last title was awarded the Mystery Writers of America's Edgar as best novel in 1954. The film industry inevitably seized on these best-sellers – Humphrey Bogart giving a definitive performance as Marlowe in Howard Hawks' 1946 version of *The Big Sleep* – and the author himself was lured to Hollywood for several years, receiving Oscar nominations for a screenplay written with Billy Wilder for James M. Cain's *Double Indemnity* (1944) and his own original, *Blue Dahlia* (1946). Like Hammett,

though, he grew frustrated by the interference of studio executives in his material and his love-hate relationship with the film industry lasted for the rest of his life. Chandler also suffered, like some of his characters, from problems with women and drink, and even a period of time spent in England in 1955 where he was fêted and admired could not halt the steady decline in his writing. Philip Marlowe, by contrast, grew from strength to strength in the public imagination thanks to movies, radio and television adaptations, causing Chandler to be asked on more than one occasion whether *he* was the model for his greatest character. He replied memorably:

'I am exactly like the characters in my books. I am very tough and have been known to break a Vienna roll with my bare hands. I do a great deal of research, especially in the apartments of tall blondes. I do not regard myself as a dead shot, but I am a pretty dangerous man with a wet towel. But all in all I think my favourite weapon is a $20 bill.'

Joking aside, Chandler had a clear vision of the hard-boiled detective as a kind of modern knight searching for the holy grail of truth, which he explained in an essay, 'The Simple Art of Murder' in the December 1944 *Atlantic Monthly*:

'Down these mean streets a man must go who is not himself mean, who is neither tarnished nor afraid. The detective in this kind of story must be such a man. He is the hero, he is everything. He must be a complete man and a common man and yet an unusual man. He must be, to use a rather weathered phrase, a man of honour...'

Opposite: A classic cover for the *Avon* edition of Chandler's *The Big Sleep*, first published in 1939.

new publishers, Collins, with whom she would remain for the rest of her life. This was followed in 1934 by probably the most famous of all the Poirot novels, *Murder on the Orient Express*, written while she was accompanying her second husband, archaeologist Sir Max Mallowan, on a dig in Egypt, and inspired by the notorious Lindbergh kidnap case. The story has, of course, been filmed, along with a number of other books about Poirot. Among the actors to have played the Belgian sleuth are Albert Finney, Robert Morley, Peter Ustinov and, most recently on television, David Suchet, who has given what many critics consider a definitive performance.

Agatha Christie would go on to write a total of 42 books about Hercule Poirot, notably *Poirot Investigates* (the first collection of short stories issued in 1924 and a *Queen's Quorum* selection among the 106 most important detective stories of all time), *Death on the Nile* (1937), *Evil under the Sun* (1941) and *Dead Man's Folly* (1956), in which the principal setting, Nasse House, was modelled on Greenway House, Christie's Devonshire home where she lived for much of her life.

However, she did not rest on these laurels. In 1922, she introduced Tommy and

An early portrait of Hercule Poirot for the paperback edition of *Dumb Witness* (1937), retitled *Poirot Loses a Client* in the US.

Tuppence Beresford, a pair of flappers turned sleuths in *The Secret Adversary* (1922), and they were followed in 1930 by the gentle, gossipy but intelligent Miss Jane Marple, 'the most famous spinster detective in fiction'. Miss Marple keeps down crime in the archetypal English village of St Mary Mead – 'There is a great deal of wickedness in village life,' she once observed – and makes her debut in *Murder at the Vicarage*. The story introduced a new element into the genre: the mystery set in a small town or village. The tall, thin, greying Miss Marple with her china-blue eyes and shrewd insight into human nature was believed to have been partly based on the author's grandmother, 'who always appeared to be intimately acquainted with all the depths of human depravity,' Agatha said, and the elderly busybody detective in *The Affair Next Door* (1897) by Anna Katherine Green, which she had read as a child. Jane Marple has been seen in films starring the unlikely if popular Margaret Rutherford and much more faithfully on television played by Joan Hickson. Christie also wrote some cases about a rather curious detective known as Parker Pyne, who specializes in romantic and marital problems, collected as *Parker Pyne Investigates* in 1934.

Reggie Fortune, the second of the famous 'Golden Age' detectives, is unlike any of Agatha Christie's creations. He is a practising doctor who is called in by Scotland Yard to help on difficult cases and uses a mixture of forensic knowledge and a single-minded ability to let the facts of a crime speak for themselves. The son of a doctor, he studied at a London hospital where he concentrated on pathology until two criminal cases were brought to his

Opposite: *Murder on the Orient Express* (1934) is one of the most famous of Agatha Christie's stories about Hercule Poirot and has been filmed numerous times.

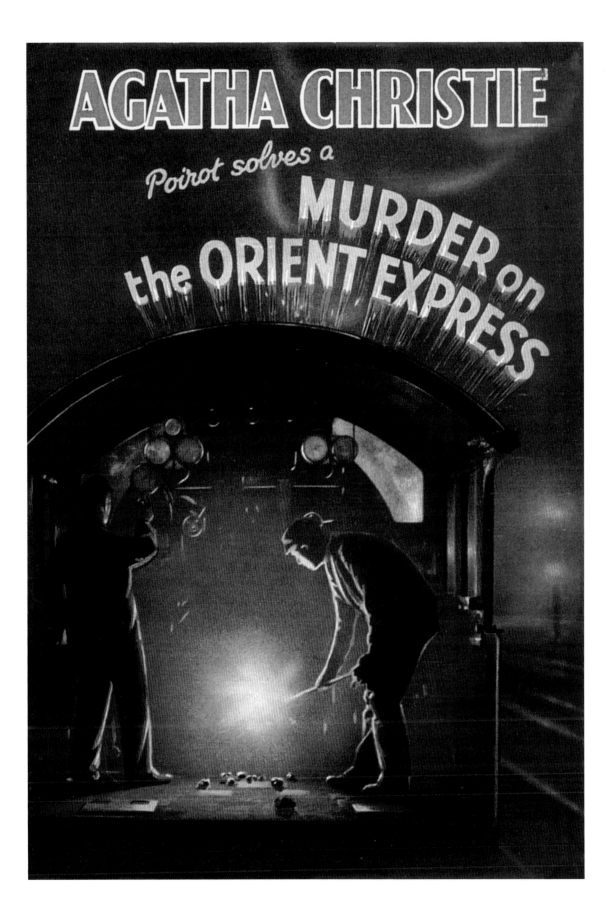

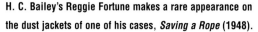

H. C. Bailey's Reggie Fortune makes a rare appearance on the dust jackets of one of his cases, *Saving a Rope* (1948).

attention and his career path was set. A gregarious man with a love of good food and fine wines, he is generous to his friends and the victims of crimes, although he can be tough both physically and mentally with lawbreakers. Reggie Fortune is not above meting out his own punishment to those who escape the law or find ways of outwitting the legal system. After his debut in *Call Mr Fortune* in 1920, he was regarded in crime story circles as the most popular detective in England between the two World Wars.

Reggie's creator, Henry Christopher Bailey (1878–1961), was born in London and was a classical scholar at Oxford where he wrote his first book, a historical novel, *My Lady of Orange* (1901), while still an undergraduate. He became a journalist in Fleet Street on the *Daily Telegraph* where he alternated as a drama critic, leader writer and war correspondent. Bailey made Reggie Fortune something of a contradiction; for although he professed himself to be one of 'the common people' he enjoyed the company of intellectuals

and drove a Rolls Royce, all facets of his character to be found in the books *Mr Fortune's Trials* (1925), *A Clue for Mr Fortune* (1936) and *Mr Fortune Finds a Pig* (1943).

Lord Peter Wimsey, the third great detective of this period, created by Dorothy L. Sayers, is a sophisticated and witty detective about whose social standing there can be no doubt. Lord Peter is an aristocrat who dresses fashionably, lives well in the heart of London's Piccadilly, has an eye for wine and women, and takes on cases because of his love of criminology. Lord Peter Death Bredon Wimsey, to give him his full title, is the youngest son of a duke and was educated at Eton and Balliol College, Oxford, where he proved himself a fine cricket player and gained a first class honours degree in modern history. After an unhappy love affair, Wimsey earned a DSO for bravery in the First World War, but returned to London suffering from a nervous breakdown. Thanks to the careful nursing of his batman-turned-butler, Bunter, Wimsey regained his health and then began to pursue his interest in crime, eventually becoming the leading amateur detective in the capital.

Dorothy Leigh Sayers (1893–1957), Wimsey's creator, was a rather more extraordinary figure than the biographical facts and interviews she gave during her life lead readers to believe. She was the only daughter of the headmaster of Christ Church Cathedral School in Oxford, and from a very early age displayed a ferocious intellect as well as a loud and flamboyant character. By the age of seven she had learned Latin and French and went on to gain a first class honours degree in languages at Somerville College, Oxford, where she was remembered for her bizarre dress sense and penchant for holding arguments in a booming voice. After leaving the university, Sayers worked briefly for a publisher before going to France to be a teacher. It was here that she first had the idea for Lord Peter Wimsey, although her initial intention was to try to get on the rota of authors producing the Sexton Blake novels. Having asked a friend to send her a selection of the books to read, she then devised a short story in which Blake hears about a man in London named Lord Peter Wimsey and asks who he is:

'Younger son of the Duke of Peterborough. Harmless sort of fellow, I think. Distinguished himself in the war. Rides his own horse in the Grand National. Authority on first editions. I've seen his photograph somewhere.

A fine period illustration of Lord Peter Wimsey and his assistant, Bunter, looking for clues in the case of *The Nine Tailors* (1934).

Fair-haired, big nose, aristocratic sort of man whose socks match his tie. No politics.'

If the story was ever submitted to the publishers of Sexton Blake, it was certainly not published. But the idea remained with Sayers until some years later when she was working at the S. H. Benson Advertising Agency writing copy for a wide range of products. She was keen to augment her salary and wrote a detective story, *Whose Body?*, in which the aforementioned Lord Peter Wimsey took the central role. As a physical model for the detective she chose a handsome young fellow student from her Oxford days, Roy Ridley, who would later become Chaplain of Balliol. Sayers submitted her manuscript to several publishers, all of whom turned it down, one commenting on its 'coarseness'. Finally, an American publishing house, Boni and Liveright, accepted the book, on condition that the authoress delete certain passages. As a result, the most English of detectives was first published in America in May 1923, and in the UK six months later. The second Wimsey novel, *Clouds of Witness*, appeared in 1926, and this time it was the critics who found certain elements of the story vulgar. In all, Dorothy Sayers wrote 11 novels and 21 short stories about the aristocratic sleuth – notably *Murder Must Advertise* (1933), set in an advertising agency; *The Nine Tailors* (1934), which Sinclair Lewis declared to be 'one of the four books in mystery stories which everyone should read'; and a collection of tales from the *Strand* and Pearson's magazines, *Lord Peter Views the Body* (1928) – before declaring that enough was enough:

'I wrote the Peter Wimsey books when I was young and had no money. I made some money and then stopped writing novels and began to write what I had always wanted to write.'

The Margery Allingham crime stories were popular in the American pulps — her story of *The Mystery Man of Soho* got front page treatment by *Thrilling Detective* in 1947.

No amount of pleading from her fans would make Dorothy L. Sayers change her decision and instead she devoted herself to poetry, plays and essays, primarily on religious themes, as well as a brilliant translation of Dante's *Divine Comedy*. For the rest of her life she refused to be drawn further on Peter Wimsey and shrouded much of her life in mystery, in particular the fact that she had given birth to an illegitimate child. Nothing, though, could deny the enduring fame of her detective, who was played on screen by Peter Haddon and Robert Montgomery, and more faithfully on television by Ian Carmichael and Edward Petherbridge.

Sayers, along with Agatha Christie, has often been described as one of the 'Big Four' female detective story writers from the 'Golden Age'. The other two are Margery Allingham (1904–1966), creator of Albert Campion, and Ngaio Marsh (1895–1982) whose 1940 book, *Surfeit of Lampreys*, featuring aristocratic investigator Lord Charles Lamprey, was described by *The Times* as 'an almost perfect classical detective story, combining an ingenious puzzle with all the attributes of a good novel'.

More than one critic has drawn attention to the fact that Albert Campion has a number of similarities with Lord Peter Wimsey. He was born into an aristocratic English family, attended Cambridge University and there made a number of friends who feature in his later life. He initially gives the impression of being a young fogey, but this proves to be merely a front to fool criminals into a false sense of security so that he can expose them to the police. A mild-mannered figure with large glasses, his early successes in *Death of a Ghost* (1934), *Flowers for the Judge* (1936) and *Mr Campion: Criminologist* (1937), give Campion an aura of confidence which causes people to turn to him whenever they are in trouble. Many seek him out at his bachelor flat near Piccadilly Circus where he is looked after by his faithful assistant, Magersfontein Lugg, a reformed Cockney burglar and larger-than-life character who Campion says has 'the courage of his former convictions'. In the later novels, Campion meets and marries Lady Amanda Fitton who helps him in several cases, and they have a son, Rupert, who makes his debut in *Coroner's Pidgin* (1945), one of the best Campion cases, set in a London preparing for the invasion of German-occupied Europe.

Margery Allingham was born in Ealing, the daughter of two professional writers, and later moved to Essex where she spent much of her life. Her first published effort appeared in the

Christian Globe when she was seven, and her first novel, *Blackkerchief Dick; A Story of Mersea Island*, about pirates and smuggling on the Essex coast, was published while she was still a teenager in 1923. It was not until after her marriage to the commercial artist and editor Philip Youngman Carter that she began to write crime fiction and he, in fact, collaborated on many stories. Allingham admitted as much in a letter written in 1952:

'Philip and I go over the plots together and we argue over every word. I write every paragraph four times. Once to get my memory down, once to put in anything I have left out, once to take out anything that seems unnecessary, and once to make the whole thing sound as if I had just thought of it.'

Such careful attention to detail earned Margery Allingham praise from her readers, the critics and even her fellow crime writers. After the publication of *The Mystery Man of Soho* (1947), which warranted front cover treatment when it filled almost the entire issue of the US magazine, *Thrilling Detective*, Agatha Christie wrote, 'Margery Allingham stands out like a shining light. Everything she writes has a definite shape ... each book has its own separate and distinctive background.'

Allingham continued to write the occasional case for Campion in the post-war years, introducing some new characters, including Charles Luke of the CID – described by one reviewer as 'a practical and extremely credible cop, the forerunner of the modern detective anti-hero' – in *More Work for the Undertaker* (1948); and the evil jailbreaker, Jack Havoc, in *The Tiger in the Smoke* (1952). When she died in 1966, her husband, who was so familiar with the private detective, was able to complete an unfinished Campion manuscript, *Cargo of Eagles* (1968), as well as write a couple of extra cases of his own, *Mr*

MARGERY ALLINGHAM

THE TIGER IN THE SMOKE

PENGUIN BOOKS 2/6

The Tiger in the Smoke (1952) was Margery Allingham's much praised story of a jailbreaker, Jack Havoc, at loose on the streets of London.

Campion's Farthing (1969) and *Mr Campion's Falcon* (1970). *Tiger in the Smoke* was filmed in 1956 with Donald Sinden, and the continuing popularity of the books was underlined in 1987 when several were filmed as part of a BBC television series starring Peter Davison and Brian Glover.

New Zealand-born Ngaio Marsh (her first name is Maori for 'flowering tree') is best known for her stories of the Eton-educated sleuth, Chief Inspector Roderick Alleyn (named after the Elizabethan actor, Edeard Alleyn, who founded her father's old school in

Dulwich), who has a remarkable technique for interviewing suspects, and whom she once famously described as looking like 'a cross between a grandee and a monk'. He was born, she explained later, in the pages of an exercise book in a London flat in 1931. 'I turned on the light, opened an exercise book, sharpened my pencil and began to write. There he was, waiting quietly in the background ready to make an entrance at Chapter Four, page 58, in *A Man Lay Dead*.'

Marsh's original intention was to be a painter, but the theatre drew her like a magnet and she became first an actress, then a playwright and finally a producer for various groups who toured New Zealand and later Britain. Despite the success of her crime novels she was to remain deeply wedded to the theatre for the rest of her life, producing many hit Shakespearian productions in both the northern and southern hemispheres. In June 1924 she met an aristocratic English family, the Rhodes, who lived in Buckinghamshire and whose life-long friendship was to give her the insight into British upper middle-class life with its country mansions, house parties and murder games that would feature in so many of her Roderick Alleyn crime novels. She immortalized the family in what is considered the most personal of her books, *Surfeit of Lampreys*, which actually brought protests from shocked readers because of the way in which the murder victim, Lord Wutherford, is despatched – a silver skewer through the eyeball while he is standing in a lift. (The title, of course, refers to the dish that was responsible for the death of an English king, and the book's dust jacket had a graphically drawn skewered lamprey.)

Perhaps not surprisingly, the theatre features in several of the Roderick Alleyn mysteries, including *Opening Night* (1951), *Death at the Dolphin* (1966) and the novelette *I Can Find My Way Out* (1946), which won a

A powerful dust jacket for Ngaio Marsh's classic story, *Surfeit of Lampreys* (1940).

prize in the first contest for best stories held by *Ellery Queen's Mystery Magazine*. In 1962, Ngaio Marsh was made a Dame of the British Empire for her contributions not to crime fiction but to the theatre, although the mystery critics agreed with American Howard Haycraft, who believed that she was one of the writers, along with Margery Allingham and Nicholas Blake, who had brought the English detective novel to 'full flower'.

Nicholas Blake was the pseudonym of Cecil Day-Lewis (1904–1972), a poet, critic and novelist who crowned his career by being made British Poet Laureate in 1968. Educated at Wadham College, Oxford, he became a teacher but found his left-wing views made him unpopular with those who ran education. Like many 1930s intellectuals he flirted with communism, only distancing himself after the

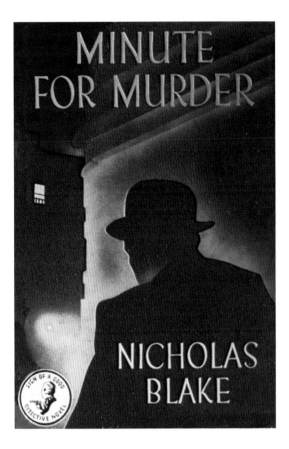

The wartime setting of Nicholas Blake's *Minute for Murder* (1947) brought back painful memories for many readers in Britain.

The dilettante American sleuth Philo Vance made his debut in the prestigious *Scribner's Magazine* in 1926 and went on to be hugely successful in both hardcover and paperback.

Spanish civil war. Never able to earn enough money from his poetry to make ends meet, Day-Lewis turned to crime fiction. In *A Question of Proof* (1935) he introduced Nigel Strangeways, an exuberant, Oxford-educated detective with a knowledge of many diverse subjects, combined with an astute judgement of character. Strangeways falls in love with the beautiful if eccentric Georgia Cavendish and they work together on several cases until her death during the Second World War.

Despite the pen-name, derived from the Christian name of his son and his mother's maiden name, it did not take readers long to guess the real identity of Nicholas Blake because of Strangeways' strong resemblance to Day-Lewis' great friend, the poet W. H.

Auden, also an admirer of crime fiction. In all, Day-Lewis produced 20 novels, all but four featuring his hero, of which the best are *The Beast Must Die* (1938), about revenge on a hit-and-run driver (and which was made into a superb *crime noir* movie, *Que la Bête Meure*, in 1969 by French director Claude Chabrol, with Michel Duchaussoy and Caroline Cellier); *Minute for Murder* (1947) set in the 'Ministry for Morale' during the war and in which Georgia Cavendish is killed during the blitz; and *The Morning After Death* (1966), which upset admirers when the author announced that he was giving up fiction to return to poetry and criticism. The Blake legacy has continued to be celebrated, the crime historian H. R. F. Keating writing shortly before

Day-Lewis' death, 'When it comes round to having a Crime Writing Laureate, Mr Blake's brow is there for the wreath.'

Many of the novels by Britain's 'Golden Age' writers were, of course, published in America, but there were also other American writers who weren't the hard-boiled practitioners yet enjoyed large followings. The suave, aesthete Philo Vance, for example, the character created by S. S. Van Dine, has been described by Steinbrunner and Penzler as 'the most popular detective in literature during the late 1920s and the early 1930s'. Indeed, when his first investigation, *The Benson Murder Case*, was serialized in the May 1926 issue of *Scribner's Magazine* it was heralded as 'A New Kind of Mystery Story'. The dilettante sleuth with his affected English accent and widespread knowledge of art, music, philosophy, religion and murder was, not surprisingly, compared to Reggie Fortune and Lord Peter Wimsey. Vance is six feet tall, with an aloof expression and a thin-lipped mouth that implies both irony and cruelty in his character. He seems to smile constantly, especially when outsmarting his best friend, District Attorney Markham, to find the solution to a murder mystery. Despite his unabashed snobbery and veneer of civility, Philo Vance is not above killing when it becomes evident the police will not be able to punish a killer he has tracked down.

S. S. Van Dine was the pen-name of Willard Huntington Wright (1888–1939), a Harvard-educated man who studied art in Munich and Paris before working as the art critic for the *Los Angeles Times* and editing the popular magazine *The Smart Set*. It was there he met H. L. Mencken and George Jean Nathan, the founders of *Black Mask*, although this did not immediately fire his enthusiasm to write detective fiction. A breakdown in his health in 1923 provided him with the time and the inclination after he read a number of contemporary crime novels and felt he could do better. Wright decided to create a sleuth who mirrored many of his own attitudes, though he felt anxious enough about possible reactions to use an old family name instead of his own. Beginning with *The Benson Murder Case*, the stories proved a huge success and made the author a wealthy man, enabling him to live like his character in a luxurious penthouse, dine at the finest restaurants and dress in the latest fashions. Wright's fame only heightened his snobbery, however, and he made enemies – not the least of them Dashiell Hammett and Raymond Chandler. Hammett took a whole page of *The Saturday Review of Literature* to damn Vance as 'a bore whose conversational manner is that of a high-school girl and he manages always, and usually ridiculously, to be wrong.' Chandler called him 'the most asinine character in American fiction'.

To be fair, millions of readers thought otherwise about the 12 cases, each with a similar title, which include *The Canary Murder Case* (1927) about the killing of a Broadway singer, considered to be the best of the cases; *The Bishop Murder Case* (1929), in which nursery rhymes feature in a series of bizarre deaths; and *The Garden Murder Case* (1937). The novels, whose dust jackets described Vance as 'America's first classic detective', were equally popular in book club editions, paperback and translations, and for 20 years they inspired a series of films in which the detective was played by William Powell, Warren William, Edmund Lowe and Alan Curtis. Wright himself scripted several Hollywood movies and was also one of the famous writers who contributed to *The President's Mystery Story* (1936), the tale of a lawyer who starts a new life by leaving his identity papers on a corpse, which had been devised by Franklin D. Roosevelt.

The next major detective to make his debut

A copy of the rare *Ellery Queen Mystery League* magazine which featured the editor in a mask on the inside front cover.

in the States was Ellery Queen, a name that served both the sleuth and his 'creator'. Queen had clearly been influenced by Philo Vance. Here again was a highly intelligent investigator who solved extraordinary crimes, but without quite the same snobbery and egocentric behaviour of Vance, although he is not above showing off his extensive forensic knowledge. Ostensibly a writer, the detective uses his intelligence and powers of observation to help his father, Inspector Richard Queen of the New York PD, solve crimes until he eventually sets himself up as a private eye. A tall, well-dressed man, he is attractive to the opposite sex and has affairs with a number of women including his secretary, Nikki Porter, but nothing comes of any of these liaisons. It was not long after the first of the 40-odd cases of Ellery Queen, *The Roman Hat Mystery*, was published in 1929, that one critic hailed him as 'the logical successor to Sherlock Holmes'. Further highly rated novels like *The*

Dutch Shoe Mystery (1931), *Calamity Town* (1942) and *Sherlock Holmes Versus Jack the Ripper* (1967) served to confirm his stature, and at the most recent count the books have sold close to 200 million copies.

Readers were initially puzzled that the Ellery Queen stories were also written by the hero, but it was not long before the truth of the pseudonym was revealed: 'he' was actually two men, Daniel Nathan (aka Frederic Dannay, 1905–1982) and Manford Lepofsky (aka Manfred B. Lee, 1905–1971), two New York-born cousins who began their careers creating advertising copy until their mutual fascination with mystery fiction prompted them to write *The Roman Hat Mystery* as an entry for a contest sponsored by *McClure's Magazine.* Although the story won the first prize, the magazine changed proprietors and another story was adjudged better than theirs, so the co-authors were forced to seek a book publisher, Frederick A. Stokes. The novel's

ELLERY QUEEN'S MYSTERY MAGAZINE

NATIONAL
MWA EDGAR
AWARDED TO
ELLERY QUEEN'S
MYSTERY MAGAZINE

Salter

35 Cents   JUNE
The Night I Died   CORNELL WOOLRICH
Bullet for One   REX STOUT

A Boy's Will   Q. PATRICK
Some of My Best Friends   STUART PALMER
Recipe for Murder   C. P. DONNEL, JR.
The Rock of Justice   MARK RONDY
Between Eight and Eight   C. S. FORESTER
Clerical Error   JAMES GOULD COZZENS

AN ANTHOLOGY OF THE BEST DETECTIVE STORIES, NEW AND OLD

Ellery Queen's Mystery Magazine first appeared in 1941
and was responsible for publishing some of the finest
crime short stories.

publication proved to be a landmark in the detective genre, and 'Ellery Queen' matured into probably the most successful collaboration in the annals of crime fiction. Asked later where the name had come from, Dannay and Lee said it had been chosen because it seemed 'unusual and memorable', and if the author and character shared the same name, readers might remember it better. The pair had also changed their own real names in the interim, and went on to turn out further novels of the ubiquitous detective, as well as writing short stories, editing anthologies and launching *Mystery League* magazine in 1933. This pulp-sized monthly which featured mainly new authors was high on quality but not on

sales and it failed after four issues. The pair used a gimmick of appearing in the magazine wearing a mask, which was also employed when they went on promotion tours for the books. Copies of this curiosity in the Queen legend are now of great rarity.

What the two men learned from this first experiment in running a magazine enabled them to have another try in 1941 with *Ellery Queen's Mystery Magazine*. Issued monthly, it developed a policy of mixing reprinted material with new fiction, and in so doing launched the careers of many top writers and also ensured its own future. In 1953, the magazine purchased the title and archives of *Black Mask*, thereafter reprinting stories by many of the great hard-boiled writers who had first appeared in its pages, including Hammett, Chandler and Carroll John Daly. The magazine won numerous awards, and in 1960 Dannay and Lee were made 'Grand Masters' by the Mystery Writers of America. The two men also wrote scripts for a number of Hollywood movies, helped in the making of an *Ellery Queen* radio series, and were involved in a number of the movies based on their detective, who was played by Ralph Bellamy, William Gargan, Peter Lawford and Jim Hutton.

A complete contrast to Philo Vance and Ellery Queen is Charlie Chan, a humble Chinese-American detective whose charm and endlessly courteous manner endear him to everyone who meets him. He is a highly regarded inspector with the Honolulu Police Department and famed for his aphorisms uttered in stilted English: 'Ancient ancestor say worry like rocking chair: it give you something to do, but it gets you no place.' Married with 11 children (one of whom, 'Number One Son', often accompanies him on cases), Chan is a chubby figure with black, closely cropped hair and eyes that are said to glow like yellow buttons when he solves a case. He is a detective who always gets his man with a triumphant flourish: 'Relinquish the firearms, Mr Jennison, or I am forced to make fatal insertion in vital organ belonging to you.' Despite appearing in only six novels, Charlie Chan was listed among the most popular sleuths of his time and for years featured in almost as many movies as Sherlock Holmes, played primarily by Warner Oland, Sidney Toler, Roland Winters and Peter Ustinov, whose metamorphosis into the detective in 1980 was attacked by a number of cultural groups who thought the role should have been played by an Oriental.

The story behind his creation reflects great credit on Earl Derr Biggers (1884–1933), an Ohio-born, Harvard-educated *Boston Traveler* columnist and drama critic. He had written a play, *If You're Only Human* (1912), and a handful of mystery novels including *Seven Keys to Baldpate* (1913) and *The Agony Column* (1916) when he began casting around for an idea for another crime novel. He realized that the Chinese had been portrayed as the villains in so many stories – especially those by Sax Rohmer – that it was time for a change. Biggers explained his reasoning later: 'Sinister and wicked Chinese are old stuff, but an amiable Chinese on the side of law and order had never been used.' The very first novel about Charlie Chan, *The House Without a Key* (1925), in which he investigates the killing of a wealthy man with a dubious past, proved how right he was. Best-seller followed best-seller, and widely held to be one of the best of his works is *Keeper of the Keys* (1932), in which a famous entertainer meets a nasty end. Magazine editors and publishers pleaded with Earl Derr Biggers for more cases of the genial detective, but his inspiration seemed to have run dry and it was left to films, radio and television scriptwriters and comic book authors to continue the legend.

More curious even than Charlie Chan is heavyweight detective Nero Wolfe, created by

Behind That Curtain (1928) was one of the all too few Charlie Chan mysteries by Earl Derr Biggers. Nonetheless, they helped to create a legend around the Honolulu policeman whose adventures were later adapted into a long-running comic strip series, co-starring his often impetuous 'Number One Son.'

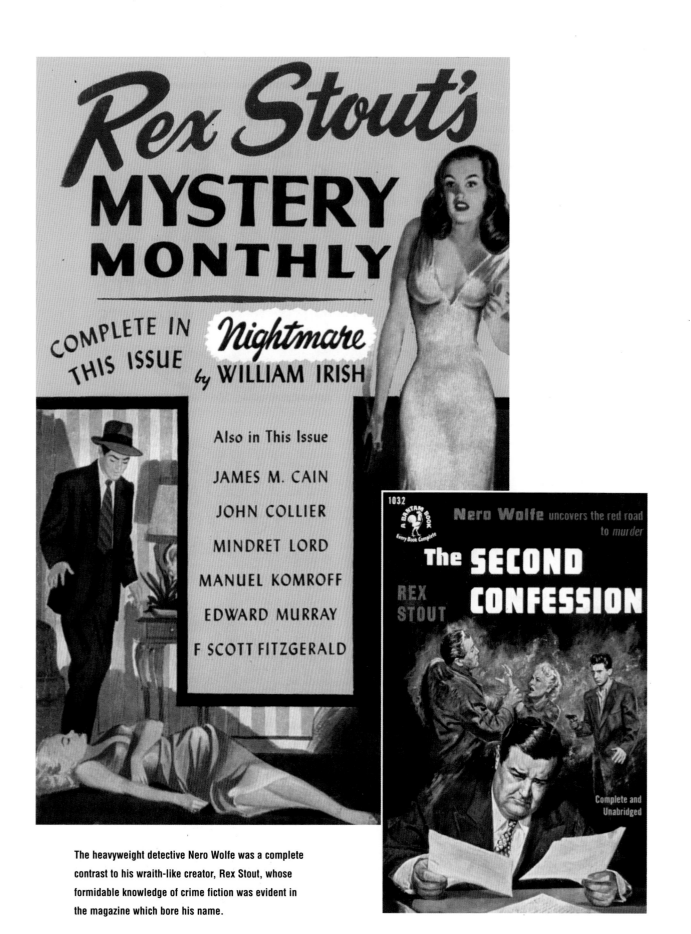

The heavyweight detective Nero Wolfe was a complete contrast to his wraith-like creator, Rex Stout, whose formidable knowledge of crime fiction was evident in the magazine which bore his name.

Rex Stout (1886–1975), who stands at a little under six feet tall, but tips the scales at a seventh of a ton. Physical activity is way down the list of Wolfe's priorities, and he dislikes leaving his brownstone apartment on New York's West Side unless it is absolutely essential in order to solve a crime. There is, though, no doubting the brilliance of this private investigator, who is rumoured to be one of a pair of illegitimate sons fathered by Sherlock Holmes and opera singer Irene Adler! He speaks seven languages, has a personal assistant, Archie Goodwin, who does most of the hard work on Wolfe's cases, chasing suspects and girls, and he retains a personal chef, Fritz Brenner, to prepare the gourmet meals that are his main delight – along with growing rare orchids on the roof of his apartment. This armchair detective *par excellence* made his debut in 1934 in *Fer-de-Lance*, the story of a murder by means of a dart tinctured with snake venom. He appeared 45 more times in a career that spanned 40 years and inspired a radio series in the 1940s, a pair of movies in which he was played by two rather less corpulent actors, Edward Arnold and Walter Connolly (which Stout so disliked that he refused permission for any more), and in a long-running comic strip series syndicated throughout America. In the 1980s, a TV series was made in America starring William Conrad.

Despite his name, Rex Stout was as thin as Wolfe was rotund. A tall, bearded, wraith-like figure whose literary skill was admired by presidents, actors and authors alike, Stout was born in Noblesville, Indiana, and was said to have been something of a child prodigy, beginning to read at just 18 months old and finishing the Bible by the time he was four. He was also apparently the state spelling champion, yet cut short his education and took a variety of jobs while selling poetry and essays to a number of magazines. The Depression hit

Stout hard and he decided to try and make some quick money by writing a detective novel. The arrival of Nero Wolfe – 'a triumphant superman detective', critic Julian Symons called him – was to give Stout a place in literary history. The sales of his titles had topped the 45 million mark in 26 languages by the time of his death. There has long been heated debate among his admirers as to which were the best Nero Wolfe titles, but Agatha Christie particularly liked *Too Many Cooks* (1938); *Over My Dead Body* (1940), which is good for the details of the detective's origins; and *If Death Ever Slept* (1957), in which Archie Goodwin comes very much to the fore in a compelling story of industrial espionage. Stout espoused a number of political causes and, apart from being President of the Writers' Guild of America and leading the fight for better royalties, fronted his own publication, *Rex Stout's Mystery Monthly*, which featured some of the best crime writers of the time and is now very collectable. Stout enjoyed presenting himself as an eccentric like his creation, and lived for 45 years in a house he had designed himself, where he grew his own food and worked for just 38 days a year – the time, he said, it took him to write a new case for Nero Wolfe.

Mickey Spillane took even less time to write a book about his ultra-tough private eye, Mike Hammer – between three and 19 days, he once claimed. Described by some critics as 'the undeniable godfather of hard-boiled', Spillane took the genre which Hammett and Chandler had inaugurated and set a new benchmark for the next generation of writers. Chandler was outraged to be mentioned in the same breath as the newcomer, commenting in the early 1950s, 'Pulp writing at its worst was never as bad as this.' He even had Philip Marlowe deliver this verdict in *Playback* (1958):

'I picked a paperback off the table and made a pretence of reading it. It was about some

I, The Jury (1947) and *The Big Kill* (1951), two of Mickey Spillane's early Mike Hammer novels which made both the author and his tough hero world famous.

private eye whose idea of a hot scene was a dead, naked woman hanging from the shower rail with the marks of torture on her. I threw the paperback into the waste-basket, not having a garbage can handy at the moment.'

Marlowe and Chandler might not have thought much of Mike Hammer, but readers did, and Spillane's American paperback publishers, New American Library, were claiming in 1953 that the five titles which had appeared since *I, The Jury* in 1947 had already sold over 15 million copies. It was an extraordinary success story for both the character and his creator, who liked to measure himself against 'the toughest of all private detectives'. Frank Morrison 'Mickey' Spillane (1918–) grew up in the tough neighbourhood of Elizabeth, New Jersey, where comic strips rather than books were the basic reading

material. Winning a place to Kansas State University, he began to write stories for the comics and legend has it that by the age of 17 he was a regular contributor to titles like *Captain Marvel*, *Captain America* and *Plastic Man*. Spillane's career was interrupted by the Second World War when he joined the US Air Force, flew P-15 fighter planes on combat missions, and completed his service with the rank of captain. He emerged from the experience a tough, abrasive figure, and tried several jobs, including working on a federal investigation into drug trafficking, before turning again to comic books. In 1947, unable to sell a concept entitled *Mike Danger*, he decided to turn the story into a novel, changed the hero's name to Hammer, and got a deal with E. P. Dutton of New York. *I, The Jury*, the story of the private eye's mission to avenge the killing of the man who had saved his life during the war and had lost an arm in the process, was a sensational best-seller, almost literally redefining the hard-boiled genre overnight. The verdict of the critics was the

The success of the Mike Hammer novels took Mickey Spillane full circle back into comic strips.

same as Raymond Chandler's, but Spillane was not in the least bothered:

'You don't read a book to get to the middle. You read it to get to the end. But if the critics blow me apart, that's fine. Every time they do, I just sell more millions of copies.'

And so he did, the subsequent novels taking readers into some of the most dangerous corners of America in the company of Mike Hammer, who kicked, beat, gouged and shot his adversaries, sometimes even when they were women. His sardonic wit matched his ruthless efficiency with a gun, as instanced when executing sex-mad villainess Charlotte, who exclaims, 'How could you?', to which he replies, 'It was easy.' Among the dozen Hammer titles, *The Big Kill* (1951) is remarkable for a startling denouement; *One Lonely Night* (1951) has a threat of communist subversion mixed in

with the sex and mayhem; while in *Kiss Me, Deadly* (1952), Hammer takes on the Mafia. The success of the books had film-makers clamouring to bring Mike Hammer to the screen with the aptly named Biff Elliott being the first in 1955, followed by Ralph Meeker and Mickey Spillane himself living out his fantasy in *The Girl Hunters* in 1963 – the first mystery writer to portray his own creation. There was also a radio adaptation in the early 1950s, followed by two television series, with Darren McGavin and Stacey Keach. In a neat twist of fate that must have delighted Spillane, comic book publishers Crestwood Publications also signed him for what proved to be a long-running comic book series, *Mike Hammer*.

For a time Spillane was referred to by his publishers as 'the most widely-read writer in the history of all mankind'. With 200 million copies of his books sold, he was certainly by far the best-selling hard-boiled author. Since the 1960s, he has returned to Mike Hammer on only three occasions and none of the books have enjoyed the same sales as the early volumes. It is a fact, too, that while the other hard-boiled writers all enjoy cult status, and the influence of Spillane's work can be seen in the novels of Elmore Leonard, James Ellroy and the other contemporary *crime noir* writers, few of his books is currently in print. It is a mystery that puzzles his admirers – one of them, crime novelist Maxim Jakubowski, referred to him recently as 'the unsung hero of hard-boiled crime writings' – but to the man himself it is of no consequence. In a line that might have come from one of his own books, when asked his verdict on the Mike Hammer novels, Spillane dismissed them in two words: 'Chewing gum'.

The Poets
of Tabloid Murder

THE POETS OF TABLOID MURDER

Rico saw the big man in the derby hat appear at the end of the alleyway. His pale, thin face registered panic and, reaching for his gun, he rushed at the figure, firing wildly. The last thing the terrified little gangster saw was a long spurt of flame and then something hitting him like a sledgehammer blow in the chest as he staggered and fell, crying out, 'Mother of God, is this the end of Rico?' W. R. Burnett, the author of *Little Caesar* (1929), did not answer the question in this climactic moment of his classic novel about the rise and fall of Chicago mobster Cesare Bandello – the hapless Rico – but his book did give birth to a

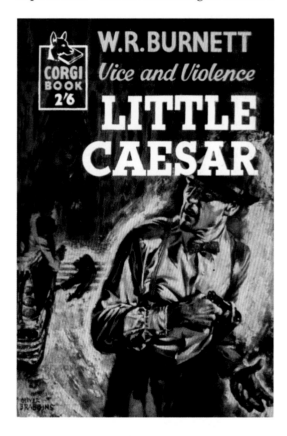

A dramatic illustration by Oliver Brabbins for W. R. Burnett's classic tale of tabloid murder, *Little Caesar*, which was first published in 1929.

new chapter in crime fiction. In the words of critic and crime *aficionado* Edmund Wilson in his famous essay, 'The Boys in the Backroom' (1941), Burnett became a leader of the 'poets of the tabloid murder'.

The story of Rico, a small-time mobster who ruthlessly gains control of the Chicago underworld, lifted the lid on the city's rackets during Prohibition. Inspired by Al Capone's reign of terror and the bloody St Valentine's Day Massacre, it graphically describes the gangster's rise to power over two other gang bosses, Sam Vettori and Arnie Lorch, while in the shadows lurks 'Big Boy', the supreme boss of the underworld who actually pulls the strings. Watching them all is Detective Flaherty, who sees Rico's rise ... and fall. W. R. Burnett, who had previously tried unsuccessfully to become a novelist and short story writer, discovered in the streets of the crime-ridden city the raw material for the tale of *Little Caesar*, which is told largely from the gangster's point of view. It has been described as 'one of the most famous of all naturalistic crime novels' and moves at breakneck speed from one graphic moment of bloodshed and violence to another. The book, which also launched the gangster story as a new element in crime fiction, was to prove the inspiration for dozens of other mystery writers as well as a pot of gold for Hollywood film-makers in the 1930s and beyond.

The author, William Riley Burnett (1899–1982) was born in Springfield, Ohio, and appears to have nursed literary ambitions from his schooldays. While he was attending the Miami Military Institute, he wrote a number of short stories and two plays, and then when working as a statistician for the state of Ohio, produced five novels, all of which were rejected by publishers. In 1929, Burnett moved to Chicago and the headlines emblazoned across the front pages of the city's tabloid newspapers at last provided his inspiration. Stories of mob killings, gang warfare and crime czars were the inspiration for *Little Caesar*, which pulled no punches in describing Rico's climb to notoriety over the bodies of others. In one brutal slaying, he guns down a rival on the steps of a church as the man is going to a service. Burnett in fact took a pragmatic view of the philosophy of the gangsters, as he explained through the words of an impoverished Italian immigrant justifying his role in racketeering:

'Look, in this country only a few have all the money. Millions don't have enough to eat, not because there ain't enough, but because they don't have the money. Others do okay, so why don't the ones without the money get together and get their hands on it?'

The book was an immediate best-seller, made a Literary Guild selection, and the film rights were bought by First National. The following year, Mervyn Leroy directed the screen version with Edward G. Robinson giving an archetypal performance as Rico that would be endlessly imitated and parodied. The book was also published in Britain and a dozen foreign languages, most of these editions having cautious typographical dust jackets, until Corgi Books of London decided to reflect this most naturalistic of crime novels with a powerfully atmospheric illustration by Oliver Brabbins.

Burnett needed no urging to continue working the rich vein he had discovered. His knowledge of the Chicago scene combined with his unromantic view of crime gave added impact to his later novels, especially *High Sierra* (1941), inspired by the true story of the killer John Dillinger and featuring a former convict providing money for a crippled girl's operation; *Nobody Lives Forever* (1946), the tale of a con man who falls for the wealthy young widow he and his gang are planning to swindle; and *The Asphalt Jungle* (1950), in which a double-cross changes the aftermath of a successful robbery. All three became very successful films, and in the interim Burnett wrote several other original screenplays for Hollywood, the titles of which speak for themselves: *Scarface* starring Paul Muni (1932), *King of the Underworld* with Humphrey Bogart (1939) and *Accused of Murder* in which Lee Van Cleef gave a memorable performance as a gangster (1956). He also adapted Graham Greene's novel *This Gun for Hire* (1936), with Alan Ladd playing the ruthless young killer.

If Burnett was surprised by the public reaction to *Little Caesar*, it was as nothing to

Gritty covers for two more of W. R. Burnett's toughest novels, *Nobody Lives Forever* (1946) and *The Asphalt Jungle* (1950).

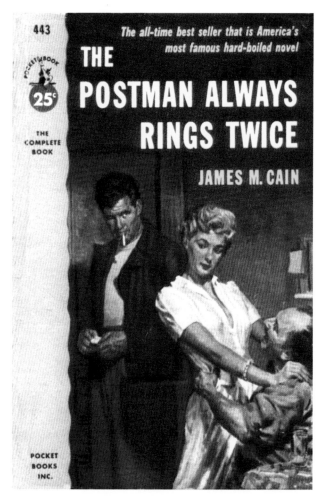

that of James M. Cain when his novel *The Postman Always Rings Twice* was published five years later in 1934. The former journalist thought of his story as being about 'a couple of jerks who discover that murder, though dreadful enough morally, can be a love story, too, but then wake up to discover that once they've pulled the thing off, no two people can share this terrible secret.' Readers, though, made it a best-seller, most of the critics thought it a triumph ('makes Hemingway look like a lexicographer,' said the *New York Times*) and it was immediately bought for filming although MGM, who had purchased the rights, had to wait for ten years before the censorship laws had been relaxed enough to permit a filmable script. (It first reached the screen in 1946 with John Garfield and Lana Turner, but a much more faithful version was

James M. Cain's classic hardboiled novel of lust and murder, *The Postman Always Rings Twice,* first published in 1934, was later brilliantly filmed in 1978 starring Jack Nicholson and Jessica Lange.

made in 1978 starring Jack Nicholson and Jessica Lange.) The story of a young vagrant and the sexy, bored wife of a restaurant owner who plan her husband's murder at a stroke became the second great tabloid murder novel and made its author famous as a 'tough guy' writer. Although this was a label that Cain hated, two of his later books, *Serenade* (1937), about a terrible murder complete with a shocking love scene in front of an altar in a Catholic church, and *Double Indemnity* (1943), also a story of adultery and premeditated murder, set the dye and he remained a personification of the tough guy writer for the

A HARD-BOILED STORY OF LOVE AND MURDER IN RENO... BY THE AUTHOR OF "THE POSTMAN ALWAYS RINGS TWICE!"

JAMES M. CAIN

Jealous Woman

COMPLETE AND UNABRIDGED

Jealous Woman (1950) added to James M. Cain's reputation as a great writer of unrelentingly powerful fiction.

rest of his life. If Cain's dislike at this label was eased to any degree, it may have been by the description of his biographer, David Madden, that he was 'the twenty minute egg of the hard-boiled school'.

James Mallahan Cain (1892–1977) was born in Annapolis, Maryland, the son of the president of Washington College, and his wife, an opera singer, who apparently inspired the youngster to dream of becoming a singer until she told him sadly that he did not have a strong enough voice. Instead he earned a BA degree and found employment as a journalist on the *Baltimore Sun*. In 1923, remembering a scandal over the burning of corpses in a country almshouse, he produced the first of

a series of dialogue sketches which later formed the basis of his first book, *Our Government*. Following a period working in New York where he contributed to *The American Mercury* and the *New York World*, Cain moved to Hollywood in 1931 to work on screenplays. It was there, he explained later, that he began to consider a novel on a theme that had interested him for some time: 'The erotic effect of murder on its participants, with its corollary, the terrible distrust the partners in this crime must have for each other for the rest of their lives.' Cain decided the story must be kept very short and terse, and the result was *The Postman Always Rings Twice*, a title suggested to him by Vincent Lawrence, another scriptwriter. Lawrence explained that he could always tell the difference between the postman and any other caller at his home, because the man with the mail always pressed the bell twice.

Not everyone was impressed by the book, though. Comparisons with Hammett and Chandler were not all favourable, and in Boston *The Postman Always Rings Twice* was seized by the police for obscenity. After a lengthy court hearing the book was released, but no bookseller in the city was prepared to display it for years. Conversely, the great French writer Albert Camus was inspired by the book to write his own brilliant nihilistic novel, *L'Étranger* (1942), while the American hard-boiled writer Ross Macdonald, who would later follow in his footsteps, wrote, 'Cain has won unfading laurels with a pair of native American masterpieces, *Postman* and *Double Indemnity*, back to back.'

Across the Atlantic in Britain, the reception for *Postman* was equally enthusiastic, but because of the shortness of *Double Indemnity*, it was published by Robert Hale in 1943 with two other short novels, *The Embezzler* and *Two Can Sing*, 'all of which rip along like bullets' to quote the publisher's blurb. Inside, the author protested once more about being called a tough guy writer and added, 'Although I have read less than 20 pages of Mr Dashiell Hammett in my whole life, Mr Clifton Fadiman [a leading US book reviewer] can refer to my hammett-and-tongs style and make things easy for himself.' *Double Indemnity* was, in fact, to be the first of James M. Cain's books to be brought to the screen in 1944 with Edward G. Robinson caught up in a plot by a scheming wife to murder her husband in a train accident. Curiously, although Raymond Chandler was widely praised for his screenplay of *Double Indemnity*, he did not think much of Cain as a writer: 'Everything he touches smells like a billy-goat. He is the kind of writer I detest, a *faux naïf*, a Proust in greasy overalls.'

Paul Cain may have shared his surname with the author of *Postman*, but their attitudes towards their work could not have been more different. Paul was an in-your-face tough guy writer, of whom *The Armchair Detective* said,

'He may just have been the hardest-boiled pulp writer of them all.' Raymond Chandler had quite the opposite view of *this* Cain and said that his work represented 'some kind of high point in the ultra hard-boiled manner'. Yet the extraordinary reputation of this man rests on just two books, *Fast One* (1932) and *Seven Slayers* (1946), plus the 18 short stories that he wrote between 1931 and 1936 for *Black Mask*. His life, too, is beset by mystery: one reference book has described him as, 'A man who emerged from nowhere and then disappeared.' He was, in fact, born George Carrol Sims (1902–1966) in Des Moines, Iowa, and moved to Los Angeles with his mother after her divorce in 1918. Two years later he was working in Hollywood as a production assistant using the name 'George Ruric' and in 1925 received a credit on Joseph von Sternberg's first US picture, *Salvation Hunters* (1925). He found employment in Hollywood erratic, and in the late 1920s, Sims moved to

Left & above: A rare paperback edition of *Fast One* (1932) by Paul Cain, described as 'the most hard-boiled pulp writer of all'. He also contributed stories such as *Chinaman's Chance* to *Black Mask*.

New York and joined the tough guy bandwagon, contributing to *Black Mask* using the name Paul Cain. His stories were set in the Prohibition era and dealt with killers, drug dealers, con men, private eyes and beautiful girls – straight from the pages of the tabloid press. Notable among these was 'Chinaman's Chance' (September 1935) about a journalist, Johnnie Gay, who has a chip on his shoulder and an eye for scandal and corruption in high places.

In 1931, Sims moved back to Hollywood to work on the screenplay of a Cary Grant movie, *Gambling Ship*, which utilized several of his *Black Mask* stories, and the following year used the whole lot to produce *Fast One*. The story of Gerry Kells, a murderous gunman, racketeer and amoral gambler, who, with his dipsomaniacal lover known only as 'S. Granquist', tries to muscle in on the west coast mob scene, the book had reviewers reaching for their adjectives. One Los Angeles scribe called it 'a ceaseless welter of bloodshed', while the *Saturday Review of Literature* thought it 'the hardest-boiled yarn of a decade'. Despite this, the book sold poorly and Sims returned to screenplays, writing the Boris Karloff film *The Black Cat*.

From the mid-1930s, however, the facts about Sims' life are blurred. He is said to have travelled extensively in America, Europe and North Africa, married at least three times – one of his wives leaping from a window of their Hollywood apartment after a drunken quarrel (she survived) – and then spent time in Spain as a beach-bum before returning to America with the intention of writing more scripts. In 1946, a second book bearing the Paul Cain by-line, *Seven Slayers*, was issued as a paperback by Saint Enterprises. It was a collection of his *Black Mask* stories and was again enthusiastically received by the critics, but failed to stir any real public interest. Thereafter, George Carrol Sims, aka Peter Ruric, aka Paul Cain, lived out his life in Hollywood in almost total obscurity working on the occasional TV screenplay until he died of cancer in June 1965. The man who had written what is now acknowledged as a classic of the tabloid murder school died alone, unknown and penniless.

Another writer whose reputation rests largely on one book, although his life was less tortuous, was Horace McCoy (1897–1955), author of *They Shoot Horses, Don't They?* published in 1935. The story of a tragic dance marathon on an oceanside pier during the Depression, infused with a mixture of fatigue and hysteria, it earned McCoy the acclaim from Geoffrey O'Brien of being 'a rare kind of

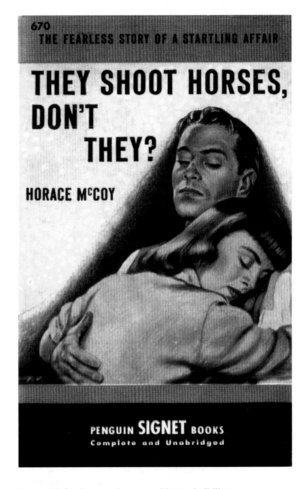

Horace McCoy became known as "the real nihilist of the hard-boiled school" for his tortured novel, *They Shoot Horses, Don't They?* published in 1935.

Frank Gruber was a prolific contributor to the pulps and creator of the streetwise private eye, Johnny Fletcher, who made his debut in *Short Stories*.

poet – the real nihilist of the hard-boiled school.' In France, he was simply classed with Faulkner and Hemingway.

McCoy's paperback publishers, Signet, endeavoured to grab custom with an intriguing biography of their author, describing him as a former 'taxi driver, war pilot, wrestler, bodyguard, bouncer and newspaperman', which was rather more colourful than the facts. He had been born in Pegram, Tennessee, and was educated at local schools before serving in the US Army Air Corps in the First World War. Subsequently, McCoy became a sports journalist on the *Dallas Journal* between 1919 and 1930, during which time he co-founded the Dallas Little Theater and wrote a number of plays. In 1931 he was lured to

Hollywood and worked on numerous pictures during the next 20 years, including *Parole* (1936), *Hunted Men* (1938) and *Queen of the Mob* (1940); he co-wrote *Rage at Dawn* (1955) with fellow hard-boiled writer Frank Gruber. The success of *They Shoot Horses, Don't They?* revealed his skill at dealing with violent death, and this was further underlined in *I Should Have Stayed Home* (1938), *Kiss Tomorrow Goodbye* (1949) and *The Corpse Was Blonde* (1950). Critic John S. Whitley compared McCoy's work to that of Dashiell Hammett, in particular the novel *Red Harvest*, writing that both men 'vividly describe the American city of the 1930s as almost totally corrupt, with violence and depravity as the casual by-products of everyday existence.'

McCoy's co-writer Frank Gruber (1904–1969) was also a prolific writer whose career spanned from the pulp heyday of the 1930s through to the cynical, picaresque works of the late 1960s. Over half of his short stories, novels, film and TV scripts had crime and detective themes, and in the 1940s and 1950s he was writing as many as four mystery novels a year under a string of pen-names including Stephen Acre, Charles K. Boston and John K. Vedder. Born in Elmer, Minnesota, Gruber attended the local high school and developed his prodigious word rate as a writer for various trade magazines before becoming a full-time freelance writer in 1934. The requirements of the pulps for fast-paced action stories suited Gruber perfectly, and he contributed to a wide variety of magazines like *Black Mask*, *Weird Tales* and *Short Stories*, in whose pages he introduced his hard-boiled, streetwise but invariably hard up private eye, Johnny Fletcher. Beginning with *The French Key* in 1940 which he apparently wrote in seven days but was voted 'best mystery' of the year, the stories represented a significant development, with Gruber's concept of the sleuth as an inner-city adventurer living by his wits. Readers also enjoyed Fletcher's assistant, Sam Cragg, a man whose name inferred his Herculean strength, the pair forming a perfect partnership of brains and brawn. *The French Key* was filmed in 1946, directed by Walter Colmes and starring Albert Decker and Mike Mazurki. Gruber also wrote another series of stories about a private detective, Simon Lash, who was a collector of rare books – like the author himself.

Later in his busy career, Gruber wrote a revealing account of his life and hard times in *The Pulp Jungle* (1967), in which he estimated he had written over 300 short stories for more than 50 different magazines, plus 70 screenplays, 150 television scripts and 60 novels. Although, he said, he was virtually penniless at times, he reckoned to have written

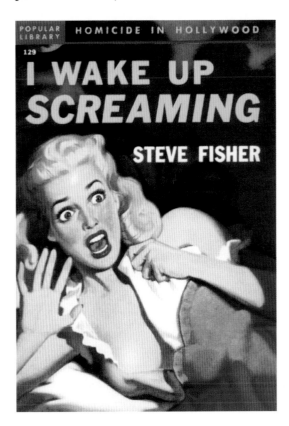

Above: Steve Fisher's story of a brutal murder in Hollywood, *I Wake Up Screaming* (1941), became one of the first *crime noir* movies.

about 600,000 words per year every year of his career, with his books translated into 24 languages and world sales exceeding 90 million copies. Frank Gruber's incredibly fertile imagination and speed of writing earned him the description of being one of the most prolific writers of all time.

One of Gruber's closest friends, Steve Fisher (1912–1980), had a similar struggle to make ends meet and he is referred to frequently in *The Pulp Jungle*. The two men first met in New York's bohemian quarter, Greenwich Village, and cracked many of the pulp markets together, in particular *Black Mask, Short Stories* and *Argosy*. Steve Fisher, though, preferred to mix his tales of tabloid murder with some sentimentality and more than the occasional flash of humour, as in 'He Worked Alone' (*Detective Fiction Weekly*, April 1927), 'What Price Murder?' (*Detective Tales*, September 1936) and 'No Gentleman Strangles His Wife' (*Black Mask*, January 1938). Born Stephen Gould Fisher in California, he began writing while serving in the US Navy, producing over 200 stories for naval publications between the years 1928 and 1932. He then moved to New York and followed his success in the pulps by selling his particular brand of compelling fiction, in which characters are pushed to their limits, to *Collier's, Esquire* and *The Saturday Evening Post*. Fisher published his first novel, *Spend the Night*, in 1935 under the pen-name Grant Lane, but later dismissed it as 'a dreadful book'. As Stephen Gould he wrote two mysteries which drew on his naval background, *Murder of the Admiral* (1936) and *Murder of the Pigboat Skipper* (1937), but, earning no real success with either, moved to Hollywood in 1940 to write scripts.

Life in the film capital suited Steve Fisher and he worked on more than 30 pictures, including *Johnny Angel* (1945), co-authored with his friend, Frank Gruber; an acclaimed version of *The Lady in the Lake* (1946) based on Raymond Chandler's novel; and *Dead Reckoning* (1947) starring Humphrey Bogart. It was here, too, that he had the idea for his classic story, *I Wake Up Screaming* (1941), set in a film studio and dealing with the brutal murder of a promising young movie starlet. The story was filmed the same year by Twentieth Century Fox and became one of the earliest classics of the *crime noir* genre as well as ensuring Fisher's reputation. It was re-filmed by the same company in 1953 as *Vicki* with Jeanne Crain and Elliott Reid, directed by Harry Horner. Fisher wrote 19 more crime novels, though none achieved the fame of *I Wake Up Screaming*. Aside from his film work, he was also one of the main scriptwriters for the popular TV series *McMillan and Wife*, and the indefatigable *Starsky and Hutch*.

The group of novels featuring the boozing, hard-boiled gumshoe Bill Crane, written by Jonathan Latimer in the 1930s, have been described by Art Scott as 'one of the most memorable and original detective series in modern mystery fiction'. Crane is based in Chicago, and while some critics have tended to describe him as an 'alcoholic private eye', he is actually a tough, resilient man who likes drink, but his consumption is actually no more prodigious than many others in his fraternity. Unlike his contemporaries, though, Crane does drink to such excess that he is inclined to fall into a drunken stupor anywhere and is often conspicuous by his hangovers and shabby brown suits that show every sign of having been slept in! The Bill Crane stories have been compared in their characterization and atmosphere to the best of Dashiell Hammett's work, especially *The Thin Man*, and they undoubtedly foreshadow the later alcohol-fuelled exploits of Mike Shayne and Shell Scott, to name but two.

Like Steve Fisher before him, Jonathan

Wyatt Latimer (1906–1983) was a former navy man who strove to become a Hollywood scriptwriter and consequently devoted more of his energy to the screen than to the printed page. Born in Chicago, he was christened after his great-great-grandfather who had served with George Washington during the American Civil War. Educated at Knox College in Galesburg, Illinois, he received a BA in 1929 and worked as a journalist on the *Chicago Herald-Examiner* and *Chicago Tribune* before wartime service with the US Navy. Latimer was inspired to write the Bill Crane stories by his experiences as a journalist, and the first of these, *Murder in the Madhouse* (1935), caught the fancy of crime fiction readers with its mixture of the grotesque, the deadly, and Crane's endless thirst which seemed to do nothing to harm his powers of deduction but merely slow them down. Among the subsequent novels in the series, *The Lady in the Morgue* (1936) was hailed as 'a masterpiece of deadpan black comedy' and filmed in 1937 with Christy Cabanne directing Preston Foster as the unsteady sleuth. Among the non-series novels, *Solomon's Vineyard* (1941), first published in England (and later in the US in a bowdlerized form as *The Fifth Grave*), is a rougher and kinkier version of Hammett's *The Dain Curse* and angered several wartime reviewers with its portrait of the sadomasochistic love-making of a luscious 'high priestess of crime'; while *Sinners and Shrouds* (1955) is generally considered the best of the author's later books, with its 'unputdownable' opening chapter in which newspaperman Sam Clay wakes up with a hangover and the corpse of a beautiful naked girl in his bed. The success of Latimer's early scripts for the movies, in particular the second version of Dashiell Hammett's *The Glass Key* (1942) and his adaptation of *The Night Has a Thousand Eyes* by Cornell Woolrich (1948), kept him busy in Hollywood, and his

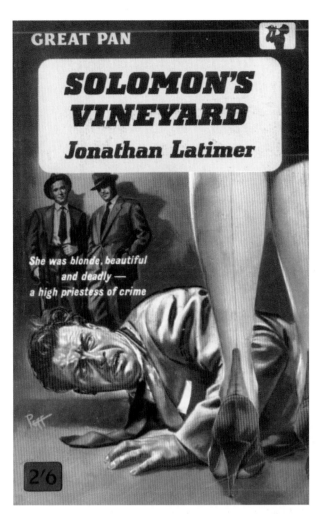

Solomon's Vineyard by Jonathan Latimer (1941) has been described as a rougher and kinkier version of Dashiell Hammett's *The Dain Curse*.

substantial contribution to crime fiction as a successor to Hammett was all but forgotten by the 1960s when he was constantly busy writing episodes for the long-running *Perry Mason* television series.

Cornell Woolrich, whose murder novel Latimer adapted for the screen, has an ever-increasing stature among the writers of tabloid murder, and was recently described by US crime historian Francis M. Nevins as 'the Poe of the Twentieth Century and the poet of its shadows'. Raymond Chandler was an admirer, too, and called him 'the best idea man, liking the *tour de force*', which perhaps explains why so many of his stories have been adapted for the screen, while Geoffrey O'Brien

has said he is 'quite simply the premier paranoid among crime writers'. A strange, tormented man who spent over half his life living in hotel rooms with little more than his typewriter and a bottle for company, Woolrich chronicled the years of the Depression and the lives of ordinary men and women unexpectedly drawn into violence and murder. Like so many of them, his own death went almost unnoticed and an obituary in the *New York Times* in 1968 got many of the facts of his life wrong and made no mention at all of his most famous novel, *The Phantom Lady* (1942). Much credit for the rescue of his reputation is due yet again to French admirers of his work.

The boy who grew up to be one of the masters of his art was born Cornell George Hopley-Woolrich (1903–1968) in New York to parents whose marriage was already on the rocks. His childhood was split between his mining engineer father who worked in Latin America and his social-climbing mother in the Big Apple. The experience of seeing Puccini's *Madame Butterfly* when he was eight years old is said to have given him a personal sense of doom that haunted him for the rest of his days. Woolrich began writing while at Columbia University, attempting to imitate his hero, F. Scott Fitzgerald, and in 1926 completed *Cover Charge*, a romantic novel set in the Jazz Age. The following year, another similar novel, *Children of the Ritz*, won a $10,000 prize offered by First National Pictures, which took him to Hollywood and a very traumatic period of his life. Here he tried unsuccessfully to be a scriptwriter and at the same time attempted to deny his evident homosexuality by marrying the daughter of the veteran English-born producer, Stuart Blackton. The marriage remained unconsummated, so the story goes, and after two weeks Woolrich fled back to New York. Here he lived with his domineering mother until her death in

1957, producing short stories and novels at a prodigious rate while scarcely leaving the security of the hotel room. After the end of the couple's love-hate relationship, Woolrich declined into alcoholism, ill health, loneliness and a bitterness that only ended with his own death.

In 1934 Woolrich had begun to write his unique style of fiction about despair, violence and murder in the same manner as Hammett and Chandler, finding a ready market in *Black Mask, Detective Fiction Weekly* and *Dime Detective*. Some were published under his own name, others as William Irish (the name of another scriptwriter with whom he had been associated in Hollywood) and George Hopley. Typical varied examples of his style are 'The Corpse and the Kid' for *Dime Detective* (September 1935); 'Cab, Mister?' for *Black Mask* (November 1937) and 'Marihuana', which first appeared in *Detective Fiction Weekly* on 3 March 1941, was reprinted in *10 Story Mystery Magazine* in May 1942, and appeared as a 10-cent Dell paperback in 1950. His first novel, and still best-known work, *The Bride Wore Black* was published in 1940. The story of a woman who seeks vengeance after seeing her bridegroom shot dead on the church steps as she goes to her wedding, it was to become the first of his 'black' series, which certain critics have argued instigated the French *crime noir* and *film noir* series. In any event, it was brilliantly filmed by François Truffaut in 1967 with Jeanne Moreau. The other titles in the series are *The Black Curtain* (1941), *The Black Angel* (1943) and *The Black Path of Fear* (1944). Under the William Irish pseudonym, Woolrich published another classic, *Phantom Lady* (1942), about the race to save an innocent man from the electric chair, which was filmed by Universal with Robert Siodmak directing Franchot Tone and Ella Raines. *The Night Has a Thousand Eyes* (1945), which focuses on the attempt of a

mind-reader to save a young woman from tragedy, was issued under the name of George Hopley and likewise adapted for the screen in 1948 by Jonathan Latimer with Edward G. Robinson and Gail Russell, directed by John Farrow. Steve Fisher adapted *I Wouldn't Be in Your Shoes* in 1948 for Monogram with Don Castle and Elyse Knox, directed by William Nigh. Alfred Hitchcock took Woolrich's short story, 'It Had To Be Murder' (*Dime Detective*, February 1942) and made it into the classic *Rear Window* (1954) starring James Stewart and Grace Kelly. Many of Cornell Woolrich's stories have been adapted for the radio in the *Suspense* series, and at least 36 films and 50

'The Poe of the 20th Century' is just one of the terms used about Cornell Woolrich, whose novel *The Phantom Lady* (1942), was published under his pen-name, William Irish.

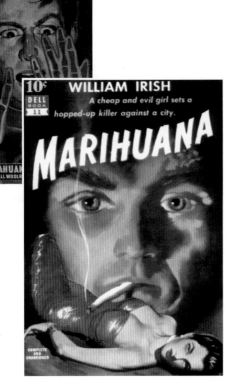

Above: Cornell Woolrich's story of drug abuse, *Marihuana*, appeared in the pulp magazine *10 Story Mystery* and a Dell paperback with different spellings of the title and a change of author credit!

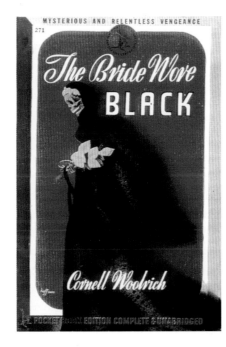

television versions of his stories have been filmed in Spain, Russia, Japan and other far-flung localities.

The period from the outbreak of the Second World War to the start of the 1950s saw the rise of a trio of tough-guy writers who have been nicknamed 'The Disciples of Chandler'. All took their raw material from the tabloid press and used it as the background for the exploits of their three very different private eyes. The men were Brett Halliday, Ross Macdonald and Richard S. Prather, and their hard-boiled gumshoes were, respectively, Mike Shayne, Lew Archer and Shell Scott.

Mike Shayne had a very inauspicious start to his career; the first novel about him, *Dividend on Death*, was turned down by four publishers before it was accepted by Henry Holt in 1939. A tall, red-headed man, very adept with his fists, Shayne started his career in New York in the mid-1930s, later moving his base of operations to Miami after the death of his young wife. There is a certain harshness about his features which disappears when he smiles, 'so that he didn't look like a hard-boiled private detective who had come to the top the tough way,' to quote from *Dividend on Death*. He is a man who likes a drink – Martell cognac, with a water chaser – and has more than a touch of the Marlowe in him with his social conscience, although he has been known to take the law into his own hands where certain dangerous criminals are concerned. Shayne numbers among his closest friends Timothy Rourke of the *Miami Daily News*, who can be an invaluable ally when he runs up against his arch-rival Peter Painter, the Miami Beach Chief of Detectives.

Brett Halliday was the *nom de plume* of Davis Dresser (1904–1977) who was born in Chicago but raised in the vast, rugged deserts

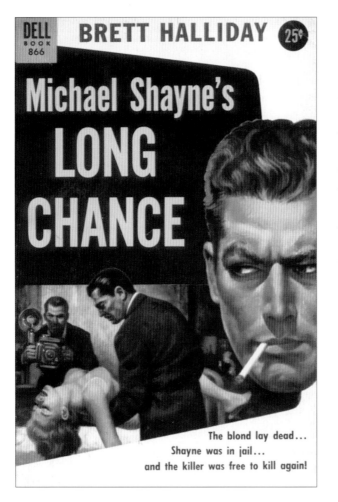

The blond lay dead...
Shayne was in jail...
and the killer was free to kill again!

Brett Halliday continued the Raymond Chandler tradition with his stories about hard-boiled private detective Michael Shayne.

of western Texas where he developed a taste for the outdoor life. While out riding, he fell from his horse and lost an eye on some barbed wire which led to him wearing an eye patch for the rest of his life. When only 14, he ran away from home and enlisted in the US Army Cavalry where he remained for two years until his true age was discovered and he was discharged. After gaining a certificate in engineering, Dresser wandered through the southwest of America and Mexico working as an engineer and surveyor. His years during the closing era of the old frontier gave him a rugged individualism and a strong sense of right and wrong, characteristics he later endowed to Mike Shayne. In 1927, the pulp boom tempted him to try his hand at writing

and he enjoyed moderate success with a number of stories about the wild west, high adventure and mystery which appeared under various pen-names.

It was a chance experience in a bar in Tampico, Mexico, however, that put him on the road to fame and fortune. Dresser shared some drinks with a tall, red-haired American who, as the tempers of other drinkers had risen, extricated them both from a bar room brawl ... and then disappeared. Four years later, Dresser saw the man again in another bar in New Orleans and before the red-head disappeared again, heard him referred to as 'Mike'. At that moment he had the idea for a new type of private eye who would ultimately become the hero of over 60 novels and innumerable novelettes, all to be published under the by-line of Brett Halliday. These, in turn, instigated a dozen movies, beginning with *Michael Shayne, Private Detective* starring Lloyd Nolan, who was replaced in the following five by Hugh Beaumont. One of these pictures, *Time to Kill* (1942), was actually based on Raymond Chandler's Philip Marlowe case *The High Window* (1942). Shayne also had a radio series featuring Jeff Chandler and a 1960s TV series of 32 hour-long episodes starring Richard Denning. In 1956, the tough gumshoe even got his own monthly periodical, *Mike Shayne Mystery Magazine*, to which Davis Dresser contributed occasionally until his death in 1977 — a death brought on, it is said, by hard drinking which rivalled that of his famous creation.

Ross Macdonald was also recognizably of the Hammett and Chandler school and, in the opinion of many, unchallenged in his time as the heir to that tradition. Indeed, his private eye, Lew Archer, more than obliquely acknowledged Hammett, deriving his surname from the murder victim, Miles Archer, in *The Maltese Falcon*. Perhaps less hard-boiled and less of a romantic than Marlowe, he has the

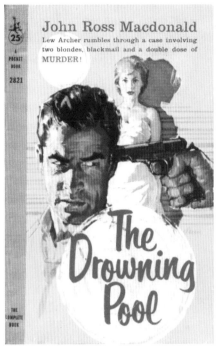

John Ross Macdonald was another admirer of Raymond Chandler whose gumshoe hero, Lew Archer, appeared in dozens of novels and short stories.

same sympathy for the victims of society as well as being uncompromisingly tough. Critic Anthony Boucher believed that Macdonald was actually a better writer than his two predecessors, and the sustained excellence of his work over 35 years helped to develop the private eye novel into a medium in which 'an author can write about people with enough feeling to be hurt and enough complexity to do wrong'. Yet, despite these influences – or perhaps even because of them – Macdonald came to be acknowledged as one of the finest modern crime practitioners and also one of the few mystery writers to be regarded as a major American novelist.

The name Ross Macdonald was actually a pseudonym for Kenneth Millar (1915–1983), who was born in Los Gatos, California, and spent much of his young life in Canada where he was taken by his mother after his parents' marriage broke down. After studying for a degree at the University of Western Ontario, he returned to the US and earned a doctorate in English literature at the University of Michigan. His dissertation was on the English poet Coleridge, and his tutor was W. H. Auden, to whom he always acknowledged a debt in acquiring his distinctive prose style and admiration of European literature. It was while Miller was serving as a communications officer on an escort carrier during the Second World War that he started to write fiction. He had been a fan of detective stories from his childhood, writing a parody of his favourite, Sherlock Holmes, 'The South Sea Company' featuring Herlock Sholmes, when he was still a teenager. In 1944 he published his first book, *The Dark Tunnel*, under his real name. Four similar crime novels followed until *The Moving Target* (1949) introduced Lew Archer, of whom Millar said later, 'I'm not Archer, exactly, but Archer is me.' Archer, in fact, becomes a private eye after

Above: John D. MacDonald developed from a prolific contributor to the pulp magazines to probably the most famous writer of paperback crime originals.

and, especially, *Black Mask*. Among his memorable stories for the latter were 'Dead Men Don't Scare', the lead story of the May 1948 issue featuring an ex-Army intelligence officer named Kestrick – shades of MacDonald himself – who is framed for murder; and 'No Grave Has My Love' about the discovery of a decomposed corpse in a hospital bed which was gruesomely illustrated on the cover of the August 1949 issue.

The launching of the Gold Medal imprint presented MacDonald with a new avenue for his talents, and he joined the list in its first year with *The Brass Cupcake* (1950). The story of a police lieutenant, Cliff Bartells, driven from his job by offending all-powerful local gangsters, it introduced one of the author's archetypal conscience-troubled characters and his girl, the tantalizing Melody Chance. The book has justifiably been compared to the work of Hammett and Chandler and is certainly in the same league as his namesake, Ross Macdonald. It was followed by over 50 more originals for Gold Medal like *Weep for Me* (1951), *The Damned* (1952) and *The Neon Jungle* (1953). Soon the author who had honed his art in the pulps was earning praise from major critics like Quentin Reynolds – 'He is certainly one of the finest storytellers around' – and being described by the *New York Times* as 'the John O'Hara of the crime-suspense story'.

It was in the early 1960s, after Richard Prather had taken Shell Scott to Pocket Books, that John D. MacDonald finally agreed to a long-standing plea by the Fawcett brothers to produce a series character for Gold Medal. The result was Travis McGee, described as a 'big, loose-jointed boat-bum', a mixture of rogue and detective, who investigates the theft of property, often on behalf of beautiful

Opposite: Novels such as *Weep for Me* (1951) earned John D. MacDonald widespread praise as a great storyteller.

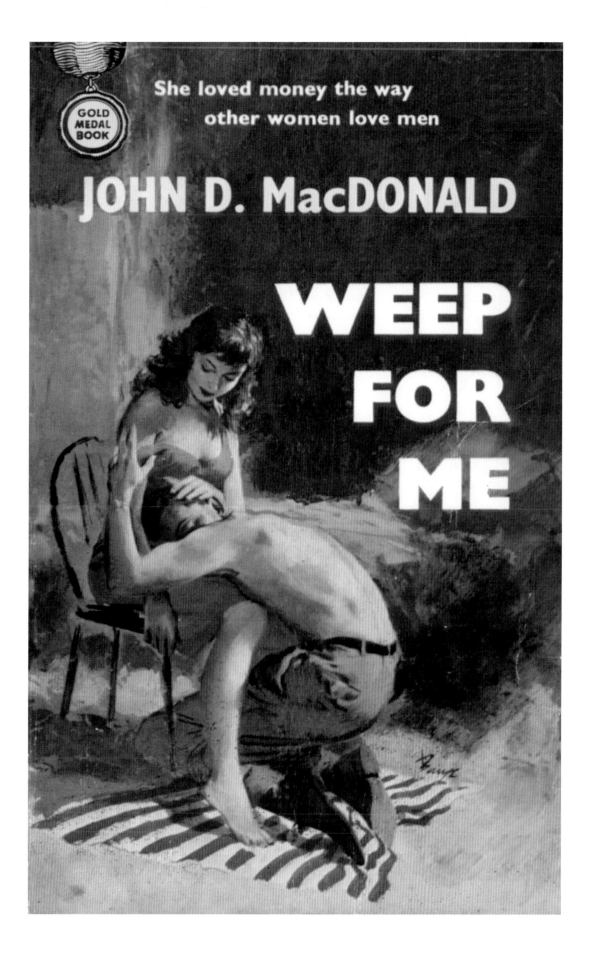

She loved money the way
other women love men

JOHN D. MacDONALD

WEEP FOR ME

women who have been conned or defrauded by criminals. Half of the proceeds is his fee for a successful outcome. Occasionally he is hired to protect individuals in danger of their lives. A former infantryman in the Korean war, McGee operates from a houseboat named the Busted Flush, so-called because it was won in a game of poker, and now based at Fort Lauderdale. Interestingly, MacDonald had intended to call his character Dallas McGee, but the assassination of President Kennedy in the autumn of 1963 made him have second thoughts. Instead he took the advice of his close friend, author McKinlay Kantor (also being published by Gold Medal) and chose the name of a famous US Air Force base. The

Contemporary crime issues featured in many of John D. MacDonald's cases of Travis McGee, the titles of which all featured colours of the spectrum.

author also did not like the use of the term 'private eye' where his character was concerned: 'I have tried to stay well clear of the word "detective" as they have licenses and are subject to lots of confining laws,' he explained. McGee's eye for a shapely figure and his active sex life got off to a good start in the first novel, *The Deep Blue Goodbye* (1964), and continued in the later capers which all had colours in the titles: *The Quick Red Fox* (1964), which introduced his friend and confidant, Meyer, a retired economist; *The Girl in the Plain Brown Wrapper* (1968) and *The Dreadful Lemon Sky* (1975). The series (which ran to over 20 titles) regularly drew on contemporary issues of crime and made use of stories of serial killers and revenge killings from the front pages of the US press. To date only two stories have been filmed: *Darker Than Amber* (1966) filmed in 1970 with Rod Taylor, directed by Robert Clouse, and *The Empty Copper Sea* (1978), made into a two-hour TV special starring Sam Elliott, that failed to inspire a projected series.

Another Gold Medal author for whom recognition is now only just forthcoming is Elliott Chaze, whose *Black Wings Has My Angel* (1953) is by any standard a quintessential hard-boiled novel. Stephen King places Chaze as one of the three great American writers of stories about the criminal mind; the other two he lists are James M. Cain and Jim Thompson. The novel describes the odyssey of an oil rigger and his hooker girlfriend on the run from the law after successfully holding up an armoured car full of money. The anguish and madness of the storyline was unlike either of Chaze's two earlier titles, *The Stainless Steel Kimono* (1947), about paratroopers in occupied Japan, and a mystery story, *The Golden Tag* (1950). In fact it was unlike anything he would write again, with the possible exception of *Wettermark* (1969), the tale of a newspaper crime reporter, Cliff

Wettermark, who is relentlessly sucked into crime by debt and appalling circumstances.

Lewis Elliott Chaze (1915–1990) was himself a newspaperman for much of his working life. Born in Mamou, Louisiana, he worked for a time as an oil rigger and then as a reporter with AP before serving as a paratrooper in World War Two. Later he spent time in Japan as a technical sergeant before returning to America and obtaining a position as the city editor and columnist on the *Hattiesburg American*. Chaze wrote mainly in his spare time, utilizing his own experiences, plus newspaper stories that passed over his desk every day, for raw material, although he only published nine books in his lifetime. *Black Wings Has My Angel* is now becoming accepted as a landmark book in the crime genre, on a par with Paul Cain's *Fast One*. Recognition for Chaze's book is long overdue. It has been reprinted once in the US (by Berkley in 1962, retitled *One for the Money*), and in hardcovers in the UK by Robert Hale in 1985.

Another writer consistently ignored by critics while selling huge quantities of books was Carter Brown, whose series of paperback originals were all adorned with beautiful girls in varying states of undress. It has been claimed that the Brown books were a publishing phenomenon with sales in tens, perhaps hundreds of millions, in editions all over the world. They were written in the same style as the pulp magazines, with plenty of violent action, lots of breezy slang and an unending procession of beautiful, willing young girls. Brown had a number of series characters including Al Wheeler, a homicide lieutenant in Pine City, near Los Angeles; Rick Holman, a Hollywood private eye regularly saving beautiful, endangered starlets; and Mavis Seidlitz, a stunning private detective whose attributes (other than her brains) usually overwhelmed the criminals she was hired to bring to justice. The creator

Elliott Chaze's *Black Wings Has My Angel* (1953) is becoming accepted as a landmark novel in crime fiction.

of this trio, whose real name was Alan Geoffrey Yates (1923–1985), had been born in London, served in the Royal Navy during the Second World War, and then emigrated to Australia in 1948. While working as a PR for Qantas Airlines, Yates began writing thrillers for a small Sydney publisher, starting with *Venus Unarmed* in 1953 which he signed Carter Brown. Within a year, he was churning out one thriller after another for Horwitz in Australia, Signet in America and New English Library in London. Although the 300 and more titles of this astonishingly prolific writer were often derided as formulaic pot-boilers, they remained consistently popular until the author's death and are now much collected for their exotic covers.

The last gasp of the hard-boiled pulp magazines nurtured two other writers destined for international fame: Ray Bradbury and Evan Hunter. Bradbury, who is now acknowledged as one of the finest writers of science fiction, was to be found learning his craft in the pages of *Detective Tales* ('Killer Come Back to Me', July 1944), *Flynn's Detective Fiction* ('Yesterday I Lived', August 1944) and *Dime Mystery Magazine* ('Wake for the Living', September 1947). Evan Hunter reversed the situation with stories of fantasy

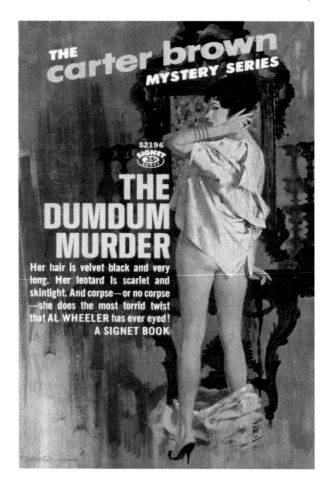

The best-selling *Carter Brown Mystery Series* written by Alan Yates have all become very collectable for the beautiful cover girls in varying stages of undress.

and science fiction for *Fantastic Universe* and *If* magazine in the early 1950s, before making a significant contribution to the group of tough novels about juvenile crime euphemistically known as 'Juvies', and then following this by creating the hugely successful series of police procedural novels set in the 87th Precinct written under the pseudonym Ed McBain.

Ray Douglas Bradbury (1920–) was born in Waukegan, Illinois, but while he was still a teenager during the Depression, his family moved to Los Angeles where he has lived ever since, although images of those early years are frequently to be found in his evocative stories. The crime and fantasy pulps were a seminal part of his early reading, and even before he had left Los Angeles High School in 1938 he was writing stories for fanzines. The following year, Bradbury made his first professional sale to the pulp *Super Science*, and followed this with 25 stories for *Weird Tales* before graduating to the *Saturday Evening Post* and publishing his first book, *Dark Carnival*, in 1947. Bradbury had been an admirer of *Black Mask* and the other hard-boiled titles for some years before he submitted his first crime stories to *Detective Tales* in 1944. The tales, he says, 'caused no immediate trepidation over in the Hammett-Chandler-Cain camp', but their acceptance prompted further tales for *Flynn's Detective Fiction*, *New Detective Magazine* and *Dime Mystery Magazine* in the next three years. Then followed the unprecedented success of his sci-fi novels, *The Martian Chronicles* (1950), *The Illustrated Man* (1951) and *Fahrenheit 451* (1953), and Bradbury did not return to the crime genre until 1985 with his first mystery suspense novel, *Death Is a Lonely Business*, written, he has explained, because of 'my greater knowledge of the field and having learned lessons from Ross Macdonald'. That same year, an anthology of the detective pulp stories was published by

Dell as *A Memory of Murder*, and there are indications that Bradbury may well write another novel in the hard-boiled tradition.

Ed McBain, the name on the covers of the 70-odd 87th Precinct novels, is probably more widely known than that of Evan Hunter. But even this is not the author's real name; he was born Salvatore Lombino (1926–) and following his subsequent rise to fame he has omitted details of a number of his early books and also guarded the information about the career which inspired his first best-seller, *The Blackboard Jungle*, published as Evan Hunter in 1954. This ground-breaking novel about a New York school full of violence and racial tension and the heartbreaking efforts of one teacher to instil knowledge into the young punks in his class was an immediate success in America and rapidly published in Britain and Europe. It became even more notorious when filmed the following year by Richard Brooks with Glenn Ford as the teacher, Sidney Poitier as a sensitive problem pupil and Vic Morrow as a knife-wielding delinquent. The soundtrack of one of the first rock 'n' roll classics, Bill Haley's *Rock Around the Clock*, added to the dynamism of the picture and, according to press reports at the time, generated violent scenes of disorder among younger audiences on both sides of the Atlantic, some of whom were said to have ripped out seats in the cinemas.

The Blackboard Jungle is often erroneously cited as the first novel to feature teenage violence and gangs. In fact, the first had appeared almost a decade earlier in 1947: *The Amboy Dukes* by Irving Shulman, which provided a realistic picture of several boy

Right: Ray Bradbury, famous now as a writer of science fiction, began his career writing hard-boiled fiction for pulp magazines like *Detective Tales* (*Killer Come Back to Me*, July 1944), *Flynn's Detective Fiction* (*Yesterday I Lived*, August 1944) and *Dime Mystery* (*Wake for the Living*, September 1947).

number of crime and fantasy stories before the success of *The Blackboard Jungle*. Raised in New York, he was educated at the Evander Childs High School and was then conscripted into the US Navy in 1941 where he served until the end of the war. He returned to New York and took a degree at Hunter College (the institution from which, it is said, he took his pen-name) and then worked in two vocational high schools in the city where he experienced at first hand the tough life that would infuse his famous book. Hunter was subsequently employed at the Scott Meredith Literary Agency, where his interest in writing gained pace and he contributed his first short stories to the pulps as Hunt Collins and Richard Marsten, followed by a pair of private eye novels as Curt Cannon, *I'm Cannon – For Hire* and *I Like 'Em Tough* for Gold Medal. In 1954 he wrote *The Blackboard Jungle* and pulp novels became a thing of the past. In the 1950s he wrote several more hardbacks on controversial social problems: *Second Ending* (1955, focusing on heroin addiction among musicians); *Strangers When We Meet* (1958, about adultery) and *A Matter of Conviction* (1959, about teenage street violence), all of which were filmed.

It was in 1956 that he took yet another pen-name, Ed McBain, to write the first 87th Precinct story, *Cop Hater*, followed in swift succession by *The Pusher* (1956), *The Con Man* (1957) and *Lady Killer* (1958). The stories are all set in a place called Isola – not unlike Manhattan, despite the author's protests to the contrary – and feature an unforgettable bunch of policemen including detectives Steve Carella, Bert Kling, Cotton Hawes, Arthur Brown and Meyer Meyer, plus their paternal boss, Lieutenant Peter Byrnes. A master criminal, 'The Deaf Man', is the thorn in the flesh of the boys of the 87th Precinct, who plans a crime and then bombards them with clues. Although he is always thwarted, 'The

Pyramid and Ace were two New York publishing houses who catered to the market for books about teenage crime with titles like *The Power Gods* by Bud Clifton and *Death House Doll* by Day Keene, both released in 1958.

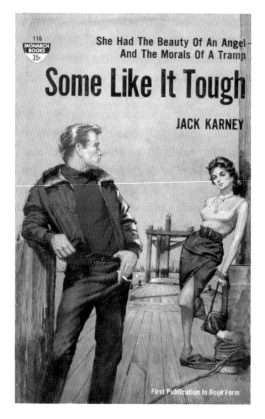

Jack Karney, author of the Monarch title *Some Like It Tough* (1959) worked in the New York District Attorney's Office.

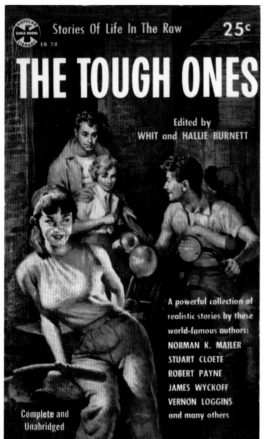

The Tough Ones (1954) was one of a number of American paperback anthologies which cashed in on the craze for stories of juvenile lawbreaking.

Evan Hunter used a number of pseudonyms during his early career, including Curt Cannon for his stories of a private eye in 1953.

Deaf Man' resists capture. McBain, like the other writers in this chapter, used the sort of stories of murder and crime that could have come from the front page of any New York newspaper, and his compelling style has produced almost 70 titles of which over 40 feature the 87th Precinct.

Perhaps one of the most extraordinary of all novels of tabloid murder is *The Scarf* (1947) by Robert Bloch (1917–1994), who is, of course, famous above all else as the author of *Psycho. The Scarf* is the terrifying story of a psychopathic strangler stalking one victim after another, *told from the killer's viewpoint.* Bloch later revealed that the idea came to him 'from nowhere' while walking along the banks of the Milwaukee River one tranquil day in the summer of 1946. When the book was published

the following year, however, a dream sequence in which the main character is seen shooting at innocent passers-by from a roof-top was cut by the publishers, Dial Press, as being 'too far-fetched'. Prophetic was probably the word that should have been used, as Bloch later explained: 'In 1966, one Charles Whitman killed his wife and mother, then ascended the tower overlooking the campus of the University of Texas armed with a rifle, and shot 46 innocent people at random, killing 16 on the spot.' The sequence was not reinstated into the book until 40 years later.

Robert Bloch was born in Chicago, the son of a bank cashier and a social worker, both of whom were fascinated by the performing arts and fostered in their son the desire to be a comedian. Instead, he began work as a copywriter in an advertising agency, and filled his spare time with writing horror and mystery stories for the pulp magazines. One of his influences was H. P. Lovecraft, and many of Bloch's early short stories appeared in *Weird Tales* and *Strange Stories* (including the classic 'Yours Truly, Jack the Ripper' [*Weird Tales*, July 1943], one of the best mystery tales of all time) as well as the occasional hard-boiled story for *Mammoth Detective*, *Detective Tales* and *Dime Mystery*. His admiration for Raymond Chandler set the style for his first novel, *The Scarf*, followed in 1954 by *The Kidnapper*, another brutal first-person narrative of a psychopath, and *Shooting Star* (1958), an even more accomplished account of a private eye's hunt for the killer of a dope addict movie idol, Dick Ryan. But the pinnacle of Robert Bloch's career came in 1958 when another newspaper story inspired *Psycho*. His attention had been

caught by a report of the appalling killings committed by Ed Gein, a Wisconsin farmer who had slaughtered a number of women and used their flesh in ghastly acts of cannibalism. Bloch admitted, 'I felt there was a book there. I tried to figure out what kind of a man could get away with murder, to develop a pattern for this imaginary character. I decided he was probably schizoid. It would be more plausible if he himself didn't know what he was doing. I came up with an Oedipal situation and the transvestite thing, which was pretty offbeat at the time.' The result was *Psycho*, written in just seven weeks, bought for filming by Alfred Hitchcock for less than $10,000 and turned into one of the most famous and commercially successful movies of all time, starring Anthony Perkins as Norman Bates.

The fame of the film won Bloch commissions to write for films and television, including the *Thriller* series and *Journey into the Unknown*,

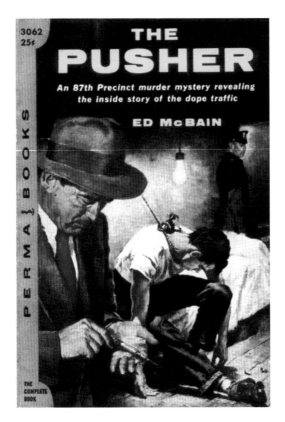

The 87th Precinct stories by Evan Hunter writing as Ed McBain have been enormously popular with readers for almost half a century.

while he occasionally wrote other novels: *The Dead Beat* (1960), about a dangerous young con-man; *American Gothic* (1974), based on the real-life crimes of the mass murderer Herman W. Mudgett in Chicago in the 1890s; and *Night of the Ripper* (1986), which 'solved' the identity of the infamous London killer. Bloch also wrote two excellent sequels to his most famous novel: *Psycho II* (1982), focusing on violence in society, and *Psycho House* (1990), about the exploitation of violence for 'entertainment'. The success of the original *Psycho* opened new doors in the film industry for Hitchcock. It also proved to be a major stepping-stone in the development of another new element in crime fiction, the *film noir* and its equally powerful literary companion, the *crime noir*, which introduced some ground-breaking new writers and also revived the reputations of some undeservedly neglected masters of the genre like David Goodis and Jim Thompson.

The huge success of Robert Bloch's novel *Psycho*, after it was filmed by Alfred Hitchcock in 1960, inspired two sequels, *Psycho II* (1982) and *Psycho House* (1990).

The Mean Streets of Crime Noir

THE MEAN STREETS OF CRIME NOIR

After dark, the cities of Los Angeles, Chicago and New York seem to be made of a menacing black and white. Harsh lights, dark shadows, black clothes, pale skins and violence constantly threaten to erupt. The same can be said of London and Paris, which explains why it was only a matter of time before hard-boiled fiction crossed the Atlantic. And in the wake of the stories by Hammett, Chandler, Cain and Burnett, writers in Europe made their own contribution to the history of crime fiction: *crime noir*, a term invented by the French to describe the phenomenon.

A legendary book about the mean streets of the Big Apple, *The Gangs of New York* by Herbert Asbury (1927) was filmed in 2002 by Martin Scorsese with Leonardo Di Caprio and Cameron Diaz.

Both London and Paris, with their bleak landscapes and anonymous crowds, proved suitable backgrounds for tense dramas in which doomed men and women careered inexorably towards their fate. Wherever the urban nightmare existed, there could be found a grim moral code which ensured that murder was never more than a heartbeat away:

'My headlights picked up the figure when I was some 50 yards from it. It looked like a woman who was lying half on and half off the kerb. The time was around midnight. It was a dark night. I drove slower. Sure enough it was a woman. I could see her distinctly now. Did I pull up at once and stop? Bet your sweet life I didn't. Why? Because I knew the dame might be dead or she could be a decoy of some gang lying in wait for a mug to stop and investigate. Then up they would come and hold you up with guns and relieve you of all your cash.'

These are not lines from a typical American hard-boiled novel, but from the pages of *The Murphy Gang* by Roland Daniel, published in London in 1934. The storyteller is a private detective and the girl isn't dead, but she leads the man into a vicious gang war from which he is lucky to escape with his life. The brutality and killing in the story are the first indications that hard-boiled fiction was crossing the Atlantic. There were, of course, those who doubted that the style *could* be repeated outside the US – much less that it would be successful – but the truth is that *crime noir* did make its mark on crime fiction worldwide and has continued to attract admirers ever since.

The author of *The Murphy Gang*, Roland Daniel, was arguably the first British writer to attempt an imitation of the roughneck American style, yet he is little remembered

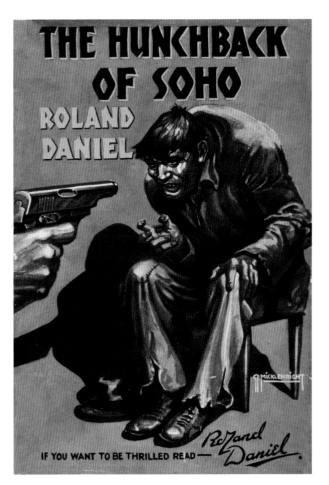

Roland Daniel was one of the pioneers of British hard-boiled writing with novels including the gruesome *Hunchback of Soho* (1943) and *Women – Dope and Murder* (1962).

today, and few of the 200 novels he wrote, at least a couple of dozen featuring hard-boiled characters, have survived. The facts that he led a quiet and retiring life and that his name was for many years believed to be a pseudonym have done little to clear the air of mystery. Yet some of Daniel's best stories, including the ground-breaking *Gangster* series, earned him comparison with Dashiell Hammett (albeit rather overblown), and his total sales were claimed to have been into the hundreds of thousands. Because his main publishers, Wright & Brown, went into liquidation in the year he died, there is difficulty in piecing together the facts. Only recently has the information come to light, and it makes for an even more extraordinary tale.

William Roland Daniel (1880–1969) was actually the son of a wealthy American who owned orange and grapefruit plantations in Florida. The boy spent his childhood in these

idyllic surroundings before being sent to England to be educated at a boarding school in Eastbourne. The young man's first love appears to have been the theatre, and after leaving school he spent several years with a touring theatre company. Tiring of the constant travelling, he decided to try writing a thriller, *The Society of Spiders*, which was accepted in 1928 by Brentano's, an American publishing house with offices in London. Daniel wrote several more thrillers for the company before it closed its British office and he switched to Wright & Brown, with whom he remained associated until his death.

Daniel's ground-breaking book was *The Gangster*, published in 1932 and inspired by W. T. Burnett's *Little Caesar*, he later admitted. Its success inspired two sequels, *The Gangster's Last Shot* in 1939 and *The Gangster's Daughter* in 1965. The author's skill at writing about underworld characters was also obvious in *The Slayer* (1936) and *Big Squeal* (1940). Among later titles that indicated he kept up-to-date on what was going on in the criminal fraternity are *All Thugs Are Dangerous* (1958) and *Women – Dope and Murder* (1962). Daniel had a liking for bizarre villains, too. In the 1930s he wrote a series of adventures for *Thriller* magazine about 'Wu Fang', indicating his love of the Far East and especially anything Chinese; and he turned out several other novels whose titles speak for themselves: *Scarthroat* (1934), *Snake Face* (1936) and, most curious of all, *The Hunchback of Soho* (1943).

According to historian W. O. G. Lofts, who managed to track down details about the elusive author after his death, Roland Daniel never lost his love of the theatre and wrote several plays, including a mystery, *The Signal*, which ran for a season in the West End of London. His last years were spent in Devon, where he continued to write until shortly before his death at the age of 88. Just one local obituary recorded his passing in Torquay Hospital, and this made only a brief mention of his crime novels and said nothing whatsoever about his contribution to hard-boiled fiction.

Two other British authors writing during the same era as Roland Daniel also produced novels that were clearly aimed at catching the new mood for tougher crime stories. The first of these was Hugh Desmond Clevely (1898–1964), the author of a series known as the *The Gang Smasher*, which was launched in 1937 and continued to be printed until the 1950s. The title character is John Martinson with his battle-scarred face, close-cropped red hair and a pugnacious square jaw, who takes on the nickname after he and his girlfriend, Sylvia, are the victims of a London gangster, Al Tortoni. Having put Tortoni behind bars, thanks to the assistance of a friend, J. D. Peters of the FBI, Martinson – described as 'a merciless hounder of villains' – then tackles other underworld figures in *The Gang Smasher Again* (1938); *Gang Law* (1939), which involves a Chicago mobster Benito Moroni; and *The Gang Smasher Calling* (1940).

Clevely was born in Bristol and, after spending his early years in a country vicarage, travelled a great deal and started writing tales

Hugh Clevely's series of *Gang Smasher* novels which began in 1937 opened English reader's eyes to the criminal underworld.

of crime and mystery in the 1930s for *Detective Weekly Thriller Library* and the *Sexton Blake* series. After service with the RAF in the Second World War, during which he rose to the rank of Wing Commander, he abandoned his hard-edged style for the more traditional crime story. Clevely's death in May 1964 was, however, as baffling as anything to be found in crime fiction. He was then living alone in the Crown and Anchor Hotel in Blandford, Dorset. On the night of 8 May, as was his habit, he bought a whisky at the bar, drank it and then set out for his usual nightly walk before going to bed. After failing to return, a search was instigated by the police and Clevely's body was found at 4.30 am, face down in a weir on the nearby River Stour. An officer reported finding two patches of blood on slabs of concrete 100 yards from the scene, with Clevely's walking stick nearby. There were further traces of blood at the river bank and smears of blood on a metal stanchion in a pothole. After hearing the evidence, the mystified local coroner went on to record an open verdict.

Death under violent circumstances was a feature of the writing of another author from this period, Richard Goyne (1902–1957), better known for a series of salacious paperback novels published under the pen-name Paul Renin, although few people knew of the connection at the time. Take this example of the Goyne style when writing as Renin:

'The silence in the shabby bedroom seemed to be screaming in his ears like a thousand demons. The light from the solitary bulb was dazzling to his horrified eyes. He felt the sweat gathering in great beads all over his body as he fought vainly to drag his gaze from the object of his terror. The thing lying sprawled on the faded rug was a woman, young, clad only in cheap, thin underwear that was gathered about her body. And where this did not cover her, one breast and part of her thighs, her skin gleamed like wax. She was lying still, a look of mild surprise on her upturned face. She was quite dead, and the boy, Frank Stanley, had killed her.'

The episode is from *Lady of Leicester Square*, published by Gerald G. Swan in London in 1939. The girl is a prostitute who has just angered the small-time crook, Frank Stanley. In a moment of blind rage, he has turned from thief to killer and his life will never be the same again. It is typical of the Paul Renin style. Goyne himself was the son a London schoolteacher and overcame infantile paralysis to lead an active life and make his mark on crime fiction, as W. O. G. Lofts has explained:

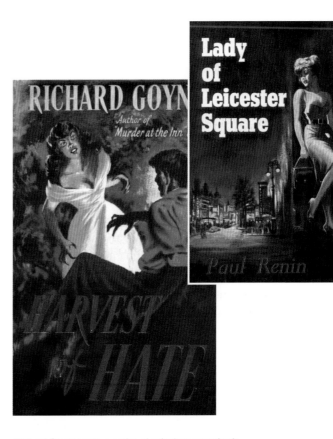

Richard Goyne wrote a series of salacious paperback novels about London vice under the pen-name of Paul Renin as well as stories about a tough private eye, Peter Parker, notably *Harvest of Hate* (1952).

'Young Goyne was a prodigy who limped. Boys of his own age shunned him at school, where he used to exploit his literary ability by producing magazines which he wrote in pencil and sold for a penny a copy. His first published work was believed to have been at the tender age of eleven and when he left school he got a job as a journalist on *The Hornsey Journal*.'

Subsequently, Goyne decided to take a gamble by becoming a freelance writer and was soon selling hundreds of crime and mystery stories to the D. C. Thompson group. In the 1930s he produced a number of sex novels under the Paul Renin by-line which all had lurid covers and were sold in shrink-wrappers (*Lonely Wives*, 1932; *Wild Oats*, 1936; *Good Time Girls*, 1940), after which he turned to hard-boiled fiction with equal facility. Other than *Lady of Leicester Square*, *The Woman in the Case* and *London Night Haunts*, both published in 1940, are now very collectable. Despite his disability, Goyne was passed fit enough to serve in the Commandos during the Second World War and later described his experiences in *Destination Unknown* (1945). Thereafter he continued to write crime stories for Stanley Paul Ltd until his death in Penrith in 1957, notably *Harvest of Hate* (1952), one of several titles to feature the private investigator Peter Parker, and *Introducing the Super* (1955), the first of the cases about ex-Superintendent 'Tubby' Greene. His obituary said no more than that he had been 'an author of numerous thrillers'.

The first British author to make an enduring mark on crime literature writing hard-boiled fiction was Peter Cheyney, who was recently referred to by Katherine Gunn as 'The King of the "Hard-Nosed" Thriller (British variety)'. Cheyney burst upon the literary scene in 1936 with *This Man Is Dangerous*, the first of what was to prove a best-selling series about private eye Lemmy Caution who, despite his name, was inclined to punch or shoot first whenever confronting the villains who peddled sex and drugs in the London underworld. Despite several reviews in the English press which condemned Cheyney's books for their violence and brutality, they were soon selling by the millions in the UK and in hundreds of thousands in America and France, as he became the first UK author to carry the hard-boiled story back across the Atlantic and over the English Channel.

When fame came to Reginald Southouse Cheyney (1896–1951) he muddied the waters about his birth and early life in several contradictory biographical pieces. In fact, he was born in the East End of London in Whitechapel, one of four boys whose father ran a market stall selling jellied eels and

The popularity of Peter Cheyney novels spread to America where books like *Sinister Errand* became *Sinister Murders* (1954) and in France where *Dark Wanton* became *La Dame Est Noir* (1948).

whelks. Leaving school at 14, the young Cheyney got a job as a clerk in a firm of solicitors but was fascinated by the stage and started submitting sketches to London theatres. His ear for Cockney dialogue earned him commissions from a number of well-known artists of the time, including George Carney and Mairie Dainton. The First World War interrupted his burgeoning career and he was forced to spend the time in the Labour Corps Records Office, although he did publish two now extremely rare volumes of war poetry. Shortly after the end of the hostilities, Cheyney met and married Dorma Leigh, a dancer who was friendly with Edgar Wallace, and he soon set out to emulate the great man. According to an entry he wrote for himself in *Who's Who*, Cheyney served for several years as a special constable in the Metropolitan Police and, as a result, in 1932 'formed and directed Cheyney Research and Investigations' which evidently undertook several cases and retrieved some stolen property. What is certain is that after a period of writing short stories as well as ghost-writing the career of ex-Detective Inspector Harold Brust in *I Guarded Kings: The Memoirs of a Political Police Officer* (1935), he discovered the formula that would make him rich and famous.

In his biography of Cheyney, *The Prince of Hokum* (1954), Michael Harrison says that the author held very right-wing political views and for a time during the 1930s was a member of Sir Oswald Mosley's New Party, though whether he joined Mosley's infamous Fascist 'Black Shirts' is open to dispute. The experience *did* open his eyes to the use of violence, and more particularly inspired him to produce some of the most violent crime stories of the time. Following the success of *This Man Is Dangerous*, Cheyney wrote ten more books about Lemmy Caution, and in 1938 introduced a second private eye, Slim Callaghan, in *The Urgent Hangman*, who also rough-housed his way through adventures full of violence and crime. Callaghan was created after a friend chided him that he could only write 'Yank gangster stories', and after the first title had appeared, the man added, 'Only Cheyney would have picked an Irish name for an Englishman!'

Cheyney, who had long before dropped his Christian names Reginald Southouse in favour of Peter, took a great deal of interest in both the promotion and presentation of his books when they were published by William Collins. At the time *This Man Is Dangerous* was being launched, he learned that the British Lion Film Corporation was producing a movie of the same title and brought a case for infringement of *his* title which, surprisingly, he won, generating a lot of publicity for the book. Cheyney also appreciated the importance of dust jackets and recommended an artist named John Pisani, who created the archetypal image of Lemmy Caution complete

with slouch hat and machine gun. Pisani was also responsible for the pictures of beautiful, seductive women featured on the front of the subsequent Caution and Callaghan capers. An American actor, Eddie Constantine, renowned for his 'tough guy' roles, portrayed Lemmy Caution on the screen in eight movies including the surreal *Alphaville*, made by Jean-Luc Godard in 1965, while Tyrone Power was the best of three actors to play Slim Callaghan on the screen.

Lemmy Caution has been acknowledged as the precursor of Mickey Spillane's Mike Hammer. But he also influenced a number of other British writers, especially Howard Hartley (the pseudonym of Leopold Horace Ognall, 1908–) who filled the hole in Collins' list after Cheyney's death with his series about tough private eye Glenn Bowman (*The Last Deception*, 1951, et al); Peter Chambers (the pseudonym of Dennis J. A. Phillips, 1924–), a star of the Robert Hale crime list in the 1960s (*Dames Can Be Deadly*, 1963, et al) and Bevis Winter (1918–), the mainstay of the Herbert

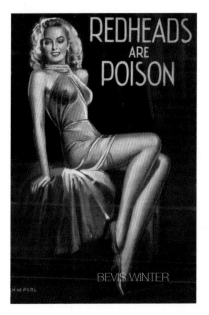

The exotic illustrations by H. W. Perl for the 'redhead' series by Bevis Winter were an invitation to hard-boiled action inside the covers.

Jenkins mystery list with his 'Redhead' series (*Redheads Are Poison*, 1948; *Redheads Cool Fast*, 1954, et al*)* who also wrote as Al Bocca, Gordon Shayne and Peter Cagney. Winter even dedicated one of the Cagney novels, *Hear the Stripper Scream* (1960), to 'My good friend and fellow conspirator, the guy who taught me all I know, one of the world's most brilliant contemporary writers ... Bevis Winter.' In particular, though, Peter Cheyney was the precursor of two other British crime writers who also ran foul of the obscenity laws: James Hadley Chase and Hank Janson.

There are few better known titles in the history of crime fiction than *No Orchids for Miss Blandish*, and certainly no more famous example of British *crime noir*. The author was James Hadley Chase, a book salesman ,turned best-seller writer, who was as

One of the most famous titles in the history of crime fiction, *No Orchids for Miss Blandish* by James Hadley Chase, first published in 1939. The book went on to enjoy even more notoriety when translated into French.

publicity-shy as Peter Cheyney was promotion-conscious and lived out much of his life in Switzerland, where he refused to give even a single interview. If the appearance of *This Man Is Dangerous* stirred up the English critics, then *No Orchids for Miss Blandish* horrified them when it was published in 1939 and provoked accusations that it was degenerate and immoral – accusations guaranteed to make it a best-seller which sold over a million copies in a year.

James Hadley Chase was actually the pen-name of Rene Lodge Brabazon Raymond (1906–1985), who was born in Hastings, the son of an Indian Army medical officer. A strong-willed boy, he quarrelled with his authoritarian father and at the age of 17 left home. Why he chose to spend the next two years as a door-to-door salesman of children's encyclopedias has never been explained beyond the need to earn money, but when he joined the book wholesalers Simpkin Marshall, he soon came to appreciate the money that could be made by successful writers. The sales figures of Dashiell Hammett, Raymond Chandler and particularly Peter Cheyney steered him towards the hard-boiled crime novel, and he was convinced he could do the same thing, as one of his biographers, Derek Adley, has explained:

'Based loosely on a brief news item Chase saw concerning a kidnapped American heiress whose ordeal had sent her out of her mind, *No Orchids for Miss Blandish* took him just six weekends to write. The magic title which sold the book is supposed to have been thought up whilst he was taking a bath. The strong criticism of his first book not only helped sales but also led to a stage adaptation produced in collaboration with Robert Nesbitt which opened at the Prince of Wales Theatre in London in July 1942 and enjoyed a long and successful run.'

James Hadley Chase also published several titles under a pen-name, Raymond Marshall, including *Lady — Here's Your Wreath* (1940).

The hard-boiled stories by James Hadley Chase proved popular in the homeland of the genre, although some were retitled by their American publisher for example, *The Dead Stay Dumb* (1940) becoming *Kiss My Fist!*. He was also a best-seller in Europe, especially in Holland with *The World in My Pocket* (1959).

The main critic of *No Orchids* was George Orwell, who described reading it as taking 'a header into the cesspool'. Detecting an analogy with the work of Peter Cheyney, Orwell said that the book had been described to him as 'pure Fascism', but he also found it 'sordid and brutal'. He counted eight murders, an unassessable number of killings and woundings, an exhumation (with a careful reminder of the stench), the flogging of Miss Blandish, the torture of another woman with red-hot cigarette-ends, a third-degree scene of unheard-of cruelty 'and much else of the same kind of cruelty and sexual perversion'. Orwell concluded his review: 'One ought not to infer

too much from the success of Mr Chase's book. It is possible that it is an isolated phenomenon, brought about by the mingled boredom and brutality of war.'

Of course it wasn't. In the half a century that followed, James Hadley Chase, who another critic referred to as the 'Faulkner of the masses', wrote 80 more sexy and violent novels which enabled him to live luxuriously in Switzerland and delight millions of readers all over the world. His ability to turn out hard-boiled stories in short order was such that he also began issuing titles under another pen-name, Raymond Marshall, the first of these, *Lady – Here's Your Wreath*, appearing in 1940. Soon, too, his books were finding a ready market in America where a number were published under new titles, a prime example being *The Dead Stay Dumb* (1940), which became *Kiss My Fist!* under the Avon banner. The success of the novels across the Atlantic was all the more remarkable because, though his stories featured the world of American gangsters, Chase had no first-hand knowledge of the country and used an atlas, guides, directories and slang dictionaries to create authentic-sounding locations, hard-boiled private eyes and violent gangsters, few of whom appeared in more than one story.

There was, however, one hiccup in the success story in May 1942. Chase, by then, was serving in the RAF where he ultimately became a Squadron Leader, but along with his publishers, Jarrolds, he was summonsed to the Central Criminal Court in London on 18 May to answer charges of 'publishing an obscene libel', namely *Miss Callaghan Comes to Grief*. A copy of the book had been purchased by the police and proceedings instituted, to which Chase and Jarrolds pleaded not guilty. Extracts from the story were read to the court by the prosecutor, Mr Christmas Humphreys, but after protests from defending counsel that these were being taken out of context, the jury were asked to take away copies and read them overnight. The following morning the 12 men and women returned and delivered a verdict of 'guilty'. Jarrolds and the author were each fined £100.

Whatever James Hadley Chase's feelings might have been about having his book labelled obscene, his service in the RAF curtailed any more writing until the end of the war. One of his first actions was to revise some of the earlier titles for republication in the UK and France. The 'Chinks' in *Twelve Chinks and a Woman* (1940), for example, became *Chinamen* and much later the title was completely changed to *Doll's Bad News*. Then, in 1949, Robert Hale took over publication from Jarrolds, although the Raymond Marshall titles remained with the imprint until 1954. After moving to Switzerland, Chase continued to produce at least a book a year until his death, while the earlier titles were constantly reprinted, issued in paperback and widely translated. The effect of the court case against *Miss Callaghan Comes to Grief* on the career of James Hadley Chase was minimal, although the story does have a strange footnote.

On that same day in May 1942 that *Miss Callaghan* was found guilty, another London publisher, Wells, Gardner, Darton & Co., were also due in court accused of publishing two obscene books: *Road Floozie*, about a footloose beauty, and *Lady Don't Turn Over*, dealing with the kidnapping rackets, both written by 'Darcy Glinto'. However, the verdict

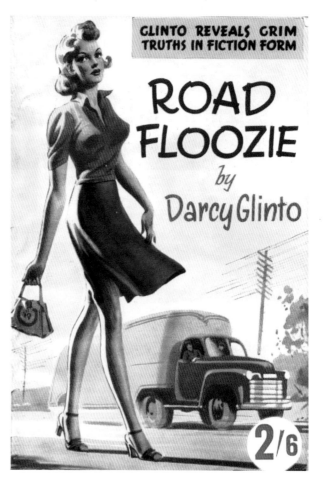

Following the success of his first novel, *No Mortgage on a Coffin* (1941), Darcy Glinto's second novel, *Road Floozie* (1942), was banned for obscenity.

against Jarrolds caused them to change a similar plea of 'not guilty' to 'guilty' and author and publisher were fined £50 on each count. The company had earlier published several American hard-boiled titles including Horace McCoy's *They Shoot Horses, Don't They?* and in 1941 launched the career of Darcy Glinto with *No Mortgage on a Coffin*. Glinto was the pseudonym of Harold Ernest Kelly (1899–1969), a prolific writer of pulp fiction for the small post-war English paperback houses, using a variety of pseudonyms including Preston Yorke, Bryn Logan and Eugene Ascher. Unfortunately for Kelly, the case did not herald the start of a success story like that of James

The American edition of one of Georges Simenon's most powerful *roman policier*, *The Fugitive* (1941).

Hadley Chase, although his Darcy Glinto novels, including *Curtains for Carrie* (1947), *One More Nice White Body* (1950) and *She Gave Me Hell* (1956), remained popular until the late 1950s.

Across the Channel in France at this time, the situation in which writers and publishers found themselves was very different. Georges Simenon (1903–1989), the Belgian-born master of the *roman policier* – and 'greatest of the "novelistic" novelists' according to André Gide – who had begun writing in Paris in 1923 and created the immortal Inspector Maigret in *The Strange Case of Peter the Lett* in 1931, was living in unoccupied France where he organized aid for refugees from Paris. Simenon's prolific flow of novels about crime and psychology had made him known around the world, and the cult of Maigret would grow ever larger thanks to film and television adaptations made after the war. In the occupied section of the country, however, there was not just the risk of a fine for breaking the rigorous German laws; a date with the firing squad was much more likely. Yet it seems probable that the tendencies towards lawlessness and the art of individual survival that were a way of life for French men and women at the time provided the inspiration for the birth of *crime noir*, just as similar conditions in America during Prohibition had inspired the work of Dashiell Hammett and his contemporaries. French readers had certainly been enjoying hard-boiled crime for some years, and in 1943 their own pioneer writer, Léo Malet, burst on the crime fiction scene.

Malet, a jaunty figure with an irrepressible sense of humour, had been reading and enjoying the novels of Hammett and Chandler for years before he began writing hard-boiled fiction in 1943. Deciding to make the most of the situation generated by the German forces occupying Paris, he created the tough and lugubrious private eye, Nestor 'Dynamite'

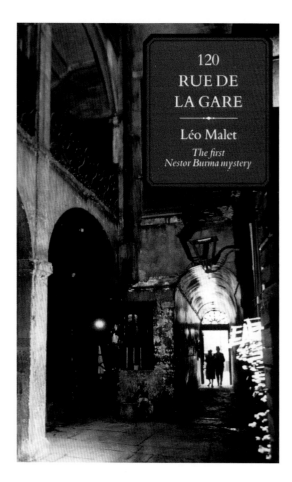

Inspired by the work of Hammett and Chandler, Léo Malet launched the French *crime noir* with his story of private eye Nestor Burma in *120 Rue de la Gare* (1943).

Burma, chief of the Fiat Lux Detective Agency, who operated on the fringes of the law – both German and French. In his first case, *120 Rue de la Gare*, 'le détective de choc' investigates the mysterious death of a French soldier who dies muttering the address of the title. The book struck a chord with sensation-starved French readers and Malet's reputation was made almost overnight.

The novel was no mean achievement for Malet (1909–), who had been born in Montpelier and received no formal education whatsoever. He was, though, gifted with a fine singing voice and put this to good effect by launching a career as a cabaret singer in Montmartre, calling himself 'La vache enragé'. The epithet was a clue to the young man's political leanings,

for apart from becoming an anarchist, he also started to contribute to a number of revolutionary magazines including *Journal de l'Homme aux Sandales* and *L'Insurge*. To keep body and soul together, Malet augmented his meagre income with jobs as an office worker, film extra, newspaper seller, manager of a fashion magazine and occasional ghost writer. In the 1930s he also joined the group of Surrealists in Paris and was a close friend of André Breton, René Magritte and Yves Tanguy. He continued to write throughout this period, even publishing several collections of poetry, but it was in 1943 with *120 Rue de la Gare* that he set French literature alight, after which he was credited with 'beginning a new era in French detective fiction'. He almost single-handedly took what was known generically as *le roman noir americain* and turned it into a recognizable national literary genre just as, in their way, Roland Daniel and the other British writers had done.

Malet dedicated his first novel to 'My friends in the Black Hole of Stalag XB' and continued to use a mixture of Resistance fighters, escaped prisoners of war, collaborators and Parisian gangsters in the early Nestor Burma novels, until the advent of peace enabled him to broaden the social background. In the 60 novels that he wrote between then and 1972, over half featured the hard-boiled private eye. He also produced several other novels under the pseudonym Frank Harding and wrote a series of novels under the general title *Nouveaux Mystères de Paris*, which ran from 1954 to 1959. The importance of Malet's work was recognized in 1948 when his Nestor Burma title *Le Cinquième Procédé* (*Mission to Marseilles*) became the first book to win the *Grand Prix de Littérature Policière*, and the *Nouveaux Mystères* series won the *Grand Prix de l'Humour Noir* in 1958. In the early 1990s a whole new programme of republishing the Nestor Burma stories was inaugurated in

France and continued in Britain and America. The author was then living in retirement in Chatillion outside Paris and reappeared in public wearing a mackintosh, glasses and a pipe that earned him comparison with Georges Simenon. It was a comparison well deserved.

The closing years of the Second World War also witnessed the emergence of the *crime noir* film. These dark, haunting pictures featuring hard-boiled private eyes, brutal police officers, gangsters, killers and any number of beautiful, terrified young women had effectively begun in 1941 with Steve Fisher's *I Wake Up Screaming*. The reception for this picture on both sides of the Atlantic despite the war was to prove the prelude for a whole series of adaptations of hard-boiled novels, in particular the works of James M. Cain (*Double Indemnity*, 1944; *Mildred Pierce*, 1945; *The Postman Always Rings Twice*, 1946 and *Out of the Past*, 1947) and Cornell Woolrich (*Phantom Lady*, 1944; *Deadline at Dawn*, 1946; *Fear in the Night*, 1947 and *The Night Has a Thousand Eyes*, 1948). Among the other important *crime noir* films of the period were two based on novels by the versatile American writer Dorothy B. Hughes (1904–1993): a New Mexico murder mystery, *Ride The Pink Horse* (1947), starring and directed by Robert Montgomery, and the chilling backstreet killings that occur in *In a Lonely Place* (1950) with Humphrey Bogart, directed by Nicholas Ray. Other important *crime noir* films include *Rope* (1948), the story of a motiveless murder written by Patrick Hamilton (1904–1962), a masterful chronicler of the squalid underbelly of London life, which Alfred Hitchcock directed with

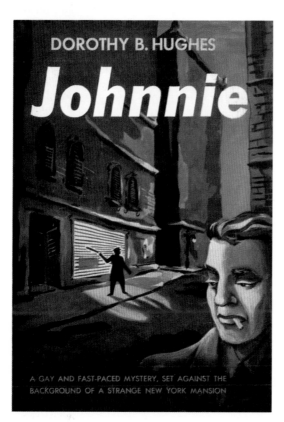

The American writer Dorothy B. Hughes had one of her finest novels turned into a brilliant *crime noir* movie in 1947.

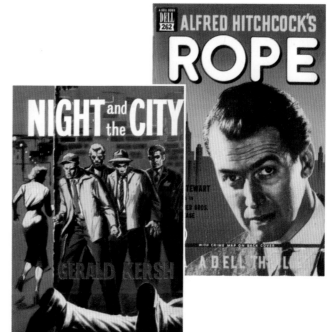

Another pair of tension-packed novels that were turned into outstanding *crime noir* movies: *Rope* (1948), based on the story of a motiveless murder by Patrick Hamilton, and Gerald Kersh's graphic picture of the London underworld, *Night and the City* (1950).

James Stewart, and *Night and the City* (1950), another novel about the London underworld, by a nightclub bouncer turned novelist Gerald Kersh (1911–1968), that Jules Dassin brought to the screen starring Richard Widmark and Gene Tierney.

In England, as the war drew to a close, a flurry of writers took up the lead of Peter Cheyney and James Hadley Chase to meet the public demand for hard-boiled fiction. A group of fly-by-night paperback firms emerged, and although the books are difficult to find today, they did play a significant role in the story of the genre. Copies with their lurid covers are now collected on both sides of the Atlantic. The first of these was Michael Hervey (1920–), an extraordinarily prolific writer, perhaps best remembered for a line warning off nervous readers printed across the covers of his books.

Hervey was born in London and, according to his own account of his life, at the age of 19 gave up a promising career as a commercial artist to go to sea. He signed on as a ship's steward and proved himself a useful linguist which made him invaluable as an interpreter. In 1939, with war imminent, he and a friend tried to work their passage back from Naples to London and were briefly interned as suspected spies! Once in England, Hervey worked for two years as an editorial assistant in the Secret Publications Division, later becoming an editor for Everybody's Books and drama critic of the *Observer*. He also began to write short stories – ultimately earning himself a place in the *Guinness Book of Records* for having written more short fiction than any other writer (3,500 tales in all) as well as producing a stream of crime paperbacks which began with *Murder Thy Neighbour* (1944), introducing hard-boiled private investigator Mike Munroe. For a time Hervey published his books under his own imprint, Hampton Press based in Essex, and it

is claimed that he sold in excess of four million copies of 60 titles before emigrating to Australia in 1951. Here he wrote more mystery stories plus a number of stage and screen plays in company with his wife, Lilyan. Years after he had left Britain, traces of his legend could apparently still be seen about the countryside, as one fan later told historian Steve Holland:

'I always recall when I think of Michael Hervey, his habit of carrying around with him small gummed labels with the legend IF YOU'RE NERVY DON'T READ HERVEY printed on them

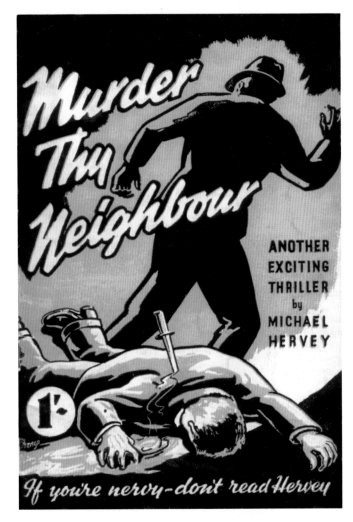

Murder Thy Neighbour (1944) was a typical Michael Hervey crime novel carrying his famous warning line.

Now Try the Morgue (1944) was one of the hard-boiled crime novels written by Elleston Trevor long before he achieved international acclaim as Adam Hall.

and he would stick these on trees, lampposts and the like wherever he went.'

If the rest of Michael Hervey's career was something of an anticlimax, quite the reverse was the case with Elleston Trevor, who cut his literary teeth writing crime and mystery paperbacks, but ended his days fêted as the author of the secret service novels about the British agent Quiller, described by *The Times* as 'one of the most consistently high-selling after Ian Fleming's 007'. At the end of his life, living in Arizona, Trevor rarely granted interviews and, when he did, denied his earlier work and insisted on talking only about recent projects. The author was born Trevor Dudley Smith (1920–1995) in Bromley, Kent, and suffered an unhappy childhood as the only son of alcoholic parents. After leaving school, he

joined the RAF and, although he was not allowed to fly because of an eye defect that made him hypersensitive to sunlight, he performed valuable service working as an engineer on Spitfires as well as beginning his literary career writing short stories for the 'Yankee Magazines' published by Gerald G. Swan. It was Swan who published his first novels, all crime stories, starting with *Now Try the Morgue* (1944), featuring a gunman-gangster character glorying in the name of Raz Berry!

After marrying Jonquil Burgess, an author of children's books, the couple settled down in Brighton to write and Trevor produced his first best-seller, *The Big Pick-Up* (1955), a story written as a challenge to J. B. Priestley, who had grumbled that 'all sorts of terrible people are writing war stories for the money'. Trevor had never been deterred by a personal lack of experience of any subject, and it is a fact that this book became accepted as the definitive novel of the wartime evacuation from Dunkirk. Several more successful war novels followed before Trevor was inspired to follow the success of John le Carré's *The Spy Who Came In from the Cold*. He selected the pseudonym Adam Hall from the telephone directory, wrote *The Quiller Memorandum* in a matter of months and did so well from the sale of the film rights and a subsequent TV series that he was able to move to America and remain there for the rest of his life, completing a total of over 80 books. In all the obituaries that marked his death at aged 75 in 1995, it was specifically stated that his first novel had been *A Chorus of Echoes* published in 1950. Raz Berry and Elleston Trevor's other hard-boiled characters had blown away on the winds of time.

Michael Storme was another ex-RAF man who took advantage of his off-duty hours during the Second World War to begin a writing career that would 'establish him amongst the most popular gangster writers of the time', according to historian Steve Holland.

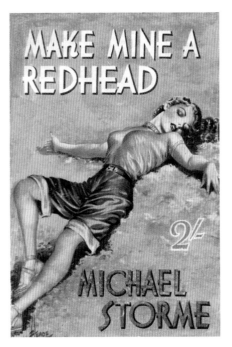

The *Make Mine* series of gangster novels by Michael Storme were always immediately recognisable by their striking 'Good Girl Art' covers by John Pollack or Reginald Heade.

Pre-eminent among his titles were the 'Make Mine' series in the late 1940s and early 1950s, about the suave, tough private eye Nick Cranley, in particular *Make Mine a Shroud* (1948), *Make Mine Beautiful* (1949) and *Make Mine a Redhead* (1952). Storme was the alter ego of George H. Dawson (1918–1979), who appears to have worked in the newspaper industry until 1939 when he became a radio engineer in the RAF and saw service in Egypt, Sudan, Tripoli and Italy. He was also on the aircraft carrier *Indomitable* when it made a last-minute dash with replacement Hurricane fighter planes for the defence of Singapore. After leaving the service in 1945, Dawson returned to London and began writing crime novels in 1947 with *Sucker for a Redhead*. The Nick Cranley who was to make him a favourite with English readers was actually based on a

real American private eye whom Dawson had met in Italy. The man was a sergeant at the Bari Aerodrome and when the two became friends, the American regaled Dawson with stories of his exploits that became the inspiration for the 'Make Mine' series, ultimately running to over 20 titles. Dawson later became a publisher, though nothing further is known of him after the end of the pulp paperback boom. The Michael Storme books are now very collectable with their outstanding cover art provided by John Pollack and Reginald Heade.

Reginald Heade was, in fact, to become inextricably linked with the most famous of the British paperback hard-boiled characters, Hank Janson, whose by-line remained an attraction for a whole generation of readers from adolescents to pensioners through the 1970s. The Janson series was created by Stephen Francis, and the early titles portrayed him as a hard-boiled reporter in Chicago who was forever running into violent gangsters and pretty girls who respectively

Cover of one of the rare paperbacks that launched the career of Britain's leading gangster 'writer', Hank Janson, in 1946.

beat him up unmercifully or lured him into bed. Francis' admiration for *film noir* and the novels of James Hadley Chase and James M. Cain was often very evident in these books. A good example is *Accused* (1952), the story of a young drifter taken on as a hired help by a sadistic road-house proprietor who keeps his wife as a virtual slave, which is an undeniable imitation of *The Postman Always Rings Twice*. Nevertheless, the name Hank Janson – chosen because Francis thought 'Hank' sounded like 'Yank' – became a byword for *crime noir*, and long after the creator had left the country to live in Spain, other writers continued the series with many of the titles republished in the States.

Stephen Daniel Francis (1917–1989) was born in Lambeth, South London, and grew up in poverty in a tenement block. These circumstances gave him a life-long empathy for all those suffering from social injustice, and while he was working at his first job as an office boy in Fleet Street he joined the Communist Party, later being ejected because of his extreme views! In 1939 he launched a magazine, *Free Expression*, and registered as a conscientious objector during the war. In 1946, after learning that a distributor was looking for gangster novels, Francis sat down and in a matter of days wrote the first two Hank Janson novels, *When Dames Get Tough* and *Scarred Faces*, published by Ward & Hitchen. Both were 64 pages long, cost one shilling and sixpence, and the print-runs of 25,000 sold out within weeks. For the third title, *This Woman Is Death*, Francis set up his own imprint, S. D. Francis, commissioned the artist Reginald Heade to illustrate the cover, and the legend of Hank Janson was up and running. Later the author explained his formula:

'I aimed at making Hank Janson seem a real living person. I invented a biography for him that he had roamed the world and had all sorts of exotic jobs which was widely accepted as true! So much so that Hank Janson fan clubs were formed and he received letters appealing for him to visit. A trademark figure was designed for readers to identify the books and there was even a song written about him, 'Hank Janson Blues' sung by the most popular vocalist of the time, Anne Shelton. When writing, I completely identified myself with Hank Janson. If a girl slapped his face my cheek stung. If he smelled rotting fish I felt nauseated and if he exhausted himself I had to gulp whiskey to revive myself.'

Sales of the books jumped into the millions during the next five years, enabling Stephen Francis to sell his interest in the character and live in Spain. Then in 1953, seven of the Janson titles were seized by the police, and the new publishers, New Fiction Press, were charged with selling obscene titles: *Accused, Killer, Pursuit, Vengeance, Amok, Auctioned* and *Persian Pride*. The first five were all gangster novels, the other two 'specials' dealing with white slavery in the Middle East. The books were described by the Lord Chief Justice, Lord Goddard, as 'grossly and bestially obscene' and he ruled – in much the same terms as Anthony Comstock had used about dime novels in the USA many years before – that if they were read by adolescents, 'it was no wonder there was so much juvenile crime'. Although an appeal by the directors of New Fiction Press against a prison sentence failed, the case against Stephen Francis collapsed when he returned to England to clear his name by producing receipts that he had not written these titles and claiming they were

Pursuit (1953) was one of the seven Hank Janson titles seized by the London police and charged with being obscene.

the work of one of his collaborators, Geoffrey Pardoe, who was now dead. While Francis may indeed not have *written* the books, it seems probable that he dictated the texts to Pardoe who then transcribed them and picked up a fee for his work. The truth of this matter will now never be known, and it is sad to relate that Francis, who had created another benchmark figure in hard-boiled fiction, selling over 20 million books, died almost as poor as he had been in his childhood, forgotten by all but a few close friends. The Hank Janson series went through several revamps in which he was changed from a journalist to a secret service agent, and it finally ceased after 18 years in 1970.

The success of the Hank Janson novels prompted a number of imitators in the UK, the most notable of whom also hid their identities behind pen-names. The first, Ben Sarto, unashamedly copied James Hadley Chase's writing style and the title of a classic Cole Porter song, *Miss Otis Regrets*, for his debut, *Miss Otis Comes to Piccadilly*, published by

The tough and beautiful *Miss Otis* was featured in a series of novels by Ben Sarto which so caught the public imagination they were featured in an episode of the top TV series, *Hancock's Half Hour*.

Such was the fame of Hank Janson that a song was written about him. The series was reprinted in America and also translated into several languages including Dutch: *The Beauty and the Beast* (1962) became *Schone Slaapster*.

Modern Fiction Ltd in 1946. Miss Otis was no simpering beauty, however, but a pretty tough cookie whose exotic figure and heavy-lidded blue eyes were more than a match for the playboys and gangsters who inhabited her world. She was created by Frank Dubrez Fawcett (1891–1968), who wrote 14 more titles including *Miss Otis Goes Up* (1947), *Miss Otis Blows Town* (1953) and *Miss Otis Says Yes* (1954). Fawcett was born in Great Driffield, began his working life as an office boy with the military publishers Gale & Polden and, after service with the British Army in the First World War, worked as a copy writer in a London advertising agency. In the 1920s, he began writing risque novels of bohemian life – *Shop Soiled* (1924) and *A Bride from the Street* (1928) were typical examples – and then branched out in the 1930s with stories of true crime for the magazines *Everybody's*, *London Opinion* and the *Evening News*. The UK paperback boom proved ideally suited to his skill at mass-producing tough crime fiction and, apart from the Miss Otis series, he wrote a number of hard-boiled tales set in London's Soho and the Bowery in New York as well as cases for the *Sexton Blake Library*. Fawcett had a particular facility with slang, and the various characters who featured alongside Mabie Otis were a colourful mob, especially the gangster Giuseppe Pelligrini and the protection racketeer, Beaky Bianco. Ben Sarto also enjoyed a moment of enduring fame when a title he had not actually written, *Lady Don't Fall Backwards*, was featured in a classic episode of the Tony Hancock TV series, *Hancock's Half Hour*, in the 1960s.

The curiously named writer 'Griff' was perhaps the biggest rival to Hank Janson and Ben Sarto. The name had been devised by Ernest Lionel MacKeag (1896–1974), who worked by day as the editor of children's magazines and moonlighted at night on the hard-boiled 'Griff' novels. Many of the titles

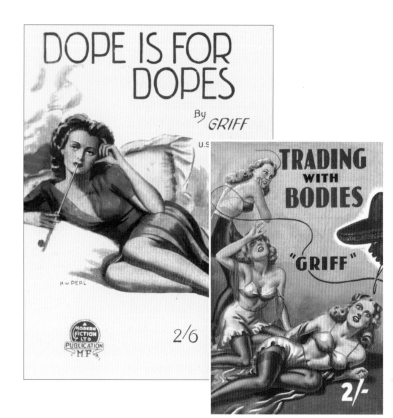

Dail Ambler was one of the few women writing
hard-boiled fiction and her Danny Spade series
was very popular for a number of years.

The name 'Griff' concealed the identity of Ernest
MacKeag whose controversial crime novels ran into
trouble with the authorities on several occasions.
Trading with Bodies was seized in a police raid in
1952 and all copies ordered to be destroyed.

featured Bill Truscott, a New York newspaperman on the *Tribune-Sun*, who later turned
private eye and specialized in breaking up
criminal organizations of vice racketeers, drug
dealers and white slave traffickers. MacKeag
was born in Newcastle-on-Tyne and as a
young man served in the Royal Navy before
joining Lloyds Newspapers Ltd as a reporter.
In 1921 he began writing stories for juvenile
publications and joined Amalgamated
Press, where he is believed to have written
over 300 episodes for a long-forgotten
detective series, *Colwyn Dane*. His first 'Griff'
story, *Rackets Incorporated* (1948), set the
style he would follow in *Only Mugs Die
Young* (1948), *Dope Is for Dopes* (1949) and
the notorious *Trading with Bodies* (1950),
with its whip-wielding cover by Ray
Theobold which was seized in a police raid in

1952 and ordered to be destroyed.

While virtually all British hard-boiled writers
used pen-names, Dail Ambler (1919–1974) was
a real person and as glamorous as the
'dolls' who appeared in the series of novels
she wrote about private eye Danny Spade. A
photograph of her, pretty and blonde in a
low-cut evening dress, adorned the back of
her paperbacks, complete with a biography
which may or may not have been true.
According to this, she had been born in
London and started working as a journalist
there before writing her first crime novel,
A Curtain of Glass, in 1954. Danny Spade
was introduced that same year in *Danny
Spade Sees Red* and continued through a
dozen more escapades in and around the
mean streets of New York. The back cover
biography continued:

'During this time Dail Ambler was asked to
write additional dialogue for the Errol Flynn
movie, *Bloodline*, and from this sold a story
entitled *Find the Lady* which took her to
Hollywood. After nine months in California,
during which she did several television shows

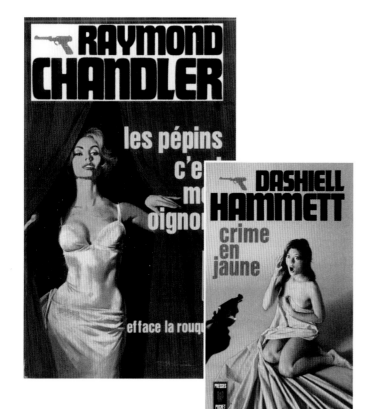

One of the most successful French partnerships in writing
le hard-boiled were Pierre Boileau and Thomas Narcejac.

Raymond Chandler and Dashiell Hammett were just two
of the American hard-boiled writers whose books were
translated into French and helped in the development of
crime noir. These two titles are *Spanish Blood* and *Dead
Yellow Women*.

and worked with top-line TV star Herbert
Marshall, she returned to England. She
subsequently wrote a play on the drug menace,
The Streeter Case, which has toured
successfully, before deciding to concentrate
on the Danny Spade series.'

At the height of the popularity of the Spade
novels, the publishers ran a competition for
readers asking them to explain 'Why I am a
Danny Spade fan' in not more than 500 words.
The top 12 entries received a signed studio
portrait of the lovely Dail. The authoress
herself appeared as the model on the cover
painted by Roger Davis for *Hold That Tiger*
(1952), which 'exposed the rackets behind the
American stage'. Despite the promising future
implied by the publisher's blurb, little was

heard of the authoress after the demise of the
series, although she is believed to have written
other crime novels under pseudonyms.

There is evidence to suggest that at least one
of the Spade stories, *The Dame Plays Rough*
(1954), was translated into French. No copy
has survived, but there is no doubt that
hard-boiled novels from Britain and especially
America were selling well in France. The
impetus that Léo Malet had given to *crime
noir* had inspired the Paris publishers
Gallimard to launch their *Série Noire* in 1945
which, under the brilliant editor Marcel
Duhamel, reprinted translations of the works
of Dashiell Hammett, Raymond Chandler,
James M. Cain and W. R. Burnett as well as
less familiar writers including Donald
Hamilton, David Goodis and Jim Thompson.
Rather appropriately, Thompson's 1954 novel
Hell Is a Woman was filmed in 1979 by Alain
Corneau as *Série Noire* starring Patrick
Dewaere and Marie Trintignant. Indeed, it was
Duhamel's interest in the work of Thompson
and his fellow American, Goodis, that led
directly to a revival of interest in their fiction.

In a matter of a few years, a whole new

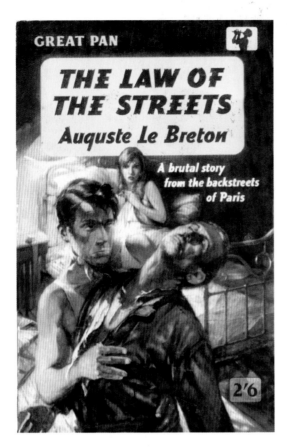

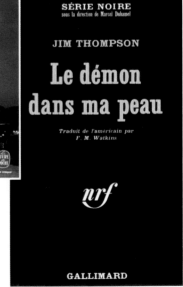

(1954) and *Le Rouge est Mis* (1954). *Rififi*, the story of a group of crooks whose mutual distrust traps them all, was famously filmed by Jules Dassin in 1955, complete with a classic robbery scene, starring Jean Servais and Carl Mohner; as was *Razzia sur la Chnouf* with a riveting performance by Jean Gabin directed by Henri Decoin. Le Breton's titles were all published in Britain and America. Albert Simonin proved himself a master of the language of the French criminal underworld and made an auspicious debut with *Touchez pas au Grisbi!* (1953). Three years later, as a result of reader demand, he issued a dictionary, *Le Petit Simonin illustré par l'example*, in which he explained the villains' *argot* and settled the argument as to what *grisbi* meant. The word was derived from *griset* or *monnaie griset*, Simonin said, and meant cash, dough, moolah – the choice was the reader's!

Today's admirers of *crime noir* have much to be thankful to the French for in reviving interest in the works of David Goodis and Jim Thompson, now widely acknowledged as

Auguste Le Breton was also the author of *Rififi* (1953), made into a classic movie by Jules Dassin.

school of French writers were developing *le hard-boiled*. Notable among these were the writing partnership of Pierre Boileau and Thomas Narcejac, Auguste Le Breton and Albert Simonin. Boileau and Narcejac made a stunning debut in 1953 with *Celle Qui N'Était Plus* (*The Woman Who Was No More*) which was filmed the following year as *Les Diaboliques* with Simone Signoret and Vera Clouzot, and directed by Henri-Georges Clouzot. The writers followed this with several more dark and murderous tales of city life, all subsequently translated into English, including *Faces in the Dark* (1955), *The Living and the Dead* (1957) and *The Evil Eye* (1959). Auguste Le Breton also produced a trio of hard-boiled masterpieces in *Du Rififi Chez les Hommes* (1953), *Razzia sur la Chnouf*

The French were largely responsible for reviving interest in the two American masters of *crime noir*, Jim Thompson and David Goodis.

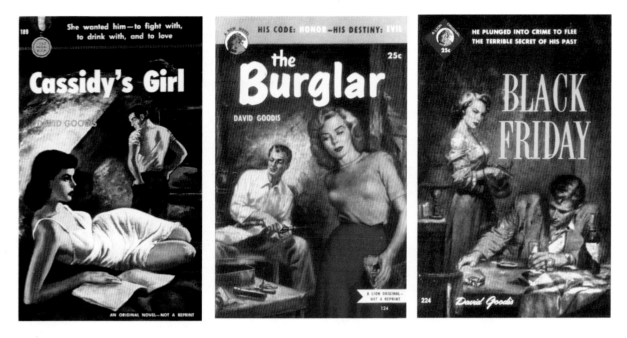

David Goodis' first *crime noir* novel, *Cassidy's Girl* (1951), sold over one million copies in its first year of publication.

Two of David Goodis' legendary Lion novels, *The Burglar* (1953) and *Black Friday* (1954).

masters of the genre. Goodis (1917–1967) was born in Philadelphia where his ambitions to become a writer were encouraged by his liberal Jewish parents. After earning a degree in journalism he worked in an advertising agency while honing his literary skills by contributing to the detective pulp magazines *New Detective* and *Big-Book Detective*, and completing his first novel, *Retreat from Oblivion*, published in 1939. After the war his novel *Dark Passage* (1946), about a man escaping from San Quentin to prove himself innocent of murdering his wife, was filmed with Humphrey Bogart and earned Goodis a six-year contract as a scriptwriter at Warner Brothers. Despite the success of this picture, Goodis and Hollywood were evidently not happy with one another and he was finally dropped by the studio and returned to Philadelphia. Here, it is said, his bitter disappointment made him into something of a recluse – and he turned his energy into writing *crime noir* novels full of violence, hatred and revenge, beginning with *Cassidy's Girl* (1951), which sold a million copies in its year of publication, *The Burglar* (1953) and *Black*

David Goodis' novel *The Dark Chase* (1947) became *Nightfall* when it was filmed in 1956 by Jacques Tourneur.

One of Jim Thompson's ground-breaking paperback originals for Gold Medal, *Texas by the Tail* (1953).

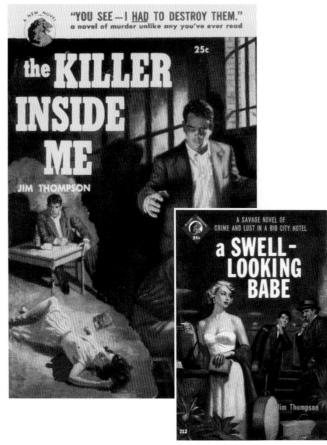

Lion also published several of Jim Thompson's novels including *A Swell-Looking Babe* (1951) and *The Killer Inside Me* (1952), which Stanley Kubrick called 'probably the most chilling and believable first-person account of a criminally warped mind I have ever encountered'.

Friday (1954). A trio of Goodis' novels from this period, *Dark Chase* (1947), *The Moon in the Gutter* (1953) and *Down There* (1956) were all destined to be taken up by the industry which had so badly used him and were filmed by brilliant French directors. *The Dark Chase* was filmed in 1956 as *Nightfall* by Jacques Tourneur with Aldo Ray, Brian Keith and Anne Bancroft; *The Moon in the Gutter* became *La Lune Dans Le Caniveau* (1983) starring Gérard Depardieu and Nastassja Kinski, directed by Jean-Jacques Beineix; and *Down There* re-emerged as *Shoot the Pianist* in 1960 with François Truffaut directing Charles Aznavour as a two-bit piano player.

It seems safe to assume that this man who ended his days so miserably will earn still greater acclaim now that his work has been returned to print. The same acclaim has also been given to James Myers Thompson (1906–1977). Here again the French found much to admire in Jim Thompson's series of paperback originals about madness, violence and obsession which were almost entirely written during the 1950s and 1960s. Jim Thompson's father was a sheriff in Andarko, Oklahoma who arrested horse thieves, foiled several jailbreaks and then had to flee to Mexico when it was discovered that he had been stealing state funds to feed his compulsion for gambling. The young Thompson grew up with a sense of insecurity and worked at several jobs including bootlegger, bellhop and oil pipe layer before turning to journalism.

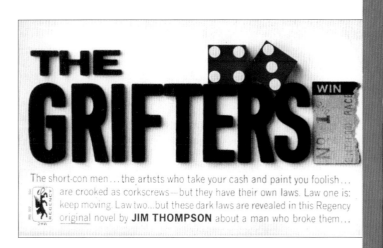

The short-con men...the artists who take your cash and paint you foolish... are crooked as corkscrews—but they have their own laws. Law one is: keep moving. Law two...but these dark laws are revealed in this Regency original novel by **JIM THOMPSON** about a man who broke them...

THE BLOODIEST
CROSS-COUNTRY RUN SINCE
BONNIE & CLYDE...
THE MOST BREATH-TAKING
CHASE SINCE
THE FRENCH CONNECTION!

BY JIM THOMPSON
THE EXPLOSIVE NOVEL!
NOW A MAJOR MOTION PICTURE!

Two more of Jim Thompson's novels that have found their way to the cinema screen – *The Getaway*, starring Steve McQueen, and *The Grifters* with Anjelica Huston, John Cusack and Annette Bening.

Like several other *crime noir* writers he felt a great affinity for the underclass and was for a time a member of the Communist Party. Then in a flurry of activity he wrote 23 novels, with ten produced in 1953 and 1954 alone. *Texas by the Tail*, *A Swell-Looking Babe*, *Savage Night* and *A Hell of a Woman* are considered the most representative of his *crime noir* style. In 1956 Thompson was recruited by Stanley Kubrick to work on *Killer's Kiss*, about a young thug who saves a girl from a lecherous dance hall owner, and the following year co-wrote one of Kubrick's greatest pictures, the anti-war tract *Paths of Glory*, starring Kirk Douglas. The film director was a great admirer of Thompson's work and referred to his novel *The Killer Inside Me* (1952) as 'probably the most chilling and believable first-person account of a criminally warped mind I have ever encountered'.

It was not until near the end of his life that the true originality of Jim Thompson's work

began fully to be recognized. In 1972, another director and admirer, Sam Peckinpah, filmed his story of *The Getaway* (1959), about a lawless ex-con and his wife, which starred Steve McQueen and Ali MacGraw. This was followed in 1990 by Stephen Frears' superb adaptation of *The Grifters* (1963), focusing on three con artists making their picaresque progress across America, with Anjelica Huston, John Cusack and Annette Bening. The picture attracted more rave reviews and received four Oscar nominations. It also confirmed the author's cult status and inspired critic Nigel Algar to observe: 'Jim Thompson did not so much transcend the genre of mystery fiction as shatter its conventions.'

The same might also be said of the entire ensemble of *crime noir* novelists mentioned in this chapter who are now so deservedly attracting a new generation of admirers and inspiring a new school of writers.

The Spies Who Came In from the Cold

THE SPIES WHO CAME IN FROM THE COLD

Harvey Birch is a tall, powerfully-built man with an alert look and an eye for a pretty girl. Accomplished at disguise, he can appear as an itinerant peddler or a gentleman of means, and handles himself and his drink with a practiced ease brought about by years of experience. Birch is a secret agent; not a contemporary character from the world of espionage, but the hero of *The Spy*, written in 1821 by James Fenimore Cooper and the very first novel of its kind in English. He is an American agent, in fact, operating during the War of Independence. In order to accomplish his mission, he has to pretend loyalty to the British, but when he finds himself caught between the Americans (who think he is

British) and the British (upon whom he is actually spying) he becomes, in the phrase now almost synonymous with the genre, the first spy in literature to be 'out in the cold'.

The spy novel has, in fact, developed as an integral part of the classic era of crime fiction. To begin with, Harvey Birch might almost have rubbed shoulders with Auguste Dupin. Then, by the middle years of the twentieth century when all the integral parts of the detective story were in place, the arrival of James Bond signalled the end of the old era of espionage and the beginning of the new. It has been repeatedly said, of course, that spying is actually the world's *second* oldest profession, and in the *Iliad* there is the account of Odysseus' night-time excursion to spy out the disposition of the Trojan forces. Not until the last century, though, did the secret agent become a hero of fiction, and this final chapter looks at the characters who plied the trade of espionage, from Birch to Bond, and their creators. John G. Cawelti and Bruce A. Rosenberg have neatly encapsulated this period of evolution in their book, *The Spy Story* (1987):

'Many individual writers contributed to the creation, the broadening and the increasing sophistication of the spy story ... in particular, the accomplishments of John Buchan, Eric Ambler, Graham Greene, Ian Fleming and John le Carré have shaped the evolution of the spy story from romantic adventure to a many-sided literary genre.'

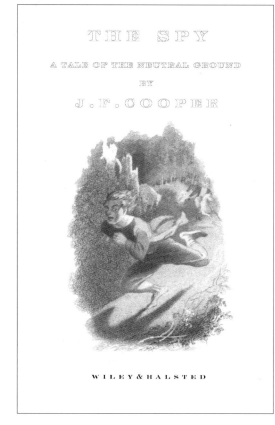

THE SPY

A TALE OF THE NEUTRAL GROUND

BY

J. F. COOPER

WILEY & HALSTED

The first fictional secret agent, the American Harvey Birch in *The Spy* by James Fenimore Cooper (1821). Birch proved himself to have the attributes of athleticism, bravery and mastery of disguise that single out the great spy.

It was perhaps appropriate that the same country which gave the world the detective story should also invent the fictional spy. It seems probable that James Fenimore Cooper was inspired by the famous case of Major André, who was captured and executed by the British during the War of Independence – and indeed he is mentioned several times in *The Spy*. Fenimore Cooper had, though, clearly made a study of the art of spying, as he explains in the introduction to his book, published by Wiley & Halsted of New York. Maintaining that a spy needed to be 'cool, shrewd and fearless by nature', he continued:

'It was his office to learn in what part of the country the agents of the crown were making their secret efforts to embody men – to repair to the place, enlist, appear zealous in the cause he affected to serve, and otherwise to get possession of as many of the secrets of the enemy as possible. These he, of course, communicated to his employers, who took all the means in their power to counteract the plans of the English, and frequently with great success. It will readily be conceived that a service like this was attended with great personal hazard. In addition to the danger of discovery, there was the daily risk of falling into the hands of the Americans themselves, who invariably visited the sins of this nature more severely on the natives of the country than on the Europeans who fell into their hands.'

Substitute the words 'foreign power' for 'Americans' and there – in a paragraph written almost 200 years ago – is a blueprint for the espionage novel. It remains a fact, of course, that Fenimore Cooper is better known for his series of novels of frontiersmen and Indians, known generically as the 'Leatherstocking Tales', than for creating the spy novel. These books, *The Pioneers* (1823), *The Last of the Mohicans* (1826), *The Deerslayer* (1841) and

THE SPY WHO CAME IN FROM THE COLD

This is, in our view, a novel of the first order —a terrible novel, of great actuality and high political import. It is also immensely thrilling.

J. B. Priestley writes:
"Superbly constructed, with an atmosphere of chilly hell."

JOHN LE CARRÉ

John Le Carré's 1963 novel which 'brought the espionage genre of age'.

others, made him the first American novelist to gain world fame, and have continued to overshadow the importance of *The Spy*. James Fenimore Cooper (1789–1851) was the son of a wealthy landowner who founded Cooperstown, and the young man spent five years in naval service before becoming a highly imaginative and prolific writer, enjoying his first success with *The Spy*. He was an apologist for American democracy, but after several years in Europe returned to the US and became a mordant critic of the shortcomings of the nation's democracy. Several of his novels have been viewed by critics as forerunners of satire of the American way of life.

In *The Spy*, Harvey Birch is seen as an outcast roaming the parts of New York State

Sir George Chesney's pioneer novel of a secret invasion of England, *The Battle of Dorking*, first published in 1871.

that are a no-man's-land in the colonial days. He is self-sufficient, carrying what he needs with him, and employing his expertise, his wits and his agility to avoid capture by the enemy. He has a slightly cynical attitude towards the Establishment – such as it is – and avoids its restrictions, occasionally even breaking them to help his mission. His clandestine existence makes him a figure of mystery, brave in the eyes of men and appealing to women, whom he charms and leaves as easily as he meets them. In an amusing episode, Birch disguises himself as a woman to fool a British colonel, revealing 'herself' when the necessary information has been extracted from the blustering lecher. 'The spy of the neutral ground' – as he is called – is a fascinating character who represents, 'one of the first attempts to analyze the professional exercise of duplicity', according to historian Michael Cox.

Despite the success of Fenimore Cooper's book, it was to be almost half a century before the next spy novel appeared, across the Atlantic in Britain. Suspicion between the various European nations, each with their vast empires, had been growing for years, with the result that Britain, France, Germany and Russia had all quietly set up their own intelligence-gathering operations. Indeed, the growing fear of military power and internal anarchy that encouraged the rise of the spy can be found reflected in a small group of novels and short stories published in the late nineteenth century, notably *The Battle of Dorking* which appeared anonymously in the May 1871 issue of *Blackwood's Magazine*. A first-person narrative, it describes the successful invasion of England by German forces, which even some clever clandestine work is unable to halt. Following hard on the Franco-German war of 1870 in which Germany had defeated France, the topical plot proved enormously popular with readers and it was quickly reprinted in paperback form, selling 80,000 copies in a month and becoming a best-seller in Britain, America and Canada. It was even subsequently translated into German as *Was England Erwartet*! At a stroke, the book launched what became known as the 'future war genre'. It was the immediate precursor of the modern spy novel.

It was not until the publication of *The Battle of Dorking* in book form in its distinctive pale purple cover that the anonymous author was revealed as a distinguished military officer, Sir George Tomkyns Chesney (1830–1895). Chesney had risen through the ranks of the Royal Engineers and in 1868 founded the Royal Indian Civil Engineering College in Staines. He was knighted in 1890 and made a General in 1892, shortly before his retirement that same year. Thereafter Chesney served as a Conservative MP for Oxford and continued to write occasional articles for *Blackwood's*

The Great War in England in 1897 by William Le Queux, which was published in 1894, is credited with playing a major part in the development of the spy story.

William Le Queux also created the first two series characters in spy fiction: Duckworth Drew in The Man from Downing Street (1904) and Gerry Sant, several of whose adventures to thwart the plans of ruthless foreign agents appeared in The Premier magazine before book publication.

Magazine warning about the poor state of Britain's defences, after having caught the public imagination with his remarkable narrative of a 'future invasion'. The impact of the book encouraged other writers to take up the theme, although 'sequels' like After the Battle of Dorking; or, What Became of the Invaders by Colonel Hanley (1872) and the anonymous Other Side of the Battle of Dorking (1873) were neither as original nor enjoyed the same popularity as Chesney's book. Chesney wrote one more novel, The New Ordeal (1879), in which war has been replaced by tournaments, with the opposing nations putting forward their champions to settle any disputes.

Sir Arthur Conan Doyle was also interested in the clandestine operations of nations – and several of the Sherlock Holmes adventures synthesized espionage with detection. The

Sign of Four (1890) features intelligence gathering on the colonial frontier rather like The Spy, while anarchist terrorism and labour agitation appear in The Valley of Fear (1915). 'The Naval Treaty', published in the Strand in October 1893, is one of the earliest short stories to feature espionage when Holmes successfully recovers a secret document. The Great Detective is also called upon by his brother Mycroft, the shadowy head of the British Secret Service, to help find the missing plans of a top secret submarine which threaten to cause an international crisis in 'The Bruce-Partington Plans' (Strand, December 1908). In 'His Last Bow' (Strand, September 1917), Holmes even comes out of retirement on the eve of the First World War to defeat the plots of a German agent.

However, the man who really deserves credit for helping to develop the spy novel is William

Le Queux, who picked up what Chesney had begun in *The Great War in England in 1897*, published in 1894, and followed this with *The Invasion of 1910* (1905), *The Man from Downing Street* (1904), *The Czar's Spy* (1905), *The German Spy* (1907) and many more. He also created the first two series characters in spy fiction: Duckworth Drew and Gerry Sant. William Tufnell Le Queux (1864–1927) was a larger-than-life figure who actually claimed to have been employed as a spy by the British Secret Service. Even after he had left the service, he was allegedly able to obtain 'secret' documents from German and Russian sources on which to base his work. He was further said to have been a pioneer expert in wireless transmission, which he used to help his espionage activity, and maintained that he began writing stories about secret agents in order to finance his work for British Intelligence. Le Queux liked his publishers to refer to him on the dust jackets of his books as 'The Master of Mystery', and this, indeed, he was. His autobiography, *Things I Know About Kings, Celebrities & Crooks* (1923), is full of anecdotes though very little detail, while the only biography about him, *The Real Le Queux* (1938) by Norman St Barbe Sladen, slavishly relates much of the same material put into the third person. The facts, such as they are, indicate that he was born in London, the son of a French father and an English mother, studied art in London and Paris, and then got a job as a reporter on the London evening paper, *The Globe*. There is probably some truth in the story that he covered the Jack the Ripper murders and he certainly visited Russia in 1912–1913 to cover the Balkan War for the London *Daily Mail*. It was in 1893, with one book, *Guilty Bonds* (1891), about a political conspiracy in Russia, already published, and another, *The Great War in England in 1897*, nearing completion, that Le Queux gave up his newspaper job.

In *The Great War in England in 1897*, Le Queux describes the French and Russians joining forces to conquer England. The invasion is assisted with information about British forces provided by a German spy, Count Karl von Beilstein, who masterminds bomb outrages and stirs up anarchist forces to assist the coalition army. After half the country has been laid to waste by the invaders, the British successfully retaliate and, during the mêlée, Von Beilstein is captured. The spy meets his death at the hands of a firing squad on Horse Guards' Parade. The book became an overnight best-seller and thereafter Le Queux, according to his own account, devoted himself to travelling around Europe looking for evidence of spies and invasion plans and carrying out patriotic activities on behalf of Britain. Whether or not he actually found any secret documents as he claimed is open to the gravest doubt; nor is there any evidence that he was ever in the pay of the government. Early in the new century, Le Queux returned to his favourite topic in *The Invasion of 1910* (1905), which is said to have accurately predicted the First World War, sold over a million copies and was translated into 27 languages, according to the author. This was followed by *Spies of the Kaiser* (1909), which suggested there was already a network of hundreds of secret agents in Britain. Following its publication, Le Queux received dozens of letters from readers denouncing wholly innocent people as spies on the flimsiest of evidence! He, though, accepted these missives as fact and renewed his urgings to the Secret Service Bureau to take action. In the interim, he had also written one of his best novels, *The Man from Downing Street* (1904), another first-person narrative in which a French plot to overthrow the British Empire is exposed and defeated by the anonymous secret agent. Another glut of spy novels appeared from Le Queux's pen during the First World War:

Number 70 Berlin (1915), *The Spy Hunter* (1917) and *The Minister of Evil* (1918). He also continued the adventures of Duckworth Drew of the Secret Service, introduced in 1903 in *Secrets of the Foreign Office* as a man possessing half a dozen nationalities and personalities:

'As the chief confidential agent of the British government, Duckworth Drew is held in fear by the diplomatic circle in Europe, and is heartily hated by all the Secret Chancelleries. The quiet-mannered Gustav Dreux, commercial traveller of Paris, would surely never be recognized as Herr Richter, wine merchant of Mannheim; as Signor Tommaso Orlandini, machinery agent of Milan; and, least of all, as Duckworth Drew of Downing Street, secret agent in the employ of the Foreign Office, and, next to His Majesty's Secretary of State for Foreign Affairs, one of the most powerful and important pillars of England's supremacy.'

Drew, in his 40s, unobtrusive and of medium height, is quite a contrast to Gerry Sant, who made his debut in 1918 in *Sant of the Secret Service*: 'Cheerful, optimistic, and the most modest of men, Gerry Sant has seldom spoken of his own adventures. The son of a certain nobleman who must here remain nameless, and hence the scion of a noble house, he has graduated through all stages of the dark and devious ways of espionage. Today the name of "Sant of the Secret Service" is synonymous with all that is ingenious, resourceful and daring.' The prolific Le Queux published a number of the Drew and Sant stories in popular journals including *The Windsor* and *The Premier*, where they remained uncollected as their author's popularity declined in the 1920s, leaving him virtually forgotten today. Although there is every reason to question how real a spy William Le Queux was, there is an argument that his contribution

to the paranoia about spies operating in Britain before the First World War did prompt the decision to set up MI5, Britain's internal security service, and its sister agency MI6, the Secret Intelligence Service. Belatedly, too, it has been acknowledged that his espionage stories anticipated almost every development in the form until the novels of Eric Ambler.

A contemporary of Le Queux, E. Phillips Oppenheim, who gloried in his publisher's epithet of 'The Prince of Storytellers', made a significant contribution to the spy story and also wrote a number of popular detective tales among his 150 books. The first of his novels, *The Mysterious Mr Sabin* (1898), was a prediction of a future conflict with Germany thwarted by the implacable character of the title. Oppenheim later called the book 'the

E. Phillips Oppenheim's spy novel, *The Mysterious Mr Sabin*, strikingly illustrated by J. Ambrose Walton, was published in 1898.

Irish Free State Government. He was tried, condemned to death, and two weeks later taken to Dublin where he was executed by a firing squad. At this time, Childers was regarded as 'the best hated man in the British Isles' – Winston Churchill branded him 'a mischief-making, murderous renegade' – and even some of his Republican friends suspected him of being a British agent. Despite this ignominy, *The Riddle of the Sands: A Record of Secret Service* had been on sale for two decades (it was not published in America until 1915) and was acknowledged as a classic. It has remained in print to this day, keeping alive the memory of the extraordinary man who wrote *the* first modern spy novel.

Four years after Childers' *The Riddle of the Sands*, another author with a great love of the sea, Joseph Conrad, wrote *The Secret Agent*, the first truly realistic and tragic spy novel. It is also the first major work to feature a double agent. Verloc is a spy and a killer, largely through laziness and inertia. He is not a man driven by evil motives yet becomes involved in an anarchist plot to commit violence in the heart of London. Verloc's wife, Winnie, who has married him solely for comfort and security, is not involved in the plot, but is dragged inexorably towards murder and suicide. Conrad based *The Secret Agent* in part on an actual historical incident and on his own experiences as a young man in Poland observing the mysterious world of Russian revolutionaries and agents.

The author was born Teodor Józef Konrad Korzeniowski (1857–1924), in Berdiczew, the son of a Polish nobleman. His father was a revolutionary with literary gifts, and perhaps inspired by his example, the young Józef joined the crew of an English merchant ship in 1878 and worked to gain his ticket as a master. In 1884, he became a naturalized English citizen and after several more years at sea, settled in Ashford, Kent, and commenced

Cover of a later American edition of Joseph Conrad's classic spy novel, *The Secret Agent* (1907), which was based on the author's own experiences.

writing the books which would make him one of the great literary figures of the twentieth century: masterpieces like *Lord Jim* (1900) and *Chance* (1914) and the superb collection of short stories *Twixt Land and Sea* (1912). Conrad returned to the world of espionage in 1911 with *Under Western Eyes*, which features the exploits of a double agent, Razumov. *The Secret Agent* exerted a great fascination on Alfred Hitchcock, who filmed the story as *Sabotage* in 1936 starring Oscar Homolka and Sylvia Sidney.

An admirer of the works of both Conrad and Erksine Childers was Scottish author John Buchan, who added a classic spy tale to the genre in 1915 with *The Thirty-Nine Steps*. This book, with its wild Scottish setting, use of mysterious clues and a plot line that fuelled contemporary public anxieties, made it 'the first major version of the twentieth-century spy story', according to John Cawelti and Bruce Rosenberg. The story also introduces a heroic agent in Richard Hannay, who becomes the object of a deadly manhunt across Scotland in the days just preceding the First World War. Hannay is wanted by the police, who believe he has murdered an American agent, and by foreign spies who want to stop him from delivering secret information to the British authorities. The information concerns a German scheme to steal British naval secrets to enable the destruction of the fleet, and ultimately the invasion of England. In this and subsequent adventures, Hannay shows himself to be exceptionally fit and good at disguise, able to pass himself off as anyone from a milkman to a chauffeur or even a film producer. He is renowned for being able to do the 'old Mashona trick' – catching a knife thrown at him in his teeth – but loses the top of his left thumb when it is shot off by an adversary, Dominick Medina. Hannay is a courageous but modest man and, curiously for someone involved in the world of espionage, rather ill at ease with women. He does age, though, in his subsequent adventures: *Greenmantle* (1916), in which he links up with a US agent, Blenkiron, to avoid a Holy War in the East; *Mr Standfast* (1919), about a German spy forced to his death at the hands of his own countrymen; and *The Three Hostages* (1924), which is again set in Scotland with the intrepid spy, now in his 50s, stalking the mastermind behind a Bolshevik plot.

John Buchan (1875–1940) was born in Perth, the son of a minister, and educated at Glasgow University and Brasenose College, Oxford, where in 1898 he won the Newdigate Prize. He studied law in London and, after a period as private secretary to the High Commissioner of South Africa, followed his inclination for writing by joining the publishing firm of Thomas Nelson & Sons. He wrote his first work, a historical romance, *Sir Quixote of the Moors* (1895), when he was just 20, and during the First World War operated as a war correspondent in France. Despite his busy life in publishing (he was the first to spot the

potential of *Trent's Last Case* by E. C. Bentley), politics (he was an MP for the Scottish Universities between 1927 and 1935), and his appointment as Governor General of Canada in 1935, John Buchan still found the time to write over 50 books of high adventure: 'Elementary tales which the Americans call the "dime novel" and which we know as "shockers", where the incidents defy the probabilities and march just inside the borders of possibility,' he once called them. Indeed, his robustious style gave rise to the expression describing this kind of book as 'Buchanesque'. He was especially pleased at the success of the Richard Hannay spy novels; the hero was modelled on one of his military heroes, General Edmund 'Tiny' Ironside, whom he had met in South Africa. To date, *The Thirty-Nine Steps* has been filmed three times: by Alfred Hitchcock in 1935 with Robert Donat; in 1960

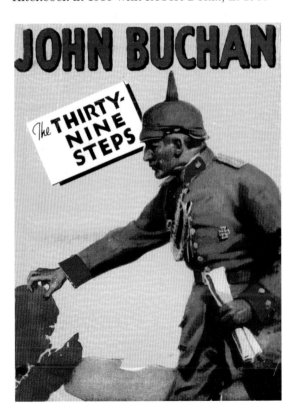

John Buchan's novel *The Thirty-Nine Steps* (1913) is one of the most famous spy stories of all time.

readers and was reprinted again in 1954 after the Second World War. Wallace's other spy, James Lexington Mortlake, works for the US Intelligence Service where he is known as 'The Black', not because of the colour of his skin, but because he always dresses in black, and when on covert operations wears a black mask! The series of episodes about Mortlake's career gathering vital information for America and Britain were first published in *Answers* magazine between 1923 and 1924, the best subsequently collected as *The Man from Morocco* (1926), and in America initially as *The Black* (1927) and subsequently as *Souls in Shadows*. In 1959, a series of Edgar Wallace films were made by director Alfred Vohrer, with Joachim Fuchsberger taking the lead role in a version of the James Mortlake story.

If neither the inept Heine or masked Mortlake managed to cause much of a stir in the spy genre, the opposite was true of Bulldog Drummond, who appeared in 1920. The adventures of this heroic, tough and intensely patriotic man written by 'Sapper', a pseudonym that ineffectively disguised the identity of Herman Cyril McNeile (1888–1937), were best-sellers for years both before and after the author's death, when the series was continued for a time by his close friend (and a partial model for Drummond) Gerard Fairlie. Captain Hugh Drummond DSO, MC – Bulldog to his friends – is a First World War officer who finds the peacetime world a little dull for his taste, so that whenever the nation is threatened, he is ready for action. The Captain is prepared to take any risk, even on occasion endangering his pretty wife, Phyllis, as he battles German and Russian adversaries, in particular the arch-villain Carl Peterson, whom he runs into in his first case, *Bulldog Drummond*. In it, Peterson is hellbent on promoting a Russian plot to bring down the British government through a paralyzing general strike. Drummond has a particular loathing for communists 'and

other unwashed people of that type', to use his own expression. He is good with his fists and a gun, never afraid to use violence or break the law, and is often contemptuous of the police when the security of the country is threatened. A master of the stiff upper lip no matter how dangerous the situation, Drummond does have a few of the traits that would later flourish in the persona of James Bond: he loves fast cars, frequents nightclubs where he plays a mean game of cards, and will take a drink – though not shaken or stirred.

Author H. C. McNeile joined the Royal Engineers and in 1915 fought in the Battle of the Somme. It was here, deep in the trenches, in the intervals between the gunfire, that he

The redoubtable Bulldog Drummond spent years tackling enemy agents and *femmes fatales* in stories such as *Bulldog Drummond* (1920) and *The Female of the Species* (1928) by Sapper, aka H. C. McNeile.

began to write short stories about a do-or-die young soldier, Sergeant Michael Cassidy. The tales were accepted by a national newspaper, but because of army regulations forbidding officers from publishing anything under their own name, McNeile opted for 'Sapper' after his military job. Back in England, McNeile had the idea for Bulldog Drummond, based partly on himself and partly on his friend, Gerard Fairlie. The success of the first book and its sequels, especially *The Female of the Species* (1928), which introduced the archetypal *femme fatale*, Irma Soldanis, Carl Peterson's mistress, and *The Return of Bulldog Drummond* (1932), made the author a wealthy man and allowed him to travel widely to find even more exotic locations for his stories. McNeile's sudden death from a war-related illness left thousands of fans disappointed until Fairlie, who had already collaborated with McNeile on several short stories and plays, continued the series in 1938 with *Bulldog Drummond on Dartmoor*, reaching a finale in *The Return of the Black Gang* in 1954. A number of actors have played Drummond on the screen including Carlyle Blackwell, Jack Buchanan, Ralph Richardson and Ronald Colman, with Warner Oland (of Fu Manchu fame) appearing as Carl Peterson.

Major Desmond Okewood, a literary contemporary of Bulldog Drummond, was also involved in a long-running battle with a sinister adversary – Dr Adolf Grundt, a German secret service agent known to British Intelligence as 'The Man with the Club-Foot' and to those under his command in the 'G' Branch of the German Secret Service as 'Der Stelze'. Okewood is a resolute, self-effacing man – 'The interesting thing about secret service yarns is what you have to leave out,' he remarks on one occasion – and when off duty he loves the company of friends, playing sport and dining at the Berkeley Grill. Of his tempestuous adversary, Okewood says, 'He is

the kind of man who glories in the blackest crimes and his revelations would eclipse those of Vidocq.' The series of novels were written by George Valentine Williams (1883–1946) also a soldier turned writer, starting in 1918 with *The Man with the Club-Foot*, continuing the following year in *The Secret Hand: Some Further Adventures of Desmond Okewood of the British Secret Service* and running on through the 1930s and 1940s until *Courier to Marrakesh* in 1944. Born in London, Williams was the son of a journalist and became the Berlin correspondent for Reuters in the early 1900s, which provided him with the background for his later series. He served in the Irish Guards during the First World War and was twice wounded, winning the Military Cross for bravery. Newspaper assignments in

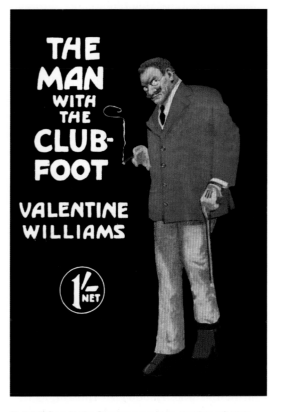

Dr Adolf Grundt, the German spy whose cunning schemes were always being foiled by Major Desmond Okewood in the series of novels by Valentine Williams including *The Man with the Club-Foot* (1918).

Europe, North Africa and America gave him further insights into the workings of espionage and he also wrote a notable biography, *Gaboriau: Father of Detective Novels*, in 1923. During the Second World War, Williams was seconded to the Political Warfare Department at Woburn Abbey. Only one of the eight novels featuring Okewood and Dr Grundt was filmed, *The Crouching Beast* (1928), directed in 1935 by Victor Hanbury, starring Richard Bird and Fritz Kortner in a complex plot to steal secret plans.

There can be no greater contrast with any of the Bulldog Drummond and Desmond Okewood books than *Ashenden; or, The British Agent* by W. Somerset Maugham, published in 1928 and now acknowledged as the first realistic novel about the life of a spy. The authenticity of this remarkable series of episodes set in the First World War is due in no small measure to the author having been a spy himself. It presents those working in espionage not as brawny heroes involved in desperate situations, with beautiful women nearly always at hand, but as ordinary people caught up in extraordinary circumstances. The book has been described as an antidote to the John Buchan school and an important stepping stone to the world of John le Carré. Ashenden is a writer who is asked to work as a secret service agent because his profession allows him to travel throughout Europe without arousing undue suspicion. The fact that he can speak several languages encourages him to accept the mission, and he senses the work will provide him with material for future books. Objective in his approach to people, Ashenden understands evil and appreciates both the good and the bad in those on either side of the political divide. Throughout his mission, which involves him recruiting and directing the operations of other spies, Ashenden never forgets the parting words of the man who recruited *him*, the mysterious

Colonel 'R' (a character who anticipates James Bond's chief, 'M', by a quarter of a century): 'If you do well, you'll get no thanks, and if you get into trouble, you'll get no help.'

William Somerset Maugham (1874–1965) was born in Paris of Irish parents, but raised in Kent by a strict clergyman uncle following the death of his mother and father. Educated at King's School, Canterbury, he studied philosophy and literature and then qualified as a doctor at St Thomas's Hospital in London. Maugham suffered badly from tuberculosis, which gave him a rapport with the men and women he met during his first practice in the London slums. These experiences fired his real desire to be a writer and inspired his first novel, *Liza of Lambeth* (1897), and later the critically acclaimed, semi-autobiographical *Of Human Bondage* (1915) with its club-footed

Another landmark in the history of spy fiction, *Ashenden* by Somerset Maugham, first published in 1928.

hero. During the First World War, Maugham served with a Red Cross unit in France and was then recruited by British Intelligence to operate in Geneva and Petrograd, where he attempted to prevent the outbreak of a Bolshevik revolution. Nearly a decade later he wrote *Ashenden*, which was hailed as another benchmark in the spy story genre. Although he never returned to the topic again, Maugham did serve with the British Ministry of Information in Paris at the start of the Second World War, fled the advancing Germans in 1940, and spent the remainder of the conflict in the USA. Alfred Hitchcock made a brilliant version of the Ashenden stories, retitled *The Secret Agent*, in 1936 starring Robert Young, Madeleine Carroll, John Gielgud and Peter Lorre.

The move towards the realistic spy novel was furthered by two other British writers, Graham Greene and Eric Ambler, who turned it into a complex and ironic tale of corruption, betrayal and conspiracy. Like Ashenden, their heroes are ordinary enough people caught in the web of espionage who often operate in what they believe to be friendly territory, though unlike their dashing predecessors they rarely save countries from invasion or thwart some fiendish international plot. The aftermath of the First World War provided a number of ideal villains for these stories in the shape of men who had profited from the conflict, wealthy manufacturers and capitalists, for example. But luck rather than bravery was more often than not what saved the lives of this new breed of anti-heroes. The concept, which would dominate the genre until the 1950s, was started by Graham Greene (1904–1991) with *Stamboul Train* published in 1932 – perhaps better known today by its American title, *Orient Express* – and continued in *A Gun for Sale* (1936) (aka *This Gun for Hire* in the USA), *The Confidential Agent* (1939) and *The Ministry of Fear* (1943).

Two of Graham Greene's brilliantly atmospheric spy novels, *Stamboul Train* (1932) and *The Confidential Agent* (1939).

'Entertainments' was the word Graham Greene preferred to use about his novels of espionage which, because of their style and mixture of the seedy and the extraordinary, evoke a particular atmosphere of what has been called 'Greeneland'. The author, who was born in Berkhampstead, Hertfordshire, graduated from Oxford and began his working life on the London *Times* and as film critic for *The Spectator*. He launched his career as a novelist in 1929 with *The Man Within*. Three years later came *Stamboul Train*, which had such a profound effect on the spy story and is all the more remarkable because Greene had never ridden on the Orient Express. His inspiration had, in fact, been Arthur Honegger's musical picture of a train, *Pacific 231*, popular ever since its composition in 1923. *Stamboul Train* is the story of the chase to capture an exiled Communist leader, and it received huge literary acclaim, as did Greene's *A Gun for*

Sale, about a paid assassin, Arthur Raven, who is pursued for the murder of a Socialist minister and decides to turn on those who hired him. The third of Greene's spy novels, *The Confidential Agent* (1939), with the central character known only as 'D', has been described by Cawelti and Rosenberg as 'one of the earliest examples of the spy who comes in from the cold a failure, the humanized spy, one who learns that some things are more important than confidential missions, and who lives to tell about it'. It was also one of Graham Greene's own favourites among his works. During the Second World War, Greene served with the Foreign Office on special duty in West Africa, and wrote a further espionage title, *The Ministry of Fear* (1943), in which a man released from an asylum where he has been confined for murdering his wife becomes involved with a curious spy ring.

All of Graham Greene's spy novels have been filmed. *Orient Express* was made in 1934 with Norman Foster and Heather Angel, and *This Gun for Hire* in 1942, starring Alan Ladd, Veronica Lake and Laird Cregar in a script changed by W. R. Burnett to an American locale. Fritz Lang directed *The Ministry of Fear* (1944) with Ray Milland and Marjorie Reynolds, and the following year Charles Boyer, Lauren Bacall and Peter Lorre co-starred in *The Confidential Agent*. Probably, though, Greene's most famous movie is *The Third Man*, which he wrote for the screen in 1950. After the release of Carol Reed's classic film about the search by an American novelist, Rollo Martins (Joseph Cotton), for his friend Harry Lime (Orson Welles) in postwar Vienna, a novelized version was published. The character of Harry Lime has become something of an icon, and Orson Welles reprised the role in a British TV series in 1951, followed in the 1960s by a second series featuring Michael Rennie.

The first espionage novel by Eric Ambler,

Uncommon Danger (1937, aka *Background to Danger* in the US), signalled another radical change from previous spy stories. In it, a victim of circumstance, a journalist named Kenton working in Nuremburg who has lost all his money, is inveigled by the mysterious Herr Sachs into carrying some documents across the German border to avoid the Gestapo. When Kenton arrives to collect his fee, he finds only the body of Sachs with a knife in the back, and is at once plunged into the middle of an international intrigue. This book, and those which followed in the next two years – *Epitaph for a Spy* (1938), *The Mask of Dimitrios* (1939, aka *A Coffin for Dimitrios* in America which was actually the author's original title) and *Journey into Fear* (1940) – quickly marked Ambler as an equally important voice in the spy field. (Greene,

Graham Greene's memorable character Harry Lime became the hero of a TV series in 1951 which was also novelized.

indeed, later referred to Ambler as 'unquestionably our best thriller writer'.)

Born in Lewisham, London, Eric Clifford Ambler (1909–1998) was the only child of parents who ran a marionette show called The Whatnots. While at school, he excelled at mathematics, which he later explained as one of the reasons he liked writing puzzling thrillers. After studying at London University, Ambler joined an advertising agency and among the campaigns he worked on was one for a chocolate laxative. He tried unsuccessfully to write plays, until circumstances brought about a dramatic change in his fortunes in 1934 when he was on holiday in Marseilles. While playing cards with a bartender, Ambler was cheated out of his money and, with nothing else to do but await the boat home, spent his time pointing an imaginary rifle from his hotel balcony at the crossroads where the bartender caught his tram home. A few weeks later Ambler saw a newsreel showing the murder of King Alexander of Yugoslavia and realized the place he had chosen for his target practice was exactly the same as that picked by the assassin. He commented later, 'I felt I had found a fresh bit of my character which was an assassin and set about writing stories that exploited the edgy mood of the times.'

Epitaph for a Spy takes place partly in an early Nazi concentration camp and features a language teacher on holiday in the south of France in whose camera are found photographs of a secret naval installation. Ambler's masterpiece, *The Mask of Dimitrios*, pitched another writer into the obsessive hunt for the evil Dimitrios Makropoulos, master of espionage and murder, who is assumed to be dead but turns out to be very much alive. The book, which is largely set in Turkey and Bulgaria, has an interesting parallel with *Stamboul Train* in that Ambler had never visited the localities which he describes so vividly. Curiously, he later received a letter

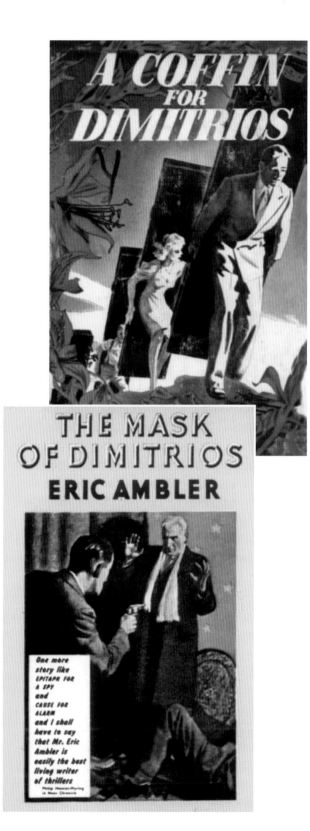

Eric Ambler's famous spy novel, *The Mask of Dimitrios* (1939), was published in America as *A Coffin for Dimitrios*, and first editions of both are now very rare.

from a drug dealer in Paris called Eliopoulos, who suggested it would be a good idea if he did not visit the city for some time! *Journey into Fear* has Graham, an engineer from a British armaments firm, stumbling onto some sensitive information and fleeing for his life on a small Italian cargo ship. During the Second World War, Ambler served initially with the Royal Artillery and was then posted to the Army Film Unit for whom he wrote numerous army training films, including one with Peter Ustinov, *The New Lot*. In the 1950s, he went to Hollywood and scripted a number of major films including the first film about the Titanic disaster, *A Night to Remember* (1958), and *Mutiny on the Bounty* (1962). Although Eric Ambler wrote several more thrillers, none achieved the success of his early quartet of espionage classics. Joseph Cotton and Orson Welles, the successful pairing in *The Third Man*, also co-starred in *Journey into Fear*, made in 1942 by director Norman Foster. Raoul Walsh directed the film version of *Background to Danger* (1943) with George Raft, Sydney Greenstreet and Peter Lorre, and Greenstreet and Lorre again appeared in the 1944 version of *The Mask of Dimitrios* with Zachary Scott. (An undistinguished remake in 1976 starred Zero Mostel, Shelley Winters and Vincent Price.) *Epitaph for a Spy* was retitled *Hotel Reserve* and made into a lack-lustre film in 1944 with James Mason, Lucie Mannheim and Raymond Lovell.

Surprisingly, there was only one major American contribution to the spy genre in the interwar years: Anthony Hamilton, known as 'America's Secret Service Agent Number 1,' created by 'Frederick Frost', another of the pseudonyms of Frederick Faust (1892–1944), aka Max Brand, creator of Dr Kildare and the many westerns which established his reputation. William F. Nolan, Faust's biographer, claims that Hamilton was 'decades ahead of James Bond', although the pictures

of him in *Detective Fiction Weekly* making his first appearance in the novelette, 'Spy!' (27 April 1935) in which he seeks to expose a plot to overthrow the King of Lithonia, present him as a rather dandified figure wearing a monocle! In fact, he likes to throw his enemies off the scent by adopting the persona of a playboy and has a beautiful assistant, Louise Curran, never far from his side. 'Spy!' proves to be Hamilton's first brush with Japan's number one agent, De Graulchier, who plots further disasters aimed at undermining the world order (and Russia in particular) in a trio of novels, *Secret Agent Number One* (1936), *Spy Meets Spy* (1937) and *The Bamboo Whistle* (1937). Although all these stories of the 'US Secret Service Agent' are full of rather stereotypical characters from an earlier era, their descriptions of a vast secret organization

Above & opposite: A significant American spy figure between the two World Wars was Anthony Hamilton, who appeared in several novels written by Frederick Frost, a pen-name of the man best known as Max Brand.

the war, all of which began with a double 0 number. With the elements of his story in place, Fleming wrote the 62,000 words of *Casino Royale* in just seven weeks. The book was published with a simple dust jacket devised by the author himself consisting of nine red hearts and the title in yellow. It was not until 1957 that the more picturesque 'upside-down' cover by Pat Marriott appeared on a reissue when the series had become an international success with fans all over the world, including US President John F. Kennedy. The unmistakable series of illustrations by Richard Chopping began with the fifth title, *From Russia, With Love* (1957), and continued through to the 'revivals' written by Robert Markham (aka Kingsley Amis) such as *Colonel Sun* (1968), and the continuing books John Gardner launched in 1981 with *Licence Renewed*. The films about the most famous spy in literature began in 1963 with a reasonably faithful *Dr No* starring Sean Connery and have continued to date with a string of actors – George Lazenby, Roger Moore, Timothy Dalton and Pierce Brosnan – meanwhile becoming ever more special-effects based.

The James Bond phenomenon prompted numerous parodies and imitations, the most successful being the American, Matt Helm – code-name 'Eric' – who, like 007, is a professional killer working for a secret government agency. Created by Donald Hamilton, Helm is described as a curious amalgam of average man, sportsman, patriot and ruthless killer, all wrapped up in the same personality. He uses a kind of psychological warfare against his adversaries and he has been known to allow himself to be deliberately captured in order to get close to his targets when he will use a gun, rifle, knife or even his own hands to finish the mission he has been sent on by his shadowy boss, 'Mac'. Helm cannot be bought off from 'making the touch' (a kill) and is always the total professional.

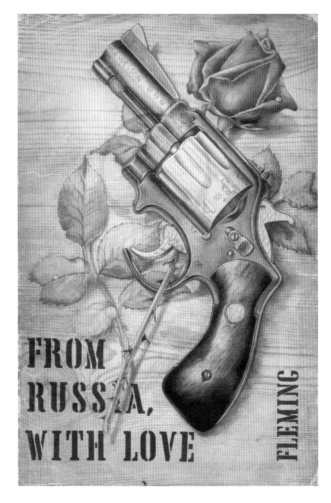

The first of the superb series of cover designs for the Bond titles by Richard Chopping which started with *From Russia, With Love* in 1957.

The price he has had to pay for his devotion to duty is the break-up of his marriage, and he is often seen in the company of beautiful women when assignments take him around America and even to far-flung places such as Hawaii and Europe. Like the Bond stories, those of Matt Helm have attracted many admirers, notably the crime historian Anthony Boucher, who detected strong parallels with Dashiell Hammett's tales of the Continental Op: 'Donald Hamilton has brought to the spy novel the authentic hard realism of Hammett, and his stories are as compelling, and probably as close to the sordid truth of espionage, as any now being told.'

Donald Bengtsson Hamilton (1916–) was born in Uppsala, Sweden, and was taken to

America by his parents at the age of eight. He studied chemistry at the University of Chicago, and after four years as a chemist in the Naval Reserve, opted for the life of freelance photographer and writer, contributing pictures and articles on hunting, yachting and photography to a variety of magazines. In 1947 he produced his first book, *Date with Darkness*, an acclaimed novel about a counterspy, and then, in 1960, introduced Matt Helm in *Death of a Citizen*, which describes his return to the activities of spy and long-range sniper in which he had engaged during the war. The series really took off with a trio of the subsequent titles: *The Ambushers* (1963), featuring the search for a Nazi war criminal; *The Shadowers* (1964), in which Helm saves a beautiful space scientist from assassination; and *The Betrayers* (1966), with a double agent plotting to blow up a troop ship packed with 3,000 US soldiers. In the mid-1960s an ill-conceived series of four Matt Helm movies were made starring Dean Martin as a glib and easy-going counterpart to Sean Connery's suave master of derring-do. In recent novels, Helm the hard-nosed killer-spy has turned into an older man operating as a trouble-shooter against sinister forces operating within American society.

The last major influence on the modern spy story – the man who is said to have 'brought the espionage genre of age' according to critic H. R. F. Keating – is John le Carré, creator of George Smiley, head of 'The Circus', British Intelligence. Short, podgy and unobtrusive, Smiley is the spymaster par excellence, a calm, reflective man, always aware of the implications of his actions yet unswerving in his determination to carry them through no matter that they may damage his deepest convictions. He was introduced in *Call for the Dead* (1961) as a rather drab figure, locked into a farce of a marriage, and referred to by one of his colleagues as, 'hopeless man, great

spy'. During the story he interrogates a middle-ranking Foreign Office official, clears him, and then when the man commits suicide sets out to find why. Smiley returns in *A Murder of Quality* (1962) to investigate a killing at a boarding school, and then stands in the shadows exhorting le Carré's other memorable creation, the doomed and decidedly unheroic spy Alex Leamas, to jump over the Berlin Wall in what became the first of the author's worldwide best-sellers, *The Spy Who Came In from the Cold* (1963). This book has been described as inventing the 'Cold War Thriller', while Graham Greene called it simply 'the best spy story I have ever read'. It was, though, with a trio of novels

American author Donald Hamilton, creator of the US agent Matt Helm, has been described as 'bringing to the spy novel the authentic hard realism of Hammett'.

about Smiley and his struggle with his ruthless Russian opposite number, Karla, namely *Tinker, Tailor, Soldier, Spy* (1974), *The Honourable Schoolboy* (1977) and *Smiley's People* (1980), that le Carré finally destroyed the myth of spying as a glamorous occupation. He showed it was actually a world full of weary victims of the espionage establishments on both sides of the Cold War, 'joes' in the Circus slang — place where social misfits have been degraded by a lifestyle dictated by meanness, bureaucracy and betrayal.

John le Carré is the pseudonym of David John Moore Cornwall (1931–), who was born in Poole, Dorset, was educated privately at Sherborne School, and then went to Oxford. According to most biographies, in 1956 he briefly taught French and German at Eton before joining the Foreign Office, where he spent five years interrogating refugees from the Eastern bloc. In the early 1960s, he was said to have been employed in the British Embassy in Bonn, working in the intelligence records section, giving him access to the files about Secret Service operations which would later inspire his ground-breaking novels. The truth about this period, which Cornwall has only just revealed, is that he was a spy himself. He started working for the secret service when he was a young student at the University of Berne (where he had gone to escape from his confidence trickster father, Ronnie) and later at Lincoln College, Oxford, where he filed reports on left-wing students. 'I really believed at last that I had found a cause I could serve,' he confessed in December 2000. 'I also longed for the dignity which great secrecy confers upon you.' After university, Cornwall's spying career blossomed. He posed as a diplomat for the Foreign Service in Bonn, was transferred to MI6 and spent several years under 'deep cover' while the Berlin Wall was being built, which gave him the inspiration for his most famous novel.

Cornwall/le Carré's career in espionage came to an abrupt end in 1963 following the publication of *The Spy Who Came In from the Cold*. Since then, success has followed success. *Spy* was brilliantly filmed in 1965 with Richard Burton as Leamas and Rupert Davies as the first George Smiley, a role now identified with Alec Guinness as a result of his appearance in *Tinker, Tailor, Soldier, Spy* for BBC TV in 1979. The author's own position as a great modern novelist and *the* espionage writer of his time is similarly assured. It is, indeed, thanks to John le Carré that the last piece in the jigsaw puzzle of the spy story, which was started all those years earlier by James Fenimore Cooper, was finally in place. The spies were *in* from the cold and the classic era of crime fiction was complete.

Opposite: George Smiley, the archetypal modern spymaster, making his first appearance in *Call for the Dead* (1961).

ACKNOWLEDGEMENTS

This book is the result of a lifetime of collecting crime fiction in magazines, books and paperbacks. Not to mention a particular fascination with the authors and artists who used their imaginations to create some of the most popular and enduring characters in *all* fiction. A gallery, in fact, of the good, the bad and the extraordinary.

Many people have helped me in the assembling of the collection upon which this book is primarily based, while others have been generous in offering their advice and providing material from their own collections, thereby enabling the work to be even more representative than it might otherwise have been. I hope that the following will accept my especial thanks: J. Randolph Cox, Lynn Munroe, Thomas Lesser, Donn Albright, William F. Nolan, Steve Holland, Mike Ashley, Mark Sutcliffe, Chris Barker and Maurice Flanaghan. I also owe a debt of gratitude to two other friends, now sadly departed to the Valhalla of crime collectors, Ken Chapman and Bill Lofts, who year after year enabled me to add to my collection of crime fiction as well as my knowledge of the genre. I only wish they had lived to see this celebration of the literature we all so admired.

INDEX

Page references in italics refer to illustration captions

A

Accused 173, 174
Accused of Murder 129
Acre, Stephen *see* Gruber,
   Frank
Ada, the Betrayed 12
Adley, Derek 164
Adventures of Heine,
   The 195–6
Adventures of Jimmie Dale,
   The 80
Adventures of Judith Lee, The . . 77
Adventures of Martin Hewitt,
   The 75
Adventures of Sam Spade, The . . 99
Affair Next Door, The 110
After Dark 16
After the Battle of Dorking;
   or, What Became of the
   Invaders 187
Against Odds 31
Agony Column, The 121
Aldine Detective Tales 60
All-Story Magazine 31
All The Year Round 17
All Thugs Are Dangerous 159
Allain, Marcel 85, 88–9
Alligator *205*
Allingham, Margery 114–15, 116
Alphaville 163
Amateur Cracksman, The 78
Amateur Murderer, The 102
Ambler, Dail 176–7
Ambler, Eric 200–2
Amboy Dukes, The 149–50
Ambushers, The 207
American Detective Series 68
American Gothic 155
Ames, Leon 7
Amis, Kingsley 206
Amok 174
Angel, Heather 200
Argosy 102, *103*, 135
Aristocratic Detective, An 76
Armchair Detective, The 132
Arnold, Edward 123
Arrowsmith's Christmas
   Annual 38
Arsène Lupin series 86
As He Comes Up the Stairs 30
Ashbury, Herbert *158*
Ashenden; or, The British
   Agent 198
Asphalt Jungle, The 129
Astounding Science Fiction . . . 144
Atherton, Sidney 76
Atlantic Monthly, The 106
Auctioned 174
Auden, W. H. 106, 117
Aznavour, Charles 180

B

Bacall, Lauren 142, 200
Background to Danger 202
Bailey, H. C. 112
Baker, Lorin 86
Baltimore Sun 131
Bamboo Whistle, The 204
Bancroft, Anne 180
Bangs, John Kendrick 72
Barnaby Rudge 15
Barrymore, John 70, 78, 88
Battle of Dorking, The 186–7
Beadle's Dime Library 23
Beast Must Die, The 117
Beaumont, Hugh 140
Beauty and the Beast *175*
Beetle, The 75–6
Beeton's Christmas
   Annual 39, 66, 69
Behind Closed Doors 23

Behind That Curtain *121*
Bellamy, Ralph 120, 190
Bening, Annette 181
Benson Murder Case, The 118
Bentley, E. C. 92, *93*, 193
Betrayers, The 207
Bid for Fortune, A 75
Big-Book Detective 179
Big Kill, The *124*, 125
Big Pick-Up, The 171
Big Sleep, The 106, 142
Biggers, Earl Derr 121
Bildad Barnacle, the Detective
   Hercules 61
Billy Blight 57
Biography for Beginners 92
Bird, Richard 198
Bishop Murder Case, The 118
Black, The 196
Black Alley Jungle 151–2
Black Angel, The 138
Black Cat, The 133
Black Curtain, The 138
Black Friday 179
Black Mask . . 78, *80*, *96*, 98, 99, 101,
   . . . . 102, 105, 118, 120,
   . . . . 132, 133, 134,
   . . . . 135, 138, 144, 148
Black Monk, The 12
Black Path of Fear, The 138
Black Shadows 40
Black Wings Has My
   Angel 146, 147
Blackboard Jungle, The . . . 149, 152
Blackkerchief Dick; A Story of
   Mersea Island 115
Blackwell, Carlyle 197
Blackwood's Magazine 186
Blake, Nicholas 116–18
Bleak House 14, 15
Bloch, Robert 153–5
Blood Money 99
Bloodhounds of Heaven 18
Blue Cross, The 82
Blue Dahlia 106
Blythe, Harry 72
Bogart, Humphrey 99, 106, 129,
   . . . . 136, 169, 179
Boileau, Pierre *177*, 178
Boisgobey, Fortune du 39
Bonham-Carter, Helena 17
Boothby, Guy 75
Boston, Charles K. *see*
   Gruber, Frank
Bowery Detective, The 49, 50
Boyer, Charles 200
Boys' First-Rate Pocket
   Library 61
Boys Journal 60
Boys of New York, The 52
Bradbury, Ray 148–9
Braddon, Mary Elizabeth . . . 28–9, 50
Bramah, Ernest 91–2
Brand, Max *see* Frost, Frederick
Brant Adams, the Emperor of
   Detectives 60
Brass Cupcake, The 144
Bravo of London, The 91
Brett, Jeremy 70
Bride from the Street, A 175
Bride Wore Black, The 138
Broadway Billy series 49
Brosnan, Pierce 206
Brought To Bay: or, The
   Experiences of a City
   Detective 35
Brown, Carter 147
Brute, The 73
Buchan, John 192–4, 198
Buchanan, Jack 197
Bulldog Drummond series . . 196–7
Bullivant, Cecil Henry 20
Burdett, Charles 7
Burglar, The 179

Burnett, W. R. . . 128–9, 159, 177, 200
Burr, Raymond 102
Burton, Richard 208
Burton's Gentleman's
   Magazine 3

C

Cages Flottantes, Les 86
Cain, James M. 130–2, 146, 169,
   . . . . 173, 177
Cain, Paul 132–3, 147
Calamity Town 119
Call for the Dead 207
Call Mr Fortune 112
Called Back 36–9
Callow, Simon 91
Calumet series 50
Camus, Albert 131
Canary Murder Case, The 118
Captain America 124
Captain Marvel 124
Cardinal Sin, A 38
Cargo of Evils 115
Carmichael, Ian 114
Carroll, Madeleine 199
Carter, John 34, 92
Case of the Vanishing Beauty,
   The 142
Case of the Velvet Claws, The . . 102
Cash Boy 151
Casino Royale 204, 205, 206
Cask, The 108
Cassell's Magazine 85, 90
Cassidy's Girl 179
Castle, Don 138
Cawelti, John G 184, 200
Celle Qui N'Était Plus 178
Chambers, Peter 163
Chambers' Edinburgh
   Magazine 33
Chambers' Journal 69
Chance 192
Chandler, Raymond . . 75, 102–7, 118
   . . . . 123–4, 132, 137
   . . . . 140, 142, 177
Charteris, Lesley *80*
Chase, James Hadley 164–6, 173
   174
Chase of the Golden Plate, The . . 81
Chase of the Ruby, The 76
Chaze, Elliott 146–7
Chesney, George Tomkyns . . . 186–7
Chesterton, G. K. 82, 85, 92
Cheyney, Peter 72, ... 162–3
Chicago Drummers' Deal 62
Chicago Tribune 100
Child of the Jago, A 75
Childers, Erskine 190–2
Children of the Ritz 137
Chorus of Echoes, A 171
Christie, Agatha . . . 4, *5*, 22, 85, 102,
   . . . . 108–10, 115
Chronicles of Don Q, The 77
Chronicles of Martin Hewitt,
   The 75
Cinquième Procédé, Le 168
Clay, Bertha M. *see* Coryell,
   John Russell
Clemens, Samuel Langhorne
   see Twain, Mark
Clevely, Hugh Desmond 160–1
Clifton, Bud 151
Cloister and the Hearth, The . . . 39
Clouds of Witness 113
Cloven Foot, The 29
Clue for Mr Fortune, A 112
Clues: or, Leaves From A Chief
   Constable's Note Book 35
Cobb Jr, Sylvanus 69
Cockeyed Corpse, The 143
Cocteau, Jean 88
Cody, Lew 9
Collins, Hunt *see* Hunter,
   Evan Collins, Wilkie 14, 15–18

. . . . 28, 33, 40, 50
Colman, Ronald 78, 197
Colonel Sun 206
Colwyn Dane 176
Comstock, Anthony 54, 56
Con Man, The. 152
Conan Doyle, Sir Arthur . . 33, 36, 39
. . . . 66, 69–70, 74
. . . . 85, 86, 187
Condon, Richard 143
Confession de Arsène
  Lupin, Le 88
Confidential Agent, The . . . 199, 200
Connery, Sean. 206
Connolly, Walter. 85, 123
Conrad, Joseph. 192
Conrad, William 123
Constantine, Eddie. 163
Conway, Hugh. 36–9
Cook, Donald 23
Cook, William Wallace. 57
Cooper, James Fenimore. 184
. . . . 185–6, 208
Cop 151
Cop Hater. 152
Cornwall, David John Moore
  see Le Carré, John
Coroner's Pidgin 114
Corpse Was Blonde, The 134
Coryell, John Russell 57, 59
Cotton, Joseph 200, 202
Coup d'État de Cheri-Bibi, Le . . 86
Courier to Marrakesh 197
Cover Charge 137
Cowan, John F.. 57
Cowdrick, J. C.. 48–9
Cox, J. Randolph 51
Crane, Walter 28
Creasey, John 72
Cregar, Laird. 200
Crime d'Orcival, Le 8
Criminals Caught 36
Crimson Crime, A. 40
Crimson Cross, The; or, Foiled
  at the Finish. 60
Crofts, Freeman Wills 108, *109*
Croker, B. M.. 29–30
Crouching Beast, The 198
Cruise of the Blue Jacket 34
Curiosities of Crime in
  Edinburgh During the
  Last Twenty Years 35–6
Curiosities of Detection 34
Curtain of Glass, A 176
Curtains for Carrie. 167
Curtis, Alan. 118
Cusack, John 181
Cushing, Peter 70
Czar's Spy, The 188

D
D for Delinquent 151
Dain Curse, The. 99, 136
Dalton, Timothy 206
Daly, Arnold 74
Daly, Carroll John. 101–2, 120
Dame Plays Rough, The 177
Dames Can Be Deadly. 163
Damned, The 144
Daniel, Roland 158–60, 168
Dannay, Frederic *see*
  Queen, Ellery
Danny Spade Sees Red 176
Dark Carnival 148
Dark Chase. 180
Dark Days 38
Dark Passage. 179
Dark Road 86
Dark Tunnel, The. 141
Dark Wanton *162*
Darker Than Amber 146
Datchet Diamonds, The. 76
Date with Darkness. 207
Daughter of Fu Manchu, The . . 194

Davies, Rupert 208
Davison, Peter 115
Dawson, George H.
  see Stone, Michael
Day-Lewis, Cecil *see*
  Blake, Nicholas
Dead Beat, The. 155
Dead Letter, The. 22, 23
Dead Mans Face, A 38
Dead Man's Folly. 110
Dead Reckoning. 136
Dead Stay Dumb, The 165
Dead Yellow Women. 99, *177*
Deadline at Dawn 169
Death at the Dolphin. 116
Death House Doll. 151
Death is a Lonely Business . . . 148
Death of a Citizen. 207
Death of a Ghost 114
Death on the Nile. 110
Decker, Albert 135
Deep Blue Goodnight, The 146
Deerslayer, The 185
Defence of the Bride
  & Other Poems, The. 23
Delf, Thomas 34
Denver Doll,
  the Detective Queen . . . 48, *49*, 61
Depardieu, Gérard 180
Design for Murder. 73
Destination Unknown. 162
Detective Fiction Weekly. . . 78, 135
. . . . 138, 202
Detective Library. 56
Detective Magazine, The. . . . 18, 20
Detective Short Story, The. 36
Detective Tales 135, 148, 154
Detective Weekly. 72, 160
Detective's Note-Book, The 34
Devil Doctor, The 194
Devil's Diamond, The 76
DeWitt, Aaron. 57
Dey, Frederic Marmaduke
  van Rensselaer 60
see also Coryell, John Russell
Diamond Coterie, The 31
Diary of an Ex-Detective, The . . 34
Dick Tracy 100–1
Dickens, Charles 14–16
Dime Detective. 102, *103*, *104*
. . . . 105, 138, 144
Dime Mystery Magazine. . . 148, 154
Dividend on Death 139
Doc Grip, the Sport Detective . . 60
Dog Detective, The. 60
Dollar Newspaper, The 6
Doll's Bad News 166
Don Q series. 77
Donat, Robert. 194
Doomsters, The 142
Dope is for Dopes. 176
Dossier 113, Le 8, 9
Double-Barrelled Detective
  Story, A 70, 72
Double Event, The 40–1
Double Indemnity . . . 106, 130, 132,
. . . . 169
Double Traitor, The 190
Double Vie de Théophraste
  Longuet, La. 85
Doughty, Francis Worcester . . 53–4
Douglas, Kirk 181
Douglas, Leal 76
Douglas, Melvyn. 88
Down There 180
Dr Nikola 75
Dr No 206
Dracula. 76
Dreadful Lemon Sky, The 146
Dresser, Davis *see*
  Halliday, Brett
Drowned, Man, The. 142
Du Rififi Chez les Hommes . . . 178

Duke 150
Dutch Shoe Mystery, The 119

E
Eaves, Hilary. 17
Edith Heron 12
Edith the Captive. 12
Eleanor's Victory 29
Ellery Queen's Mystery
  Magazine 82, 116, 120
Elliott, Biff 125
Elliott, Sam. 146
Ellis, Edward S. 47, 66
Ellroy, James 125
Ellson, Hal 150
Embezzler, The. 131
Empty Copper Sea, The. 146
Encyclopedia of Mystery
  and Detection 9
Epitaph for a Spy 201
Esclaves de Paris, Les. 8
Everybody's 175
Evil Eye, The 178
Evil Under the Sun 110
Experiences of a Barrister 34
Experiences of a Lady
  Detective 26
Exploits of Elaine, The 74
Exploits of Juve, The. 89
Expressman and the
  Detective, The *22*
Eyre's Acquittal 30

F
Faces in the Dark 178
Fairbanks, Douglas 77
Fame & Fortune Weekly 54
Fantastic Universe 148
Fantômas 89
Far and Near series. 57
Farenheit *451* 148
Farewell, My Lovely 106, 142
Farewell, Nikola. 75
Fargus, Frederick John
  see Conway, Hugh
Fast One. 132, 147
Faust, Frederick *see* Frost,
  Frederick Fawcett, Frank Dubrez
  see Sarto, Ben
Fear in the Night. 169
Female Detective, The 34–5
Fenn, George Manville. 40
Fer-de-Lance. 123
Ferval, Paul. 9
Fiction Factory, The 59
Fifth Grave, The. 136
Fighting Against Millions 59
Find a Victim. 142
Find the Lady 176
Finney, Albert. 110
Fisher, Steve. 135–6, 169
Five Cent Comic Weekly, The. . . 54
Five Cent Wide Awake
  Library 54
5 Murderers 105
Flash Gordon 100
Flashlight Detective Series . . 66, 68
Fleming, Ian 204–6
Floating Prison, The 86
Flowers for the Judge 114
Flynn's Detective Fiction 148
For the Defence 33
Ford, Glenn. 149
Forrest, Steve. 7
Forrester, Andrew 34–5
Foster, Norman. 200
Foster, Preston. 136
Four Just Men, The 195
Francis, Stephen. 174–6
  see also Janson, Hank
Frank Reade Library. 54
French Key, The. 134
Fresnay, Pierre 86

From Russia, With Love 206
Frost, Frederick 202–4
Fuchsberger, Joachim 196
Futrelle, Jacques 81–2

G

Gaboriau, Émile 8–9, 32, 39
. . . . 50, 51, 57, 198
Galton Case, The 142
Gambler, The; or,
    The Policeman's Story 7
Gambling Ship 133
Gang Smasher series 160
Gangs of New York, The 158
Gangster, The 159
Gangster's Daughter, The 159
Gangster's Last Shot, The 159
Garden Murder Case, The 118
Gardner, Erle Stanley 102, 103
Gardner, John 206
Garfield, John 130
Gargan, William 120
Garnett Bell: Detective 20
German Spy, The 188
Getaway, The 181
Gielgud, Sir John 199
Gift, The 4, 6
Gilbert, John 86
Gillette, William 70
Girl Hunters, The 125
Girl in the Plain Brown
    Wrapper, The 146
Glass Key, The 136
Glinto, Darcy 167
Glover, Brian 115
Gold Bug, The 6
Golden Spike, The 150
Golden Tag, The 146
Good Time Girls 161
Goodis, David 155, 177, 178–80
Gould, Nat 40–3
Gould, Stephen 135
Goyne, Richard 161–2
Graham's Magazine 3, 6
Grant, Cary 133
Graves, Peter 142
Great Impersonation, The 190
Great War in England
    in 1897, The 187–8
Green, Anna Katherine 22, 23,
. . . . 31, 110
Greene, Graham 129, 199–200
Greene, Hugh 76
Greenmantle 193
Greenstreet, Sydney 202
'Griff' 175–6
Grifters, The 181
Gruber, Frank 134–5
Guilty Bonds 188
Guinness, Sir Alec 85, 208
Guinness Book of Records 170
Gun For Hire, A 199, 200
Gunmaker of Moscow, The 69

H

Haddon, Peter 114
Half-Dime Library 47–8
Halfpenny Marvel 72
Hall, Adam see
    Trevor, Elleston
Halliday, Brett 139–40
Halsey, Harlan Page 50, 60
Hamilton, Donald 177, 206–7
Hamilton, Patrick 169
Hammett, Dashiell . . . 22, 75, 96–101
. . . . 102, 106, 118, 120
. . . . 132, 136, 177
Hanley, Colonel 187
Hannay, Richard 193–4
Harding, Frank see Malet, Léo
Harlem Jack,
    the Office-Boy Detective 52
Harris, Julie 142
Harrison, Michael 163

Hartley, Howard 163
Harvest of Hate 162
Haunted Men 134
Haycraft, Howard 106, 116
Hear the Stripper Scream 164
Heldman, Richard Bernard
    see Marsh, Richard
Hell is a Woman 177
Hell of a Woman, A 181
Henderson, William 35
Hervey, Michael 170
Hickson, Joan 110
High Sierra 129
High Window, The 106, 140
His Darling Sin 29
His Royal Nibs 57
Hitchcock, Alfred 138, 154, 169
. . . . 192, 194, 199
Hold That Tiger 177
Hollowdell Grange 40
Homolka, Oscar 192
Honeyman, William
    Crawford 35–6
Honourable Algernon Knox,
    Detective, The 190
Honourable Schoolboy, The 208
Hopley, George see
    Woolrich, Cornell Hornung,
    Ernest William 78
House Without a Door, The 53
House Without A Key, The 121
Hudson River Tunnel
    Detective, The 52
Hughes, Dorothy B. 169
Hume, Fergus 32–3, 57
Hunchback of Soho, The 160
Hunt, Septimus 12
Hunted Down 15, 36
Hunter, Evan 148, 149, 152–3
Huston, Anjelica 181
Hutton, Jim 120

I

I, The Jury 124–5
I Can Find My Way Out 116
I Guarded Kings: The
    Memoirs of a Political
    Police Officer 163
I Like 'Em Tough 152
I Should Have Stayed Home . . . 134
I Wake Up Screaming 136, 169
I Wouldn't Be in Your Shoes . . . 138
If 148
If Death Ever Slept 123
If You're Only Human 121
I'll Fix You 150
Illustrated Man, The 148
I'm Cannon - For Hire 152
In a Lonely Place 169
Innocence of Father Brown,
    The 85
Inspector Dickens Retires 190
Inspector French's
    Greatest Case 108
Interference 30
Introducing the Super 162
Invasion of 1910, The 188
Invisible Pickpocket, The 36
Irish, William see
    Woolrich, Cornell
Irish Police Officer, The: The
    Identification & Other Tales . . 34

J

Jacob Street Mystery, The 91
Jailbait Street 150
Jakubowski, Maxim 125
James Boys series 54
Janson, Hank . . . 12, 164, 172–4, 175
Jimmie Dale, Alias the
    Gray Seal 80
John Thorndyke's Cases 90
Johnny Angel 135

Journey into Fear 201, 202
Journey into the Unknown 155
Joyce, James 88
Judith Lee: Some Pages from
    Her Life 77

K

Karloff, Boris 133, 195
Karney, Jack 151
Keach, Stacey 125
Keating, H. R. F. 118, 207
Keene, Day 151
Keeper of the Keys 121
Keith, Brian 180
Kelley, Hickey and Company,
    the Detectives of
    Philadelphia 61
Kelly, Grace 138
Kelly, Harold Ernest
    see Glinto, Darcy
Kersh, Gerald 170
Kidnapper, The 154
Killer 174
Killer Inside Me, The 180, 181
Killer's Kiss 181
King, Stephen 146
King of Crooks, A 20
King of the Underworld 129
Kinski, Nastassja 180
Kirkwood, James 190
Kiss Me, Deadly 125
Kiss My Fist 165
Kiss Tomorrow Goodbye 134
Knowles, Patric 7
Knox, Elyse 138
Kortner, Fritz 198
Kummer, Frederic Arnold 73

L

Ladd, Alan 129, 200
Lady - Here's Your Wreath 165
Lady Audley's Secret 28–9
Lady Don't Turn Over 166
Lady in the Lake, The 103, 106
. . . . 135–6
Lady in the Morgue, The 136
Lady Killer 152
Lady of Leicester Square 161
L'Affaire Lerouge 8, 9
Lake, Veronica 200
Land O' Leal, The 30
Lang, Andrew 39
Lange, Jessica 130
Last Days of Tul, The:
    A Romance of the Lost
    Cities of the Yucatan 22–3
Last Deception, The 163
Last of the Mohicans, The 185
Last Stroke, The 30–1, 31
Latimer, Jonathan 136
Law and the Lady, The 18
Lawford, Peter 120
Lawson, W. B. 57
Lazenby, George 206
Le Breton, Auguste 178
Le Carré, John . 171, 185, 198, 207–9
Lea, Charlton 62
Leavenworth Case, The 22, 23
Leblanc, Maurice 57, 85, 86, 88
Lee, Christopher 195
Leonard, Elmore 125
Lepofsky, Manford see
    Queen, Ellery
Leroux, Gaston 85–6
Leslie, Rolf 81
L'Étranger 131
Letters Left at the
    Pastry Cook's 27
Lew Archer,
    Private Investigator 142
Licence Renewed 206
L'Illustration 85
Lindridge, James 12, 14
Lippincott's Magazine . . . 31, 68, 69

Little Caesar. 128–9, 159
Little Sister, The 106
Liza of Lambeth. 199
Lofts, W. O. G.. . . . . . . 62–3, 160, 161
Log Cabin Library. 56, 57
Lombino, Salvatore see
    Hunter, Evan
London Night Haunts. 161–2
London Opinion 175
London Society 69
Lonely Wives 161
Long Goodbye, The 106
Lord Jim. 192
Lord Peter Views the Body 113
Lorre, Peter. 199, 200, 202
Lovecroft, H. P.. 154
Lovell, Raymond. 202
Lowe, Edmund 118, 190
Lust of Hate, The 75
Lynch, Lawrence L. 30–1
Lyons, Harry Agar. 195

M
MacDonald, John D.. 143–6
Macdonald, Ross . . . 131, 139, 140–2
MacGraw, Ali 181
MacKeag, Ernest Lionel
    see 'Griff'
Madame Midas 32, 33
Madden, David 131
Maggie, the Child of Charity;
    or, Waits on the Sea of
    Humanity. 57
Magnet Detective Library, The. 57, 68
Make Mine series. 172
Malaeska; The Indian Wife
    of the White Hunter 47
Malet, Léo. 167–9, 177
Maltese Falcon, The. 96, 99
Mammoth Detective. 154
Mammoth Monthly Reader,
    The. 57
Man from Downing Street,
    The. 188
Man from Morocco, The 196
Man Lay Dead, A. 116
Man with the Club-Foot 197
Man Within, The 199
Maniac Father, The. 10
Mannheim, Lucie 202
Markham, Robert. 206
Marsh, Ngaio. 114, 115–16
Marsh, Richard. 75–7
Marshall, Herbert. 177
Marshall, Raymond see Chase,
    James Hadley
Marsten, Richard see
    Hunter, Evan
Martel, Charles see
    Delf, Thomas
Martian Chronicles, The. 148
Mask of Dimitrios. 201–2
Mask of Fu Manchu, The 194
Masked Venus, The 28
Mason, James. 202
Mathers, Helen 29, 30
Matter of Conviction, A 152
Maugham, W. Somerset 198–9
Max Carrados 91
Mayhew, Horace. 27
Mazurki, Mike. 135
McBain, Ed see Hunter,
    Evan
McCoy, Horace. 133–4
McGavin, Darren 125
McGovan, James 35–6
McLevy, James 35–6
McMillan and Wife 136
McNeile, Herman Cyril
    see 'Sapper'
McQueen, Steve 181
Meeker, Ralph. 125
Melina the Murderess 12
Mémoires de Vidocq. 2, 3

Memory of Murder, A 149
Merry Wives of London,
    The. 12, 14
Messenger-Boy Detective
    Among the Bowery
    Sharps, The. 52
Michael Shayne,
    Private Detective 140
Midnight Club 190
Mike Hammer 125
Mike Shayne Mystery
    Magazine 140
Mildred Pierce 169
Milland, Ray 200
Millar, Kenneth see
    Macdonald, Ross
Millie Lynn - Shop
    Investigator 20
Minister of Evil, The. 189
Ministry of Fear, The 199, 200
Minute for Murder. 117
Miracle Man, The. 80
Miss Callaghan Comes
    to Grief 166
Miss Otis series 174–5
Mollie Maguires and the
    Detectives, The 22
Money: How To Get, How To
    Keep, and How To Use It. 27
Monsieur Lecoq 9
Montgomery, Robert 114, 169
Moon in the Gutter, The 180
Moonstone, The 14, 16, 17–18
Moore, Kenneth 194
Moore, Roger 206
More Work for the
    Undertaker 115
Moreau, Jeanne 138
Morley, Robert 110
Morning After Death, The. 117
Morrison, Arthur 74–5
Morrow, Vic 149
Mostel, Zero 202
Mountain Mystery A: or,
    The Outlaws of the Rockies. . . 31
Moving Target, The. 141, 142
Mower, Jack 74
Mr Campion series 114, 115
Mr Fortune series 112
Mr Justice Raffles 78
Mr Standfast 193
Much Darker Days. 39
Mulhall, Jack. 74
Muni, Paul. 129
Munro's Ten Cent Novels. 50
Murder at the Vicarage 110
Murder from the East 102
Murder in the Madhouse. 136
Murder Must Advertise 113
Murder of Quality, A 207–8
Murder of Roger Ackroyd,
    The. 109
Murder of the Pigboat
    Skipper 135
Murder on the Links 109
Murder on the Orient
    Express 110
Murder or Manslaughter 30
Murder the Admiral 135
Murder Thy Neighbour 170
Murders in the Rue Morgue,
    The. 2, 3–4
Murdoch, Emma see Lynch,
    Lawrence L.
Murphy Gang, The. 158
Musick, John R. 54
Mutiny on the Bounty. 202
My Lady of Orange 112
Mystère de la Chambre
    Jaune, Le. 85, 86
Mysteries of London, The . . . 12, 13
Mysteries of the Night, The. 60
Mysterious Affair
    at Styles, The 108, 109

Mysterious Mr Sabin, The . . 189–90
Mystery League 120
Mystery Magazine, The. 72, 73
Mystery Man of Soho,
    The. 114, 115
Mystery of a Hansom Cab . . . 32–3
Mystery of a Motor Cab. 33
Mystery of Dr Fu Manchu . . 194–5
Mystery of Edwin Drood,
    The 15, 16
Mystery of Marie Roget,
    The. 4, 5
Mystery of the Sleeping Car
    Express, The. 108
Mystery of the Yellow
    Room, The. 85, 86

N
Name is Archer, The 142
Narcejac, Thomas. 177, 178
Nathan, Daniel see
    Queen, Ellery
Ned Kelly and His Bushmen . . . 39
Neon Jungle, The. 144
Nevins, Francis M. 137
New Detective. 179
New Detective Story, The 31
New Exploits of Elaine, The. . . . 74
New Idol, The 86
New Lot, The 202
New Ordeal, The 18
New York Detective Library 52
New York Fireside
    Companion. 49, 50
New York Ledger 69
New York Nat, The Knife
    Detective 52
New York Nell, the Boy-Girl
    Detective 61
Newell, Wedgewood. 88
Newgate 12
Newman, Paul 142
Nicholas Goade, Detective. 190
Nicholson, Jack 130
Nick Carter series 58, 59–60
Night and the City. 170
Night Has a Thousand Eyes,
    The. 136, 138, 169
Night of the Ripper 155
Night to Remember, A 202
Nightmare Town 99–100
Nine Tailors, The. 113
Niven, David. 78
No Mortgage on a Coffin. 167
No Orchids for
    Miss Blandish. 164, 165
No Proof, A Detective Story 31
Nobody Lives Forever 129
Nolan, Lloyd 140
Nolan, William F. 96, 202
Norwood, Eille 70
Nouveaux Mystères de Paris . . 168
November Joe; The Detective
    of the Woods 77
Now Try the Morgue 171
Nugget Library, The 57
Number 70 Berlin 188

O
O'Brien, Geoffrey. 137
O'Brien-Moore, Erin. 23
O'er Land and Sea Library 61
Of Human Bondage. 199
Oland, Warner. 121, 195, 197
Old Cap Collier
    Library 34, 49, 51, 52
Old Detective's Pupil; or,
    The Mysterious Crime of
    Madison Square 59
Old Electricity, the
    Lightning Detective 60
Old House of West Street, The 10, 12
Old Humphrey, the
    Dwarf Detective 52

Old King Brady 52, 53
Old Opium, the
    Mongolian Detective 52
Old Sledge, Blacksmith-Detective 52
Old Sleuth, the Detective; or,
    The Bay Ridge Mystery 50
Old Sleuth Library 50
Oliver Twist 15
On Crime Writing 142
One for The Money 147
120 Rue de la Gare 168
One Lonely Night 125
One More Nice White Body 167
One of a Mob 41, 42
Only Mugs Die Young 176
Opening Night 116
Oppenheim, E. Phillips 189–90
Orczy, Emma Magdalen,
    Baroness 80–1
Orient Express 199, 200
Orlando Chester 69
Ornum & Co's Fifteen Cent
    Romances 51
Orwell, George 165
Other Side of the Battle of
    Dorking 187
Our American Cousin 18
Our Government 131
Ousby, Ian 18
Out of the Past 169
Over My Dead Body 123

P
Pace That Kills, The 42
Packard, Frank L. 78, 80, 81
Paget, Sidney 66, 69, 74
Painted Woman, The 73
Palas et Cheri-Bibi 86
Parfum de la Dame en
    Noir, Le 86
Parker, Eleanor 17
Parker Pyne Investigates 110
Parole 134
Paths of Glory 181
Pattern for Murder 143
Pearls are a Nuisance 105
Pearson's Magazine 77, 80,
. . . . 91, 113
Penzler, Otto 9, 34, 118
People's Magazine 78
Perfume of the Lady in Black,
    The 86
Perkins, Anthony 154
Perry Mason 137
Persian Pride 174
Petherbridge, Edward 114
Petit Simonin illustré
    par l'example, Le 178
Petit Vieux des Batignolles,
    Le 8
Phantom Lady, The . . . 137, 138, 169
Phantom of the Opera, The 85
Philp, Kenward 49
Pinkerton, Allan 20–2
Pioneers, The 185
Plastic Man 124
Poe, Edgar Allan 2–7, 15, 28
. . . . 33, 57, 69, 85
Poirot Investigates 110
Poitier, Sidney 149
Politan 3
Posthumous Adventures of
    Shylock Holmes 72
Posthumous Papers of the
    Pickwick Club 14
Postman Always Rings Twice,
    The 130, 131, 169, 173
Powell, David 88
Powell, Robert 194
Powell, William 118
Power, Tyrone 163
Power Gods, The 151
Prather, Richard S. 139, 142–3

Premier, The 189
President Fu Manchu 194
President's Mystery Story,
    The 118
Prest, Thomas Peckett 10–12
Price, Vincent 202
Prichard, Hesketh 77
Priestly, J. B. 106, 171
Prince of Hokum 163
Prowse, Robert 62
Psycho 153, 154
Pulp Jungle, The 135
Purloined Letter, The 4, 6
Pursuit 174
Pusher, The 152

Q
Que la Bête Meure 117
Queen, Ellery 36, 82, 119–20
Queen of Hearts, The 17
Queen of the Mob 134
Queneau, Raymond 88
Question of Proof, A 117
Queux, William Le 187–9
Quick Red Fox, The 146
Quiller Memorandum, The 171

R
Rackets Incorporated 176
Raft, George 190, 202
Rage at Dawn 134
Ragged Edge, The 151
Raines, Ella 138
Rainham, Thomas 150
Ralph the Bailiff 29
Rathbone, Basil 70
Rawlinson, Herbert 74
Ray, Aldo 180
Raymond, Rene Lodge
    Brabazon see Chase, James
    Hadley
Razzia sur la Chnouf 178
Reade, Charles 39
Real Lady Hilda, The 30
Real Le Queux, The 188
Rear Window 138
Recollections of a Detective
    Police-Officer 7, 33, 34
Recollections of a Policeman . . . 33
Recollections of a Sheriff's
    Officer 34
Red Harvest 99, 134
Red Light Will, the River
    Detective 60
Red Thumb Mark, The 90
Red Triangle, The 75
Redhead series 163–4
Reefer Boy 150
Reeve, Arthur B. 73–4
Regester, Seeley 22–3
Renin, Paul see Goyne, Richard
Rennie, Michael 200
Retreat from Oblivion 179
Revelations of a Lady
    Detective 26–7
Revelations of a Private
    Detective, The 34–5
Revenue Detective The; or,
    Old Rattlesnake 60
Rex Stout's Mystery Monthly . . 123
Reynolds, George W. M 12, 13
Reynolds, Marjorie 200
Reynolds, Quentin 59, 144
Richards, Frank 73
Richardson, Maurice 75
Richardson, Sir Ralph 197
Riddle of the Sands,
    The 190–1, 192
Ride the Pink Horse 169
Rideal, Charles F. 36
Road Floozie 166
Robinson, Edward G 129, 132,
. . . . 138

Rogue's Life, A 18, 27, 28
Rohmer, Sax 194–5
Roman Hat Mystery, The 119
Romance of Elaine, The 74
Rope 169–70
Rosenberg, Bruce A. 184, 200
Rouge est Mis, Le 178
Rough Justice 29
Rouletabille Chez les
    Bohémiens 86
Royal Magazine, The 81
Royal Prisoner, A 89
Royal Yacht, The 69
Running Down A Double 60
Russell, Gail 138
Russell, William see
    Walters, Thomas
Rutherford, Margaret 110
Rymer, Malcolm James 12

S
Saint, The 80
Salvation Hunters 132
Sant of the Secret Service 189
Santa Fe Sal the Slasher 61
'Sapper' 196–7
Sarto, Ben 174–5
Saturday Review of Literature,
    The 118
Savage, Richard Henry 28
Savage Night 181
Saving a Rope 112
Sawney Bean, the Man Eater
    of Midlothian 12
Sayers, Dorothy L. 72, 112–14
Scandal in Bohemia, A 69
Scarf, The 153, 154
Scarface 129
Scarlet Pimpernel, The 80, 81
Scarred Faces 173
Scarthroat 160
Scientific Detective Monthly 73
Scott, Zachary 202
Scrambled Yeggs, The 143
Scribner's Magazine 118
Sea and Shore Series, The 57
Seaside Library, The 50
Second Ending 152
Secret Adversary, The 110
Secret Agent, The 192
Secret Agent Number One 204
Secret Agent X-9 . . . . 100, 101
Secret Detective: or, One Night
    in a Gambling House 34
Secret Hand, The: Some Further
    Adventures of Desmond
    Okewood of the British
    Secret Service 197
Secret Service 54
Secret Service: or, Recollections
    of a City Detective 34
Secrets of the Foreign Office . . . 189
Sellers, Peter 195
Serenade 130
Servais, Jean 178
Seth Jones: or, The Captives
    of the Frontier 47
Seven Keys to Baldpate 121
Seven Slayers 132, 133
Sexton Blake Library . . 72, 160, 175
Shadowed by Three 30–1
Shadowers, The 207
She Gave Me Hell 167
Shell Scott Mystery Magazine . . 143
Sheppard, Bithia Mary see
    Croker, B. M.
Sherlock Holmes Detective
    Library 68
Sherlock Holmes Versus Jack
    the Ripper 119
Shooting Star 154
Shop Soiled 175
Short Stories 134, 135